D1086831

Salting Roses

**Center Point
Large Print**

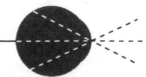

This Large Print Book carries the Seal of Approval of N.A.V.H.

Salting Roses

Lorelle Marinello

CENTER POINT LARGE PRINT
THORNDIKE, MAINE

This Center Point Large Print edition is
published in the year 2011 by arrangement with
Avon Books, an imprint of HarperCollins Publishers.

This book is a work of fiction. References to real people, events,
establishments, organizations, or locales are intended only to provide
a sense of authenticity, and are used fictitiously. Though many of the
author's ancestral roots live in Alabama soil, this town of Shady
Grove—and there are three others in Alabama—and all its inhabitants
are drawn from the author's imagination. Any resemblance to folks,
living or dead, is purely coincidental. All other characters, and all
incidents and dialogue, are drawn from the author's imagination and
are not to be construed as real.

The text of this Large Print edition is unabridged.
In other aspects, this book may vary
from the original edition.
Printed in the United States of America.
Set in 16-point Times New Roman type.

ISBN: 978-1-60285-968-5

Library of Congress Cataloging-in-Publication Data

Marinello, Lorelle.
Salting roses / Lorelle Marinello. — Center Point large print ed.
p. cm.
Originally published: New York : Avon, 2010.
ISBN 978-1-60285-968-5 (library binding : alk. paper)
1. Single women—Fiction. 2. Family secrets—Fiction.
3. Heiresses—Fiction. 4. Alabama—Fiction. 5. Large type books.
I. Title.
PS3613.A7482S25 2011
813'.6—dc22

2010046135

In loving memory of my Papa and Nana,
W. Louis Moore and Velma Louisa Orr

Acknowledgments

A writer's thank-you list begins long before the birth of a novel. It is my firm belief that writers don't come out of the womb knowing how to put words on a page. A writer may be born with an innate desire to string words together and an overactive imagination, but like any other profession, writing requires study and practice of craft as well as creative vision.

I would like to thank the many mentors who have had a hand in my education. Thank you, Donna Kordela and Phyllis Gebauer for offering soft-spoken encouragement in my fetal days. To Marian Jones for your vigilant green pen. A special thanks to Jenny Crusie for sharing your wisdom on craft and the business of writing so generously. Jenny, your words kept me sane during the long wait. To my ever-patient critique partner and dear friend, Cheryl Howe, who respected my voice and my vision. To Jennifer Stevenson for giving me fresh eyes during the BIG revision and beefing up my wimpy soul with your amazing strength. I want to be you when I grow up. Thanks to the girls in the Wet Noodle Posse's basement who have been there through the ups and downs with unflagging optimism.

Thanks to Stef Feagan for making me put on my iron underwear and revise and Janet Mullany for her advice and for sharing many a hearty chuckle during the publishing journey.

Since a writer does not live alone on a desert island, I want to thank those who have been in the trenches with me on a daily basis: my husband, Frederick; my sister, Cyndi, who has cheered me on my whole life and never stopped believing in me; my children, Seth, Selena, and Sarah, who never complained about me sitting in front of the computer for endless hours. To my local writer's support group who kept my chin up: Mary Leo, Cheryl Howe, Sylvia Mendoza, Cathy Yardley, Ara Burklund, Ann Collins, Judy Duarte, and Chris Marie Green.

My thanks would not be complete without heartfelt thanks to my agent Anne Hawkins for her enthusiasm for the story from the outset. I also want to thank the patient folks at HarperCollins for their support. Thanks to Jennifer Pooley, Amanda Bergeron, and Carrie Feron, Liate Stehlik and the hardworking folks in the marketing and art departments for helping me to make my dream come true.

Chapter 1

Gracie Lynne Calloway began her small life in Shady Grove, Alabama, fast asleep in a coal bucket on the front porch of 1854 Peachtree Lane. At 8 A.M., she was carried in with the morning paper and a short note . . .

Uncle Ben,

You always said I'd give the devil a run for his Bible. Guess you were right. I remember how you liked babies. Could you mind her for a spell? I know you two will get along just fine. If Auntie Alice says you don't know nothing about raising children, tell her I said you are better than any mama I know.

Say a prayer for me,
Rita

. . . And between the ham and the eggs and two pots of coffee, she was given her name. She had the beautiful and glamorous Grace Kelly to thank for the first part, her Uncle Ben to thank for the last—and Rita to thank for the coal bucket.

Gracie liked her name well enough, but she

would gladly have traded the coal bucket for a flesh-and-blood mother. Not that her uncles, Ben and Artie, hadn't done a fine job of raising her. Gracie could pitch and hit a baseball better than most guys she knew. And with Aunt Alice's well-meaning interference from next door, she could set a table with edible food, but she knew better than to advertise the fact. At Gracie's advanced years, being a good cook was the equivalent of being a marked target, and that could only lead to one thing: marriage—something Alice risked her knees in prayer for every night.

Alice was Ben's next-door wife. She said things were more peaceful with her and Ben under separate roofs. Peaceful or not, living apart they hadn't produced any new Calloways. Alice let it be known that all her hopes had settled on Gracie. With each passing year since Gracie's eighteenth birthday, Alice's hopes had become an unfettered war. Today was a milestone birthday for Gracie—number twenty-five. Once again Alice would be working the years toward her cause.

In general, birthdays were something Gracie approached with caution. She couldn't remember one that didn't make her stomach go funny. When it came right down to it, the date they'd ear-marked for her birthday was the day she'd been abandoned on Ben's porch. No one had ever thought to change it since her real birth date was a mystery to everyone—but Rita. Being cast off by the one person who should love you above all others was hardly a cause for celebration, in Gracie's mind.

Alice would be poking the candles into her cake about now and shooing Uncle Ben away from the leftover icing. But Gracie was in no hurry to endure another reminder of her unceremonious arrival in Shady Grove.

Gracie trudged down the canned goods aisle to Draper's front window and flipped the CLOSED sign face out. Across the street, prissy Darla Watson paused while buttoning down the Clip and Curl's peppermint-striped shades to twiddle her fingers at Gracie.

Gracie jumped back into the shadows. Not once in Gracie's ten years at the market had Darla so much as lifted an eyelash in her direction. Gracie took extra pains to make sure she stayed invisible to folks like Darla, who, bless her black heart, never failed to make Gracie's "sad circumstances" a topic of conversation whenever Gracie's back was turned.

Gracie ventured one last peek through the window, thinking she must have dreamed the whole exchange. Sure enough, Darla had disappeared, but Artie rounded the corner and was making his way in her direction. He had a slight hitch to his gait, a war injury from the time he and Ben served in Korea. Today he moved slower than usual, pausing as he struggled to get air into his tarred lungs.

Gracie swallowed her concern and unlatched the door. "Alice chase you out of the house?"

Artie hobbled through the doorway. "You mean that hurricane in the kitchen?"

"That bad, huh?"

"Pink icing. I'm supposed to get sprinkles to match. I sure hope you got pink, or she won't let me back in the house."

Gracie closed the door and cut a path down the baking aisle. She plucked a tiny bottle off the shelf and handed it to Artie. "Pink, huh?"

"For your female side—the one that don't play ball. Alice said to put it on *her account*—like she's one of them big-dog celebrities she's always yammerin' on about."

Alice was the self-appointed balance in Gracie's life. She took it as her heavenly duty to outweigh her male counterparts, Ben and Artie. Now that Gracie had risen to the role of star pitcher on the Grove Gators women's baseball team, Alice embraced her role with a fervor that exceeded her devotion to the Lord. Gracie just wished she'd find another more worthy victim to help into everlasting happiness.

Artie's footsteps kept pace behind her as she headed toward her office in the back corner of the market. "If I know Alice, she wouldn't trust anyone but herself to get pink sprinkles. You

12

blackmailed her into giving you the job, didn't you?"

"I knowed you was down here hidin'. And Alice knowed that I was the only one who could ferret you out."

"I'm not hiding—I'm working." Gracie kept moving, thankful that Artie couldn't see her face. She needed a couple more minutes to put a lead bucket over her thoughts before he turned on his X-ray vision.

Artie huffed and puffed at her heels. "You'd think twenty-five was the ugly birthday. Wait till you get as old as me. Folks down at the DMV don't want to take your picture no more. Next thing you know, they're handin' you a bus pass. That's when you buy yourself a spot in the Big Man's parkin' lot."

It wasn't the first time Artie had mentioned dying. Gracie glanced over her shoulder and watched him take a shaky breath but swallowed her fear and the scolding on the tip of her tongue. "You know darn well that's not what's eating me."

"What I know is, it ain't worms—but it might as well be. This dark hole ain't no place for you to spend the rest of your life."

Gracie shimmied past a pallet of dog food and into her office, then took a seat behind her desk. "You never said boo about my job before. It's not so bad. It pays the bills and nobody bothers me."

"That's just it—nobody's ever gonna bother you here. You're gettin' too bossy. Somebody with more kick needs to take you down a notch once in a while. I'm gettin' too old for the job."

"Stop it, you hear? I don't want to listen to another word about you getting old. You know what I think?"

Artie planted himself in the chair across from her. "I sure do, but you's gonna tell me anyway, so have at it."

"I think . . . Alice has been slipping mind-altering drugs into your tea. 'Cause I swear I hear Alice's echo ringing inside your skull. Sounds like church bells to me."

"What you hear, Gracie Lynne, is your birthday clock tickin'."

"I know the difference between a tick and a traitor's bellyaching. I see the marriage statistics bandied about every day in the tabloids on the front checkout counter. Fact is, I consider myself lucky. I can dump my shiftless man and nobody cares."

"You ain't got a man." Artie rapped his cane on the top of her desk.

Gracie glared at him and jutted out her chin. "I'm just saying *if* I had one, that's all. Three years ago, Ben and Alice pooled their money and bought me that fancy hope chest. Last year, I got a set of spoons, so I figured this year, it'll be forks. Next year, it'll be knives. By the time I'm

14

thirty, I'll be able to set a table. Unless, I shoehorn some poor fool into marrying me and end the anticipation altogether."

"They're savin' the knives for last, after you hook yourself a somebody. Don't want you to scare him off."

Gracie met Artie's steady gaze. "I suspected as much."

A silver brow lifted over his right eye. "You got any particular fool in mind? And don't say Skip Evers, 'cause I know you better than that."

Skippy could qualify as lots of things—best friend, even first-kiss material, but never husband—despite the fact that they'd grown up in the same sandbox. The last thing she figured to hear from Artie was a question about her love life. He was here for a reason, but she was pretty sure matchmaker wasn't it.

Gracie eyed him suspiciously over the top of her desk. "I figure Santa Claus ought to fit the bill. He works out of town, and he's only got the one red suit. I won't be bothered with much laundry."

Artie put on his sorry face. "Uh-huh. That's what I thought. You got your yearly case of my-mama-don't-love-me blues."

"You're wrong. I gave up on Rita a long time ago. I'm just working myself up to the excitement over the forks, that's all." Gracie crossed her arms over her chest and kept her eagle gaze trained on Artie, willing him to retract the accusation. He knew how the mention of Rita on her birthday set her back up. It wasn't like him to be mean-spirited.

But Artie just kept looking at her with that sad, wise half-grin of his. "This ain't about forks. I came down here to put a smile on that pretty face, but I can see you's already worked yourself into a misery over the mama you ain't never had."

"Oh, for monkey's sake, if you aren't the most mule-headed—"

What began as a chuckle in Artie's chest, ended as a choking cough.

Gracie rushed around the desk and held out a cup of water. "One smile, coming up." She cracked the biggest smile she could muster. "There. You satisfied?"

He swallowed and offered her a weak smile. "You know, you could almost scare somebody away with that fearsome face of yours."

Alarm buttons went off in Gracie's head. She backed against the edge of her desk. "And just *who* would I be scaring away? Alice didn't invite her churchy friends, did she?"

Artie shifted in his chair and dodged her gaze. "You know I don't step in the way of Ben's doings—"

"Not that Delilah Perkins? Every time she sets eyes on me, her nose grows wings and takes to the sky."

"The Widow Perkins is out at the graveyard lightin' candles around her poor husband's grave tonight, so's he won't haunt her no more." He chuckled to himself, then looked up at Gracie. "So, you can quit your wallowin'?"

"That depends on who's coming to my birthday celebration."

The teasing glint was gone from Artie's eyes. "You know how when you was a mousy thing and them hoity-toity Parnells wouldn't let you play with their little girl? You came home and cried buckets on my shirt . . ." Artie paused, his eyes glazed over with the memory.

Gracie felt her stomach clench. She could still see Mrs. Parnell's icy blue gaze narrowing down at her as Gracie stood on the Parnells' freshly swept back porch in her patched overalls and holey sneakers. She could still hear the cold edge of the woman's haughty voice telling her that little Shelly Ann Parnell didn't keep company with dirty bastard children. But what Artie didn't know was that Mrs. Parnell had carried her animosity one step further. She'd chased off Gracie's other girlfriends by spreading ugly lies to their mamas. The next week, Gracie played sick so she didn't have to go to her ballet lessons. After that, she spent more time playing with boys who admired her for her skill with a bat and ball. Other than Artie's niece, Chantel, she didn't have any girlfriends. She'd been hungry for female companionship until the Parnells moved away.

Another cold ripple ran through Gracie's belly. She leaned across the desk toward Artie. "They're not moving back from Atlanta, are they? 'Cause Shady Grove doesn't need their sort."

"You can pop your eyes back into your head 'cause they're not coming back."

Gracie heaved herself into her seat. "That's a relief. Now, go on. But don't scare me like that again, you hear?"

Artie shot her an apologetic look. "Well, I was plenty mad at the way they were pecking at my little chick."

"I remember. Ben stopped you from going over there and giving the Parnells what for. First time I ever saw you two fight." She'd never been so proud of Artie. That was the day she knew he loved her like she was his own. It didn't matter that their blood didn't match and their skin wasn't the same color.

Artie's gaze turned sheepish. "Ben was right, honey. I was wrong. It would have made things worse. But I did something just as bad."

"What's that?"

"I let you believe all folks with money are nasty, selfish folks. That ain't the whole truth, so I'm comin' clean. You hear what I'm sayin'?"

Artie's middle initial was *T*. He claimed it stood for Theodore, but Gracie knew better—

the *T* was for truthful. Artie started to twitch if a lie slept on his tongue too long. He wasn't exactly twitching, but the whites of his eyes were showing more than usual.

Gracie raised one brow, a look he'd perfected and she'd adopted. "Arthur Dubois, you are being mighty mysterious. Is that all you came down here to tell me?"

Artie's gaze got even quieter. "You need to get yourself home. That's all. Can't say no more."

Sam Fontana let the rented Town Car roll to a stop in front of 1854 Peachtree Lane. It wasn't hard to find. Shady Grove was stuffed into what resembled the letter *I*, with the long middle being Pecan Street, and Peachtree and Parnell forming the arms and legs on the opposite ends. The tiny lanes, which laced between, were little more than dog tracks speckled with clapboard shotgun shacks sandwiched by truck gardens. From there, the lanes petered out into red-clay paths that wandered into a dense green tangle of trees and kudzu.

The exact population of Shady Grove depended on which end you entered from. The sign in front of the First Methodist Church at the east end claimed the town boasted two thousand and twelve residents, while the one planted firmly in front of the First Baptist at the west end claimed only eighteen hundred and fifty. The fact that the residents had differing opinions on their numbers reinforced his belief that he'd entered an alternate universe.

When Kate Hammond had handed him her missing granddaughter's address, he was sure her steel-trap-of-a-brain had finally come unsprung. He double-checked the number one more time. No mistake. This was it. 1–8–5–4 could easily be the year it was built. Conrad Hammond's precious daughter had been raised in a dilapidated house where the paint was so faded the color was a mere memory—just one of many facts that did not bode well for Gracie's smooth transition to the Hammond lifestyle.

Sam cut the motor and grabbed the bouquet of flowers from the front seat. Conrad Hammond's long-lost daughter would probably be so excited, she wouldn't notice the daisies were slightly wilted from the heat.

Before he lost his nerve, he climbed out and glanced at his watch one more time before he punched the doorbell. Ben Calloway had phoned his hotel and warned him not to show up early. He'd insisted that he needed time to give Gracie the news himself, which was fine by Sam. He didn't want Conrad's daughter fainting at his feet.

Chapter 2

When Gracie came downstairs, pink streamers and clusters of balloons were draped over the doorways of Ben's drab living room. Alice had outdone herself. There was even a fancy cardboard sign with HAPPY BIRTHDAY linked together in glittery letters and another that Gracie recognized as a leftover from the Sunday school graduation party that said CONGRATULATIONS.

Artie tottered out of the hall. "Don't you look nice in your new party dress. Turn around and let me take a look at you." He motioned for her to twirl.

Heat rose to Gracie's cheeks. She tugged at the scooped neckline to hide what little was showing of her womanly parts. "Don't you start. I feel half naked already. I'm only wearing this to make Alice happy."

"Well, you look like a fine ladybird with the right amount of feathers. As much as it pains me to say it, maybe Alice is on to somethin' with that new dress. You look pretty."

Gracie raised a skeptical brow Artie's way. "Pretty? I'm not sure you know the meaning of the word. Alice's new frilly kitchen curtains are *pretty*." He knew darn well how she preferred indifferent comments when it came to her appearance, if any at all. He also knew, better than anyone, that Gracie dallying in front of a mirror only led to trouble. She'd start looking for things that weren't there—like a family resemblance to Rita or Ben, an occupation that invariably set her in a nasty mood and ended with her crying on his shoulder. It wouldn't be long before she'd end up speculating on who her daddy was and if he shared her gray-green eyes, fine brown hair, and arrow-straight nose.

"Arthur Dubois, you know, and I know, that I've never been *pretty* in my whole life."

Artie's self-satisfied grin said otherwise. Gracie gave up trying to stare him down and retreated to the safety of Ben's chair.

But before she could settle in, Artie fluttered his hands at her and shooed her toward the door. "Someone's knockin'. You go on and answer it. And remember what I told you—put on your smiley face."

Gracie shot Artie a hard look as she marched to the door. "You want to tell me what's going on?"

"The river's rising, girl, and there ain't no boat. Sometimes you just gotta jump in and swim like hell."

Gracie paused with her hand on the handle. "Last time you said that, we were down by two in the ninth and I had a stomachache, which turned out to be *the flu*."

"And you hit a home run before you parked your cookies on that sassy catcher's new glove. Saved the day. Now, go to it, girl."

Cautiously Gracie peered through the door's cameo. In the fading light, she caught sight of the back of a tall man in a ball cap. The relief was so immediate that Gracie was able to produce one more smile. "It's just Skippy. Shame on you, Artie Dubois, for scaring the daylights out of me."

After twenty years of waltzing into the Calloway household unannounced, Skippy had suddenly taken to ringing the darn bell. Short of cutting the wire, there was nothing Gracie could do to talk him out of his nasty new habit.

Gracie swung the door wide. "Get yourself in here, Skippy. We've all got clothes on."

A tall stranger swiped a Yankee's ball cap from his head. "Miss Calloway?"

Gracie's tongue lost its way as she struggled to work his dark features into Skip Evers's paler image. "Excuse me, I thought you were . . . our neighbor."

The stranger's hair was inky like a night river, slicked back and swimming over the collar of his crisp blue Oxford shirt. He didn't seem at all surprised by her confusion. He deftly juggled his briefcase and a thirsty bouquet of daisies to his left hand and extended his right toward Gracie. "Sam Fontana, private investigator. I represent Katherine Hammond, your grandmother."

Gracie inched away from his big hand. "I'm afraid you're mistaken, Mr. . . . Fontana, was it? My grandma's name was Calloway. She passed on before I was born. Now, if you'll excuse me, I've got folks waiting in the kitchen."

She started to close the door, but he blocked her move with his arm and gestured toward the sofa. "Perhaps you're uncle hasn't had time to explain . . ."

Gracie sent a panicked glance over her shoulder to Artie, but he'd disappeared. The remainder of Gracie's patience went with him. She turned back to the stranger and shot him a hot look that had been known to shrivel hulking belligerent ball players. "Maybe I should talk slower. *You* . . . don't seem to be *hearing* me, *mister*. I-don't-know-any-Hammonds." Gracie's words waded out of her mouth like sated ants out of a honey jar. Even she could hear her own voice twang. Why was he looking at her funny?

A twinkle sparkled in his eyes. He was laughing at her. Heat rushed to her cheeks. Suddenly, she had the urge to rubberize his shin, but before she could unleash her frustration on the stranger, Ben's big palm landed heavily on her shoulder and drew her back.

"Come on in, Mr. Fontana. You're just in time for the cake." Ben's drawl had a nervous tick as it jumped past her ear. "Gracie, honey, why don't you go on and help Alice in the kitchen?"

24

Gracie shrugged off his grip and tipped her head back to check Ben's face for caginess. Sure enough, his gaze dodged hers. He was hiding something all right. She glanced back at the stranger. His dark features were dipped in a frown and aimed at Ben. She wasn't the only one in the fog.

Before she could take Ben to task, the stranger took advantage of the lull and thrust the daisies at her and flashed another of his bold grins her way. "Happy Birthday, Miss Calloway. Your father was a good friend of mine. It's an honor."

Her stunned gaze volleyed back and forth between Ben and the stranger. All the apprehension she'd felt when Artie showed up at the market came rushing back. "Ben, what's he talking about?"

Alice's mushroom sandals pumped across the floor with a familiar soft hiss. Ben reached out with his free arm and corralled her to the door. "Alice, this here's Sam Fontana. He came all the way from Connecticut to wish *Our* Gracie a happy birthday."

Ben stepped aside so Alice could do the proper with the Yankee visitor. Darned, if the man didn't flash his bright teeth and pour on the charm when he grasped Alice's hand.

And wouldn't you know, Alice blushed like a ripe peach. "All the way from Connecticut . . . how nice. Welcome, Mr. Fontana. We've got plenty of cake to go around, so don't you worry your sweet tooth a minute. And look, you brought flowers, too. Why, isn't that mighty thoughtful of you. Gracie, honey, let me put those in water before they drop dead."

Gracie glanced at the daisies. "You're too late." Carelessly she tossed the stranger's shabby gift to Alice then inserted herself between Ben and the mysterious Mr. Fontana. "Now just a minute, Ben . . . Rita never said anything in her letters about my daddy—"

Ben ignored her and herded the man toward the kitchen. "This way, Sam. Hold on to your tongue 'cause Alice makes the best Sally Lunn cake you ever tasted. She won't give us any until we've sung the birthday song and blown out the candles."

"But, Ben, Skip's not here—"

"We'll save him a slice. Now step aside, Gracie, so our guest can help us celebrate your big day. After we've had our cake, Sam and I are going to have a talk. You'll get your answers when we're done, so hush yourself till then."

Gracie's surprise must have shown on her face. Sam Fontana shot her an apologetic look that sent the blood rushing to her cheeks. Ben's gruff ways rarely unsettled her. Most times she had to admit she'd earned the rough side of his temper.

Gracie swallowed the lump in her throat and

followed Ben into the kitchen. The last thing she wanted were more looks of pity from the mysterious Mr. Fontana.

Artie was seated at the table, looking even more tired than he had a few minutes ago. He raised his chin her way and locked his gaze on hers. "Make a wish, girl. Not one of them no-account ones. Make it big." Then he offered her an encouraging smile and cocked one brow, reminding her that this celebration was not just for her but for all of them—Alice, Ben, and himself. With a family as small as theirs, there were few occasions to celebrate. They looked forward to this day every year.

Alice reached across the table between them and lit the candles. "Don't just stand there, Ben Calloway, shut the lights off and get ready to snap the picture."

The room went dark, except for the blazing cake. Ben positioned himself beside the stranger who stood at Artie's back. "Smile now, girl, or your aunt will make me stand here all night."

Gracie kept her gaze on Artie as the camera flashed. *A big wish,* he'd said. As long as she'd been a kid, she'd only had one that qualified as big—*Rita coming home and being her mama.* But that wasn't what Artie was hinting at. She thought about things that might match Artie's definition of big—the Braves winning the series, attending a playoff game, shaking Tom Glavine's hand . . .

all things she might enjoy—but not her heart's desire.

Ben's wish would involve a big fish. Gracie didn't care much for fish, big or otherwise. Alice's wish was easy to figure—she'd want Gracie to land a husband before her next birthday, but there was no way Gracie was going to ask for that . . . So, Rita was it.

Gracie focused on the dancing flames, took a big breath, and blew with all her might. The camera flashed again. When all the candles were out and she'd glanced up, it was the handsome Mr. Fontana who caught her gaze. She wouldn't exactly call the curve of his lips a smile. It was more like a knowing grin. Gracie suddenly felt a heat wave blow beneath the hem of her new dress. A warm flood rushed to her cheeks. Gooseflesh prickled the backs of her arms. If she glanced away first, she'd look like a chicken. Then he'd know how nervous his glances made her feel.

To her relief, Ben shoved a plate at Mr. Fontana and steered him toward the living room.

Gracie steadied her hand and accepted a slice of cake from Alice, then reached for a chair beside Artie. "He says he's a friend of my daddy's— How do I know he's telling the truth?"

Artie waved her off. "The answers you's lookin' for got to come from Ben. You go on out there and nail his tail, you hear?"

Ben had positioned himself on the sofa, next to Mr. Fontana. His plate was already empty. If Gracie knew his sweet tooth, he'd be heading back to the kitchen for another slice of cake. "Nailing Ben's tail," as Artie put it, was not so easy. He'd had years of practice dodging Alice's inquisitions. Gracie would get quicker answers out of the stranger.

Gracie took a seat in Ben's chair and eyed Sam Fontana over her plate. She'd say he was handsome, if she were in a better mood. He'd perched himself on the edge of the piano bench with his legs spread wide and his forearms resting on his thighs. His hat with the chopstick New York Yankees logo lay alongside his briefcase. His attention was on his plate. With the dexterity of a surgeon, he removed the icing, then cut the cake into neat bite-sized pieces. Gracie didn't realize she was staring at him until he flipped his gaze up to hers. And there it was again, that sly grin lurking in his dark eyes.

Gracie self-consciously checked her neckline and quickly shifted her gaze to his briefcase. *New and pricey. Definitely not a blue-light special.* In the raggedy surroundings of their secondhand living room, the smooth-as-glass leather smelled like freshly minted money. A closer look, and sure enough, the name *Hammond* was stamped beneath the handle in fancy gold letters. It was a hard-sounding name, stiff as bricks, and more than a little intimidating. Not a name she'd choose. Rita must have felt the same way, or she wouldn't have run off and left Gracie in a lurch.

She ignored the flutter in her chest and forced herself to look him square in the eye. "So, Mr. Fontana, why didn't my daddy come himself?"

Ben rocketed out of his seat and reached for Mr. Fontana's plate. "How about another piece of cake?"

The teasing light disappeared from Sam Fontana's gaze. He glanced at Ben briefly. "No, thanks. I'd like to answer Gracie's question."

Ben's face colored up, but Alice had rushed in to his rescue. "Come into the kitchen, Ben Calloway, and I'll cut you a big slice. Let the nice Mr. Fontana chat with Our Gracie." Alice stopped beside Gracie. "I just knew that blue dress would look good on you. I said to Marjorie Finks it would. She wanted me to buy the pink one, but I told her the blue would go better with your eyes. Don't you agree, Mr. Fontana?" She hurried Ben off to the kitchen, without giving Mr. Fontana a chance to reply.

Sam's gaze followed Ben and Alice as far as the kitchen, then abruptly bounced back to Gracie. "To answer your question—your father passed away. Recently."

Gracie felt like she'd been sucker punched. She'd had a daddy a whole twenty minutes of her small life. Considering Rita's track record as her mama, she shouldn't feel cheated, but she did.

He leaned forward on the edge of the bench. His masculine features wore a worried expression. "I know this comes as a surprise. I want to reassure you that your grandmother, Katherine Hammond, is anxious to meet you. Your father's sudden death came as quite a blow to her—to all of us, in fact."

"Where did you say you're from?"

"Connecticut."

"This grandma, you say I have, is from there, too?"

"That's right."

Rita had run off to New York but ended up in Connecticut—that much Gracie knew. There was a chance that he was on the level. Gracie was busy drawing a mental picture of her fictitious grandma when the doorbell rang.

Ben took the interruption as a chance to burst back into the living room. "You best answer the door, girl, and give Mr. Fontana's ear a rest."

"Don't go away, Mr. Fontana, I have a few more questions for you." Gracie shot Ben a warning glance and hurried to the door.

"Happy birthday, Gracie." Skip Evers shoved a lumpy package with a lopsided bow at Gracie. "That's so I don't have to listen to you bellyache about your fingers burning during ball practice."

Gracie hugged the present to her chest. A baseball glove was all she'd ever get from Skippy and that was just fine by her. She reached out to give him a hug, but Ben snatched Skip away. "Say hello to Mr. Fontana from Connecticut, Skipper. He's come to see Our Gracie."

Skip beamed brightly and offered his hand to the Yankee. "Connecticut? That's a long way to come for a birthday party. Where'd you say you know Gracie from?"

The stranger accepted Skip's grip, but his gaze reached for Gracie. "We have a mutual friend."

"That so, huh? Well, welcome to Shady Grove."

From the look on the Yankee's face, Gracie guessed he was sizing Skippy up and figuring out what part he played in her life. The possibilities drew a thoughtful frown on Sam's face. Gracie had to admit, though it was a darker look, it was no less handsome.

Gracie lost her chance to drill Mr. Fontana with more questions. Ben maneuvered their guest and Skippy into a conversation on the merits of fishing with live bait. Gracie was left to Alice's updates on the new line of fall dresses at Marjorie Finks's dress shop.

When the cake had been wiped clean from their plates and Skippy had gone home, Alice enlisted Gracie's help in the kitchen while Ben hustled the visitor onto the screened porch out back. It was clear Ben had no intention of letting Gracie in on their conversation.

Gracie stacked the plates in the sink and tried to sneak a peek at the men on the porch. Artie had always been there to point Ben gently in the right direction, but he'd disappeared without even finishing his cake. "Where's Artie? I'd feel a whole lot better if he was there."

Alice poked her head out of the fridge. "He's got better things to do than spy for you. He's resting."

Gracie started toward Artie's door, but Alice cut her off. "Let him be. I expect he's tired from his walk."

Alice was right. Artie was practically falling asleep in his chair after Alice cut the cake. He'd only taken two bites. Next time he went to the doctor, she was going to tag along.

Gracie marched back to the sink, picked up a dish towel, and glanced toward the porch. "Ben has turned into a regular chatterbox. Most days, I hardly get two words out of him. Now he and Mr. Fontana are sharing secrets, like two twelve-year-old girls."

Alice's gaze went all soft and drifted from the hot soapy water toward the back porch. "Mr. Fontana is so handsome and he has a nice smile, don't you think?" Then she was back, looking Gracie square in the eye. "And he has good teeth. You can tell a man by the condition of his teeth.

33

If he smokes too much or drinks, it shows. The Lord won't hide a man's vices for him. No, siree."

It was a known fact in the Calloway households that the Reverend J.D. Adams had good teeth, the finest measure of a man in Alice's book. Ben kept his in a jelly jar beside his bed at night. Enough said.

Through the screened window, Gracie caught a glimpse of the Yankee's smile. It was nice, she'd give him that, but she'd learned from Shelly Ann Parnell's mama that nice smiles didn't add up. Gracie reached for a handful of knives. "They could be caps. Maybe he's got a cousin who's a dentist."

"Oh, you *are* a cynical child. Where's your faith? Artie's responsible for this. He's made you distrustful of your fellow man. I blame myself for letting you grow up in a house full of men." Alice reached for Gracie's dish towel to wipe at the corners of her eyes.

Gracie offered her a brief hug. "We've been all through this. Your job at the church was a sacrifice I was willing to make for the folks of Shady Grove, and they thank me for it every Sunday. Shady Grove First Methodist has never had a finer secretary. Reverend Adams says so often enough. Why, I think he'd have you admitted to sainthood if he was a priest."

Alice's face matched the roses printed on her apron. "Don't be blasphemous, child."

"Artie took care of me just fine. I've got all my fingers and toes. And I was never good at ballet dancing. Besides, you would have been bored sitting through baseball practice."

"Baseball practice won't get you a man."

Gracie rolled her eyes. The argument was so old, she was sure it must have been scrawled in the Old Testament. Apart from the celebrity gossip rags, the Bible was the only reading material Alice paid homage to.

Gracie stole a quick glance at Sam Fontana. "Who's to say I want one?"

"If any man would be impressed with your arm, it would be Skip Evers; and I don't see him cutting a path to your door with anything but an empty stomach. He didn't look twice at you in that new dress. But that handsome Mr. Fontana took a good eyeful. And he has such nice teeth . . ."

The fact that Shady Grove was short on men like Sam Fontana hadn't escaped Gracie's notice. Unlike Alice, she counted it as a blessing. Men like Sam Fontana made her nervous.

Gracie dogged Alice from the sink to the table and back. "If I had a grandma and a daddy somewhere, you'd think Rita would have told us in a letter."

Alice set to scrubbing the cake plate with more enthusiasm than necessary. "Rita was never one to take much score in other's feelings. We just figured the day you arrived on our doorstep was

God's way of bringing you where you belonged. Poor Rita, I suppose losing a mama at age fourteen does things to a girl. Lynne did the best she could with her."

"Do you know who my daddy was, Alice?" Gracie had asked the question a thousand times before she was twelve. Suddenly something always needed mending or washing. Finally, she'd stopped asking.

But the answers were being whispered in the next room, and she was tired of waiting. She crossed her arms and eyed her aunt. "The truth, Alice. Let's have it."

Alice picked up a dish towel and swiped feverishly at invisible crumbs. "Like I told you before, Rita ran off to New York City with Tom Robbins's boy. He came back, but she didn't. Ben will tell us soon enough, I expect."

Tom Robbins's boy, Woody Robbins, had a freckled face and red hair. He'd been married for twenty years. Every one of his five kids had the same pumpkin-red hair and spotty skin, not to mention ears like bats. She'd ruled him out years ago.

Gracie parked herself at the counter in Alice's way. "Ben would have told us by now, if there wasn't something to hide. I've had an uneasy feeling all day."

Alice paused in her wiping and narrowed her gaze on Gracie. "No one in our family has ever had the sight. God wouldn't have allowed it. What you feel is Mr. Fontana's admiration. When a man notices you, you feel different, that's all."

Gracie snatched a quick peek at the porch. Ben reached out and handed the Yankee a piece of paper, which quickly disappeared into Sam Fontana's briefcase. When the stranger looked up, his gaze collided with hers. He flashed her another grin before she ducked out of view.

"They're passing notes. Now, are you going to tell me, or do I have to march in there—"

Before Alice could give her a straight answer, Ben stepped into the kitchen. He was alone. His smile wavered when it landed on Gracie. "Have a seat, Gracie girl."

Gracie pulled a chair from the kitchenette and plopped herself into it, then crossed her arms over her chest. "Okay, let's have it. I'm tired of all this mystery."

Ben waddled back and forth across the yellowed linoleum, massaging his neck between nervous glances. "First off, I guess I should tell you Rita ain't your mama."

Suddenly the birthday cake felt like lead in Gracie's stomach. *Rita wasn't her mama?* She'd have to admit, she'd entertained the thought once or twice when she was feeling sorry for herself. After all, Rita had never showed much interest in filling the role. A few token gifts in twenty-five years weren't much to hang your heart on. At first, Gracie had seen the presents as promises of love. But as she grew older and Rita never appeared along with the frilly packages, she knew they were just guilt gifts, each a more painful reminder than the last that she wasn't worthy of Rita's love. Along about age twelve, she stopped opening the gifts. Ben took to hiding the presents to keep her spirits from disintegrating into weeklong bouts of tears.

Cautiously, Gracie opened her mouth to speak, but Ben jumped ahead. "Now, don't go gettin' yourself all worked up until I finish. I might not be able to start again. The truth is, I never met your mama. She might be a fine woman. It ain't my place to say. As for your daddy . . . well, I'm sorry to report that Sam was telling the truth, he's gone to his maker. I feel bad about that."

Ben shot a nervous glance Alice's way, then took a shaky breath. "The fact is, he left you some money and Mr. Fontana is here to see that you take it. That about fills the pot."

Money? That's what this fuss was all about? Artie's visit to the market suddenly made sense. She thought about his warning. Then she thought about the Parnells and the humiliation she'd suffered when the girls she'd counted as her friends deserted her. Darla Watson and Shelly Ann Parnell had smeared her new Barbie lunch pail, which Alice had bought her for her birthday, with peanut butter and honey, then set it on an anthill in the schoolyard. When the lunch bell rang, Darla and Shelly gathered a circle of girls around her and taunted her with names like *Love Baby*, and others too ugly to recall. She didn't need to impress the likes of Darla Watson. The last thing she wanted was to draw more attention to herself. She'd spent years working herself into the background so folks would leave her be.

The fact that she'd had a daddy—something she'd always wished for—and that he'd left her some money, did give her pause. But all this time he'd known where she was, and he hadn't come to get her. Why? Gracie knew the answer without even asking—*because she wasn't worth coming for, that's why.* There was no other explanation. The money was just his guilt talking—like the frilly birthday presents Rita had sent over the years.

She didn't want to be anybody's charity case. She didn't need her daddy's money. She had the things she wanted. "Tell Mr. Fontana to give it to the church. They need a new roof on the Bible school."

Alice squeezed Gracie's shoulder. "Oh, Gracie . . . that's real considerate of you, and I don't want to be un-Christian, but you know, you might put it in your hope chest. Young couples need money to buy houses and things. It's time to think about such and the like. I'm sure the Lord wouldn't begrudge you a home."

Ben's smile was still missing. He paced while Alice fluttered. "They'll be plenty left over after she puts a new roof on the school, I expect."

Alice stopped her fussing and placed a warm hand on Gracie's shoulder. "Well, that's very generous of Our Gracie's daddy. I'll say a prayer for his soul."

Gracie was still waiting for Ben's smile to surface. He'd never looked so uneasy. Gracie tried to smother her panic. It was just money, guilt money at that, nothing to get worked up about. She felt her lips tremble when she opened her mouth to speak. "How much will be left over, Ben?"

Ben's face turned crimson and his kerchief emerged from his pocket. He wiped as he spoke. "More than a day's wage." Ben could tell big fish stories all day long without stumbling over a word. This was different. He was practically choking on what Gracie suspected was an ugly truth.

Beads of perspiration popped out on Gracie's upper lip. She ignored Alice's eagle eye and swiped at the moisture with the back of her hand. "Ben Calloway, how *much* more?"

" 'Bout six hundred and fifty million, give or take a bit."

Chapter 3

Gracie hadn't slept a wink. The ridiculous sum Ben had spouted at her hung in the air like a bubble in a comic strip. *Six hundred and fifty million dollars.*

She could barely wrap her mind around the amount. What did one person do with that kind of money? She'd seen plenty of reports on TV about folks who'd won the lottery; their stories were littered with divorce, broken friendships, even murder and suicide. The whole business sickened her, but not just for the obvious reasons. Those poor suckers had become a public spectacle. The envious world standing by expecting them to make a big show. When their new lives toppled and fell to ruins, the same wishful folks were there to pick at the leavings, confident in the fact that they would have made wiser choices and not become fools. But Gracie had a theory of her own: Money was the best maker of fools. It was like a slippery friend who promised you a good time and made you forget about the things that really mattered—things most folks took for granted, like love and loyalty, even generosity—until it was too late. She'd worked hard to gain the love and respect that came naturally to most folks. She didn't want to risk losing a single friendship over something as fickle as money.

Gracie's good fortune, as Alice called it, was further complicated by the fact that she wasn't just Jane Doe who'd made good on the weekly lottery pool. She had another history that guaranteed a crowd—*she was somebody's kidnapped baby*. If she knew anything about the general population, she knew they craved a juicy story where the underdog wins. Such things didn't happen all that often in real life. Thanks to Alice's subscription to *People* magazine, she'd already figured out that she would be a prime target for a made-for-TV movie, some screenwriter's million-dollar ticket to fame and fortune.

And then there was the fact that no one seemed to be considering her feelings on the matter. Had her father even thought of her longer than the moment it took him to sign a piece of paper condemning her to become a public spectacle? If he'd known about her, why hadn't he come to find her? She knew the answer without asking. *Because he was embarrassed by her.* It was the story of her life—first Rita, now her daddy.

Gracie had been petrified with disbelief when Ben dropped the bomb. Time had stopped while Ben's words, traveling through her subconscious, tripped silent alarms. Then she'd caught sight of Alice in her peripheral vision. Poor Alice had gone sheet white. Gracie snapped to in time to lower Alice into a chair. Ben had dithered in the background looking sheepish while Gracie fortified Alice's nerves with cooking sherry.

Ben had refused to answer her questions with more than a noncommittal shrug. This morning, even Artie had played dumb. She needed facts to see just how bad things were. Gracie decided to take advantage of the early hour and made a trek to the other side of the tracks to what the residents of Shady Grove fondly dubbed The Temple—the Shady Grove Library, a small brick Greek Revival building that sat on the corner of Parnell and Pecan streets.

Willa Snow, Shady Grove's librarian, was as old as dirt but sharp as spring grass. Half the time she could be seen dozing at her desk, her mouth cocked open with her tonsils baiting flies. But Gracie wasn't fooled—the white-haired spinster was playing possum. If you didn't return a book on time, you could bet she'd be at your door the next morning to poke you with her bony finger and deliver a lecture that would make the most hardened sinner repent. Consequently, not many books strayed past the shiny white pillars of Willa's castle.

Gracie caged the butterflies in her stomach and marched up the neatly swept steps. Her goal was the back room where the periodicals were stored in heavy leather-bound books the size of suitcases. Blessedly, she caught Willa in the middle of her morning doze. As Gracie tiptoed past the front desk, she prayed Ben's big fish story was for once as mythical as the two-hundred-pound granddaddy catfish in Miller's Pond.

The musty smell of aged paper and mildew hit her as soon as she stepped through the narrow doorway. The room had once been a storeroom. The walls were bare brick with only two narrow windows that had been painted shut back when dinosaurs roamed the earth. Willa's solution to the airless room was a fan in the far corner.

Gracie located the yellowing volumes of the *Atlanta Constitution*, then wrestled the leather tome to the table, frantically thumbing to October 1970. Midway through, the bold headlines jumped off the page at her.

KIDNAPPED BABY FEARED DROWNED

Late yesterday, financier Conrad Hammond's baby daughter, Katherine Hammond, was taken from her home. The kidnapper and his car were found in a nearby river twelve hours after the child was reported missing from the nursery by her mother, Lillian Hammond. The four-month-old heiress to the Hammond fortune is thought to have drowned along with her kidnapper, but the baby's body is yet to be recovered. Hammond says he will continue the search until his daughter is found. The financier has offered a reward of one million dollars for information leading to her recovery. The kidnapper was identified as Eddie Fry, a golf instructor at Fairfield Oaks Country Club where Hammond is a member . . .

Good gravy! Ben had left out a few important details—on purpose, no doubt. Gracie read the last line again. *Fairfield Oaks Country Club.* The tattered note Rita had left behind on Ben's doorstep had been scrawled on a piece of Fairfield Oaks stationery; its looping logo implanted clearly in her childhood memory.

When she was six years old, she'd begged Ben for the stained piece of paper so she could put it in her treasure box. Each birthday she pulled it out and reread Rita's words: *Could you mind her for a spell?* And every year she wondered when Ben's *spell* would be up and her mama would come and collect her. Finally, the ritual became too painful, and she'd buried Rita's note in the backyard in a coffee can.

Now she knew the answer to her question. Rita was never coming—Little Gracie Calloway was a damn heiress, richer than even Shelly Ann Parnell. But she could go Shelly Ann one better— she was a Yankee, something Shelly Ann would never be.

Gracie's morning trip to the library had stirred up more questions than it had answered. And wouldn't you know—Ben, true to his wishy-washy self, had scooted out the door while she was gone, taking the day's newspaper with him. She decided to anchor herself to the same kitchen chair where Ben had dropped the six-hundred-and-fifty-million-dollar bomb, to try to digest the fact that someone she didn't know wanted to give her enough money to bankroll a small country.

As far as Gracie was concerned, Martians had taken over the Calloway households and sucked out folks' brains along with their good sense. To prove her theory, Alice came hurrying through the back door armed with a bottle of 409 and a gleam of purpose in her eye.

"Don't just sit there, child. Now that you're somebody, we've got to be ready for company. You never know who might drop by. Someone is bound to want to interview you."

She whirled across the room and attacked the stove top like it was the hood of a prize automobile, sneaking occasional glances Gracie's way. "That was nice of Ben to show your Mr. Fontana a little hospitality after your party last night. I do believe he is finally learning some manners. About time, I must say. Particularly now that you've got yourself a proper suitor."

Gracie recognized the calculated intent flickering in the corner of her aunt's gaze. "He's not *my* anything. You're swinging at curve balls that will never make it past first base."

Alice scurried around the fringes of Gracie's vision, humming happily. The longer Gracie let the silence go, the deeper trouble she was going to be in. Once Alice's imagination got to galloping, it never ran out of wind. Now was time to head it off before it raced out the gate into gossipy Marjorie Finks's pasture.

Gracie blocked Alice's path to the sink. "He doesn't even like me."

Alice ignored Gracie's glare and darted around her. "Of course he does. He brought you flowers and he wants to give you all that money."

Money. Finally a subject Gracie could attack without guilt. "It's obscene that anyone should be that rich. What the hell do people *do* with that kind of money?"

Alice shot her a warning look that said, watch your mouth, young lady, but it disappeared as fast as it came. "How 'bout I fix you a nice steak. A good piece of meat will help clear your thinking."

Gracie glanced up at Alice, who now was perched over the refrigerator on a step stool. "You shouldn't be up there. You might have one of your dizzy spells, then I'd have to take that Yankee's money just to pay your hospital bill."

Alice backed down the stool's steps slowly.

Once she hit the floor, she shot to Gracie's chair beside the table. "You have to accept the money, Gracie Lynne. It would be impolite to refuse. Besides, your daddy left it to you. You can't insult his good name. What would folks think?" Up came her scolding finger.

Gracie cringed. *Oh Lordy, here it comes.*

"They'd think we'd raised you to be an ungrateful nobody, that's what they'd think. And for your information, missy, my dizzy spells are firecrackers under your lazy uncle's fanny. They're nothing to worry about. It's the other reasons you need to be thinking of."

There was no arguing with Alice when she brought out "what will folks think." But Gracie couldn't back down on this one. She braced herself for a storm. "We're not talking hemlines here. That much money is a lot of trouble. I've seen enough of your celebrity magazines to know what those rich folks have to deal with. I'm just not prepared to take it on. I'm getting a migraine just thinking about it."

She really was getting a headache. Gracie rubbed her temples for good effect.

Alice shot her a worried glance and opened her mouth to speak, but Gracie cut her off. "Besides, I've got my job at the market. I make a nice living. There is nothing I want, I can't buy myself. Go ahead, name one person who is better off with millions of dollars."

48

"That's the devil's advocate talking, young lady. Your daddy didn't leave the money to his shiftless second wife and her spoiled daughter. He knew you'd do better. You keep the market's books neat and tidy. You'll just get a bigger book, that's all." With that said, Alice attacked her next victim, the clean Formica tabletop.

Gracie popped out of her chair and followed Alice around to the other side. "*What* second wife and spoiled daughter? I have *a sister?* Why did nobody tell me?"

Alice scrubbed harder, avoiding Gracie's gaze. "Only a half, mind you."

Gracie shuffled Alice's disapproval under the rug. *She had a sister.* The same blood ran in her veins, just a little farther north on the map. It was almost too much to hope for. She'd always wanted to be part of a big family, but since Rita showed no signs of coming home, it hadn't even been something to get worked up about. Gracie retreated to her chair again, her legs suddenly shaky. "And my mother? Where is she?"

Alice stopped her circling. "I haven't heard about your mama. Don't you go getting any sentimental ideas about any of them, you hear? They are most likely poison. If they weren't, Ben would have . . ." Alice faltered and turned away. "Well, I can't say, is all."

"*Ben.* I should have known. So, when did he let you in on my birthday surprise? Or have you been sharing secrets with Mr. Fontana all along?"

"I haven't said two words to Mr. Fontana. Shame on you, Gracie, for thinking such a thing." Alice rushed to the sink and busied herself with rinsing out the sponge. Her lips were set in the stubborn line they assumed when she'd spoken out of turn and wanted to take something back.

Gracie followed Alice to the sink, then reached over and shut the water off, forcing her aunt to look up her way. "I need to know, Alice."

Alice was ready for her with a mulish frown. "Ben told me about them the night before last. I wormed it out of him with pie. You might try doing the same with that nice Mr. Fontana. He looks like a man who appreciates pumpkin." The stubbornness melted from her gaze. "And don't forget the nutmeg. I'll bet he's the sort who likes extra spice . . ." Then she was gone—carried off in the ether, most likely, by the sound of wedding bells.

But Gracie wasn't through. *"Alice—"*

The soft fleshy skin stiffened over the hard angle of Alice's jaw. "You didn't need to associate with *their* kind. Even your own daddy agreed."

Gracie crossed her arms and mimicked Alice's stony stance. "What kind is that?" Gracie knew what Alice's definition of *their kind* was, but she wanted Alice to say it so she could build her case against the handsome Mr. Fontana with the good

50

teeth. So far, Alice wouldn't admit that the money he was trying to foist on her was trouble, even though Alice had preached to Gracie all her life on the vice of selfishness and greed.

"You know, the kind that's self-indulgent and doesn't pay the Lord his due respect."

"You mean like those hoity-toity Parnells? Don't you worry. I have no intention of being one of them. I don't want the money Mr. Fontana is pushing on me, but I wouldn't mind a sister."

"I think it's time we paid a visit to Reverend Adams. Perhaps J.D. can talk some sense into that thick head of yours."

Alice had the Reverend Adams wrapped around her little finger. The bachelor preacher had blessed her when she'd rescued him from the clutches of the Widow Perkins. She had explained very patiently to the grasping Delilah Perkins that the reverend was devoted only to the Lord—*and herself*, but Alice left out this tiny detail. Those close to Alice were aware of his adoration, even Uncle Ben, who didn't seem bothered by the fact that his next-door wife had a platonic relationship with the preacher.

Alice's finger was at the ready. She wasted no time wagging it in Gracie's face. "I know just what he'll say."

"Me too." Gracie weathered Alice's storm with her hands planted firmly on her hips. But her refusal to budge didn't slow Alice down.

She continued to wave her finger in Gracie's direction. "He'll say you need to think of the others, those you could help with the money. God don't give you these opportunities without a reason. He opened a door, Gracie. Don't slam it in his face."

"You're right, that's just what he'd say. Guess we can save ourselves a trip and the Reverend Adams's time, now that we know his mind."

Alice gaped back at Gracie. Confusion tugged at her soft pale skin. It would take her a few minutes to digest the fact that Gracie had just agreed with her while refusing her advice all in the same breath, a trick she'd learned from Ben that never failed to throw Alice off the track long enough for them to make an escape. But for some reason, the usual relief Gracie felt when she managed to outwit Alice was missing this time around.

Gracie slipped in the back door of the market just before lunch. She couldn't wait to get to work. Here, at least, she was still the same old Gracie. The familiar sound of Jimmy's voice calling out a price to check-stand two and the smell of pasteboard boxes and fresh produce were signs that life was still as it should be. So far, the news of her new identity had yet to spread beyond the Calloway household. Her fervent hope was that Sam Fontana would realize he'd gotten the wrong girl and would pack his bags and take his handsome face back to frosty Connecticut. Yesterday would fade into a distant memory.

Gracie closed her office door quietly and seated herself at her desk. She glanced at the photo propped on the corner. Artie and Ben stood beside her on the front steps. Gracie was all of five years old. She had a smile as big as Texas on her face. One of her hands was tucked into Artie's; the other gripped Ben's thumb. They were a family—maybe not like most folks but in every way that mattered. Sam Fontana couldn't change that. *But the money was a different matter* . . . Money was like magic: tricky.

A sharp knock sounded on the door. Gracie glanced up from the photo. "Come on in, Jimmy."

Sam Fontana stepped into her office and plopped a picnic basket on her desk. "Jimmy said it was okay to bother you."

His tall frame sucked up the empty space in the tiny room. The purposeful gleam in his eye was aimed at her.

Gracie shot to her feet, raced around the desk to close the door, then raced back. "What are you doing here? I figured you'd be long gone by now."

"I guess the news sort of came at you out of the blue. Sorry about that. Ben said it would be better coming from him. Thought maybe you might want to talk."

Gracie glanced at the door nervously. "You didn't say anything to Jimmy, did you?"

"Not a word. I told him I was friend of the family and that Alice had sent me on a mission of life and death." His teasing grin exposed a glimpse of his straight white teeth. "Evidently you forgot to eat breakfast. She assured me you were weak with hunger—near starvation, from the sound of it. I promised her I would make you eat, even if I had to spoon the food into your mouth myself." He was exaggerating, of course, but not by much, knowing Alice's flare for the dramatic.

Gracie eyed Sam's large hand on the basket handle and tried to quiet the flutter in her stomach. "It's a trap, you understand."

Sam flashed her a devilish look and lifted the lid. "For whom?"

There it was again, that disarming smile that could melt butter on a cold day. She dodged his gaze and focused her attention on the basket. "For both of us."

"Is it working?" The tone in his voice dared her to look up.

Gracie crossed her arms over her stomach to hush the grumble. "What did she pack? Let me guess—fried chicken, pickled okra, cornbread, and pie. Am I right?"

Sam opened the lid and unloaded the contents on the desk. "Almost."

He looked way too satisfied with himself. Gracie gave in to her curiosity and leaned over the desk to peer into the basket.

Sam dug to the bottom and produced a triangular piece of aluminum foil. "It's my lucky day. Pizza." He seated himself in a chair opposite hers and speared Gracie with a triumphant look. "By the way, Alice said to tell you she's on to your tricks."

Heat flooded Gracie's cheeks. Alice had no business mixing Sam Fontana up in their personal battles. She retreated back to her seat. "I'm going to have to speak to the reverend. Alice has too much free time these days."

Sam reached into the basket and pulled out two Cokes and handed one to Gracie. "Homemade pizza, my favorite."

"Like I said, a trap."

He was intent on neatly peeling away the layers of foil from a slice but spared her a brief sideways glance. "She did warn me about your cynical side. Alice is a tough cookie. Actually, I feel flattered she went to so much trouble."

"You won't after you take a bite of that."

Sam held up the steaming triangle, eyeing it from side to side. "Why? What's wrong with it?"

"Salt and ketchup. It's Alice's own recipe. Even Ben won't touch it, and he eats just about anything."

Sam shuddered and tossed the pizza into the

garbage can on the side of her desk. "You've ruined my fantasy."

"Good, then we're square. Have some chicken."

Sam accepted a leg and took a bite. They ate in silence, but Gracie could feel his attention fix on her.

When she glanced up, he was staring back. The teasing grin she was beginning to associate with the cocky Yankee was gone. Something besides lunch was on his mind.

Gracie folded her napkin into a neat square, watching him out of the corner of her eye. "It wasn't just Alice who sent you over here today, was it?"

He took his time wiping his fingers and disposing of his lunch before he glanced up her way. "I'm going to be straight with you, Gracie. Today, I'm flying back to Connecticut to see your grandmother. I've got a private jet waiting. I would like you to come with me. You could see where you were born. I know Kate is anxious to meet you."

Leave Shady Grove, go to Connecticut—he didn't know what he was asking.

She popped out of her chair and began to pace behind her desk, trying to think of a way to stall an answer to his invitation. "What about my mama and my sister? You keep mentioning my grandma, but no one says boo about my mama. And Alice told me I have a sister."

"Half sister, technically. Your grandmother thought it would be best to keep your existence quiet for now. The media would have a field day if they found out about you. Believe me, you don't want that. Not yet."

Gracie stopped cold. "I don't want that *ever*." Visions of catty Darla Watson and Marjorie Finks came to mind. Gracie stifled a shudder. "Are you saying my mama and my sister have loose lips?"

Her question hung out there all by its lonesome while the Yankee shifted uneasily in his seat.

"People don't always act like themselves when large sums of money are involved."

So, the Yankee wasn't totally clueless, after all. Nonetheless, Gracie felt disappointed. Sam only confirmed what Alice had told her earlier. Her mama and her sister were like all the rest.

Gracie put on an indifferent face. "You don't have to tell me. Since last night, Ben and Artie have been avoiding me, like I've got some kind of sickness. Artie's holed up in his room—*resting*. Ben rushed off to work at the crack of dawn without his breakfast. And Alice is home baking pizza when she should be at work. The last thing I want is another body to look after."

"Don't worry—Kate is quite capable of looking after herself."

Gracie avoided his gaze and busied herself repacking the basket. "Tell my grandma I'm grateful for her interest and I'm sorry for the loss of her boy, but I have folks to attend to down here."

"Alice said she would look after Ben and Artie for a few days."

"She did, did she? But who's going to look after Alice? She's not been herself lately. I *can't* go, and that's that." Gracie felt the blood whoosh in her ears. She swallowed the lump in her throat and shoved the picnic basket into Sam's empty hands. "If my grandma gives you a hard time, tell her I'm partial to wearing cleats in the house and they would scratch up her nice wood floors. That should quiet her down. Alice is terrified of folks messing up her floors."

"I don't think Kate is worried about her floors, but I'll pass the message along. Can I bring you anything from Connecticut?"

"I've got everything I need right here. Thanks."

He set the basket on his chair and reached into his back pocket, drew out a dog-eared snapshot from his wallet. He held it in front of her. "That's your father and me when I was twelve. He was one of the good guys, Gracie. For the record . . . he cared about you, more than you'll ever know. He's why I'm here . . . and he's why I'll be back."

Harriet Ackers's cluttered bungalow was a refuge of sorts for Gracie. She looked forward to delivering Harriet's groceries on Wednesdays and spending time with the salty ex-army nurse. Their friendship began when she caught Gracie snitching peas off her garden fence. Gracie was all of seven years old. It was summer and she'd spent the morning at Miller's Pond swimming until she thought hunger would bore a hole clean through her stomach before she reached home.

A shortcut ran between the most fruitful truck gardens in Shady Grove—and Harriet's was the prize: the sugar peas fresh off her vines, Gracie's favorite. It was hotter than usual that day. Gracie stopped to rest for a spell in the shade of Harriet's back fence. That's when she spotted Harriet's peas. Once she'd tasted one plump sugary pea, she couldn't stop. She'd just about filled her stomach and was beginning to feel a bit green herself when Harriet reached over the fence, grabbed her by the scruff of the neck, and hauled a terrified Gracie into her kitchen.

Harriet locked the door and plopped down on her kitchen stool, crossing her hamlike arms over her round belly. From her guard station, she ordered Gracie to fix them both lunch. That day, Gracie learned how to make fluffy buttermilk biscuits and creamy chicken gravy; how to whip heavy cream without turning it to butter and pluck the tops off strawberries without wasting the fruit.

She had done such a good job that Harriet promised not to tattle to Ben about Gracie's thievery. But she had given herself away when she cooked the same meal for Ben and Artie weeks later. Basking in their praise, she'd confessed to stealing Harriet's peas. Ben punished her by sending her off to Harriet's two afternoons a week to pull weeds in her garden. By then, Gracie didn't care—she and Harriet had become fast friends.

Harriet hadn't been the only one to enjoy herself that afternoon. Gracie found someone who listened to her without judging her. Harriet didn't mind if Gracie put her elbows on the table or if she tucked her napkin in the neck of her T-shirt. She didn't care that Gracie had dirt on her face. When Harriet laughed, she'd slap her knee and say things like *Hot damn* and *Hell's bells*.

She let her poodle-dog Gigi eat at the table off a plate, same as Gracie. When Gigi went to heaven, Gracie helped Harriet bury her in the back garden and say the eulogy while they both cried until their eyes were nearly swollen shut. Then Harriet had filled two bowls with her home-made vanilla ice cream and poured a whole can of Hershey's chocolate syrup on top in honor of Gigi.

Harriet had loved her sweets. But Gracie hadn't known then that Harriet was pushing toward diabetes. Gracie parked her Jeep and tucked Harriet's prescription into the top of the grocery bag.

She knocked on Harriet's door and poked her head inside. "Put your clothes on, Harry. I've come with your groceries."

"Gracie, honey, you are a blessing. Set them in the kitchen. I'll be right out. I'm fixing Bobo's hair. Hold still, you naughty dog."

Bobo came bounding into the kitchen and launched himself into Gracie's arms, barely giving her time to set the groceries on the table. He stood nearly as tall as Gracie on his hind legs. His silver-gray topknot flopped sideways, weighted down by a pale blue satin ribbon. Gracie held his front paws as they did their ritual dance, with Bobo trying to kiss her on the lips and Gracie dodging his tongue.

"There's not an ounce of the postman's mutt in him, but he refuses to act like his royal-blooded self. I give up." Harriet waddled into the room, supported between two canes. Slowly she eased herself into a La-Z-Boy in the corner of the big square kitchen and smiled back at Gracie as she caught her breath. "Open that last canister on the end of the counter, Gracie, honey. I made you something for your birthday."

Harriet had been baking again. Doc had told her to stay away from sugar because of her diabetes, but Gracie didn't have the heart to scold her. Gracie carried the canister to the table and made a big show of opening the lid and inhaling the rich chocolaty aroma.

"I figured Alice would bake you a cake, but I know you like cookies better. They're coconut chocolate chip, your favorite. Happy birthday, Gracie."

Gracie gave Harriet a hug and took a big bite of the cookie. "The best ever. Thanks, Harry."

"You're mighty welcome. I made an extra batch for my nephew, you know, the one up in Montgomery. David. Fine boy and smart, too. He's been busy working his fingers to the bone making buckets of money. He promised to come visit me and Bobo this weekend. Did you remember my chicken?"

Gracie unloaded the chicken from the bag and set it on the top shelf in the fridge, where Harry could reach it easily. "I had Jimmy set aside the biggest one. Four pounds, like you said."

"That's fine. And the potatoes?"

"Right here. You want them in the fridge, too?"

"In the pantry, second shelf."

"I hear Alice bought you a dress for your birthday."

"You know Alice."

"Yes, I do." Harriet's voice was full of expectation.

Gracie glanced over her shoulder from the refrigerator and paused. "You look like the cat who swallowed the canary. What else did you hear?"

Harriet looked a bit sheepish. She didn't

normally pass along gossip. "Not much. Just that you had a picnic lunch delivered today . . . by a good-looking young man."

"Where did you hear that?"

"From Marjorie Finks. She called to say the slippers I ordered were in. It took her five whole minutes to get around mentioning the slippers. She went on and on about the handsome stranger with the basket. She was standing in the check-out line when he wandered in asking for you. Thought I should warn you that you're on her radar."

Marjorie Finks. Should have known. "Alice sent him over with the basket. He's leaving for Connecticut. I don't expect we'll be seeing him again anytime soon. Marjorie will just have to find someone else to gossip about."

"Connecticut is a fair piece." Harry's smile turned thoughtful.

"You ever been to Connecticut, Harry?"

"Once, a long time ago."

"What's it like?"

"Cold, snowy. Folks didn't have much time to talk. They were too busy keeping warm. I always meant to go back in the fall to see the leaves. It should be beautiful this time of year."

Gracie pulled up a chair at the table and smiled absently in Harriet's direction. "I've heard that, too."

The conversation was dead on arrival. Harriet

was going to think she was bored and trying to wiggle away. Even Bobo had gone to sleep.

Gracie felt like a fraud, smiling when she didn't feel much like it. She'd always been herself around Harriet. Like most folks in Shady Grove, Harriet knew about Rita and Gracie's unheralded arrival on the Calloway's front porch. But she'd never held Rita's so-called mistake against Gracie. She even knew of Gracie's yearning for Rita's return. Unlike other folks, Harriet never tried to talk Gracie out of her dream.

She wanted to tell Harry about her predicament, but something inside her held her back. If Harry knew, then Gracie would have to admit it was real. She'd have one more person thinking she was crazy not to want her daddy's money. Not that Harriet was a greedy capitalist or anything like that. But she took special pride in her nephew's accomplishments. Apart from Bobo, he was all she talked about.

Gracie picked at a loose thread on the hem of her shirt. "Harry, you ever seen that guy on TV who shows up on folks' doorsteps with a check the size of Texas?"

"Wouldn't that be something?" Harriet glanced briefly in Gracie's direction, but Gracie could tell her mind was someplace else. Probably on her nephew and the chicken dinner.

"What do you suppose folks do with all that money?" Gracie persisted.

"Spend it as fast as they can, I suppose."

"On what?"

Harriet rolled her gaze back toward Gracie as if considering Gracie's question. "If they're smart, they start out with things they need."

"What about you, what would you spend it on?"

"Me? Bobo's teeth, I guess. He's got bad breath. His teeth need a good scrubbing, but that vet in Goshen charges an arm and leg to clean teeth. I don't need much else. What would I do with a fancy car, or a fancy house, or new clothes?"

The phone rang. Gracie bounced out of her chair and grabbed it on the second ring. "Hello, Harriet Ackers's residence." A male voice on the other end of the line asked for Harriet.

"It's for you." Gracie handed the phone to Harriet and watched her face light up.

"David. What a nice surprise. Gracie brought me fine chicken. I'll make those baked potatoes you like with the cheese and . . ." Harriet paused. The excitement disappeared from her eyes. "Oh, well, surely I understand. The chicken will keep in the freezer. I'll save it for next time. I know how busy you are. I do understand. Bye."

The look on Harriet's face broke Gracie's heart. She wanted to roast Harry's nephew, but she put on a sunny smile instead. "How about I bake the chicken and we have supper together tonight? Sort of a belated birthday party. As I recall, you owe me a game of Scrabble."

"That's mighty sweet of you, Gracie, but I know you got plenty to do. What about Artie and Ben? They must be expecting you at home."

"Alice made her fried chicken today. There's nothing Ben and Artie like better than cold chicken. And I can't think of anyone I'd rather have dinner with."

"Not even that good-looking man who delivered your lunch . . . ?"

"Especially him."

Harriet leveled Gracie with a concerned look. "Did he say something to you that made you think he was being disrespectful?"

Gracie wandered across the room, putting more space between her and Harriet's curious gaze. "No. He has a cocky sort of grin that makes me feel . . ." Gracie hunted around for a word to describe how Sam Fontana made her feel.

"Like a woman?"

Darned if Harriet hadn't hit the nail on the head. But Gracie wasn't ready to admit it. She offered Harriet a noncommittal shrug. "Uncomfortable."

Harry's eyes danced with speculation. "Well then, let's hope he comes back."

"That's what's worrying me."

Chapter 4

Sam pulled out of the rental-car parking lot and nosed his way through the throng of morning commuters toward the Hammond estate. Kate Hammond's attorneys had kept a lid on Gracie Calloway's rise from the dead barely long enough for him to unload the bad news on Conrad's reluctant daughter, then hop an early morning flight home. By the time he'd landed at the Westchester County Airport, the newsstand was littered with headlines. HAMMOND BABY FOUND ALIVE IN SWAMP. CAN HAMMOND HEIRESS BE SAVED FROM FAMILY CURSE? And his personal favorite: LOST BABY HEIRESS RAISED BY ALLIGATORS, courtesy of The International Queen of Sensation and Dirt on the Rich and Famous, Paula Knightly. Just the bait he needed to convince Gracie to own up to her Hammond roots.

Sam suppressed a yawn. He was dragging more than usual, despite the sugar rush from the leftover slice of birthday cake Alice had forced on him. He'd hurriedly consumed the pink lump of goo with a cup of cold coffee on his way to the airport. Katherine Hammond wanted to hear all the gritty details in person and wouldn't be put off another day. She'd arranged for her private jet to pick him up in Montgomery and fly him to Connecticut. Only by sheer luck and cunning had he managed to dodge Kate's chauffeur, take a quick detour to his office for a shave, and arrive under his own steam.

Two familiar rent-a-cops hovered near the entrance of the Hammond estate. So, Kate had taken his advice, after all, and called for protection from the media. Sam nodded to the men, then punched the intercom button. "It's the big, bad wolf, Jonesy. Open up."

"Welcome back, sir. Chivas on the rocks?"

"Make that two fingers."

"Yes, sir."

"You're my man, Mr. Jones." Sam tapped his fingers on the roof of the car while the massive iron gates eased open. Once free, he followed the curving row of neatly pruned junipers up the long winding drive.

Jonesy met him at the door with drink in hand. "How's the old lady treating you?"

Martin Jones's smile dimmed slightly. "A sunny retirement would be treating me considerably better, sir."

"Bones aching this fall? Perhaps you can sell the old lady on a trip to the Keys. You were always a very persuasive fellow. So where's she hiding?"

"The *old lady* is here." Kate sounded more annoyed than usual.

Sam turned and offered her a lopsided grin. She was eighty but stood easily erect. Her silver hair hugged the back of her head in a neat French roll and was engineered to add stature to her petite height. As usual, she was dressed in a pair of carefully pressed gray slacks and a matching cardigan. The only feminine details she allowed herself were an antique comb, said to be a gift from the late Queen Mother, and the thin ruffle of lace at the neck of her prim white blouse. Apart from the fine lines in her face, she could pass for sixty-five with ease.

"Good morning, Kate."

"God save me from insolent fools. Martin Jones, you are free to go to Florida, or wherever it is you have in mind. You are no longer in my employ."

Shock registered on Jonesy's weathered features, but he recovered quickly and rearranged his expression into a quiet mask. "Yes, Mrs. Hammond. Shall I instruct Cook to serve your lunch in my absence?"

Jonesy knew, as did Sam, that Cook performed domestic duties outside the kitchen with stubborn defiance.

Kate Hammond glared at Jonesy, then at Sam, as if he had something to do with her domestic predicament. "Damn you, Jones. How did Conrad put up with you all those years?"

Sam kept his smile to himself. Quite a ballsy

question, considering Kate had been trying to lure Martin Jones from Conrad's household for the past five years since her own butler, Ellis, had retired. Jonesy came from a long line of domestic servants. Rumor had it that his uncle had served royalty. Martin Jones had been with the Hammonds before Gracie Calloway was a twinkle in Conrad's eye.

With a slight measure of emotion, Jonesy bowed his head. "Mr. Conrad had a generous heart, madam."

Kate Hammond tempered her glare at Jonesy's sadness. Her shoulders slumped for a brief second, then righted themselves to a stalwart position. "Yes, his Achilles' heel. If it weren't for his heart, we wouldn't be in this damnable position. Mr. Jones, you may serve in fifteen minutes."

"Yes, madam." Jonesy flashed Sam a brief triumphant smile, then disappeared down the long marbled hall.

Kate Hammond lifted her imperial chin and zeroed her gaze on Sam's. "Cook made your favorite, lamb curry, today. You better have something good for me, young man, or you won't get any lunch. Get rid of that drink. It's too early for strong spirits."

Sam followed her into the dining room and set his glass on a silver serving tray beside the table. "That all depends on what you call good, Kate."

"Don't be coy, Mr. Fontana. It doesn't suit you. I pay you to give me the facts."

"I've located your granddaughter, but she doesn't seem to want any part of Conrad's money."

Kate waved away his response. "That's nonsense—of course she wants it. Only a fool would turn down a fortune."

Sam smiled to himself at the irony of his situation. Was Kate forgetting he'd done just that when Conrad had offered him a job with a clear path to the top? The ink had barely been dry on his MBA. "My guess is she's more concerned with the fact she's been left in the dark all these years by folks she trusted. Ben and Conrad have had eight years since they met and struck a deal to bring her up to speed."

She quietly considered his words and offered him a brief sympathetic smile. "She's not the only one who feels that way, I see. Let me assure you, if you were left out of the know, Conrad had good reason. I did not find out myself until the attorneys delivered the emended trust. Now, tell me what else did she have to say?"

"She asked me to extend her thanks to you. Let's see, how did she put it . . . . 'Tell my grandma I'm thankful for her interest and I'm mighty sorry for the loss of her boy, but I'm partial to wearing cleats in the house and they would scratch up her nice wood floors.' "

"Cleats?"

"They're shoes with spikes—"

"*I know* what they are. Good God. It's as bad as I thought."

"Actually she was barefoot the day I met her. She's not so bad—once you get past her hostility toward Yankees."

"Impertinence doesn't suit you, either. Have a seat, Mr. Fontana."

Sam ignored his own chair and drew hers back.

Kate accepted his gesture with a chilly nod, then waited until he was seated before she resumed her interrogation. "I suppose she insists on being called something plebeian, like Kathy."

"Her name is Gracie, after Princess Grace, I was told."

"She's a bottled blonde like that mother of hers, I presume."

"Not at all. She's a brunette with grayish eyes. Interesting combination." Sam hid his smile when Kate's gray-green eyes flashed his way. "Here, see for yourself." Sam pulled a Polaroid snapshot from his pocket and handed it to her.

Before he left, Ben Calloway had slipped him the picture of Gracie blowing out her birthday candles. She was a full head shorter than Sam's six feet—but fearless when mad, just like the woman sitting opposite him.

Kate studied the picture in silence for a few

minutes before she scowled back at him. "She looks like a waif. Her hair needs a good trimming. Who is that woman standing in the background?"

Sam suppressed a smile; she'd spotted her rival. He'd wondered how long it would take. "That's Alice, Gracie's aunt. She lives next door. She's a great cook."

Quietly she set the photo on the table beside her plate, out of Sam's reach. "That explains her waist size."

"Be nice. She might just be the key to your salvation."

"Don't be silly—this is business. No one is being saved here. It's too late for that."

Kate Hammond put up a good front, but Sam knew better. Conrad's death had hit her hard. Apart from his second child, Clare, who was little more than a ghostly pawn for her social-climbing mother, Marcia Hammond, Conrad's second ex-wife, she had no other family but Gracie. In a few years, her own fortune might go Marcia's greedy way too, just as surely as Conrad's would if Gracie didn't step up to the plate.

Kate's gaze drifted away from him toward the view. "Have you made arrangements for the blood test?"

"I haven't told her yet."

Kate's attention snapped back to him. "If she

73

wants the money, she will have to be tested. You know that. I thought I made it clear."

"Like I said, she doesn't want the money."

Kate's attention snapped back to him. "What? That's ridiculous. She must be a fraud."

"According to Alice, one of Gracie's uncles believes money is responsible for the social injustice in the world. Gracie appears to have adopted his view."

"Good God. A bleeding-heart liberal. What next?"

"Lillian. She's back from Monte Carlo. That's where you sent her, isn't it? I hope it didn't cost you much. She claims she wants her daughter back. She's not being shy about whose shoulder she cries on. She's had offers from an alphabet of networks for her side of the story."

If Kate was surprised by the news, she didn't show it. She sat straight-faced while he delivered what he hoped was the last in a string of obstacles.

"But it looks like wife number two is going to give Lillian a run for the money and has offers of her own. Marcia is screaming foul ball from the top of her lungs because her baby was left out of the deal."

When he finished, Kate offered him a strained smile. "I'll handle Lillian and Marcia. I want you to return to Alabama and talk some sense into my granddaughter."

"She has plenty of sense—more than the average

bear—that's the problem. Twenty-five years in Shady Grove has given her time to figure out the truth about the lies the rest of us tell ourselves."

"I have no idea what you mean. Use your overabundance of charm to sway her. Court her, if need be. Whatever it takes, Mr. Fontana."

Gracie had missed her chance to hammer Ben with questions about the article she'd found at the library that morning. Shortly before dinner, the Widow Perkins's kitchen pipes had conveniently sprung a leak. Ben had scurried into the shower, then out the door. Gracie figured now was as good a time as any to start looking for answers.

She tiptoed up the stairs, pushed open the door to Ben's room, and flicked on the light. Artie's snores echoed from the room below. Gracie avoided the squeaky floorboard at the end of Ben's bed and crossed the worn braided rug to the nightstand.

Rita's young face peered at Gracie out of a dusty picture frame. Unlike Gracie, she was tall and leggy with dark brown eyes. For years, the photo sat on Gracie's dresser. She'd spun girlish dreams of Rita returning to sweep her off to a cozy house with bright curtains and a slobbery dog. By age twelve, Gracie had buried that dream and banished Rita's smiling face to Ben's room. Now, more than ever, Gracie figured she deserved some answers for the years of suffering she'd endured on Rita's behalf. Ben was avoiding her, which meant he had the answers and wasn't sharing.

Gracie drew open the slim drawer. A few old photos of herself and Artie that hadn't made it into frames lay on top. A dog-eared western, bookmarked with Sam Fontana's business card, came next. Another stab of betrayal hit her, but Gracie continued her search and rummaged to the bottom. There were no secret letters from Conrad Hammond, or Rita, for that matter. Chances were, Ben had been expecting her to snoop and had hidden the evidence.

Gracie shoved the contents back inside and slammed the drawer, then yanked the pillow out from under the coverlet and stretched out on Ben's bed. Gracie could wait Ben out. Another hour wouldn't matter.

Gracie was entertaining images of Delilah torturing Ben with her nonstop chatter when the phone jingled on the nightstand. She pounced on it before it could wake Artie. "Hello."

"Gracie?"

She jolted upright. *Sam Fontana—surprise, surprise.* "Ben's not here."

There was a long silence before his voice reached out to her again. "Then maybe you can answer my questions." His tone shifted from surprise to a teasing reminder of his crafty grin.

Gracie glared at the receiver. "I seem to be

having trouble coming up with answers to my own questions. I doubt I can answer yours." She hadn't meant to let her own frustration seep into her reply. For a moment, she felt herself teeter between tears and indignation. Why did Sam Fontana have that effect on her?

"Maybe I can help . . . you." The words were light, but the warmth of his voice said more. Gracie felt heat flood her cheeks.

"What was your question, Mr. Fontana?"

"It's *Sam* to you, *Gracie*."

Another pause. Gracie refused to react. Dangerous territory led in his direction. Silently, she let the warm familiarity drift away.

When his voice came again, it was all business. "The phone number Ben gave me for Rita is out of service. Any idea where I could get ahold of her?"

Rita was missing. Nothing new. She'd been missing for twenty-five years. But the urgency in Sam's voice said finding Rita was important. "Sorry, Yankee, I can't help you. Ben's got more secrets than Hank Aaron's got home runs." Gracie paused. She could hear him breathing on the other end of the line. He might have questions for Rita, but Gracie figured she'd deserved first shot at the answers. "What do you want with Rita?"

"Just need to verify a few details regarding your arrival in Shady Grove. Routine procedure. Nothing to worry about."

"I'm not worried, Sam Spade, but it sounds like you are. Could you be thinking you've got the wrong girl?"

"Don't get your hopes up, princess. When do you expect Ben home?"

If she wasn't worried before, she was now. Gracie frowned at the clock. It was past eight. Ben had been gone over two hours. Sam's frustration mirrored her own, but she figured she had more cause. "When Ben gets home, all depends on Delilah Perkins's pipes."

"Delilah, huh?"

He was poking at something she wasn't ready to put a name to. Another flood of warmth rushed to Gracie's face. Gracie glared at the receiver. "It's not what you're thinking."

"What's that, Gracie?" Sam's voice was hot in her ear.

She packaged his name with the devil's. "Ben and Alice have their differences, but he wouldn't cheat on her."

"I'm sure you're right. When Ben gets home, have him give me a call at my office. He has the number. Good night, Gracie. Sweet dreams."

Gracie glared at the receiver, then dropped it into the cradle. He'd done it again—this time with her help. She was thinking dirty thoughts about Sam Fontana, things that would try Alice's knees on Sundays for years to come.

Chapter 5

The rain had cleared out of Shady Grove before dawn. Gracie perched on the top of the bleachers and glanced at the field. Puddles dotted the red clay, the worst ones being at first base and home plate, a fact that didn't improve her mood. Ben had been dodging her for two days, and her anger had settled into a hollow disappointment. Maybe she shouldn't even think of him as her uncle anymore—but the thought depressed her more than the muddy puddles.

Gracie slammed down the palm of her hand on the aluminum bench. The metal rang out in the morning quiet. On the heels of the racket came the soft shuffling of footsteps behind her, followed by Artie's familiar voice.

"I thought I'd find you here. You practicin' your curve ball like I showed you?"

"What are you doing out of the house?"

"Just needed a little fresh air, that's all. Looks like you need some, too."

Gracie climbed down to the bottom bench so Artie wouldn't have to climb up. He was already out of breath. She noticed the way he clutched the seat of the bench as he sat, then cursed herself for not taking the Jeep this morning so she could give him a ride home.

"I just thought I'd see how the field looked after the storm last night. Jerry is going to get an earful for not filling in those holes. Look at the size of those puddles. A child could drown at first base."

"It ain't holes you're worried about, and you ain't drownin'. No, girl, you were born under a lucky star. You could have drowned. Folks thought you did, but you cheated the Big Man. And now you can do just about anythin' you want, anythin' at all. Even fill in that little ol' hole over there, if that's what floats your boat."

"Arthur Dubois, what are you rattling on about? You fall and hit your head on the way over here?"

Artie waved his cane in Gracie's direction. "Nope. I came to knock some sense into yours. But I can see, I'd be wastin' my time 'cause you got holes on your mind. Or maybe they's in your head and the stuff I taught you done fall out."

"What are you saying?"

Artie tapped her head gently with the crook of his cane. "Don't sound hollow. Lean over and let me check your ears, see if I can spy that tree over there."

"Is this about Ben and Alice lying to me—"

"It ain't. But just so you knows what's what, nobody lied to nobody. They was just tryin' to protect you from the big, bad Yankees. You should be thankin' them. You could have been shipped off to one of them fancy boardin' schools, had your ass froze off in New Hampshire or some other frosty place."

"What do you mean?"

"Rita was feeling pretty low about the time you was to graduate high school, so she called Ben. I guess you was 'bout seventeen." Artie paused and glanced at her sideways out of his good eye.

Gracie steeled herself for the truth. "Go on."

"Well, one thing led to another, and Rita up and tells him that she was just caught in a bad situation and that you ain't hers."

"I wish she'd kept it to herself."

"Ol' Ben, he had to know just how bad. So, he sets off for Connecticut. Was gone a whole week. Met your daddy. Ben convinced him you wouldn't be happy up in Yankeeland."

"Why didn't Ben tell me? Why didn't my own daddy tell me himself?"

"Now, tell me truthfully, girl, would you really have wanted this trouble then? You were so full of yourself. You had yourself your first sweetheart."

"Johnnie Bean? Some sweetheart he was. He married Marianne Talbot two months after graduation. I could have done without him. And what makes you think I want this trouble now?

There is no good time to find out you're some-body you're not."

"Well, you got it. And you don't look no different to me today than you did last week, 'cept maybe your face is stretched a bit longer. Come to think of it, girl, you look a little like that ol' horse over in Mrs. Simpson's pasture. What's his name?"

"Bullshit."

Artie slapped his knee and shot her a sideways smile. "And up popped two big ol' ears. I take that back. You ain't a horse at all, you's a mule. Bill Buckley—most stubborn ass I ever knowed. Uh-huh. That's you."

If Gracie had a thousand fingers and toes, she still couldn't count the number of times she'd heard Artie tell stories about his favorite mule, but she'd never been put in old Bill Buckley's shoes.

"This isn't my dream, Artie. You know that."

"And I say, you's long overdue for somethin' big."

"Okay, Artie. What's that?"

Artie leaned back and looked her full in the face. The white hairs that speckled his temples stood out stark against his warm brown skin. "Take the money, girl."

"You better check my ears now, because I know I didn't hear you right. We are not talking bets on a pool game down at Banjo Jimmy's. We're talking big money."

"I know. But, honey, its just paper, and you can do good things with it just as well as bad. I know I done told you folks with money are mean, evil sons-of-bitches, and some of them are, like them hoity-toity Parnells. They weren't good enough to shine your shoes. But some of them do good."

"Like who?"

"Well, let's see now . . ."

"You have to think hard because no one comes to mind."

"You could be one. You wouldn't waste it on fancy clothes you ain't gonna wear, or fancy jewels you don't need, and the like. No, siree. You'd fix them holes in the field so Little Jackie Brown don't fall in and drown while her mama is watchin' her play ball. And just maybe 'cause you fixed that hole, some kid from Shady Grove will make the cut someday and play ball in the World Series."

"But not Jackie."

"You never know. Times and people change. You could help things along . . ."

Gracie glanced over at Artie. "You're smooth, old man, but not smooth enough. I want to go on being plain ol' Gracie Lynne Calloway. Nobody bothers me in the back room of the market. Why do I need to be some snooty Katherine Hammond from Greenwich, Connecticut, who folks point their finger at? I haven't got the accent or the inclination to be a Yankee."

"And I ain't got the right skin color to be your uncle, but I am. What have I been tellin' you all these years? When you gots the walk and you gots the talk—"

"—You are the man. Ain't nobody can say different."

"Damn right. You're still Gracie. The money is just handy window dressin'."

Artie broke into a coughing fit and Gracie didn't have the heart to give him a long list of the folks who would tell her otherwise. She ran up to the filling station and got him a Coke, then walked him home.

Katherine's second ex-daughter-in-law, Marcia Hammond, hadn't improved with age. The years sat on her hips and middle with comfortable satisfaction. Unwisely, she'd covered them in lumpy ochre polyester. Her dislike of Conrad's second wife was no secret. Ellis, her former butler, would never have let Marcia slip past the front door.

Kate shuddered and turned an angry eye on Mr. Jones as Marcia steered her daughter, Clare, into the room, then maneuvered herself into a chair opposite Kate's.

"Conrad's will is ludicrous. He can't be serious—"

"Whether the will is ludicrous or not, remains to be seen," said Kate.

"Clare has been robbed of her rightful inheritance . . . *by a dead child*. I need your support on this, Katherine. Surely you know Conrad was grieving when he wrote that will. He just never got around to changing it, that's all."

"I know nothing of the sort. You're suggesting my son was out of his mind. I assure you, he was quite sane when he wrote that will. The child was discovered when she was seventeen. He had plenty of time to consider all of the possible repercussions." Kate pinned his son's second bad choice of wives with a meaningful look.

But Marcia, true to her thick skin and unperceptive nature, didn't blink at the insinuation. She threw her bulk out of her chair and retreated to Clare's side. "She can't be more than a backwater hick—a nobody. What sane man chooses a stranger over his own child? Surely, you don't mean you're going to let it stand?"

Kate settled back in her chair, pretending ease she didn't feel. "Nonsense, Clare has a generous trust fund. Besides, he was thinking of his own child—one who gave him a great deal of joy in the short time he had her."

Marcia latched on to Clare's shoulder in a possessive gesture. "Lillian's—*not mine*."

Kate ignored Marcia and glanced over at her

granddaughter. Clare sat fashionably thin and silent on the couch, lost among the cushions and her mother's venom. What Clare needed was freedom, a life without Marcia running it. Kate had tried to loosen Marcia's control over Clare, but she met with her mother's stubborn disapproval. Conrad refused to get involved, beyond writing a check.

More money would not do Clare any good. Clare would end up giving her share to her mother to manage. And Marcia would only waste it on parties in hopes of gaining entrée into homes where she didn't belong.

At least Lillian knew what she was and didn't pretend to be anything else, not around Kate anyway. When she came for money, she got to the point. Kate admired that small aspect of her character. But for Marcia, pretense was her middle name. She even used it on herself.

Kate rose from her chair and crossed the room to stand adjacent to the foyer. She glanced back at Marcia. "Lillian's daughter is the one you need to convince, not me."

"*What?* Surely you don't really believe the girl is legitimate?"

At first, Kate had her doubts, but the Polaroid snapshot tucked into her breast pocket said otherwise. Gracie Lynne Calloway was the spitting image of herself sixty years ago, right down to the dimple in her left cheek.

Kate ignored Marcia and turned toward her granddaughter. "Not only is she alive, but I think Clare should meet her sister—don't you agree, Clare?"

For the first time since she arrived, Clare's face lit up. "Really, Nana? I'd love to—"

"Absolutely not. It's time to go, Clare." Marcia latched on to her daughter's arm and hoisted her out of her chair toward the door, where, for once, Martin Jones had conveniently positioned himself.

When the door was closed firmly, Kate marched past Martin Jones. "Next time that woman appears at the gate, do not let her in. If you do, I will dismiss you immediately. Mr. Fontana will not come to your rescue a second time."

"Yes, madam. But Mr. Fontana has just arrived—"

"Oh, for goodness' sake! His timing is as bad as yours." Out of the corner of her eye, she caught sight of Sam seated comfortably on the sofa, sipping coffee with an oversized sandwich balanced on a plate in his lap. "How long have you been lurking, Mr. Fontana?"

"Let's see, I came in on the part where your sanity was called into question. Rest assured, Conrad did not write his will until after he'd confirmed Gracie's identity. The blood check is just to make piranhas like Marcia keep their distance."

"Are you saying I'll have to put up with more of these performances?"

"It shouldn't be long. Gracie Calloway's uncle, Artie Dubois, is ill." Sam Fontana's voice faded along with his grin. "He's run up a hefty medical debt."

"I'm not going to ask how you acquired this information."

"That would be best."

Kate seated herself opposite Sam. "So, this will work to our advantage?"

"You sound desperate."

Despite his persistent grin, Kate couldn't help but like Joe Fontana's son. He was on her side, but most important—*on her son's side*, and maybe the only one who was. She gave in to her exhaustion and slumped into her chair. "You just witnessed the opening performance of the season. Things will get worse if my grand-daughter waffles too long. You saw the circus train of reporters skulking outside my front gate, I assume. Even your rent-a-cops, as you call them, haven't been able to keep all of them away. We aren't the only ones waiting for her to make a decision. The networks have found something better to advertise than the new fall season."

"I wouldn't worry. Gracie Calloway isn't in a position to say no."

But when Sam glanced Kate's way, she couldn't help but notice his grin was gone.

· · ·

Sam set the receiver into the cradle and stared blindly at the familiar landscape of brick buildings lined up outside his office window. Conrad Hammond had more tricks up his sleeve. Why was he surprised? Sam had just inherited a house—*in Shady Grove,* of all places. The attorney's secretary said the messenger would deliver the key within the next half hour. A plane was being readied for a late afternoon flight; he'd be back in Alabama by sunset. That gave him fifteen minutes to pack, five to order dinner, and the rest to break the news to Kate Hammond. In a few short hours, he'd have the honor of telling Gracie her father had been spying on her—*for eight years.* He could already hear the fireworks.

Sam punched Kate's number. "Hey, Jonesy, is the boss in?"

"Sure thing, Mr. Fontana. I'll let her know it's you."

"Here she is. It's Mr. Fontana, madam."

"That'll be all, Mr. Jones. Close the door on your way out." Kate's voice paused while a door clicked shut in the background. "Insolent man."

"Insolent, huh? Never been called that before."

"Not you, Mr. Fontana. That poor excuse for a butler. Every time I turn around, he's there— lurking with that infernal smirk. I feel like an

89

unwanted guest in my own home. If not for Conrad's allegiance to the man, I'd dispose of him posthaste, along with *that woman*."

"Murder is against the law."

"It won't be murder—it will be self-defense."

"I'm sure it will. Which woman?"

"Marcia. She's set the worst sharks of the media on us. Paula Knightly—of all the barracudas to tattle to—"

"Give it a few days. Some celebrity will step out of line. The world won't know we exist."

"Well, it will be your world soon, Mr. Fontana. I don't plan to be here forever."

"I could swear I asked Jonesy to put me through to Battle-ax Hammond, but he's connected me to some wallflower with a weak stem."

"This is no joking matter, Mr. Fontana."

"No, it's not. It seems Conrad bought a house in Shady Grove and set up a part-time house-keeper. I'm assuming you knew nothing about this?"

"Shady Grove? Housekeeper? Good God, not another one of his women. Save yourself a great deal of trouble, Mr. Fontana. Don't procreate."

"Keep that up and you might be at war with my mother someday. I'm expecting a key any minute from the attorney's office. I'm off to Alabama."

"He was a good and predictable child." Kate's

voice sounded more forlorn than it had in days.

"Katherine, are you okay? Lillian's not rattling your cage, too, is she?"

"We've been spared for a day or two. Lillian has the flu. Set up a meeting with the girl by the end of the week. Bring her here. I have no intention of traveling where alligators roam the streets. The sooner we get this over with, the better. I expect a progress report from you tomorrow, Mr. Fontana."

A sharp click echoed from Kate's end of the line. Sam stared at the receiver. "Alligators?"

Chapter 6

Gracie snuggled the quilt around her shoulders and set the front porch swing swaying. It wasn't so much the evening temperature that made her want the familiar warmth of the Calloway family heirloom around her. The real chiller keeping her up nights was her new identity.

Across the street, a light went on in Edna McCoy's bathroom, then promptly went out. Gracie curled her legs under her and peered into the night. Spent leaves shivered on an errant breeze, then broke loose and floated onto the front walk with a hollow *clack*. As if summoned by her fears, a car rounded the corner and came to a stop at the curb. Gracie huddled deeper into her quilt. A bold moon beamed at her from the crown of Edna's scarlet oak. It was the second full moon this month, a blue moon, bringing with it trouble in the form of one tall Yankee.

The slam of the car door shook the quiet. Gracie flinched, then forced herself to take a slow calming breath as Sam Fontana stepped out of the shadows into the moon's glow. The dry leaves crackled under his heavy footsteps as he moved up the walk. Before he reached the porch steps, he paused and glanced up. He was looking for signs of life inside the house. When his gaze finally adjusted to the dark and rounded on Gracie's, he shot her a sleepy echo of his signature grin.

His usual self-assured stride was tired as he climbed onto the porch. "Let me guess. Ben told you I'd be back, so you decided to wait up to welcome me."

Gracie returned his challenging grin with a sassy one of her own. "My, but you *are* a dreamer, Mr. Fontana. Ben didn't say anything about you stopping by."

"It's Sam. Ben isn't much of a talker. But me— I'm pretty much a call-'em-as-I-see-'em kind of guy. I'd say you've got about six hundred fifty million reasons why you can't sleep tonight. Or maybe I should make that six hundred fifty million—*and one*."

"What's the *one* for?"

Sam eased himself down onto the swing, his warm thigh pressed casually against her bare toes where they peeked out from under the quilt. "Me," he said, with a confidence that sent her teeth snapping together. "*I'm* the one."

She could see his even white teeth shining through the darkness. But what really made her uneasy was the husky melody of his voice. It did things to her that it had no business doing— like making her wonder what it would be like to chase away her fears with the moist warmth of his lips and the solid feel of his shoulder.

Sam's gaze danced at her through the dark. "I'll bet you've been keeping yourself up with a thousand ways to fry my liver. I can't say I blame you."

Gracie forced her gaze away from his mouth and shrank toward the cold arm of the swing. "I take it back. You're not a dreamer at all, Mr. Fontana. You're just plain crazy."

Sam laughed. "You've got it in your head that I'm here to turn you into some kind of subversive capitalist. That couldn't be further from the truth. I happen to agree with your father. Shady Grove has given you the guts you're going to need to handle your inheritance."

"I've got a job. Pays just fine. And don't try to sweet-talk me into forgiving my daddy for not letting me in on the secret of my heritage. I haven't forgiven Ben yet. I'm not likely to cut a total stranger any slack, even if he happens to share my blood. Which, I'm not saying he does; I'm just entertaining the possibility, you understand."

"Coming through loud and clear, princess. You need to assimilate. No problem."

Gracie eyed him through the darkness. Why was he being so damn agreeable? She raised her chin a notch and shot him a suspicious glance. "More sugar, Mr. Fontana, won't work on me. I need details and dates, not fancy words."

"A blood test would be a good start. As to the

details of your kidnapping, well, my pop worked on your case for years when the trail was a lot fresher. Ben claims Rita came into the story after the fact and that she doesn't know how Eddie got his hands on you. Instinct tells me there's a missing link before Rita came into the picture. Rita gave up the goods to Ben, then he struck a deal with Conrad. That's all I know. The lady Rita was rooming with is pushing ninety. She can't remember her own name, let alone Eddie Fry dropping a crying baby on her porch twenty-five years ago. I'm afraid Mr. Fry took most of the answers with him into the river the night you were kidnapped."

"Can't say I'm suffering any grief over Mr. Fry's sorry end. But I like my blood where it is —in my veins. I don't need money that bad. Like I said, I have a job. Pays just fine."

Sam's lips twitched in the silence. "I'm not a big fan of needles myself. But, if it'll make you feel better, I'll be there to hold your hand."

How did a thickheaded Yankee get so perceptive? She wasn't afraid of much. It seemed silly that a little ol' thing like a needle could make her feel sick to her stomach. She wasn't about to embarrass herself in front of a man she hardly knew. Gracie had learned years ago that if she couldn't make herself invisible, a tough exterior was her second best defense. She sat up a little straighter, trying to add inches to her

95

small stature. "I don't need my hand held."

Despite his ready grin, Gracie felt the fight leave her. Knowing the chain of events that had brought her to Shady Grove wasn't going to change things. "It's taken me nearly twenty years to come to peace with who I am. Now you want me to entertain a whole new possibility. Tell your fancy attorneys and the Hammonds they are going to have to cool their heels while I catch up."

Sam's deep chuckle was like a sip of fiery brandy. It made her burn from her toes that were still trapped beneath his thigh, to the tops of her ears. She was grateful for the cover of darkness when Sam tipped his head back and let out a soft throaty hoot of laughter that set the swing gently rocking. "Princess Gracie, you are just the breath of fresh air the Hammonds need. I'll find a way to persuade you."

His shoulder brushed her bare one where the quilt had dropped away. Gracie quickly yanked the barrier back. "You think you're so smart, but you don't even know me. I'm nobody's princess and I've never been anybody's fresh air."

Sam reached over and tugged the quilt up higher, then tucked it under her chin. "That's where you're wrong—I know you better than you think. Good night, Gracie. Sweet dreams."

Sam let the car glide to a stop at the end of Parnell Street. The house, strategically lit from all sides,

96

glowed out of the darkness. The two-story Italianate Victorian loomed slightly above the street, peering out at the world through unblinking glossy green shutters behind a crisp white picket fence. Like royalty, it sat a safe distance from its neighbors, surrounded by a lawn that rolled and stretched on two sides. By Hammond standards, it was modest, but in Shady Grove the place was the damn Taj Mahal.

Sam felt the uncomfortable need for a haircut and a tie as soon as he stepped through the front gate. No mistake, the house had the Hammond stamp of organized perfection written all over it. Not a blade of grass was out of place. Two magnolias stood guard on either side of the walk, symmetrically trimmed, not too tall or too wide. Twin knee-high boxwood hedges lined the brick walk leading to the wide porch steps. The bright brass door handle and knocker gleamed with royal Hammond shine.

This was just the sort of display of wealth Gracie was suspicious of . . . and now it belonged to him—not exactly the best ticket into Gracie's confidence.

Conrad had wanted him to embrace the finer things in life, be the son he never had. Sam knew he'd disappointed him when he'd chosen to follow his own father's footsteps into investigative work.

Sam paused with the key in his hand. The pieces

were beginning to fall into place. Conrad had strategically arranged for the attorneys to wait until Sam had accepted the job as the Hammond emissary before they dropped the bomb. It wasn't an oversight; there was no such thing in Conrad's world. He and Gracie Calloway were swimming in the same damn fish bowl. For the first time, he had the urge to turn and walk away—to dump it all back in Kate's lap. But he owed Conrad a debt. And then, there was Gracie . . . No matter how tough she pretended to be, she was scared. If he backed out, Kate would send an army of attorneys, which would only terrify Gracie more.

Ben had advised him to level with Gracie before someone else spilled the beans. But despite the cozy conversation they'd shared in the swing, Sam hadn't been able to bring Gracie up to date on Conrad's latest secret. He was still reeling from the surprise himself. When he'd boarded the plane that afternoon, he'd fully intended to break the news to Gracie ASAP. But she'd looked so vulnerable wrapped in her quilt that he'd lost his nerve.

What other secrets did Conrad have waiting for him? The large brass key felt cold in his hand. Quickly, he shoved it into the lock, swung the door wide, then flipped the light switch. *Shazam!*

Sam staggered back a step. As familiar with the Hammond lifestyle as he was, he'd say

Conrad had outdone himself. Just as he had his carefully restored Tudor estate in Greenwich, Conrad had left his golden touch on his Shady Grove home—from the pegged and polished wood floors to the detailed moldings. But even Conrad's generosity during the last days of Sam's father's battle with cancer wasn't going to buy Conrad into his good graces this time. How was he going to explain all this to Gracie? He'd been making headway in gaining her trust. At least she hadn't flat out refused to take the blood test. She'd entertained the idea with a pale face, despite her fear. How could he justify Conrad living right under her nose, and not just in any old house but a house that so obviously represented the wealth and privilege that had shunned her as a child?

Sam pushed the door closed with his elbow and set his bag down in the foyer with a *thump*. There was another key on the key chain. From the size of it, he'd say it didn't belong to just any wussy door. Instinct guided Sam toward the back of the house. There was an office with a private bath and another door that could have been a good location for a closet, except the hardware was heftier—actually vaultlike, with metal studs where the hinges were attached. Sam inserted the key. A tiny green light flashed. The front door wasn't alarmed, but this one was. Interesting.

Sam gave the key a full turn—a soft hiss, like an air seal was being broken—stilled his hand on the handle. He made a quick mental list of Conrad's interests: *Flying*—the house was too small to house anything built by the Wright Brothers; *Greek antiquities,* nope—too hard to acquire these days; *baseball*—Conrad had dragged him to auctions more than once and asked his opinion on a few choice items. And given Gracie's interest . . .

There was only one way to find out . . . Sam pushed the door wide. Motion-sensor lights threw the room into a sparkling glow. That was Conrad, always big on surprise and drama. Sam took two steps and stopped dead. All four walls were covered, floor to ceiling, with glass cases filled with enough baseball collectibles to fill a small museum. In the center of the room stood a lonely mahogany library table with a single cream-colored envelope with Gracie's name scribbled on it. Conrad's elves had been very busy.

Chapter 7

Gracie took the stairs two at a time, then stopped short in the empty kitchen. Ben had escaped again. His breakfast dishes, the missing morning paper—more reminders that he was running scared.

Gracie poured herself a mug of Ben's swamp coffee, then hacked off a slice of her birthday cake. She had other things to worry about besides the size of her thighs. If sugar took the edge off her black mood, then she'd damn well eat cake, breakfast, lunch, and dinner.

Her fork was barely to her mouth when Alice's familiar footsteps raced up the back steps and into the kitchen. "There are six news vans lining the street. Come see."

The media was close to God in Alice's book. Katie Couric sneezed during the Macy's parade one year, and Alice sent her a fancy box of tissues and new wool hat, then waited patiently for a thank-you note to arrive. Sure enough, one did, and Alice had been starstruck ever since. There was nothing that could put her in a tizzy faster than a brush with fame.

Gracie set her fork down and glanced calmly at Alice. "Is Edna McCoy salting Vera Hatfield's roses again?" The feud had been going on for nearly twenty years. It had started when Edna's late husband had openly admired Vera's prize-winning China rose, *Cramoisi superieur*, over the back fence one day while the spinster school-teacher was gardening in what Edna claimed was an indecent pair of short shorts. A week later, when the newsmen rolled in to do a feature story on the rose that had won the state prize, Vera's rosebush was dead, murdered by salt. Vera pointed a finger at Edna. Two days later Edna's Yellow Lady Banks had gone the way of the shaker. A reporter from Kentucky was quick to pick up on their surnames. Soon Shady Grove was swarming with a host of rabid TV news-casters all looking to capitalize on the feud. Gracie had been six years old at the time, but the pandemonium was still branded in her memory. She was in no mood to feed Alice's chatter this morning.

But Alice latched on to Gracie's arm and dragged her out of her chair into the living room. "No, silly. Look there. The cameras are pointing at us."

Gracie reached to pull the curtain back, but Alice batted her hand away. "Wait a minute, Gracie. You don't want the world to see us naked, do you? We need to put on some lip-stick." Alice reached into the pocket of her apron, produced a tube of coral red, and smeared it deftly over her mouth, then offered it to Gracie.

Gracie waved her away and peered out the window. Sure enough, Alice was right. A succession of car doors slammed outside. Several reporters rushed toward the front gate. Gracie jumped back. "I smell a dirty rat."

Alice craned her neck toward Artie's room. "I'm not a bit surprised. Probably a whole family of them living down the hall. Hush now, or you'll wake them up."

"I mean—*a Yankee.*" Gracie tried to steer Alice away from the window, but she slipped out of her grasp, pulled a comb from her pocket, and set to work on her hair.

"Gracie, we tried to raise you with a proper mind. Not all Yankees are rats. That nice Mr. Fontana, for starters."

"He's just the one I was thinking of."

Alice stopped fussing with her hair. "What do you mean?"

"How else would they find out about me? He must have spilled the beans to pressure me into saying yes. And to think I believed him when he said he didn't want the media involved—"

"Nonsense. I'm sure Mr. Fontana did his best." Alice was just paying her fear lip service. Her attention was focused out the window. She poked her head over Gracie's shoulder and reached past her to part the curtain. "You're a celebrity now. All these years I've had to put up

103

with Marjorie's bragging about her grand-daughter doing this and that. Won't she just split her pants when she finds out we're going to be on TV."

Gracie turned abruptly, blocking Alice's view. "It was you, wasn't it, Alice? You called them so you could show Marjorie up."

"Now you're being ridiculous, Gracie Lynne. I wouldn't even know who to call." Alice shot her a quick miffed look, then turned her attention back to the scene outside.

Gracie felt chastised, but it didn't change the fact that the number of vans outside was growing by the minute. Someone was responsible and Sam Fontana seemed the most likely source.

"I'm going to call Mr. Fontana and tell him to get the dogs off my porch. Then we'll see what he has to say." Gracie nudged Alice away from the window, but Alice refused to give up her spot.

Alice pushed closer. "Look there. Isn't that Chantel coming up the walk? They took her picture. How do you like that? She's stealing your show. I wish you'd put on your new dress this morning. You look so pretty in blue. You might as well take advantage of your good fortune."

There was no use in talking to Alice. "I've got to call Mr. Fontana." Gracie started for the kitchen, then turned around and gave Alice a stern look. "Don't open that door."

"But Gracie, honey, that would be rude. Manners mark a lady for life. On my word— isn't that Paula Knightly, *in the flesh?* Wait till I tell Marjorie . . . I'm so tired of hearing about her granddaughter being runner-up for Miss Georgia, I could die. She'll turn pea green." Alice made a beeline for the door before Gracie could stop her.

Cameras flashed in Alice's face. Voices volleyed in the background. "Miss Hammond, how about a short comment on your kidnapping? Miss Hammond, what do you plan to do with the money? Is it true you were raised by alligators?"

Gracie grabbed Alice's arm, then Chantel's, and yanked them into the living room and slammed the door. She turned to scold Alice, but she had gone sheet white.

"Quick, Chantel. Help me get her to the chair before she melts on the floor."

"You better getta rope, 'cause as soon as she comes back to her mind, she's gonna head right back out that door, if I know your Alice."

Alice's color returned in record time and she waggled her finger under Chantel's nose. "Your lazy uncle is still asleep. Don't you think I don't know what you're up to—I saw you posing for the cameras out there." Alice refused to stay put and headed for the window again.

"There she goes. What'd I jus' tell you, girl?"

Gracie jumped into her path and turned her toward the kitchen. "Alice, why don't you make us some tea?"

Chantel tagged after Gracie. "Don't bother yourself on my account, Miss Alice, I just came to deliver this letter for Mr. Fontana. He said I was to give it to Gracie and nobody else." Chantel withdrew an envelope from beneath the cover of her sweater.

Gracie stared at the fine ivory linen paper. Her name was scrawled across the front. Not Katherine Hammond, just plain old Gracie Calloway.

Chantel poked at her with the envelope. "It's from Mr. Conrad, the man I been keeping house for. Now that he's plowing the Lord's south forty, I don't have to keep it a secret no more." Chantel's gaze drifted around Ben's living room, then circled back to Gracie. "Guess I'll be lookin' for another job to fill my time."

Gracie glared at the envelope. "But I don't know a Mr. Conrad . . ."

"Sure you do. He goes to your ball games. I've seen you talkin' to him after the game. You shook his hand. Me and Artie was there. He wears funny shoes with tassels on them and a Yankee's hat, like your Mr. Fontana."

It was Gracie's turn to sit in Ben's chair. *"Conrad?* As in *Conrad Hammond?"*

"Don't know no Mr. Hammond, but Mr.

Fontana is Mr. Conrad's friend. He's stayin' at the . . . house."

"He's my daddy?"

"What you say, girl? Mr. Conrad can't be *your* daddy. You don't look nothin' like him. He's tall and skinny, all stiff-like. I'd be checkin' my mama's barn for a different horse."

Gracie glared at her best friend. She'd had almost a week to make the connection between the names. Mr. Conrad had sent two dozen roses to the market. His card claimed it was for the great game she'd pitched. Though she'd only shaken his hand once in a feverish moment of victory, she'd kept the roses on her desk at work and not taken them home. There would have been a string of questions from Alice. She'd asked around after him so she could send a proper thank you, but no one she knew seemed to know his direction. Gracie figured it was on the other end of town where the houses stretched out on bigger lots and folks kept their business to themselves—the Parnell side, which Gracie avoided out of habit.

She'd dried the pretty petals and put them in a box to remind her what it was like to get something as fine as roses. Now she felt like a plain fool. Mr. Conrad and Conrad Hammond were one and the same—like Katherine Hammond and Gracie Lynne Calloway . . . The joke was on her, but she didn't feel like laughing. She felt the birthday cake settle in her stomach like a lump of clay.

Chantel waved her hand in front of Gracie's face. "Mrs. Alice, your Gracie looks a little pale, even for a white girl. I'll hold her head down; you get some whiskey."

Alice's *Lordy me*'s drifted off to the kitchen between incantations of Paula Knightly's name.

Chantel's big hand pressed against the back of Gracie's head. "Take a nice deep breath, Gracie Lynne, and let the juices come back to your brain—along with some sense. You know, you are some kind of funny, girl. All this fuss over a silly letter you ain't even opened yet."

"And I'm not going to open it." Gracie ducked away and launched herself out of the chair. "I've had enough surprises for one week. You can take it right back over to Mr. Fontana."

"Can't do that. I got to get my mama to a hair dressin' appointment. You'll have to give it to him yourself." Chantel grabbed Gracie's elbow and forced the letter into her hand. "Consider yourself *de*-livered."

"Fine, Miss Smarty, what's the address?"

"Don't need no address. It's the Parnell place."

Sam settled into Conrad's leather wing-backed chair and glanced at his watch. Chantel left thirty minutes ago. As much as he'd wanted to know what Conrad had said in his letter, he'd resisted

108

the urge to steam it open. Gracie would fill him in on the pertinent details—or, more than likely, throw the thing back in his face.

She didn't like him, and that fact intrigued him. Most women found him attractive, even charming, until they found out what he did for a living. Being a P.I. was not a sure road to wealth. Besides the lousy hours, his schedule changed at the drop of a hat. He'd left more than one date twiddling her thumbs in a movie. His relationships rarely lasted more than one night. He'd come to accept the pattern as a hazard of his job.

Gracie, on the other hand, liked her world ordered, predictable, the same way Conrad had. He was counting on that stubborn predictability to deliver her to his door.

Hurried footsteps scurrying up the front walk told him he wasn't to be disappointed. Sam waited in his chair for her knock. What he heard instead was the door banging open, then slamming shut as footsteps pounded into the hall.

"Sam-*mule* Fonta-*na!*" Gracie's long drawl bounced across the foyer into the living room.

Sam didn't bother to get up. "Gracie—"

She spun her petite frame toward his voice. Her chocolaty hair flared out around her shoulders. She hadn't dressed to impress him in her soft gray T-shirt and raggedy jeans, but she did.

Sam met her frown with a winning smile. "You got your letter, I take it?"

"That's not all I got. Get your doggy friends off my porch and out of my yard." Gracie waved the unopened letter toward the window. Her gray eyes flashed, and he was reminded of Katherine.

"What dogs are those?" Sam crossed the room to peek through the shutters. One by one, media vans swerved to a stop in front of the house. A woman he recognized as Paula Knightly's leggy blond assistant gathered a tribe of cameramen at his front gate. Evidently, the tenacious Paula had abandoned Kate's doorstep in favor of Gracie's. Great. The local sheriff hadn't taken his warnings about the possibility of a media circus seriously. One reporter positioned himself behind a tree, while another set his tripod up on top of his van and boldly aimed his camera at the front door.

Gracie followed him to the window. "They don't listen any better than you do. Look at those fools. They're like hungry ants at a picnic, crawlin' all over the place. Go on out there and tell them to shoo."

Sam spun around to face her. "Your wicked stepmother promised them dirt, and they're here to find it. Until something more sensational comes along, you're the new queen of the moment. Let's face it, babies don't come back from the dead and inherit fortunes every day." Sam closed the shutters and wandered back to his chair. "Would you like a drink? A soda or something?"

"But I haven't said I want to be queen. You go tell them that."

Sam wiped the teasing grin from his face and stared back at Conrad's daughter. Beneath her eyes were pale blue shadows that said she hadn't slept well. "Have a seat, Gracie. *Please.*"

Sam eased into his chair. Gracie scowled at him but followed his lead.

"Look, Gracie, you really don't have a choice. Names are being changed, documents signed as we speak. It's already your baby. But don't worry, Conrad was never a guy to suffer fools. He has a regular bunch of Einsteins managing his money. You won't have to worry about a thing. Smile. Attend a few charitable functions. Be a face for the Hammond family." As soon as the words were out, he knew he'd said the wrong thing.

Her gray-green eyes darkened to smoke. "Did your mama ever have your ears checked? You don't hear so well. I said I don't want your *damn money.*"

"It's not mine, princess. It's yours. All six hundred fifty million." Sam leaned forward and balanced his gaze on hers. "Most people would say you're nuts . . . but I can't say I blame you. Conrad didn't have much time to relax."

"I'm not afraid of work, if that's what you're thinking. I started sweeping out the Blue Jay

Club after school when I was twelve. I was hired on at the market when I was sixteen. Artie didn't want me working around the club after that."

Sam suspected Artie saw what she had yet to see: she was a beauty, a real looker. Men would notice. A honky-tonk wasn't a place for a young girl, even in the off hours. His respect for Artie went up a notch. "You and Artie are pretty tight, huh?"

Gracie's shoulders dropped slightly and she leaned back in her chair. "He was one of the hottest sax players around—until his lungs went south. Artie worked nights and took care of me during the day. He's always been there for me when other folks didn't have the time."

Other folks, meaning Conrad. He could see her side, but Conrad deserved a chance, just the same. Sam motioned toward the letter. "Why don't you open the envelope, see what Conrad has to say."

"Don't you mean . . . *Mr. Conrad?*" Gracie's voice regained its steely edge.

"Look, I didn't know about that until last night . . . or about this house." Sam glanced around the richly appointed room, then circled back to Gracie. "Conrad played his cards close. He was all about control. Don't take it personally. He was that way with everyone."

Gracie rocketed out of the chair. "That's just how I take it. That man sent me flowers—two

112

dozen of the biggest roses I've ever seen, in a crystal vase—I'm talking *Waterford*. And don't look at me like I shouldn't have a clue about good glass. I gave it to Alice. She thinks Skippy won it for me at the church carnival."

Sam shot Gracie a look of disbelief. Skip Evers's suspicious glance at their first meeting played over in Sam's mind. If Evers wanted more from Gracie than a winning season, he now had six hundred and fifty million reasons to hurry his decision.

A fortune hunter was the last thing Conrad would want his daughter to fall victim to. It was Sam's job to see that such an event never happened.

Sam closed in on her. "If Mr. Evers comes at you with a ring, promise me you'll make him sign a prenup before you say *I do*. Purely professional advice, you understand."

Gracie threw him a saucy smile even Scarlett O'Hara would be proud of. "And disappoint Alice? Why, Mr. Fontana, I do declare you have a streak of meanness . . . despite your nice teeth."

Her thick, honeyed drawl caught him off guard. She was naive, but worldly, feminine, and tough—sometimes all at once. With Gracie, he felt like he was standing in quicksand.

But Sam wasn't in the mood for games, even with Gracie. He stepped forward, pressing into her space. "I think Alice will understand that I have your best interests at heart."

"I came over here to give this back to you." Gracie held Conrad's letter at arm's length.

The edge of the envelope grazed his stomach. Sam stopped short. He could see Conrad's choppy handwriting on the front. Conrad had addressed it personally—gone the extra mile for Gracie, like he had for Sam when his dad was dying.

Anger came at him out of left field. Sam shoved the letter back. "He never gave up on you. You owe it to Conrad to open that envelope."

Gracie glanced down at the letter, leveled Sam with a glare, and slumped into her chair. "Okay, Fontana, you win this inning . . . but if I open this, you'll blast the peanut gallery outside. Deal?"

Sam nodded. "I'll do my best."

Gracie slipped one thin finger under the flap and ripped the envelope open. Sam turned his back and wandered to the window. Behind him, he could hear the soft shuffle of paper. Conrad could be long-winded on the written page. In person, he was short and to the point, a get-it-done kind of man who was uncomfortable with emotion.

Another shuffle of paper and a sharp intake of breath were followed by a burst of laughter. Sam spun toward Gracie. She leaned back in her chair, relief smeared from one corner of her mouth to the other.

"What?"

She was practically beaming. "Let's see how the crown fits on your head. In six months, I can dump all of this on you. And you can see how you like being *king*."

"What are you talking about?" Sam snatched the stack of papers from her hand. He bypassed the handwritten note on top and thumbed to the second page, then the third and fourth. It was a legal document drawn up by Conrad's attorneys. She was right. *Damn. "That sly bastard."*

True to his word, Sam had distracted the news folks while Gracie slipped out the back and through the alley toward home. When she got to her neighborhood, she took a shortcut through the Sphinkses' garden. Alma raised a hand full of clothespins to say howdy as Gracie hopped the fence, then raced up the back steps and tumbled into the kitchen.

Ben was sitting down to the table with a sandwich. "God Almighty, girl, is the devil on your heels, or have you been snitching Harriet Ackers beans again?"

"Reporters." Gracie glanced toward the living room window. The street was blessedly empty. Gracie turned back to Ben. "Well, look who's talking to me."

"Why shouldn't I talk to you?"

Gracie pulled up a chair and sat down opposite

Ben. "I don't know. Seems I've had the plague lately."

"You're starting to sound like Alice. All that female double-talk gets a man all turned around in his head. What's your beef, girl? Give it to me plain and simple."

"You know damn well what you did was shifty. I'm just waiting for you to say it. Time to eat crow, Ben."

"It was for your own good, and I ain't gonna apologize for taking care of my own. As far as I knew, you were Rita's child. I did what I thought best."

"For Rita . . . or for me?" Ben didn't say much about Rita, but Gracie knew from Artie that something had died in Ben when Rita ran away.

"You weren't the only one hoping Rita would come back. I missed that girl more than words can say. She's all I got left of my sister." Ben glanced away. Gracie spotted a bit of moisture in the corner of his eyes. "I promised her mama I would keep her safe. I didn't do such a good job. I wanted to do better with you." Ben paused.

"You did just fine with me." Gracie felt her anger slide away and a lump form in her throat.

He avoided her gaze, smoothing the edge of the tablecloth between his index finger and thumb. "When she told me you weren't hers, I was just as surprised as you. I thought it was God's way of showing me up for the mistakes I made with her. I could have given you back to your daddy, but you'd have been miserable and I knew you'd find a way to come right back. Rita was restless here in Shady Grove. From the day she was born, she wanted to spread her wings and see the world. But you were different. You were a timid little thing. Never could stand change. Artie said you needed toughening up. He thought I should send you off to college when you graduated high school instead of letting you hibernate in Draper's back room. I couldn't bring myself to push you out of the nest. Partly because I didn't want to lose you, like I lost Rita, but partly because I still hoped she would come back—if not for me, at least for your sake."

"Artie knew that was a losing battle, because I didn't want to go away to college."

"That didn't stop him from giving me hell for not making you go. Maybe if I'd made Rita go, she would have turned out different . . ."

The part of Gracie that was still angry with Ben was the part of her that was jealous of his love for Rita. Her whole life Ben had been making excuses for Rita, while he made it clear he expected more of Gracie. Rarely did he show her the kind of unconditional affection she craved from him. Gracie suspected that's why she'd been afraid to leave Shady Grove. She was afraid he would forget her and she'd no longer have a place to come home to. She wondered if Rita was thinking the same thing.

"When were you planning on telling me the truth about my daddy?"

Ben shrugged but still refused to look at her. "I would have gotten around to it when the time was right."

"When would that have been?"

"When you were married with a husband and children of your own. Now, if you don't mind, I've got to get to work. The Widow Perkins got a leaky water softener." Ben pushed back from the table and stood up. His sandwich was half eaten.

Gracie blocked his path. "Hold on a minute."

"Shouldn't you be at work?" Ben glanced at his watch and glared at her.

Gracie glared right back. "Jimmy told me to take the day off on account of my daddy dying, but I know he was just trying to avoid the stir of all those reporters who showed up this morning. Now, sit yourself back down. I'm not done yet."

"You're getting mighty bossy. I'm telling you, it will go bad for you when you get a husband."

Gracie waved Conrad's letter in front of Ben. "Mr. Fontana sent this letter over from the Parnell house this morning." Gracie paused, waiting for Ben's reaction. Had he known her father had taken up residence in Shady Grove?

Ben sank back into his seat and cast her a sheepish look that said it wasn't any secret to him.

There was no escaping the instant disappointment she felt. But despite his deception, he still owned a large piece of her heart. She'd wanted her suspicions to be wrong.

She glared at Ben. "Ben Calloway you should be ashamed of yourself. But I'm going to forgive you—just this once."

Ben ducked Gracie's gaze and took a bite of his sandwich, then chewed in silence.

"*I said,* I was going to forgive you."

Finally, Ben looked up at her and swallowed. "That's mighty generous of you. Why's that?"

" 'Cause of the letter."

"Here we go again. More woman-talk." Ben reached for his sandwich and took another bite.

"My daddy says here, I can give it all to Mr. Fontana in six months." Gracie added extra wattage to her smile. She wouldn't let Ben's trickery dim the relief she felt. Eventually folks would forget about the money and things would go back to the way they'd always been; Delilah Perkins would rope someone else into fixing her pipes; Alice would give up trying to marry her off to Sam Fontana; and Artie would stop talking about dying. She would be safe in Shady Grove where she knew the enemy.

"Let me see that." Ben grabbed the letter, then drew his glasses from his shirt pocket and started to read.

Gracie settled back in her chair, smiling to

herself as the lines of his face deepened to valleys.

He turned the pages slowly, wetting his finger with his tongue before going on to the next page. When he finally looked up, his frown was gone. "You read this all the way through?"

"The important parts. Why?"

"The only quick way out of this is if your blood don't match your daddy's. Maybe your mama had more than one stallion in her barn. You'll have to go to Montgomery to get yourself tested. One of them DNA tests. Mr. Fontana will take you, I expect."

Gracie thought back to the night in the swing. Her breakfast picked up the sudden jittery rhythm of her heartbeat and danced in her stomach. "He did say something about wanting my blood. I thought he was just rattling my cage."

"Nope. Says right here, you got to ante up." Ben was wearing the smile she'd worn moments ago.

She knew it was too good to be true. Apart from baseball, she always ended up with the short end of the stick. "What if my DNA doesn't match? I'm free, right?"

"As a bird. Now, I got to get to the Widow Perkins's softener." He started toward the door.

"Uncle Ben, just how big an alley cat was my mama?"

"It's not my place to say. Never met the

woman." Ben pulled his comb from his back pocket and smoothed his hair, then stopped short. "I almost forgot." He hurried back across the kitchen to the drawer beside the stove, then leafed under the potholders and pulled out a manila envelope. "Your daddy wanted me to give this to you when I felt you was ready. I guess you aren't gonna get any more ready than you are now." Ben reached into the envelope and pulled out a slim black checkbook.

Gracie glared back at Ben. "What's that for?"

Ben latched on to her hand and pressed the cool black leather into her palm. "You might be able to give back your daddy's money, but *this* belongs to you. It's your christening money. Your daddy invested it for you when you were born. I guess in Connecticut they welcome you into the world with more than a teething ring."

Gracie eyed the tailored leather cover suspiciously. The name *Katherine Hammond* was pressed into the lower left-hand corner in gleaming gold letters. Just like Sam's briefcase, it squeaked of a world that had shunned her. "I could use something to chew on right about now."

"Well, now you can buy yourself a whole house full of chew toys."

Gracie flipped the cover open and checked the balance. The number one at the head of the line wasn't much to get excited over. It was the string of numbers behind it, six in all that sent her heart into a tailspin. "This is a joke, right?" Gracie checked the balance again. "How long have you known about *this?*"

Ben sidled toward the door. "Got to run. The widow gets antsy if I'm late."

"*Ben Calloway,* come back here and explain what I'm supposed to do with this."

"Anything you want. Think of it as a practice run. Maybe the money can teach you a few lessons that I ain't been able to—starting with a plain old-fashioned thank you. Now, I got to go. Don't hold supper for me."

Gracie frowned at the empty doorway. All questions led back to Sam Fontana. Why did he have to be her link to the puzzle? Him and those eyes of his. Soul-reading eyes that skated past lies with hardly a blink.

Down the hall, Artie's coughing whipped away her disturbing thoughts. Gracie slipped the letter into her back pocket and dialed the doctor's number. She reminded herself to breathe as she waited for the receptionist to pick up on the other end. Artie was getting worse. Any fool could see that, but Alice, Ben, and Chantel were going about their business like always. Artie needed her here.

The Hammonds and their fancy attorneys could wait. Not one of them had swooped down from New England to welcome her into their family.

They'd sent a stranger. Gracie knew from past experience, when folks overlooked you it was because they were embarrassed by you. She didn't want to be anybody else's shameful secret. No amount of money could tempt her to weather more hurtful slurs than the ones she'd endured already. She'd seen the papers, despite Ben's efforts to hide them. They were calling her *Gator Girl*, saying she'd been raised in the swamp by alligators. She knew who the real alligators were and she didn't want any part of them.

Chapter 8

Artie hadn't said two words to Gracie as she bundled him into her Jeep and carted him off to the doctor's office. Once inside, she positioned herself between Artie and the examining room door. "I have a few things to say to Doc. Don't you think I don't know the two of you have been keeping secrets."

Artie's bottom lip was pushed out more than usual, a sign that he was going to put up a fuss. She refused to let him scare her off with his cantankerous mood. Let him pout. That was fine by her. She had stuff to pout about, too. Her new checkbook was burning a hole in the bottom of her purse, for one. As it turned out, she had over a million dollars between her savings and checking accounts. So far she hadn't come up with any ideas of how to put a dent in the balance.

Gracie picked up a magazine and leafed through the pages. *Modern Maturity* held no secrets for her. She felt old beyond her years. Disgusted, she tossed the magazine onto the table and grabbed up a dog-eared copy of *Time* magazine. Jennifer Aniston's sleek hairdo was reported to have set off a craze of flat hair. Poor Darla Watson's business would surely suffer.

Gracie whipped through the pages, working from front to back. Folks were rattling on about the verdict in the Simpson case. She'd had her fill of that nonsense from Alice, who daily refused to read another word but had no qualms about turning Gracie's ears blue with the shame of it all.

On her second pass through the pages, Artie snatched the magazine away. "What you want to create a tornado in here for, girl? I told you I could do fine all by my lonesome. Ain't no reason for you to be hangin' around creatin' drafts. Why don't you go on and pester Mr. Fontana. He enjoys it."

"He'd rather kiss swamp mud. The truth is he's just being nice because he's afraid I'm going to make him king, and all. You know I can't stomach kiss-ups."

Artie cupped his ear. "Say what? Kissing? You and Mr. Fontana?"

Gracie pressed her hand over Artie's mouth. "*Hush* yourself, Arthur Dubois. The whole world can hear you."

But it was too late. The receptionist's head popped up from behind her counter. Her baby blues widened to the size of quarters.

Gracie hid the heat in her cheeks behind a curtain of hair and hissed at Artie, "I have been doing no such thing, Arthur Dubois, and you know it. You better have the doctor check your hearing."

"You is full of vinegar today, girl. What's eatin' you?"

Gracie felt her chin wobble. She quickly buried her tears beneath her anger. "Besides your pestering? This damn checkbook, that's what."

Artie let out a soft chuckle. "Your daddy sure tricked you, didn't he? Must be heavy, all that paper."

"I need a way to lighten it. Got any ideas?"

"I'll bet there's a half dozen folks in Shady Grove who'd be glad to help you do just that. Moses Day, for one."

"And what would he do with it? He'd head straight for the Blue Jay and drink himself silly, that's what. Then Burgess would be on my tail about having Moses taking up space in his jail. I didn't say I wanted to throw it away. There's a difference between giving and throwing."

The doctor poked his head out the door and called Artie's name. Artie was out of his chair in a flash. "I can see you gots a serious problem. I'll let you think on it while me and Doc make bets on who's gonna win the Series."

Gracie launched herself out of her chair and started toward the doctor. "I need to have a word with the doctor myself—"

Artie turned around and placed a hand on her shoulder, pushing her away gently. "Now, hold on. It ain't none of your business. I'm a grown man and I don't appreciate you treatin' me like no child, you hear? You go on now. I'll see you later." Artie's voice had a serious edge that he saved for the times when he was disappointed in her.

Gracie jerked back. A lump in her throat cut off her protest. Artie wouldn't look at her after that. The lemon-sized lump began to feel more like a grapefruit.

Doc glanced at Gracie and nodded briefly, "Gracie Lynne," then swung an arm over Artie's shoulder. "Good morning to you, Arthur, old man. You won't believe what the wife surprised me with this morning—Series tickets."

"You's a liar. This is the first Series in two years, and Atlanta is at the bat. There ain't no tickets to be had. Your wife has been scalped."

"I checked. They are the genuine article." The doctor reached into the pocket of his white coat and withdrew the tickets. "My son is taking me next week. Guess we'll have to reschedule our appointment to collect my winnings, 'cause Cleveland is going to whoop the Braves."

"I have half a mind not to pay my bill. You's a mean, ungrateful devil, throwin' a man's dream in his face." Artie turned back to her before he closed the door. "You go on now, Gracie. I'll walk home. I still gots two legs."

Damn him. There was something he wasn't telling her and the doctor was in on the lie.

Gracie picked up another magazine. Out of the corner of her eye she spied the receptionist staring in her direction. The doctor's niece was new on the job. Word around town was this was her big break from the pet-sitting business in frosty Philadelphia.

Gracie smiled back, abandoned her magazine, and sidled up to the counter. She'd fix Artie. If he wouldn't let her talk to the doctor, then she'd pay his bill. Gracie fished her new checkbook out of her purse. "How much does Artie owe y'all?"

The receptionist eyed the shiny black leather. "I really can't say—not without Mr. Dubois's permission. I'm afraid that's confidential information for authorized family members only."

Gracie stared at the girl in disbelief. She'd paid Artie's doctor bills in the past without the third degree. She pierced the girl with a sharp look, then realized, Artie had sworn her to secrecy. He was shutting Gracie out. Why? Was he afraid folks would call him a leech if he accepted money from her?

Artie had put shoes on her feet lots of times when Ben was running short of cash. There was one year when she'd gone through four shoe sizes. She knew it hadn't been easy for him to come up with the money for the special shoes to fit her skinny feet.

Gracie opened her checkbook, ignoring the name scribbled in the top right corner. "You got a pen?"

The receptionist fumbled around her desk, then handed Gracie what she'd asked for.

"Thanks. Now we play twenty questions. Just so you know, I usually win in three." Gracie pointed to the word processor sitting on the desk. "Does the number there have two or three spaces before the decimal?"

The girl's face turned bright red. "I can't—"

"I hear Doc is hoping to remodel the office. Put in a new air-conditioning system. It must get mighty hot in here come July." Gracie eyed the dinosaur fan on the counter. It had one speed—slow and hot. The girl's smug expression waffled between wishful and desperate.

"Now, is that two or three spaces?"

The receptionist straightened in her chair and tipped her nose higher. "Neither."

Gracie checked her face for truthfulness. "Fine. One, then."

"Nope."

Good grief! How much did Artie owe? Gracie barely hid her surprise. "Okay, four it is, then."

The girl shot her a smug look. She was warming up to the game a little too much.

Artie owed at least a thousand dollars, maybe more. He hadn't said a thing to her. Gracie felt a stab of pain. He knew she had plenty of money.

She swallowed her disappointment and looked down at the checkbook.

Now she needed the first number. The rest in between didn't make much difference. The doctor could send her a refund. It would serve them all right for being so secretive.

Gracie held the girl's gaze. "You tell me when I'm getting warm. Two thousand?"

The girl shook her head and looked away.

Gracie couldn't help but sag with relief. "I'm too high, right?"

Once again the girl swished her blond ponytail from side to side.

"*Holy smokes!* Artie owes Doc more than two thousand dollars?"

This time Gracie received an enthusiastic nod.

"Is it more than three but less than five? Four—"

The girl's gaze snapped to the monitor, but her mouth remained closed. She was done playing.

"Four thousand dollars it is, then. You can put whatever's left over in the kitty for next month's bill." Despite Gracie's confidence, her hand shook as she scribbled out the number. How could Artie owe that kind of money and not tell her? When she got to the signature line, she stopped and stared at the name engraved on the check. She hadn't thought that far ahead. She was going to have to sign her name *Katherine Hammond*.

Her hand was poised over the line. She suddenly became conscious of the receptionist's eye on her pen. Hurriedly, she scribbled the unfamiliar name in the proper place, tore off the check, and slapped it down on the desk, then rushed out the door before her knees made a fool out of her.

The recent storm had been kind to the northern seaboard. The airport traffic was light for a weekday afternoon. Sam shook the pilot's hand. "Don't disappear. I won't be long."

"Sure thing, Mr. Fontana. I'll be ready to go after lunch."

Sam climbed down the stairs of the Hammond company jet to the tarmac. A black limo sat in the shadow of the hangar. Martin Jones popped the trunk, then rushed to Sam's side and reached for his briefcase and carryon. "Welcome back to Connecticut, sir."

"Thanks. I'll keep the case. The old lady's got you wearing two hats today, eh?"

"It's just me, the old lady, and the gardener. Glad you're back." Jonesy paused, eyeing the jet expectantly. "Miss Hammond isn't joining us?"

"Miss Calloway? Not yet. And I wish you weren't seeing me, either. In fact, the Bermuda Triangle is looking pretty good right now."

The drive to Katherine's estate took twenty minutes. The front gate was devoid of reporters.

Some other poor sucker was media lunch bait today.

Jonesy punched in the security code, made short work of the drive, and parked in front of a pair of towering glass doors.

"Thanks, Jonesy. I can find my way from here."

Jonesy raised his hand in a brief salute. "She's expecting you in the library. I'll be back as soon as I get rid of the hearse."

Sam offered him a nod and helped himself to a bottle of water from the minibar. His mind was wandering over Gracie's response to Conrad's letter when he heard a soft but purposeful click on the marble hall.

"Where's my granddaughter, Mr. Fontana?"

Sam turned away from the window. Kate's usual tidiness was missing. She stood in the archway, elegant but disheveled. Puffy bags darkened her eyes. Her blouse gaped from the waistband of her slacks. Wisps of silvered hair fluttered at her temples. She raised her chin a notch and fixed Sam with a haughty stare.

Sam offered her a salute with his pilfered bottle of Perrier. "You look lovely and positively middle class, Kate. Congratulations."

Momentarily flustered, she hurried to the window in the far corner of the room and seated herself in a lone chair, then turned her eagle glare on him. "You deserve a good thrashing. The girl, where is she?"

Kate wasn't as tough as she pretended. The last few days had taken a toll on her. Sam offered her a bold smile, hoping it would set her back up before he dropped Conrad's latest bomb on her. "Your granddaughter is wrestling with more of Conrad's secrets."

"Are you telling me she's a weakling?"

"Not at all." Sam abandoned his bottle on a table and braved her space.

Kate sagged deeper in her chair. "I can't keep the wolves from her door forever. I'm feeling my age."

Sam offered her his arm. "Do you feel up to a walk?"

Kate pinned him with a half-caliber glare. "Those heathens in the South have warped your good sense. Do I look like I need exercise? I'm exhausted from wrangling with Marcia and the attorneys."

"You look like you could use some fresh air."

Begrudgingly, she grasped his arm. "I look as bad as that, do I?"

There was no snowing Kate Hammond. She knew she looked like she'd been through hell. Instead of offering her false reassurances, Sam threw her a charming grin. "I can see your grand-daughter in you. You must have given them a run for their money in your day."

Kate rose to his bait. "I think I will be indignant for the both of us. You, young sir, need to learn some manners. It's no wonder she chose the alligators over your company."

"I'll win her over."

A twinkle of mischief curved her lips as she accepted his arm. "Don't be so sure of yourself. She's my granddaughter, after all. Hammonds aren't fools."

Sam led Kate through the French door onto the patio and down a cobbled walk. When they'd reached a secluded area in a circle of boxwoods, he steered her to a bench in a sunny spot. "Have a seat, Kate."

She perched herself carefully on the edge of the concrete bench and glared up at him. "If I catch a chill, you will have more than my granddaughter to deal with. Marcia and Lillian will be your problem as well. I assume you have a good reason for bringing me on a this adventure."

"It's a garden Kate, not Kilimanjaro." Sam took off his jacket and offered it to her.

When she had settled it over her shoulders, she looked at him expectantly. "Your reason, Mr. Fontana?"

His head was still spinning over Conrad's dirty trick. He wanted her input on the situation but had resisted telling her over the phone. She wasn't going to like Conrad's surprise any better than he did. "Conrad left a last request, which I would prefer the rest of the world didn't know about just yet."

Now he had her attention. Kate's sharp gray eyes narrowed. "Are you saying he emended his will again, and didn't give me a copy?"

"He left a letter—to Gracie. It was waiting for me in Shady Grove. I contacted the attorneys. Seems they are fully aware of the situation and have special instructions from Conrad. If the press gets wind of the situation, Marcia and Lillian will have more ammunition to aim at us." Sam began to pace.

"What situation is that, Mr. Fontana?"

Sam stopped and stared blankly at Kate. He still couldn't believe Conrad had done this to him. Now he knew how Gracie had felt when she'd found out about Ben's secret arrangement with Conrad. "Your granddaughter can dump the whole enchilada on me—in six months." He let his words hang while Kate digested the news. Her face was surprisingly calm. She'd known, or at least suspected, Conrad's latest move.

Gently, she patted the bench beside her. "Sit, Mr. Fontana. You're making me dizzy."

Sam seated himself beside Kate. "The house, and the collection, took me by surprise. I want you to know, I fully intend to hand them over to Gracie when the time is right."

"I can see why Conrad wouldn't want Marcia and Lillian to know about this special arrangement between you and my granddaughter. But I suspect there is another reason why he set things up this way."

A lively twinkle in her eye told him he didn't want to hear her answer, but he found himself asking anyway. "What other reason?"

"Conrad was a silly romantic, even as a boy. I suppose that would explain his hopelessly blind attempts at marriage." Kate's gaze wandered off with her thoughts.

Sam leaned forward, inserting himself into her line of vision. "Back up. You lost me."

"You and my granddaughter, Mr. Fontana. He's matchmaking."

A similar suspicion had crossed his mind when he'd discovered Conrad's baseball collection in Shady Grove. Bait is what it was, and Conrad had left it in his control. He had yet to show it to Gracie. He wanted her to base her decision about the money on deeper convictions than a room full of balls, bats, and gloves.

"Tell me, *Mr. Fontana,* do you find my grand-daughter attractive?"

Sam stared blankly at her and made a mental note to keep Alice and Kate apart. "Why me?"

Kate let out a resigned sigh. "You were like a son to Conrad. Is it so strange that he would think you a good choice for his daughter?"

"I'm a Yankees' fan and the one responsible for ruining her life. I'm one step up from dirt, as far as your granddaughter is concerned."

"It's good to know she has standards." Kate swept him with a quick appraising glance. "Dirty or not, I'd say you're redeemable. With a few manners, you'd make an admirable candidate for my future grandson-in-law. My son was rarely wrong."

"Do I have a say in this?"

Kate didn't respond. She looked fragile and tired. Her mind had wandered off down Memory Lane. Sam didn't have the heart to bring her back.

Her lips softened into a sad half smile. "He was always a precocious child. Not in a troublesome way, so I encouraged him. But he kept me on my toes, and he loved surprises."

"He knew me well enough to realize I don't. Not this kind." His words were lost to the fall breeze.

Kate's gaze had drifted across the lawn. For a second, pain was visible on her face. Then her gaze snapped back to Sam's. "Losing a child is an unnatural order I wouldn't wish on my worst enemy. I grieved for my son when he lost that child. But now that I've lost him, I understand his pain even more. If this Gracie Calloway is really his daughter and she doesn't accept her role, it will make the tragedy even greater—and you, Mr. Fontana, will need protection from some very persuasive fortune hunters. I suggest you return to Alabama and work harder to convince her."

• • •

The sun had barely slipped below Edna McCoy's roofline when Gracie poked her head through Artie's bedroom door. A magazine lay facedown on the covers lumped over his belly. His bifocals angled to one side of his face. He was fast asleep. Gracie tiptoed to the bed and leaned forward to pluck his glasses off his nose.

His brown hand shot up and latched on to her wrist. "Have a seat, girl. Tell me about your day."

She'd played this game with Artie before. He was after some answers. Chances were, he wouldn't rest until he got them. Gracie shrugged. "Not much to tell." He'd started the game, so he could go first.

Quietly, he folded his hands over his belly and gave her a sideways look that said he wasn't buying. "I seen the way you been playin' Alice lately. Don't think you can slip off my hook so easy, you hear?"

He was trying to reel her in on the you-paid-my-doctor-bill hook, which shouldn't have been baited in the first place. They'd never had secrets from each other before.

She returned his look. "Alice is happy believing what she does. I know better than to tell her otherwise."

He made a show of settling in against the pillows. "Guess you need a story to loosen that tongue of yours."

Gracie leaned against the bedpost on the end of the bed. "Go on, I'm listening."

"Little Jackie Brown's mama dragged her into the doctor's today. She sliced her ear with a pair of shears, trying to cut her hair off. Says she gonna be a boy from now on so she can play on a team just like her twin, Skinny Jimmy." He paused, looking harder at Gracie.

She knew what he was thinking. She'd set Jackie up for a fall by telling her about how when she was her age she'd made it onto an all-boys team in Troy. Gracie's charade had lasted until the second inning when she struck out some spoiled mama's boy. The sissy-baby snatched her ball cap off her head. And despite her new haircut, his mama pegged her for a girl right off. Gracie's all-boy team had had to forfeit the game. Girls having the right to play ball had been Gracie's hot button ever since. This was payback.

Artie raised one gray brow her way. "Jackie only needed three stitches and a tetanus shot. But her hair looked like some kinda mess. Darla Watson's gonna have to work miracles to make her back into a girl again."

Great. One more thing for Darla to whisper about at church. Gracie returned his one-eyed glare. "Are you trying to raise my blood pressure?"

"Just thought I'd warn you 'cause her mama

says she gonna send you the bill for the doctor and a haircut. Word is you's Shady Grove's new Santie Claus."

Gracie made a move to rise off the bed. "I don't have to take this."

"Sit tight. I ain't done. Then it'll be your turn."

Gracie leaned back and crossed her arms over her chest. "I'm still listening, barely."

"While Mrs. Brown was carryin' on about Jackie's hair, Moses Day come in sportin' a shiny new pair of stylish shoes even Elvis would be proud of. My, but they sure were fine."

"Are you angling for a new pair of shoes?"

"Not me. Moses's brand-new shoes already give him a nasty ol' blister."

She'd run into Moses outside the doctor's office with her checkbook still smoking in the palm of her hand. Wily old Moses spotted her desperation right off. Next thing she knew, she was at the shoe store.

"I told him to pick the sneakers. He accused me of being a cheapskate and insisted on picking out the most expensive ones in the store—hand-stitched Italian leather, stiff as stone. Serves him right if he got himself a damn blister."

"Doc gave him some ointment and some Band-Aids. So, Moses hops onto the same train Jackie's mama's ridin' and says for Doc to send you the bill. Then what do you know, Doc's secretary pops up and says she's already gots more than enough of your money 'cause you's paid my bill, and then some." Artie paused. But Gracie knew better than to rise to his bait too soon. There was more coming down the line.

He smoothed the blanket under his chin. "You almost lost that poor girl her job, buttin' in like you did, when I told you to stay out. Doc was plenty mad. But I explained what she was up against, and he agreed you got a mule stripe down your back a mile wide. I didn't even have to mention your big ol' ears."

Gracie pulled her checkbook from her back pocket and tossed it onto the bed. "Take a look. Even Moses's fancy shoes and your doctor bill didn't make a dent. So, I paid Harriet Ackers's poodle's vet bill. Bobo has receding gums, evidently. I figured it was a good way to repay her for snitching her beans."

Artie shifted back to his one-eyed glare. "What else did you figure?"

Gracie launched herself off the bed, jammed her hands in her back pockets, and started to pace. "How do you expect me to unload all this money? You told me I could do good with it. Now you're yammering on about how I'm causing trouble. What are you doing with a doctor bill the size of Texas anyway? Far as I can see, the doctor has done nothing but give you a few sleeping pills."

"That's between me and the doctor. I'm

yammerin' 'cause you's not using the brains God gave you. You ain't dreamin' big enough and you ain't done nothin' that matters to Gracie Calloway. If it don't matter to *you,* how you gonna know if it's the right thing to do?" Artie voice petered out. He said all he was going to say. One brow curved over his right eye, like a big gray question mark.

Gracie felt the frustration of the day slip over her mood. He was right; the things she'd done so far hadn't made a real difference to anyone— not even her. And she'd spent nearly five thousand dollars, more than she spent in a year just living.

Chapter 9

When opportunity knocked, Sam knew enough to answer before Gracie could nix his chance. When Chantel had shown up on his doorstep bright and early saying Artie needed a ride to Gracie's game, he'd offered to play chauffeur in hopes of a chance at breaking down her resolve. As long as she kept her bat on the other side of the fence and didn't aim any balls at his head, he'd even dutifully cheer when appropriate and admire her tight white pants from a distance.

Seats were filling up fast. Artie tottered up the steps to the fourth row. "If we sit here, she won't see us right off." Sam slid onto the bench beside Artie. "She doesn't like me much, does she?"

Artie rested his hands on his cane and glanced Sam's way. "Well, let's see . . . you come here all the way from Connecticut thinkin' she's gonna melt like butter in your hand 'cause you're offerin' her piles of money. I guess she surprised you, huh?"

"She's not your average material girl who prefers to spend her weekends at the mall. I've got that much figured out."

Sam glanced in Gracie's direction. She'd tied

her silky brown hair in a ponytail. Though she was wearing her uniform, she looked every inch the girl he'd met in the pretty blue dress. She had curves, instead of boyish angles. Nice curves.

Artie leaned close to his ear. "You know, not all poor folks is greedy." Then he lowered his voice and nudged Sam with his bony elbow. "And not all girls are attracted to handsome, cocky white boys, neither."

The old man was hunched over in his seat looking thin and tired, but confident that he'd called Sam's number. Maybe he was right; Sam had expected Gracie to show him gratitude and be charmed straight out of the gate by his winning smile. He'd never had to work at being likable. "You're saying she plays by different rules. Are they yours?"

"I can only be blamed so much for what goes on in her head. She come to us the way she is. She's the most stubborn girl I know. But she's got a heart that's big enough for everybody—but herself. That's Our Gracie."

Sam glanced to where Gracie sat beside her teammates, waiting for her turn at bat. The number twelve took up the width of her back. She was a full head shorter than the other team members, but Sam already knew her size was deceptive. He'd bet she could out-hit and out-throw any girl on the team.

He kept his gaze fixed on Gracie. "What do you mean, 'but herself'?" Sam wanted to say more, but he reined in his concern. She seemed confident enough to him.

"The sun used to come up just to see that girl smile. Then she went off to school. Ever since, she's been Rita's cast-off baby, in her mind. Don't matter that we all told her otherwise." Artie paused for a breath. "Jus' so you knows, I'm on your side. It's high time she stopped hidin' in Draper's back room."

For someone with as much spunk as Gracie, the market did seem too tame an existence. Now he understood why. "So, the money's just an excuse?"

"The Parnells put her off rich folks, for sure. But havin' her picture in the paper is a whole lot more scary for Our Gracie than balancin' a checkbook with a few extra zeros."

Artie pressed his handkerchief to his mouth and coughed. Sam thrust out the Coke he was nursing. Artie accepted the cup and took a long swallow. "You came along at just the right time —like one of them white knights."

"Slow down, old man. I'm okay with the fact that I've never met a woman who wants to hook her caboose to my engine. I'm doing this strictly as a favor to a friend."

"Might have started out that way, but now you's worryin' about whether she likes you or not. Seems to me, you're lookin' to pull into the station." Artie gave him a thoughtful glance, then swerved his attention back to the game.

Sam's gaze took a detour to the sidelines where Gracie was warming up to bat. As the next batter stepped up to the plate, Gracie paused next to the fence beside Evers. When the pitch came, the batter sliced at the ball, popping it into the catcher's glove. While the crowd offered sympathetic shouts to the batter, the umpire motioned for Gracie to take her turn.

Confidently, she stepped up to the plate. Her back was turned Sam's way. He took the opportunity to admire all the visible parts that made up Gracie Calloway—from her small wrists to the tight set of her jaw as she tried to stare down the pitcher. His gaze was on its second trip over her round behind when he heard a loud crack as her bat connected with the ball, then she was gone. His gaze didn't catch up with her until she emerged from a cloud of dust on second base.

Artie hoisted himself out of his seat and clapped. "That's the way to do it, Gracie girl."

Sam joined him and let out a loud whistle. The crowd behind them was noticeably quiet. When he and Artie sat down, he glanced at the rows of spectators. A few offered halfhearted claps of support for the team, but several pointed to Gracie while they whispered to their neighbors.

Sam frowned at the few who were brave enough to meet his gaze.

Artie's face was calm, but Sam could tell he wasn't happy with the crowd's response.

The next batter stepped up to the plate. Artie nodded in her direction. "That's Mary Beth. She's got a nice swing, but her bat is allergic to the ball. Let's see what she's got today."

The first pitch was low and inside. Mary Beth jumped back and threw the pitcher a hot look. The next ball was dead-on. Mary Beth took a swing at the ball but missed. Shouts of encouragement raced through the stand as the umpire called out "Strike one." On second base, Gracie stretched toward third, her attention volleying back and forth between Mary Beth and the pitcher. Gracie grabbed her chance and raced to third. Again, no cheering from the crowd—only dirty looks from the pitcher that said she wouldn't be caught off guard again. Gracie flashed her a devilish grin. Sam knew she'd try to steal home the first chance she got.

Mary Beth took a low whack at the next ball. Her cheap hit landed between the pitcher and third. Mary Beth raced to first while the pitcher dove for the ball. Gracie dodged her and skidded into home inches ahead of the throw. It was a daring play that could easily have cost the team a third out but won a run instead.

Artie clapped, then glanced back at the quiet

crowd. "Folks seem to have lost their manners all of a sudden."

Sam could count six hundred fifty million reasons why they'd lost their manners and knew it wasn't going to help his cause one bit.

Gracie gave Mary Beth a thumbs-up and a big smile before she dusted herself off and made her way to the dugout. The fact that Gracie loved the game was clearly posted on her face. Sam could imagine Conrad watching Gracie make a daring play, seeing pride spread across his features when she pulled it off. The reason why Conrad chose Gracie to step into his shoes was becoming more apparent. She had the guts to take a calculated risk and she liked to win.

Sam stood and let out a loud whistle of approval. Gracie turned around and waved, but it was clear she was waving to Artie. All she had to offer Sam was a long cool look before she turned back to the game. He gave her a thumbs-up anyway, then joined Artie on the bench.

Artie nodded in her direction. "That'll be the only run you'll see cross the plate today. Most of them girls don't believe in themselves enough to really put out. See that girl stepping up to the plate? She joined the team last season, hopin' to charm our man Skippy."

The girl cast a dreamy glance back at Skip Evers before she settled in for the pitch.

"What about Gracie? Ben said he was expecting Evers to pop the question."

Artie shrugged. "Won't do him no good."

The old man sounded pretty sure of himself. "Yeah? How's that?"

"I seen the way she looks at you." Artie captured Sam's gaze with a sideways glance.

Sam laughed. "Yeah, like I'm her worst nightmare."

"Nope, like you's a dead man." Artie's grin was cemented into the lines of his face.

Sam cocked one brow Artie's way. "And that's good?" When he didn't answer right away, Sam let his gaze shift back to the field and Gracie in her dirt-smeared uniform.

Artie leaned forward, inserting himself into Sam's peripheral vision. "Now, that all depends . . ."

Sam met his loaded grin. "On what?"

"On how sweet you like your sugah."

Artie's suggestion affected him more than he was willing to let on. Sam offered him an indifferent shrug on the slim chance that he might fool the old man. "I'm not much on sweets. Bad for the teeth."

"Alice got to you already. And here I was thinkin' you was a smart boy. You listen to me. When we gets older, teeth don't matter so much. What we need is a bit of sweetness to cut out the bite of life. You'll see."

Sam glanced back toward the dugout. Gracie was rubbing shoulders with Evers at the fence. The fact that Evers's nearness bothered him was purely professional. He didn't want some fortune hunter making short work of Conrad's daughter.

"What are Evers's financial prospects?"

"Prospects? Our Skippy? Let's see he done some deputy work, but mostly he helps out at the family's hardware store since his daddy passed on. He's a fine catch, as catches go 'round here. Doesn't drink, goes to work regular. Got manners and roots. A girl could do worse." Artie cocked one tired eye at Sam, but Sam kept his attention on Evers and Gracie.

"If he suddenly decides to come at Gracie with a diamond ring, let me know."

Artie's response was cut off by a fit of coughing. He pulled a handkerchief from his pocket and covered his mouth. When he removed it, Sam noticed spots of blood before Artie buried it in his pocket.

Sam held out a pack of gum and offered Artie a stick, careful to keep his gaze fixed on Gracie. "You've seen a doctor about that cough?"

"Ain't nothin' he can do."

Sam turned toward Artie and waited for him to say more, but the old man's lips were buttoned tight.

"Does Gracie know?"

Artie bowed his head a moment, then met Sam's gaze. "Nope. But now's not the time to tell her. She's got bigger trouble to deal with."

"Bigger than you dying? I doubt that. How long have you got?"

"I figure, when the Lord is ready, he'll tell me."

From the look on Artie's face, Sam knew the doctor's prediction wasn't good. Time was growing short. Sam remembered when his dad had told him he'd been diagnosed with cancer. The grief had been immediate and overwhelming. It took a week and a tough talk from Conrad before he'd finally been able to put on a brave face for his parents' sakes. There was never a good time to get the sort of news Artie was going to have to deliver.

"In case you haven't noticed, she doesn't take surprises well. Who's going to tell her?"

Artie's face closed up. "Not you, you hear? I'll tell her myself, when the time is right. I swaddled her and spooned grits into her sassy mouth. I'll know when she can take it."

Sam nodded, relieved he didn't have to give Gracie the news. "Okay. But if you're waiting for a lull, this is it. Things are only going to get more complicated from here on out."

Chapter 10

The media-feeding frenzy had settled around Draper's Market since Sam had reminded the local deputies of their duty to keep them away from Peachtree Lane. At first Jimmy had been happy with the attention and the increase in business, but the local customers were beginning to complain about the reporters sucking down their supply of Twinkies and Cokes, and they were threatening to take their business to Goshen.

When Gracie slipped though the back door, Jimmy raced past her toward the front. "We're out of ones and fives. Hotfoot it down to the bank, girl. I got a riot brewing on checkout one over the last box of cupcakes."

"But Jimmy—the street is crawling with reporters—"

"Ones and fives, you heard me." Jimmy wasn't just in a temporary panic; he was mad—and not much ruffled Jimmy's feathers.

Gracie plopped her purse on the corner of the desk and locked the office door, then opened the safe and set the cashbox on the desk.

Since yesterday, Draper's had accumulated five crisp stacks of fifties, bearing Ulysses

Grant's grumpy face. But Andy Jackson had Grant beat. There were fifteen stacks of twenties. Most were dog-eared and limp. Chances were the good folks of Shady Grove had rifled their mattresses in desperation to keep the Yankee locusts from gobbling up their supply of junk food.

If this continued, Jimmy's wife would be going to Florida to visit her fancy sister, and those new freezers he'd been hoping for would be humming on aisle five before the month was out—all on account of her *not* being Rita Calloway's abandoned love baby anymore but some freak sideshow heiress who'd risen from the dead.

Gracie's fingers stumbled as she counted out the stacks. She took a deep breath and started again, remembering Artie's words. *It's just paper, girl.* At least it had been—until this week. Today, the paper felt oily, dirty. Its odor overpowered the smell of Jimmy's stale cup of coffee on the corner of her desk. Gracie paused in her counting. *Money had a smell.* She'd forgotten . . .

She'd come home from Sunday school after a particularly nasty boy, Timothy Driscoll, had poked fun at her hand-me-down shoes. When she was done sobbing, Artie sat her on his knee and pulled a dollar bill out of his pocket and made her sniff it. "You smell that, girl?"

Gracie had held the worn paper against her nose. "I don't smell a thing."

Artie reached over and pressed his calloused thumbs against her eyelids, forcing them closed. "Sniff again. Breathe deep this time. What you smell now?"

Gracie did as she was told because Artie always had a purpose, even if most folks didn't understand what it was. She'd sniffed so hard she had to cough to catch her breath. "Smells like dirty paper, that's all."

"You sure? You don't smell no lollipops or no fancy new furniture? No new Cadillac? How 'bout a new pair of skates or that bicycle you been eyeing in the window at the hardware store? You smell any of those?"

"Nope. Just paper."

"Then what's you carryin' on about? Only difference between you and that nasty boy is he gots more paper than you. He still goes to the doctor when he's sick, same as you. He bleeds when he stubs his toe and needs a Band-Aid, same as you. And the green beans on his plate is the same grassy color as the ones on yours."

Just paper—that was the only difference between Gracie Calloway and Katherine Hammond.

She could live with that. Gracie took a long, slow breath, then finished counting and loading the money into the zippered bank pouch and locked the safe.

Silently she unbolted the door, jammed Jimmy's

154

old fishing hat on her head, and slipped past the crates of produce, pausing briefly to peer out the back door into the alley to give a listen for reporters before she darted out. She scurried along the back wall of the market with her head down, past the dry cleaners, the five-and-dime, stopping at the end of the block behind the yarn shop to scope out the street ahead.

Alice and Marjorie Finks's voices carried through the screened door of the Sharp Needle. They were at it again. She recognized their tone even before the words figured themselves into her brain. Alice and Marjorie had been measuring each other's accomplishments since high school. Their bickering was enough to squash any regret Gracie harbored for not having more girlfriends.

Marjorie's high-pitched cluck dropped an octave. "Those Yankee reporters are calling her Gator Girl, you know. It's just shameful. You can't take this sitting down, Alice Calloway. It reflects badly on all of us."

Gracie knew she should move on. No good came from listening at doorways, but she stayed put, waiting for Alice to land Marjorie with a snappy comeback.

Marjorie paused long enough to catch her breath and shift into high gear. "It doesn't help, with her traipsing around in boys' clothes, looking like a swamp rat. My poor dear Alice, the Lord has given you a heavy cross to bear. But don't you worry yourself a minute, we are here to help you, aren't we, ladies?"

Gracie's cheeks flooded with heat. *Swamp rat?* She glanced down at her jeans and sneakers. So what if the hem of her pants was frayed a bit. Celebrities paid big money for jeans like hers. And her sneakers were just starting to get comfortable. The last thing she wanted was Marjorie Finks nosing into her business and putting ideas into Alice's head. She eyed her destination on the opposite corner but hesitated, giving Alice another chance to call Marjorie on her nastiness. A mumbled series of milk-toast bless-your-hearts echoed through the open door, then the rapid click of knitting needles covered the awkward silence.

It wasn't like Alice to let Marjorie slip by. Why didn't she put Marjorie in her place?

Slowly Alice's voice rose above the din of clicking needles, but her words lacked her usual fervor. "Lord knows, I've done my best with the girl."

The disappointment in Alice's words sent a prickly stab of guilt through Gracie. She hadn't made it easy on Alice, that's for sure. Rather than be the daughter Alice wanted, she'd escaped to the ball field while Artie and Ben had covered for her. She'd never really considered how her determination to play ball made Alice appear to her friends. Pretty soon, the prickly stab steeled into a large lump in the back of Gracie's throat. She edged toward the corner of the building, anxious to run, until she heard Alice's voice rise.

"Why would she want to bother with Shady Grove cast-offs? I expect, with all that money her daddy left, she can afford Versace and that Italian fellow—whatever his name is—Oscar somebody. I can't think of it right now. Ben bought me some of his perfume last Christmas."

Oscar de la Renta? Good grief, Alice knew her better than that.

The clicking of needles stopped. A long pregnant pause was followed by the scrape of a chair. "The reverend needs me to go over his sermon." Alice's drawl squeezed into sharp pecks the way it did when she was on the edge of tears. "He's preparing one especially with Gracie in mind. Since she's putting a new roof on the Sunday school, it's only right. I don't want to keep J.D. waiting."

Gracie knew for a fact that the reverend practiced his sermon with Alice Saturday evenings. It was only Tuesday. Gracie frowned at the screen door. Her daddy's money had turned Alice into a chicken-baby and a liar. Gracie knew as soon as Alice's words caught up with her, the guilt would take a toll on her nerves and everyone in the Calloway households would suffer along with her.

Gracie turned away from the yarn shop and

cut across the street. By the time she stumbled into the bank, sweat trickled between her shoulder blades.

Darrell Johnson bobbed up from behind the manager's desk, raced around the front counter, and ushered Gracie into his private office. "Well, hey there, Gracie . . . or should I call you *Katherine* now?"

Good Lord, even Darrell had caught the disease. Freshman year of high school, they'd raced each other for the number one spot in Mr. Jennings algebra class. He'd been one of the few people in Shady Grove she could count on to treat her like an equal.

Gracie whipped the hat off her head. "Gracie is fine."

Darrell hesitated, then sent her a hundred-watt smile. "Gracie, it is, then. I want you to know, your money is safe with us. You won't have to worry about a thing. We've got the latest security devices. Come have a look."

Gracie yanked the bank pouch out of her purse. "Maybe some other time, Darrell. Jimmy sent me to fetch change. Business at the market has picked up lately."

Darrell looked like a largemouth bass trolling for bugs. He snapped at the air twice before sound came out. "The market—? I thought you were here to . . ." His smile dimmed, but he caught himself and beamed again. "Can I get you a Coke . . . or a cup of coffee, maybe? It's not just big banks that offer their special customers perks. No, siree. Why, we have cup holders and key chains. We even have—"

"I don't need a cup holder or a key chain. Thank you, Darrell. Just some change." Gracie handed him the zippered pouch and felt her disappointment put down roots. Darrell smelled money everyday and he hadn't figured out the truth. What were the chances other folks would buy into Artie's *just paper* theory? She could hardly go around asking folks to close their eyes and sniff a dollar bill.

Chapter 11

After Alice's set-to with Marjorie at the yarn shop and Gracie's disillusioning trip to the bank, Gracie was eager to start the six-month clock ticking. She hurried through Sam's back gate and banged on the kitchen door.

A latch clicked overhead, then heavy footsteps beat across the upper deck. Sam Fontana leaned over the rail and peered down at her in his boxers and T-shirt, his dark hair tousled from sleep. "Does anyone in this town ever use a phone?"

Gracie leaned back and frowned up at him, trying to ignore the way his shoulders stretched the white cotton of his shirt. "You need to shake a leg. We've got things to do. I need to be at work this afternoon, so hurry yourself up."

Sam settled casually against the rail. "What sort of things, princess?"

There it was, his smug smile, the one that made her teeth grind together. He'd caught her gawking and wasn't going to let her forget it.

Gracie whipped the letter out of her pocket. "Says here I've got to have a blood test." The thought of a needle poking into her arm made her empty stomach churn. She'd been in such a rush to get started this morning that she hadn't had any breakfast. The churning became an angry rumble. "Hurry it up, before I change my mind."

"The key is under the blue pot. I'll take a shower."

"Great. I'll make breakfast." Gracie managed a smile before her tongue stuck to the roof of her mouth. Her mind was suddenly filled with images that would make Alice call out the snake charmer—like Sam Fontana with warm and soapy water streaming over his body . . . Lord, help her.

Gracie jammed the key into the lock and stepped into Sam's kitchen. Someone with more vision than the stuffy Parnells had transformed the space into something she'd only seen in Alice's home decorating magazines. The counters were silver-gray stone on top of dark cherry cabinets. Sleek stainless steel appliances blended into the background. The notion that Mrs. Parnell would feel outdone in the fancy kitchen gave Gracie a sense of satisfaction.

Upstairs, the water hummed in the pipes. Gracie set her purse on a barstool near the center island and opened the mammoth refrigerator. There were eggs, orange juice, milk, oleo, a package of English muffins—and a Mason jar of Alice's homemade blackberry preserves with a note rubber-banded around the middle.

Dear Mr. Fontana,

Gracie especially wanted you to have these fine preserves and hoped you'd accept them along with her apology for not being more hospitable on her birthday. I suspect she was just overcome with her good fortune, and all. Bless your heart for being so patient.

Sincerely,
Alice Calloway

First the pizza and the picnic lunch and now jam. Good grief. No wonder he was looking at her in that cocky way. He probably thought she'd come over here to kiss up.

The sound of running water overhead ended with a jolt of the pipes. Gracie wadded up the note and crammed it into her pocket, then set to scrambling Sam's eggs.

She'd just popped the muffins into the toaster when she caught a whiff of aftershave. Gracie said a prayer as the sweet scent mixed with the smell of eggs and toasting muffins. "Hope you're hungry."

Sam's voice moved closer. "You've got a hidden domestic streak."

Gracie spun around. "Hidden? Are you saying I'm not girlish enough? 'Cause I didn't see

162

anything in those papers that says I have to cook and sew."

"Not at all. But your grandmother will be impressed."

Gracie spooned his eggs onto a plate, then returned to butter his muffins while keeping him in the corner of her eye. "Impressed by what?"

"Your . . . skills." Sam settled on a stool at the island behind her. "Because she doesn't know her way around the kitchen or the sharp end of a needle." He topped his statement off with a slightly wicked smile. "As to the girlish part, you've got nothing to worry about."

Gracie met his grin with a blush, then turned away. "I didn't say I don't know how to cook or sew. I just prefer doing other things, that's all. You sure do like to twist folks' words." She tossed his muffin beside his eggs and shot the plate across the slick countertop in his direction, then took the seat opposite his.

He caught the plate easily with the edge of his thumb. "My apologies. We all have hidden talents we sometimes hope people won't recognize."

"So what are your hidden talents?"

Sam's gaze drifted away for a moment, then returned to Gracie. "Your father thought I would make a good CEO."

Gracie shook her head. "I can't see you in a

Sunday suit and tie. And I'm pretty sure ball jackets and jeans wouldn't cut the mustard in a fancy New York office."

"Two points. You're right, I hate ties."

"Don't let Alice hear you say that. Even your nice teeth won't help you out of a long lecture on the duties of a gentleman."

Sam grabbed another muffin. "I'll remember that."

Gracie set down her fork. "You do realize if the blood test says Conrad isn't my daddy, you're it, and I'm free? From what I hear, my mama didn't spend her nights knitting booties."

"Don't get your hopes up. My guess is you were Lillian's insurance policy. Even though you disappeared, she still came out of the marriage with a fair settlement—all things considered."

Gracie's appetite suddenly went south. A boatload of reporters had found their way to Shady Grove to see Gracie, but her own mama had yet to put in an appearance. It occurred to Gracie that kidnapping wasn't all that much of a tragedy if the people who lost you didn't want you back. Quietly, she asked the question that had been on her mind since the whole mess began. "So, where is my . . . a . . . Lillian?"

Sam stopped chewing and reached for his coffee cup, eyeing her silently across the counter.

Gracie's impatience got the better of her. "*Well?* She's not dead, too, is she?"

"Nope. She's got the flu. You'll be hearing from her soon. I guarantee it." Sam stacked his dishes and carried them to the sink. "We better get going, if you have to work this afternoon."

Gracie latched on to his arm. "What are you not telling me?"

Sam exhaled a long breath. "Lillian's made an art out of living well on borrowed favors. When she wears out her welcome, people buy her off with limos, or trips to Monte Carlo, or cash. She hops from one unused summerhouse to another, one step ahead of her creditors."

He made her mama sound like a glorified version of Moses Day. "My mama's *a leech?*"

"Pretty much. And—"

"And *what?*"

Sam was beginning to twitch, which could only mean more bad news. "Conrad's second wife has filed a suit against you for a chunk of the estate on behalf of her daughter—your sister. We expect Lillian to throw her hat into the ring soon. She and Marcia have been at war for years. The attorneys are prepared. Don't worry."

Gracie dropped her grip on his arm and stepped back. "*My own sister is suing me?* When were you going to tell me this?"

Sam held her gaze with his. "Don't take it personally, Gracie. It's just about the money, not about you."

Gracie lifted her chin, reminding herself that

she didn't know the Hammonds from Adam. She shouldn't give a fig about them and their greedy ways. But it hurt, just the same.

"Let's get this blood test over." Gracie grabbed her purse and tromped to the door. The Parnell kitchen didn't look so perfect anymore. It looked messy, like her life. Gracie took a small measure of satisfaction out of the fact that she'd been the one to create that mess.

As they rolled back into Shady Grove, Gracie was feeling proud of herself. She hadn't puked or passed out when the nurse asked her to roll up her sleeve. She'd even managed a tiny smile. She could still feel the warmth of Sam's hand on hers. If she'd squeezed his a little too hard, he hadn't complained. He'd thrown her his best smile when the needle hit her vein, probably knowing his sass would get her back up enough to see her through the ordeal.

He'd been on his best behavior on the way home. She'd rewarded him by letting him buy her a burger and fries. By the time they hit Pecan Street, Gracie was feeling, if not gracious toward Sam, at least temporarily at peace with her situation—until they drove past Draper's Market. Reporters huddled outside in groups with cameras hugging their hips as they guzzled cans of Coke and waited for another photo op.

Gracie ducked low in her seat and motioned Sam

down the street. "Double back through the alley."

Sam turned the corner and slowly backtracked through the alley to the market's rear entrance. "So take the day off. I'll call for more security. Tomorrow things will settle down."

She returned to her seat. "Jimmy needs me. Besides, what would I do until they decide to give up and go away—sit on the couch, eating ice cream and watching TV? I'd be fat and crazy inside a week."

Sam glanced over at Gracie with a look of disbelief that quickly dissolved into resignation. "At least let me walk you inside."

Gracie checked for loose cameras, then stepped out of the car and into the alley. She glanced back at Sam. "Thanks, but I'll be fine. I'm going straight to my office and locking the door." She needed space from the Yankee. Her stomach was feeling fluttery every time he smiled at her. And more than once today, she'd found herself wondering what it would feel like if he leaned over and kissed her.

Gracie relaxed as soon as she heard Jimmy's salty voice barking from the front of the store, directing traffic through the checkout counters. She shimmied past a pallet of dog food and tiptoed toward her office. She'd barely reached the doorway when a short stocky man burst from behind the sacks and lunged at her with a microphone. "Just a few quick questions—Miss Hammond, what does it feel like to have all that money?"

Gracie stumbled backward, caught herself, then darted for the front of the store. "Jimmy, how did this . . . this weaselly worm *get in?*"

The reporter dashed around her, blocking her path. "When are you and Fontana tying the knot? Was that the reason for the blood test this morning? When's the baby gator due?"

Gracie's face burned with heat as the sea of faces crowding the checkout counter turned her way. Even Jimmy froze. They were all waiting for her to answer the man's last question.

Gracie lunged in the man's direction, pointing toward the door. *"Get out—"*

"Come on, honey. Give me a break." The man raised his camera and snapped her picture again. "Just one statement—"

Gracie covered her face with one hand and tried to push him away with the other, but the idiot refused to budge. Then he did something worse —*he laughed*.

Gracie felt her temper let go at its roots. The days of frustration channeled themselves into her fist. She aimed for his nose and made a home run when her knuckles glanced off his bone and came to stop on his right eye. His laughing face crumpled in surprise. He tumbled backward, spewing blood over the cereal display —just as Burgess, Shady Grove's duly elected sheriff, swaggered through the front door.

Chapter 12

Sam tossed his keys onto the kitchen island beside the remains of their breakfast. He smiled to himself as he set the dishes in the sink and turned the water on. He'd caught Gracie looking at him with a hungry look more than once today. If he didn't miss his guess, she liked him more than she pretended. The woman under her tough exterior was leaking through. He'd almost given in and kissed her.

A soft knock sounded at the back door, interrupting his thoughts. Sam crossed to the door. "Chantel. I didn't expect you until tomorrow."

"I know, and I'll be here, for sure. But I come 'bout Gracie. She hauled off and popped some reporter in the nose. His eyes swelled up as big as apples, on the spot. He claims he can't see and is gonna sue. The sheriff dragged her off to the jailhouse. Burgess was plenty mad. She's gonna need help."

"*What?* I just left her there—ten minutes ago. Where's the jail?"

Chantel's mouth split into a wide grin. "On Pecan Street. Middle of the block. She's tough when she's mad."

Sam raced back to the sink, shut the water off, and scooped up his keys. "Not as tough as you think. Chantel, you working today?"

"No, sir."

"Work's here if you want it."

Chantel peered past his shoulder and frowned. "Yes, sir. It sure is. You let Gracie cook, I see."

"She offered."

"Uh-huh. But she didn't offer to clean up? Gracie's never been much for dishes. I'll do it. But you should make her pay me, Mr. Fontana, sir, if you don't mind me sayin' so. Her havin' that big money, and all."

"Call me Sam. Sir makes my hair turn gray. And I'll pay you as soon as I spring Gracie from the cell block."

Chantel wandered to the sink, then looked back over her shoulder at him. "You ain't so bad for a Yankee, you know that? Gracie, she's one lucky woman. Yes, siree. Mighty lucky."

The sheriff's office smelled like Lysol and mildew. Gracie crossed her arms over her chest and slumped down in the hard oak chair. The sheriff paced the floor on the other side of the table. Burg's gun waggled on his wide hips when he walked. Sixteen years of doughnuts hung over his belt, hiding the buckle.

Burg stopped opposite Gracie and ran his big hand along his jaw. "What you want to haul off and hit the guy for, Gracie? Now he wants to charge you with assault. This puts me in an awkward position, with me and Ben going fishing on Saturday."

"Tell that reporter I'm going to charge him with harassment. He jumped me and stuck a microphone in my face."

"Did he touch you? If he touched you, I could make him back down."

"He's just got a little ol' black eye, Burgess. He deserved more."

"You could offer him money, now that you're rich. He'd drop the charges in a flash, I'll bet. Then you wouldn't have to clog up my jail. Judge ain't gonna be happy to see you, either. He and Ben go way back."

"Money. That's what started all this. I told them I don't want it. Everybody's gone deaf, even Artie. I just want to go back to being me. Nobody used to bother me at the market. They hardly knew I was there. That's the way I like it." Gracie felt the tears burn behind her eyes, but she blinked them away.

Burgess was looking at her like she was crazy. *"Don't want it?* Why the hell not?"

Gracie shot forward in her chair and leaned across the table. " 'Cause of folks like that reporter fellow. I don't want to be on TV, or go to Paris, or New York, like Alice says. I don't want to wear high heels and ride on elevators.

Do you know, they have buildings in those places that are over eighty stories? *Eighty.* I like it here in Shady Grove with my feet on the ground. There isn't a building over two stories tall, not counting Widow Perkins's attic, of course. And since it's haunted, I have no intention of ever checking it out, even if she claims Harry stashed a signed 1933 Series ball up there."

"You're afraid of heights. How about that? I didn't think you were afraid of anything."

"Only a fool isn't afraid of anything, Burgess."

"How are we gonna get you out of this mess? That guy is real hot under the collar. My job could be on the line here."

Velma, Burg's secretary, poked her head in the door. "Mr. Fontana from Connecticut is here to see Gracie. He says he represents her daddy's family. Should I let him in?"

Burgess sagged with relief. "Send him in. Somebody's gotta rescue this girl before I starve to death. Lulu's running a special today on chicken fried steak and I'm gonna miss it."

When Burgess turned back to Gracie, his face was ten sides of serious. "Now listen up, little lady. A Mr. Fontana is coming in here and I want you to cooperate with him, you understand? This ain't doing nobody no good, you being in here. Pretty soon folks are gonna accuse me of police brutality for locking you up. They could care less what happens to that Yankee with the shiner.

You know how things work around here. Smile nice when you step outside, you hear?"

The door opened again and Sam stepped through. "Gracie. Sheriff."

Burgess stuck out his hand, grabbed Sam's and pumped it up and down like he was waiting for water. "Boy, am I glad you're here, Mr. Fontana. We got ourselves in a pickle."

Sam smiled back, then shot Gracie a questioning glance. She didn't need reading lessons to hear what he was saying with one raised eyebrow: *Her fist had bought her just the sort of attention she'd been trying to avoid.* She crossed her arms over her chest, refusing to be intimidated by his glare, then sat back while he turned his Yankee charm on Burgess.

"The New York office called the newspaper and dealt with the matter. They're also sending an attorney from Montgomery to deal with the reporter, in case there is any misunderstanding."

Velma popped her head in the door and flashed Gracie a bright smile, then turned to Burgess. "The Yankee newsman wants to drop the charges. And there's an attorney on the line waiting to talk to you, long distance."

Burgess clapped his hands, then reached out and gave Sam's hand a hard shake. "It's been a pleasure, Mr. Fontana. Gracie, you see Velma and she'll give you back your pocketbook. And remember what I said, smile on the way out."

Then he was gone, and Gracie was alone with Sam.

"I suppose *the New York office* paid to get me out of this?"

"I don't know. They didn't say, and I didn't ask. If they did, you, or the estate, will get a bill. Eventually."

"And what if that little blood test I took today comes back saying my mama was sleeping in someone else's barn? Then what?"

"Then I'll take it out of my expense account. Right now, let's get out of here before more press shows up and I have to play bodyguard."

Gracie refused to budge. Never in her whole life had she been so mortified as when Burgess had slapped handcuffs on her in front of a store full of familiar faces. She hadn't asked for this trouble. She'd told Sam more than once, but he didn't seem to be hearing her.

"I bet you're just so proud of yourself, Sam Fontana, calling New York City, and all—"

Sam leaned in real close. "Not really. I figured if you were terrified of someone sticking a needle in your arm, you might be slightly bent out of shape by being thrown in jail."

His voice was steady and gentle, not at all what she deserved for her sassy tone, but she couldn't help herself.

"I'm going to be the laughingstock of Shady Grove. Alice will be embarrassed in front of her friends. Marjorie Finks was standing right there. All on account of some fool reporter. You know what he asked me in front of all those folks?"

"We can press charges against him. Make him disappear in a dark hole."

"He asked me if I was *pregnant*—in front all those people. Now, why would he ask me such a thing?"

"The blood test. Someone must have followed us. Don't worry, I'll take care of it. And I think you underestimate Alice's loyalty. She would have plugged that reporter, too."

Gracie felt salt from her tears sting her eyes as hot embarrassment flooded her face. Gracie nodded and tried to summon a smile. "Take me home, Sam."

Chapter 13

Gracie sank lower into Ben's chair and aimed the remote at the TV with her good hand. A quick surf through the channels made it pretty clear that other folks out there were having worse days than she was, but she felt inclined to wallow a bit longer. The bag of ice on her right hand was beginning to melt.

Nothing was broken, just bruised knuckles—and the annihilation of her pride. Thanks to the mouthy reporter, half the town thought she and Sam Fontana had been going at it like rabbits. They'd be counting the days, waiting for her belly to pop out with proof so they could say how they were right about how wild oats ran in the Calloway family. If she didn't produce Sam's baby, they'd say she'd committed an even bigger sin and gotten ridden of *the poor thing,* bless its little heart. Either way, she was doomed.

Gracie flipped the channel, searching for a recap of last night's Braves and Indians game, but her own face flashed across the screen, followed by shots of the back of Sam Fontana's head. The picture was taken behind Burg's office. A clip of the reporter's face—after she'd punched him—followed with a close-up of his swollen eye. The newscaster laughed as he topped off the report with an old photo of her as an infant in her father's arms, then finished up with shots of the clinic where Gracie had gone for her blood test.

A cold ripple snaked through her belly. *The whole world was laughing at her.* Gracie rocketed out of her chair. She needed to talk to Sam. *Now.*

Before she reached the door, Artie tottered out of the halo of kitchen light into the dim living room, towing a portable oxygen tank behind him. "Don't worry, Gracie, you're just the new toy on the block. Everybody wants to have a turn at you. It'll wear off."

Gracie stared at the clear plastic tube running across Artie's face. "When did you get *that?*"

"That ol' doctor played a mean trick on me today. Said he was goin' to put me in the hospital if I didn't hook myself up. Since you paid my bill, he thinks he can milk more money out of me."

Gracie's gaze jumped from the plastic tubing to a white bandage on Artie's forehead. "What's that for? Did he have to knock you out to get you to agree?"

Artie lowered himself into Ben's chair. "Just sort of ran out of breath. Bumped my head. It's nothin'. Didn't even need stitches."

Gracie kept a careful eye on him while he

inhaled his next breath through the clear tube. She had to admit he was breathing easier. At least her money was good for something.

"Did Chantel take you to the doctor?"

"Chantel got extra work today, so I told her to go on. I stuck out my thumb and guess who stopped?" His sassy grin was back.

"Who?"

"The Widow Perkins. Gave me a ride there and back, then helped me all the way up the front steps. Even sweet-talked her way inside. First, I thought she was after my body, but as soon as she realized you weren't here, she cut out the door fast as fire."

"I was in jail. The Widow Perkins won't be offering you any more rides."

"What'd you do, salt somebody's roses? I thought you learned your lesson when it back-fired on you the first time." The whites of Artie's eyes glowed in the dim light, but his surprise was just for show. He knew the score.

"I'm never going to live my adventure in the Parnell garden down, am I? Why is it every time I try to stick up for myself, it backfires on me? I'm just not cut out for revenge. The Parnells' roses are gonna live forever 'cause I dusted them with Epsom salts instead of table salt. And now, the whole world thinks I'm a snooty heiress 'cause I popped some smart-mouthed reporter in the nose."

"Say *what?*"

"Don't tell me, Artie Dubois, you haven't heard 'cause it was even on the news just now. I put Edna and Vera in the shade."

Artie settled back in his chair, crossing his arms over his belly. "I know, but I need a good story."

Gracie perched herself on the end of the couch closest to Artie. "A reporter waylaid me in the market. I told him to shoo, but he kept on with his microphone and nosy questions. Put me to shame in front of everyone . . ." Gracie's throat closed up and her eyes blurred with tears.

"So you punched the sorry ass. Used your right hook, just like I teached you." Artie raised his fist and jabbed at the air.

For a moment, it was like old times—just her and Artie sharing the day. Gracie managed a watery smile. "I gave him my best shot. He landed in the cereal display, so I know he didn't get all that hurt. But before I can say boo, the wormy man is swearing to sue, and Burgess slapped me in handcuffs."

Artie was beaming. "And you gots your pretty face all over the news. Some big fighter man's trainer gonna be callin' you for a contract, and you don't know what to say."

"I don't plan on making a habit of punching folks. It's just that, that reporter said some things . . . that were downright snake-like."

"I'm just pullin' your leg, girl. You don't like being in the spotlight 'cause you think someone's gonna poke fun at you. That's all over now. It's time for you to stand up and say Gracie Calloway's somebody and she's got somethin' to say. This is your chance, girl. Folks is listenin'. Why you wastin' your words on a some pea-brained reporter for?"

Artie broke off in a coughing fit. Gracie jumped out of her chair and ran to get him some water, but Artie had it under control before she got back.

"Didn't that doctor give you any medicine for your cough? Lord knows, I paid him enough—"

Artie took a sip of water and struggled with a smile, then gave up and sank back in the chair exhausted. Gracie didn't have the heart to poke at him again. She'd write checks in her new checkbook till it was all gone, if she could make Artie get well.

He rolled his head her way and glanced at her from his best eye. "Did you know, that lucky-dog doctor got tickets to the playoffs next week? That's as near to heaven as a man can get. In my next life, I'm gonna be a doctor—with a horn. Gotta have a horn. Lord knows I miss playin' nearly as much as you miss being Little Miss Nobody. But I ain't ever gonna play again jus' like you ain't gonna be Miss Nobody no more."

• • •

Sam leaned over the rail for the second time that day. Gracie's silhouette hovered in the yellow glow of the back-porch light. Gold danced off the top of her fine, straight hair like a halo. It never ceased to amaze him how unaware Gracie was of her womanly attributes. He smiled down at her, admiring the way warm shadows curved around her breasts and hips.

Gracie stepped off the stoop and glared up at him. "I need to talk to you, Sam Fontana."

Even through her honey-thick accent, he recognized her I-mean-business tone. What she had to say wasn't going to be sweet. Sam rested one hip on the rail and crossed his arms over his chest as he peered down at her. "You don't have an urge to cook, do you? I was thinking about calling out for Chinese."

"Only *you.*"

"That sounds . . . promising." Sam wiggled his dark brows at her.

Gracie's stubborn frown stayed in place. "It's not, so don't get your hopes up, *Yankee.*"

So, they were back to Miss Scarlett and the damn Yankee again. He wondered briefly what had set her off but then realized he was happy she'd come around to save him from a dull evening. "You know where the key is."

"Yes, I do." Gracie pulled a shiny gold key from her back pocket and inserted it in his door.

"Remind me to call a locksmith."

Gracie craned her head back at him and her halo slipped into shadow. "Won't do you any good. There's only one in town. Billy Mead. Billy and I are thick as thieves."

"Why am I not surprised?" Sam hurried across the deck into the bedroom, grabbing a T-shirt off the bedpost as he went. Then, remembering how she'd eyed his chest that morning, he went back for a second shirt with buttons. He yanked the soft white cotton down over his head, jammed his arms into the sleeves, buttoning and muttering as he hurried to the door. "You're asking for trouble here, Fontana. She's got an in with a locksmith. And she's got a right hook Ali would have been proud of, not to mention she—"

"She what?" Gracie was waiting for him at the bottom of the stairs. Her nose was pressed to the first in a row of photos leading up the stairwell.

Sam hurried down before she could climb up. "I expected you to be in the kitchen boiling oil for the next wave of invaders."

"I thought I'd start with you." Gracie eyed his shirt before her gaze skittered back to the photos hanging along the wall. "Some of these are pretty old. Who's this guy?"

Sam peered over her shoulder. The black-and-white photo looked like something straight out of a James Cagney movie. His dad was leaning against Conrad's antique Rolls, a Fedora tipped down over one eye. He'd been in his mid-forties then, still tall and lean with a perpetual smile.

Sam felt a matching smile tug at his lips. "That's my pop. He and Conrad were pretty thick after you were kidnapped. Pop didn't think you were dead, either."

"That was mighty considerate of him." Gracie stole a sideways peek at Sam, then turned back to the photo. "You look just like him, you know."

Sam covered the catch in his throat with a laugh. "He was a great guy." Sam stepped back, putting some distance between himself and the photo. "He died nine years ago. Cancer."

Gracie's gaze followed him. "I'm sorry, truly."

Sam shrugged, shaking off her intent interest. His dad's death wasn't something he could talk about easily. "Yeah, well, what ya gonna do? Something's gotta get you. Just wish it had been something besides the big *C*."

The look of sympathy she shot him was almost his undoing. "Breast cancer took Ben's sister when Rita was fourteen. Ben raised Rita, like he raised me."

Gracie moved on to the next photograph. Sam lagged behind, listening to the way her words flowed softly together as she drifted up the stairs. She was captivated by the faces of people she'd never met. Amazing, and sad in a way.

"Ben talked about his sister so much, I used

to dream about her and pretend she was my guardian angel." Gracie's gaze touched his briefly. "Her name was Lynne, like my middle name."

Sam nodded in understanding. "Roots."

"You're catching on, Yankee." She glanced at him over her shoulder, her gaze lingering long enough for him to detect a small measure of admiration, before she moved on to the next picture.

Sam's dad stood beside Conrad; each man held a twenty-pound bass clutched by the gills.

"Your daddy has nice teeth. Alice would approve."

Then Gracie went silent. Her attention had shifted to the largest photograph in the middle of the row—Conrad holding baby Gracie in his arms, with Lillian standing by his side. The wind had brushed a short dark wisp of Gracie's hair against Conrad's cheek. He was smiling, almost laughing. Sam had stared at that picture years ago and wondered about the baby in Conrad's arms. She didn't look like much, but Conrad seemed to think she was something special. That had been enough for him and his dad to endure Conrad's dark moments.

Sam reached over and touched Gracie's arm to distract her from her thoughts. "So, what brought you all the way over here, if it wasn't to cook me dinner?"

Gracie stepped down until her stormy gray

gaze was level with his. It was like getting sucked inside a tornado. He couldn't look away.

She pointed at the photo. "That picture was on the news tonight for the whole world to see."

"It's not the first time. Don't worry. Pretty soon some fool will step out of line and no one will remember who Katherine Hammond was."

"Don't look so calm—your picture was up there, too. They caught you smuggling me out of the sheriff's office this afternoon. Someone followed us to Montgomery, too. They got shots of your thick head."

Sam ran a mental tally of the day. Nothing suspicious registered in his memory. "Must have been a lone camera. I wouldn't worry."

Gracie crossed her arms over her stomach and tapped her toe. "What kind of private investigator *are* you? You didn't even see the guy, did you?"

What could he say? If he told her his attention had been on her, she'd short circuit. It was safer to play dumb. Sam shrugged and offered her a blank look. "Can't say I did."

"You don't care that your picture was on the news?" Gracie's cheeks were starting to glow again.

Sam offered her a bold smile. "Did he get my left side or my right?"

"The back."

"Well, there you go. Only my mother would recognize me. I'm safe."

"Your arm was around my waist and your name was connected to mine. Folks *were laughing*."

Gracie's stubborn chin had a scary wobble to it, a good clue that she'd been made fun of before and she took it hard, even harder than the invasion of her privacy.

Sam erased his teasing grin. "I'll call the station in the morning and find out who the photographer was. He'll get something better than a black eye. I promise. Now, can we go downstairs? I want to show you something." Sam offered her his arm, but she hesitated, staring back at him like he was offering her a snake.

"Don't worry, you're going to like this surprise."

Tentatively, she laid her hand on his arm and moved a little closer. "My right fist is sore, but I still got my left—just so you know."

Sam stifled a chuckle. "I'll remember that." He had no intention of ending up like the reporter with the shiner. Silently, he led her down the stairs. When they reached the door, he pulled up short. "Now close your eyes."

"What for?"

"Just do it, without any sass for once."

Gracie flashed him a hot glance that reminded him of Kate, then closed her eyes. "Okay, they're shut. Hurry yourself up. I don't have all night. I've got to get my beauty sleep. I might be on camera tomorrow."

"Are you going to keep talking? I might change my mind. I can guarantee you'd be sorry." Sam shoved the key into the lock and waited for the slow hiss of air and the green light.

"Fine, but no tricks now."

The only trick he wanted from Gracie was a kiss, a genuine you-make-me-hot kiss. Her fresh scent and her light touch on his arm channeled his thoughts in one direction. But then he remembered her left fist bunched against her thigh. Sam shoved the door wide but kept a close watch on her face. "Okay. Open 'em up."

He couldn't help but smile when her jaw dropped, then abruptly slammed shut. For once, she was speechless.

Sam pressed gently on the small of her back. "Conrad left us more than one surprise. Go on. Take a look around."

"Holy smokes! Where'd he get all this stuff?" Gracie broke free and rushed toward a display case. "*Look at that.* There's a ball from the '82 Series . . . *signed by Ozzie Smith himself.* I had the flu that year. Artie stayed home with me instead of going down to the Blue Jay. The Cardinals whooped the Brewers in game six." Gracie spun around to take in the whole room. "It must have taken ages to collect all this stuff."

"Just money. Conrad started seriously collecting eight years ago. He dabbled before that, just as a hobby."

Gracie narrowed her gaze at him. The significance of the timing hadn't passed her by. She was still wounded over Ben and Conrad's silent deal. Her expression dissolved into confusion, then edged toward tears.

Sam's tongue went hungry for a joke. He couldn't even find a bad lie to lighten her mood. "He wanted to share something you had a passion for. Is that so hard to understand, princess?"

Gracie blinked in disbelief. "So, he waited until he was dead. Maybe I'm just slow, but that makes no sense."

"Conrad was a complicated man. He always maintained control. His own emotions were subject to the same rules, particularly after he lost you. If he couldn't limit the depth of his emotions, he kept them at a distance whenever possible, especially from himself. I'm sure he was planning on sharing this with you someday. He just hadn't figured out how. What if you weren't suitably impressed?"

"Believe me, I would have been plenty impressed, *if* he'd had the guts to show this to me himself." Gracie wandered along the walls, stopping every few feet. "Well, it's a good thing I didn't have a yen for Barbie dolls."

Sam chuckled. "For that, I *am* thankful."

Gracie's gaze circled back to his. "You're right. You would look out of place in a pink room full of dolls."

"Yeah, but I wouldn't have a hard time giving it up." Sam braced himself for her reaction.

Gracie's antenna went up. "Are you crazy? Why would you ever want to do that?"

He was on shaky ground here. Maybe this wasn't such a good idea after all. But Gracie was waiting for an answer. The longer he put off his response, the steelier her gaze grew. Sam forced himself to relax and smile. "All this was meant for you."

Gracie crossed her arms tightly over her chest and glared at him suspiciously. *"Me?"*

"Frankly—it's a bribe."

"If this is another one of your jokes, Sam, I'm not laughing."

Sam lost his nerve. What was it about Conrad's daughter that made him reluctant to lie? "Look, Gracie, you know, and I know, what that blood test is going to say."

She shot him a dark look, then set off along the row of display cases. Sam tagged behind, watching the sway of her hips and the lights dance in her hair. He caught the faint fragrance of honeysuckle and found himself wondering which part of her body had had the honor.

Then Gracie came to an abrupt stop and whipped around. "He has a signed glove from *the Babe?*"

Sam glanced at the case, then smiled back. *"I . . .* have a glove signed by *the Babe."*

189

Gracie shot him a dark look. "Yes, *you do.* You're a mighty lucky man."

"Mighty lucky, that's me."

Gracie gave the room one last, longing glance, then headed for the door. Sam locked up and set the alarm. He could swear he'd heard her mutter the word *thief* as she passed by, taking her sweet scent with her. He found himself wondering why he suddenly felt like he'd been robbed as well. Then he reminded himself that Conrad rarely played fair.

Chapter 14

Kate Hammond folded her gloved hands primly in her lap and stared out the car window at her son's ridiculously impractical sprawling Tudorbethan-styled mansion while she waited for Martin Jones to open the passenger door. It wasn't that she couldn't manage the simple task herself. Her stubborn decision to remain seated was due to the fact that the recalcitrant Mr. Jones had been slow to deliver her breakfast this morning and she was determined to make him pay for her frigid eggs.

She sat quietly fuming as he skirted the car at a lazy pace. When he opened the door, he offered her his hand in what was clearly a last-minute gesture. "We've arrived, madam."

"I can see that, Mr. Jones." Kate stepped past him into the early morning drizzle. "Let's get this over with. Do not dawdle, Mr. Jones."

"Yes, madam." Jones took her order as a cue and set off up the serpentine walk, leaving her to fend for herself on the wet bricks.

The walkway was longer than she remembered, even though it had been only weeks since she'd last been to the estate. She'd been avoiding the house since Conrad's death, but she couldn't put it off any longer. It was here that she hoped to find some remnant of the past that might sway her recalcitrant granddaughter.

"Mr. Jones, you may start with the kitchen." The painful business of sorting through Conrad's personal possessions could wait until later.

Kate headed for the stairs, barely pausing on her way to the nursery. If she kept moving and remained focused on her goal, she could maintain control. But as soon as she stepped through the door, she knew her task wasn't going to be so easy. Memories of the rainy afternoon her granddaughter was discovered missing had been kept alive in every detail—the crib, the rocking horse, the paintings—all handpicked by Conrad and a team of designers. Her son had refused to change a thing, convinced that someday his daughter would come home.

The detective the police had sent in a rush that long-ago afternoon was young and looked to the more experienced police officers for guidance. A quick phone call and a fiery complaint put Sam Fontana's father on the case—unfortunately, too late. Even the FBI admitted to being bewildered by facts that didn't add up.

Had she known what the course of events would be, would she have done things differently? She'd done the best she could. Conrad never blamed her. He told her he would have done the same thing, including paying the ransom money. Eddie Fry had asked for a paltry sum in Conrad's estimation—five hundred thousand dollars. He would have paid ten times that much without blinking an eye. Retribution would have come later, when the child was safe.

By the time they realized their chances of finding the baby were slim to none, Joe Fontana's firm belief that Gracie was alive pulled her son from a suicidal funk and focused his energy on her recovery. Kate would be forever in the detective's debt.

Kate crossed the room and dragged back the pale yellow drapes and let daylight flood the room. But the nursery looked as gloomy as ever despite the toys and carefully chosen decorations.

A car crunched along the gravel drive. Kate turned toward the window in time to glimpse the flash of a red sports car. *Lillian.* What next?

Kate had expected a face-off, but not here. Lillian despised the house. Too soon the click of Lillian's heels echoed down the hall. Kate braced herself.

Her son's first wife was like a shiny bauble. She glittered in so many places, the tarnished ones were barely noticeable, except to the trained eye. The overbright lipstick and the alluring half-shutter of her eyes were more the result of lack of sleep than artful planning.

Before Lillian could locate her in the large room, Kate launched her attack. "How was

Monte Carlo? Not to your liking? It has become rather plebeian since Princess Grace passed on, I suppose—"

"You lied to me, Katherine. You said Conrad had not forgotten me. You said, 'Go off and enjoy yourself, Lillian. I'll take care of the details, Lillian.' "

"All of which was true. Conrad did not forget you . . . or your loyalty. The trip to Monte Carlo was on me. I take it Lord Devon was not in a generous mood?"

"He gave me the flu. To make up for it, he proposed." Lillian turned away but glanced back as if trying to gauge Kate's reaction.

Kate remained near the window, refusing to rise to Lillian's bait. "He was on his deathbed, I trust. And you accepted. Are congratulations or condolences in order?"

Lillian threw Kate a smug smile, then strolled across the room, letting her fingers glide carelessly over her daughter's toys. "Your celebration is premature, Katherine. I turned him down. My daughter needs me."

"Your daughter is twenty-five. She's managed to become an adult without your assistance. What makes you think she'd welcome, or need, your interference now?"

"He didn't change a thing. Why am I not surprised? Even you have to admit his obsession was unnatural." Lillian plucked a fluffy pink rabbit out of the crib. She chose the last gift Kate had given her granddaughter before her kidnapping. "Of course, she'll want my help. Every girl needs a mother to teach her how to be a woman. It's an art." Lillian glanced at Kate. "Well, for some of us."

Kate resisted the urge to grab the rabbit. "She has a strong distaste for lies, I understand, and . . . an excellent knowledge of firearms."

Lillian's smile turned cold. "You and Conrad must have had many good laughs. Tell me, how long have you known where she is?"

Leave it to Lillian to hit on the one sore point she had with her son's planning. Underneath Lillian's practiced indifference was a keen brain. She'd survived quite well on her ability to detect the smallest prevarication. Kate had to admit her son had left a questionable trail to his lost daughter's location. Kate was only just learning the extent of his subterfuge. Somehow she had to convince Lillian that Conrad's deception was in the interest of protecting their daughter.

Lillian's smile widened to a lethal limit. "Need I remind you, kidnapping is a felony, Kate? I'm sure there are plenty of questions left that people, besides myself, would like answers to."

"It won't work, Lillian. If you try to involve the media in your witch-hunt, it will backfire on you

195

. . . and your daughter. I promise you. Think of the child. You've heard nothing but malicious gossip, which, if you follow, will lead you to embarrassment. I'd reconsider Devon's offer, if I were you. He may withdraw it permanently if you make a spectacle of yourself."

"Conrad hid my daughter from me—*in a swamp.* You still haven't answered my question, so I'm going to assume you've known of her whereabouts since the beginning."

Kate abandoned her post by the window, moved around the crib into Lillian's path, and snatched the rabbit away. "Don't be ridiculous. I'm as surprised as you to find my grand-daughter alive."

Lillian backed off slightly.

Kate took advantage of her silence. "I hardly think the pain and depression Conrad suffered after that miscreant Mr. Fry stole his child was an act. I have Joe Fontana to thank for the fact that my son survived the worst of the ordeal. Once she was located, you can hardly fault him for doing everything in his power to prevent the incident from happening again."

"Perhaps he should have thought of her safety sooner. There was always one more deal that had to be made—one more business trip before we could take that trip to France. Where was he when she was kidnapped? Oh, yes. *Japan.* You sent him yourself, didn't you? It took him thirty-two hours to fly home. For thirty-two hours I was alone, not knowing if my child was alive or dead. For *thirty-two hours,* I was questioned—*like a criminal.* The few friends I had, disappeared. Do you know why?"

"Mr. Fry left few secrets behind. I'm well aware of what he was."

"But you failed to share your knowledge with me, dear Kate. Every one of my so-called friends had had private lessons with Eddie Fry. They swore he was the Fairfield County cure-all for the absent husband—a charming man who said all the right things, laughed at your jokes, even dried your tears. But best of all, he made you feel desirable for a few hours a week."

Kate knew about loneliness. She'd lost her husband at an early age. She could never quite trust the men who professed love for her. Money always colored the equation. She did not want to fall victim to a string of failed marriages, so she learned to live with the emptiness of her position and channel her energies into the company and her son, in that order.

Guilt was an old friend. Inevitably it found her when she was alone, particularly the weeks since Conrad's death. She'd blamed herself for driving him to work harder. When he'd married Lillian, he'd changed. His young wife had charmed him from one social event to the next.

He'd abandoned his careful watch over Hammond Industries in the early days of his marriage. The company had taken several hard financial hits. The Hammonds almost lost their controlling interest in the company. Kate had publicly humiliated him in the boardroom in order to get his attention, an action she regretted to this day.

Years of experience told her Lillian's interest in her daughter was not purely maternal. Lillian had had years to build on the resentment that blossomed the day her daughter was kidnapped. Kate placed the rabbit back in the crib, regretting she hadn't had the foresight to head off Lillian's anger.

Lillian snatched a doll out of the crib and moved toward the door. "I'm her mother. I plan to be part of her life. Your attorneys have no say in the matter."

"We'll leave that up to my granddaughter, shall we?"

Lillian paused in the doorway and glanced back. *"My daughter,* Kate. You seem to continually forget. If you interfere, I can assure you, you will regret it."

Kate returned to the window. When Lillian emerged from the house, she wasn't alone. Martin Jones marched alongside her, holding an umbrella in one hand and a large yellow envelope against his chest with the other. When they reached the driver's side of the car, he opened the door and handed her the packet. Seconds later, she was gone. As Martin Jones hurried toward the house, he had a bounce to his step for the first time in weeks.

Kate crossed the room slowly, forcing herself to remain calm as she hit the intercom button. "Mr. Jones, get Mr. Fontana on the phone. Then report to me promptly in fifteen minutes."

Sam fought the tangle of sheets and swiped at the phone. "Fontana here."

Kate's voice penetrated his sleepy haze. "Lillian is officially on the warpath. She's on her way to Alabama."

Sam rolled over and blinked at the clock. Nine A.M. He rarely slept so late. The images of Gracie in the collection room had kept him up most of the night.

"Mr. Fontana, are you there?"

"I'm here." Sam rose to a sitting position.

"I want you to protect my granddaughter."

Sam stifled a chuckle, remembering Gracie's threat of her left fist. "Lillian is the one who'll need protecting. Have you seen the news lately?"

"You know very well I don't subscribe to gossip. Tell me. What has she done?"

"A reporter pushed too hard. Turns out, your granddaughter has a strong right hook."

"Mr. Fontana, what am I paying you for? I thought you were taking care of things."

"That would require me spending time with your granddaughter, twenty-four-seven."

"Well, then do it—unless you're afraid of her, too."

"She's already complaining about being a bug under glass. Me, twenty-four hours a day, might make her even more determined to dump this in my lap for good. A photographer took shots of us leaving the sheriff's office. The rag sheets have wasted no time tying our names in smutty knots. Let's just say, it's not winning me any Brownie points."

"Well, put the man out of business. That's what you're there for."

"I'm working on it."

"See that you do." *Click.*

Sam stared at the receiver, then dropped it back in the cradle. The day had barely begun and already two women wanted to light a match to him and a third was on her way. If not for the debt he owed Conrad, friend to friend, he'd blow the whole deal off—give Gracie the house, the collection, and walk away.

No sooner had the words entered his brain than a small voice called him a liar. Gracie's soft curves bathed in the golden glow of the porch light flashed through his memory. He'd witnessed her laughter, her anger, even her tears. Each version of Gracie Calloway fascinated him. She wasn't a cloned debutante or a seasoned one-night stand. She was all the things the people in Shady Grove had made her—a product of a quiet Southern town with an unorthodox upbringing. Last night, he'd been tempted to kiss her, but he'd resisted, not just for her sake but for his, too.

Chapter 15

Before Gracie stepped out the back door, she'd already drawn a mental picture of Alice in a steaming pot of boiling water, then a few hungry cannibals were tossed into the scene. The smoking incinerator in Alice's back garden helped complete the grisly image, adding a hazy layer of gray dust and a *gawd*-awful smell. The slap of the brisk morning chill against her exposed legs did nothing to cool her temper. Self-consciously she held the hem of her dress down and charged into Alice's kitchen.

Alice spun away from the pantry where she was hanging up her apron. "My, my, don't you look pretty this morning, Gracie."

Gracie crossed her arms and drummed her toes on the linoleum. "Where did you put my jeans . . . *and* my T-shirts?"

Alice turned back to the pantry. "What a difference . . . your hair is all combed and you're wearing that pretty new dress. Lavender goes so well with your eyes. I knew it would when I picked it out."

"*Alice—my clothes*. Where'd you put them?"

Alice fluttered to the sink and started wiping the bleached porcelain. Her gaze darted out the window to the garden. "Could be in the wash. I heard Artie say he was going to do some washing today. Aren't you supposed to be getting to work? Or have they fired you for hitting that poor reporter? Gracie, honestly, I don't know what you were thinking—I'm going to have to hide my head for days with the shame."

Gracie rolled her eyes at Alice's attempt to sidetrack the conversation. "Artie hasn't gotten out of bed yet. The only thing hanging in my closet is this dress and the blue one you gave me for my birthday, so I figured it was you. Besides, I heard you and Marjorie talking the other day . . ."

Alice froze for a moment, then launched herself into a flurry of filling the teakettle and lighting the stove. Still, she refused to look Gracie's way. "I hear you had a nice breakfast with Mr. Fontana. He's such a nice young man. Smart, too, I'll bet. I can always tell by the eyes. There's somebody home in that man's head. An important fact when you're picking out the father of your children. You don't want to end up with a half-wit, like Doddie Smees. That boy of hers ain't got the brain God gave a turkey. All on account of her marrying Brewster."

"Brewster was struck by a bolt of lightning when he was a kid. He can't help being simple."

Sure enough, as soon as the topic changed, Alice poked her head around. "It was no such thing. It was the *white* lightning his daddy brewed out on Parker's swamp that struck him."

"Never mind about Brewster Smees. I want to know what you're doing sending Mr. Fontana preserves with notes saying they were from me . . . *and where'd you put my clothes?* I can't go to work dressed like this. Folks will think I'm getting above myself, that 'cause my daddy was rich I've changed, which is just not true."

The kettle started to whistle. Alice used the distraction to turn her back on Gracie. "That was a fine batch of preserves. It's only right that we should share our good fortune. Don't want folks saying we don't know how to do the proper when someone new moves into town. And besides, Mr. Fontana is here on your account, so it's our duty to see that he feels welcome."

"He's not settling in. He'll be gone soon enough."

Alice poured a cup of tea and set it on the table beside a plate of freshly baked muffins. "Have a seat, Gracie."

Gracie eyed the carefully arranged place settings and reluctantly pulled out a chair. Alice had been expecting her. Not a good sign. "I can take care of Mr. Fontana just fine without your help. We've come to an understanding."

Suddenly Alice was overcome. She fluttered to the refrigerator. When she returned with a carton of milk, tears wet the corners of her eyes.

She pulled a tissue from inside her sleeve and dabbed at her cheeks. "My heart is so relieved to hear that, you just don't know."

Gracie narrowed her gaze at her aunt. "Am I missing something here—besides my clothes? What is it that you're so relieved about? Because I've got a feeling it's not just me who's burning Mr. Fontana's toast."

"Gracie, you didn't."

"The preserves hid the charcoal flavor. Now, let's have the truth. I've got to get to work; so do you, for that matter. The Reverend Adams will be wondering where you are."

"Yes, well, that's what I wanted to talk to you about, Gracie, honey." Alice's voice dripped with extra sweetness. She had that coy look in her eye. Suddenly, the freshly baked muffins made sense.

The tea sloshed out of Gracie's cup onto the table. "Don't tell me you quit your job on account of my new circumstances?"

Alice reached for a sponge and wiped up the spill. "Why, no, honey . . . not exactly." Alice fidgeted then and covered Gracie's hand with both of hers. "You see, Ben and me . . . well, we split up a long time ago—divorced actually."

Gracie jerked away. *"Say what?"*

Alice dodged Gracie's question and kept on going. "At first, my living next door was just temporary, then I got so I liked it, and so did

Ben. It was convenient. We got married too young. Folks did in those days. We'd always been the best of friends—like you and Skippy, so we figured why not. Well, we just didn't suit as husband and wife, is all."

Gracie felt a cold chill roll from the top of her head to the pit of her stomach. "Why are you telling me this *now?*"

"The Reverend Adams has asked me to marry him. And I've said yes."

Gracie stared at Alice's animated face. Surely, she hadn't heard her right.

Alice's lips continued to move. Gracie tried to catch up with what she was saying.

". . . J.D. has been waiting such a long time. Well, he doesn't want to wait any longer, and neither do I. We're no spring chickens. J.D. is planning to retire next year and we thought we'd do some traveling while we can still make it off the front porch. Besides, that Delilah Perkins has been making herself quite forward lately and I'm worried she might—Well, J.D. is a man, and men have their needs . . ."

Gracie shot out of her chair and glared at her aunt, who started wringing her hands. "But what about Ben? He's sure to be broken-hearted. I know he doesn't say much, but—And Artie is feeling so poorly . . . I'm at work all day—"

"I know this comes as a shock, but I figure you don't need me here so much anymore, what with Mr. Fontana and your daddy leaving you that money . . ."

"How come you and Ben never told me you got divorced? Who am I, Loose Lips Lucy? I can keep my tongue between my teeth. First my daddy—*now this*. Got any more surprises? Because I'd just as soon as get it out on the table so I can deal with it all at once."

"Well, there is one more tiny thing—nothing to fret about, really. Your mama called last night. She claims she wants to see you." Despite her reassurances, Alice wore her worried frown.

Gracie could hear Chantel singing to herself in the Parnell kitchen—something about how her man had done her wrong and how he was going to pay. Gracie might not have the lungs to hit the high notes, but she was singing the same tune. Alice's breakfast confession was a direct result of Sam Fontana's appearance in Shady Grove. No amount of sweet talk could hide the fact.

Gracie blew through the kitchen doorway at full speed. "Where is he?"

Chantel spun around and planted one hand on her hip. "Ain't you supposed to be at the market?"

"I'm heading that way—just as soon as I give that man a piece of my mind."

Chantel shook her head but went on wiping

the counter. "Bitin' his head off ain't no way to get sugah."

"Who says I want *sugah?* Whatever put that fool idea into your head?"

Chantel's gaze drifted longingly over Gracie's new dress. "You're all fancied up, girl. And I know you hate to wear dresses 'cause you give them to me as soon as Alice ain't lookin'."

The dress did make Gracie feel pretty, but slightly naked . . . particularly when she thought about Sam Fontana and those big dark eyes of his that seemed to see right through her. Pretty soon, one thought led to another until her mood took another hit.

She turned her frown on Chantel. "She stole my clothes. I had no choice."

Chantel's eyes widened to the size of saucers, never a good sign. "So that's what I smelled burnin' in her backyard. Made quite a stink."

"*What?* Alice *burned* my clothes?" Gracie remembered Alice's smoking incinerator. "It's his fault. None of this would be happening if he had stayed in Yankeeland where he belongs. Where is he?"

"Upstairs."

Gracie started toward the dining room. "Thanks."

Chantel latched onto Gracie's arm. "Hold on, now. You can't go marchin' up there. He's taking a shower."

Gracie jerked free. "We both know I've seen a boy's naked backside. One more isn't going to hold any surprises."

"Uh-huh."

"Chantel Dubois, you don't know a thing about boys."

"I know that he ain't no boy. I got eyes in my head. But you go on now. Do what you like, Miss Smarty Pants. I'll make myself scarce." Chantel plucked an apple out of the fruit bowl and bit into one side. "It's my break time. Think I'll wander out to the front porch, read me a magazine. Tell Mr. Fontana to holler if he needs me."

Gracie glared after Chantel's retreating back. She did have a point. There was nothing about Sam Fontana that said *boy*. Then she thought about Alice burning her clothes and her plans to marry the Reverend Adams now that Gracie was *taken care of*. That was all the fuel Gracie needed to push her up the stairs to Sam Fontana's bedroom.

The room screamed of neatness, apart from the tousled bed. No clothes thrown helter-skelter or shoes to trip over. She hoped Alice didn't get wind of Sam Fontana's neat streak. She'd burn more than Gracie's clothes. She'd set fire to Ben's house and make her homeless so she could be even more indebted to Sam Fontana and her daddy's generosity. The thought put a new match to Gracie's anger. She marched toward the sound of running water.

The bathroom door stood ajar. Steam drifted out into the room along with the sweet smell of spicy soap. Gracie took a deep breath and knocked. "Sam Fontana . . . I want to talk to *y-o-u*." Chantel said to give him sweetness. Heck, she'd give him a whole hive. The honey would be so thick in her voice he'd be mired in goo—

The rushing water on the other side of the door came to an abrupt stop with a loud bump of the pipes.

"You should call Ben. Your water pressure is sky high. You're going to burst your pipes."

There was a long pause before Sam's voice came back her way. "Did you come over here to drum up business for Ben?"

"Why no, *sugah* . . . I came over here to tell you—*I've had enough*." Gracie's temper got the better of her. She was out of honey. All she had left were bees—the nasty stinging sort. She pressed closer to the door, resisting the urge to throw it open. "Just so you know, I'm quitting—crying uncle."

"No, you aren't. I understand the photographer met Burgess's pet alligator this morning and grabbed the first gray dog back to the Big Apple." A deep rumble of laughter echoed against the tiled walls.

Why was he so set on being her white knight? It made it hard for her to put him in his place. The fresh scent of soap sifting through the open door worked a new kind of sweetness over her tongue. "I didn't come about the photographer. Alice is getting married to the Reverend Adams. I didn't even know she and Ben were *di-vorced*." Gracie felt her throat close up.

"Toss me a towel, would ya? On the shelf to your left." The shower door clicked open. Sam's voice lost its echo as he moved closer.

Gracie got a glimpse of his bare back and bolted for a towel. Then, squeezing her eyes shut, she thrust it through the doorway.

Another chuckle rumbled out with the steam. "You ever had a boyfriend, Gracie?"

Gracie squeezed her eyes tighter. The moist curve of his shoulder replayed in her mind. She felt a warm rush of heat seep over her skin. It wasn't just the vision that prickled her skin; it was the gentle prodding in his voice that poked at her. "Sure. I've had plenty of boyfriends, just none worth keeping, that's all."

"That's not what I was asking." Suddenly the muffle was gone from his voice. His rich baritone was broadcasting inches away.

The image of his bare shoulder expanded to a wide-angled shot. Without opening her eyes, she could see the rest of Sam Fontana, from his tight buttocks to his muscular thighs and thick curling

211

chest hair as it made a soft path down his stomach into dangerous territory. Then it hit her: She'd been storing up images of him all week; otherwise she'd never be able to draw such a clear and tempting picture. She'd never made it to third base with any boy, let alone to home. But suddenly, she was wondering what it would be like with Sam Fontana. *Oh, Lord. She was in trouble now.*

"Open your eyes, Gracie." The gentle tone of his voice tugged at her resistance.

She squeezed her eyes tighter. If she opened them, he'd know the truth—she was a big chicken when it came to a boy's naked anything. Gracie took a step back, then jutted her chin in the direction of his voice. "Why?"

"Because I'm going to kiss you and I want you to look at me."

"Why would you want to do a fool thing like that?" Gracie kept her stubborn expression trained on his voice.

"You need it—badly. Somebody's got to do it." Sam's voice had honey of its own.

She could feel his body heat through the thin cotton of her dress. Gracie's eyes flew open. "I've been kissed before, don't you think I haven't—"

"*Gracie*—" Sam stepped even closer, but Gracie stubbornly held her ground.

If she ran, she'd embarrass herself and he'd

win. She stood a little taller and tried to still the jitterbugs racing from her fingertips to her toes. "If you think this is going to make me change my mind—"

"Hush up, Gracie, and hold still." Sam's warm fingers made contact with her chin and gently held her mouth steady.

Gracie scowled at him but closed her eyes and leaned forward to give him access to her lips. He'd see she was a woman of experience. She knew how to kiss. What she hadn't gained from experimenting with Johnnie Bean before he became enamored with Marianne Talbot's cleavage, she'd learned from Hollywood when she and Alice got together to watch "those female movies," as Ben called them. Gracie tried to drum up a vision of a Hollywood hunk, but Sam's image kept getting in the way.

He let out a soft, sexy chuckle, then pressed his mouth to hers. No bones about it—Sam Fontana was all business. He didn't waste time saying howdy with just his lips—he led her mouth in a dance that required she use her tongue to keep up with him. When he snaked his free arm around her back and pulled her closer, she slipped her arms bravely over his bare shoulders. Then instinct took over, at least that's what she figured it was, seeing how she'd never kissed a nearly naked man and Alice didn't own any R-rated videos.

Her fingertips roamed his supple skin. Not bad. In fact, he felt so good she found herself pressing her breasts to his chest when her nipples strained against her bra. Gracie's breath grew ragged, and so did Sam's. But she was a long way from wanting to stop when he cried uncle and jumped away.

"Okay, that's enough for lesson one." Sam turned his back to her and set his hands on his hips. He leaned over, his sides heaving in and out like he was trying to catch his breath.

Gracie stole a lungful of oxygen for herself, then glared at him. "Looks like you're the one out of practice, Yankee boy."

"You're not ready for lesson two." Sam struggled with his words between breaths.

"Says who?" Gracie didn't even try to hide her relief. She figured she'd won the inning and she wanted to crow.

Then Sam spun around to face her, and she wasn't so sure. "Says me."

Though the warning lights were going off in her brain, the heady feeling of success egged her to pitch one more ball over home plate. "Seems to me you're the one who's running scared."

Sam shot her a dangerous look. "You forget— I'm *I*-talian. It's in my blood." He was throwing her Southernness back in her face.

With that said, Sam marched toward his open

suitcase and grabbed a pair of fresh briefs, then turned his back and dropped his towel.

Gracie felt her jaw open with a snap. Chantel was right—she'd seen lots of naked boys' backsides, even a few front sides on hot summer days as a kid at Miller's pond, but never any quite like Sam's. He had one tight butt, nice and round and all muscle, the kind that didn't require a belt to hold up his pants.

Gracie drew a sharp breath that could be heard across the room. A familiar chuckle echoed back at her. Sam pulled on a pair of faded jeans before he turned to face her. But the light blue denim next to his warm tanned skin couldn't erase the image of what she'd just seen. It only made it more tantalizing.

Gracie kept a wary eye on him as he padded toward her in his bare feet, hands set on his hips in what Gracie recognized as a challenge. Suddenly she didn't feel so brave staring at his muscled chest with its deceptively alluring covering of soft hair snaking into his pants. And damned if he didn't know it and use it to his advantage.

Sam raised his chin and smiled wickedly at her. "If I kiss you again, you might think I was after your money."

"I came over here to give it to you, you fool—to beg you to take it, if I have to. Alice thinks she can run off with the reverend now that I'm taken care of. What's Ben going to say? He and Alice may not sleep under the same roof, but she's been a part of his life since they were kids. This is going to break his heart."

"Seems to me everyone has been tiptoeing around, trying not to rock your world a little too long. It *needs* rocking. Tell me, princess, have you ever seen Ben kiss Alice? I mean really make her hot and bothered."

Gracie stared back at Sam. She was dumbfounded. He was right. She couldn't come up with one instance in the past twenty-five years where Ben had shown husband-like affection to Alice, not even a peck on the cheek. Their relationship was more like hers and Skippy's, brotherly-like. But there was nothing brotherly about Sam's kiss. It had shut-the-door-and-pull-down-the-shades written all over it. Now she knew the difference. "Do you suppose the Reverend Adams has kissed Alice like that?"

Sam's lips curved into a sly grin. "Like what?"

Gracie shot him her stormiest frown. "Like the way you kissed me. Is that why you did it—to shut me up? Teach me a lesson?"

Sam's grin flattened out. "You know, there's a lock on that door and Chantel hasn't made the bed *yet*. We could move on to lesson two . . . I'm sure *an experienced* girl like you will catch on fast."

He was trying to scare her. And he was doing a

damn fine job. Nearly as good as the thoughts of what she and Sam could be doing on her daddy's Egyptian cotton sheets in the big four-poster bed.

Gracie mustered the last of her bravado. "I'll have to take a rain check. I've got to get to work. I'm not through with you, Yankee boy. We've got things to settle." Gracie backed slowly toward the door. To her relief, Sam didn't come after her, but he looked like he wanted to. She couldn't be sure if it was to turn her over his knee or begin lesson two.

When she reached the door and was about to head down the stairs, his voice called her back. "Gracie?"

She poked her head into the room. "What?"

"Nice dress." Sam threw her an approving nod.

Gracie offered him a big smile. "Sam?"

Sam's expression was soft and hopeful—one big olive branch. "Yeah?"

"Nice ass. But I'll need more than sweet words and a little ol' kiss to make up for Alice burning my clothes. I'll need a steak with all the trimmings." Gracie didn't stick around to catch his reaction. She could hear it booming behind her as she flew down the stairs and out the front door.

Chantel jerked out of her rocking chair, but Gracie kept her feet moving and shouted over her shoulder. "You were right, Chantel. He ain't no boy. And he's got a damn fine ass."

"What'd I tell you, girl? But you're runnin' the wrong way."

"Tell that Yankee, I'll be back for lesson two —and my steak."

Sam skidded to a halt in the doorway and watched Gracie sprint down the brick path toward the front gate. The hem of her dress bounced above her knees, giving him a good glimpse of her creamy thighs. "A devil in a blue dress. Why do I feel like I've been sideswiped? Christ, she's twelve going on thirty-five."

Chantel popped out of the leafy shadow on the corner of the porch and paused beside him. "It's lavender. My favorite shade."

Sam stared after Gracie, still feeling dazed. "Goes with her eyes."

"Uh-huh. Yes, sir, Mr. Fontana. Our Gracie is one of a kind. The Lord done broke the mold after He made her." Chantel glanced back at him over her shoulder, eyeing him from head to toe. "But I hope he didn't break the mold after he made you. I hear you got some sweet kind of ass, Mr. Fontana, sir. And yours is spoken for."

"Who's paying you?"

Chantel slipped past him into the house. "Guess my break time is over. I'll just put some fresh sheets on the bed." Chantel paused behind him. He could feel her eyes on his backside. "And defrost some of that Yankee broil for your supper 'cause Alice burned all Gracie's clothes and she ain't got nothin' to wear but two of the finest dresses I've seen. So, I figure you ain't got a chance." Chantel's shoes slapped against the wood floor as she made her way toward the kitchen, alternately humming and singing.

Sam absently picked up the melody as he watched Gracie disappear around the corner. By the time the second chorus rolled through his head, he realized he was singing Percy Sledge's old hit song "When a Man Loves a Woman," and he wondered why the words rolled off his tongue so easily when he thought of Gracie Calloway. Just like Percy, he was doomed.

Chapter 16

Sam's kiss was still burning on her lips when Gracie slipped through the back door of the market. He'd been unnerved by their kiss, even more than she had. Why else would he push her away, then try to scare her off? For some reason, the notion made her feel more inclined toward Sam, despite Alice destroying her wardrobe. She felt pretty in her new dress, still slightly naked, but definitely feminine and surprisingly powerful when she thought of the open admiration in Sam's gaze as she made her escape.

Gracie let the door close softly against her back while she paused to listen for unfamiliar voices at the front of the market. The hum of reporters she'd heard all week was gone. Sam's rent-a-cops were doing their job, bless their mercenary hearts. As much as the idea of protection rubbed her the wrong way, she was thankful for the quiet. Sam Fontana had scored another point in his favor. She might just owe him a steak, instead of the other way around.

Gracie followed Jimmy's voice down the hall to her office. "Just make yourself comfortable, Melinda. Here, I'll get that. Don't want you to strain yourself. Gracie used to make deposits

Monday, Wednesdays, and Fridays, but I can do that."

Gracie glanced at her watch. She was only fifteen minutes late. Jimmy never worried about such things as long as she got her work done. She hurried through the doorway. "Hey there, Jimmy. What's up?"

Startled, Jimmy bumped his head and dropped the cash drawer he was unloading from the safe. "Good Lord, girl. You about sent me back to the farm. I thought you was one of them confounded reporters."

"Nope, just me, Jimmy. Hey there, Melinda. How's the baby coming along?" Melinda was about to hatch her fourth child. The sight of Melinda's swollen belly dimmed Gracie's smile a shade. Even though Gracie had managed to miss most of sex ed, she knew kisses, like the one Sam Fontana had given her that morning, could get a girl the kind of trouble Melinda had —four babies in six years.

But Melinda didn't seem to mind. She offered Gracie a proud smile. "This is going to be a big boy. My feet are so swollen, I can't stand up more than two minutes without them cramping into knots."

Jimmy handed the cash drawer to Gracie without looking her in the eye. His usual pasty complexion turned ruddy where it met his collar. "I thought you could handle the front today. Most of the reporters have gone home. I'll show Melinda what to do here. Lucky for us, she's good with figures."

Gracie glanced from Melinda to Jimmy, hoping she'd heard him wrong.

Jimmy hurried around the desk. "You make yourself right at home, Melinda, you hear? The cupboard on the right is for your personal things."

He was giving her Gracie's space—pushing Gracie out of her hidey-hole to a place where folks could poke at her.

Gracie stared at Jimmy. "Is this because of the reporter with the broken nose?"

"Nope. This is to help Melinda's feet. I figured you'd understand." Jimmy nodded toward the door. "Check stand two, Gracie."

This was Jimmy's way of telling her that now that she had money, she didn't need Jimmy's dingy office in the back of the market anymore. Melinda did. The scuttlebutt was that Melinda's husband had been laid off work last week. Jimmy was only doing what Gracie would have done had she been in his shoes. Melinda had mouths to feed.

Gracie grabbed Melinda's apron off a hook and tied it tight over her flat tummy. "Okay, Jimmy. But I'm off at five. I have shopping to do. All I have is this dress—"

Jimmy turned back to Melinda. "Five o'clock. Fine, Gracie."

She picked up the cash drawer and headed

toward the front. The thought of smiling all day at folks who whispered about her behind her back made Gracie want to run. Sure enough, as soon as they loaded their groceries onto the turnstile, their sidelong glances swung toward her belly. They were quick to hide their curiosity when they caught her looking back.

Her last customer was the crowning glory of her afternoon—Moses Day limping along in his new shoes. Word was, he'd been on the wagon for a whole week. Jimmy wouldn't sell him anything with alcohol in it, not even cough syrup. Moses was in an ornery mood when he sidled up to her checkout counter with a bottle of apple juice and a Twinkie. "Those shoes you bought me done gave me a damn blister."

Gracie rang up his items. "I told you to pick the sneakers, Moses."

"They make my feet sweat. What you still doing here, girl?"

"Working."

"What the hell for?" Moses leaned over the produce scale and peered down at Gracie's feet. "I don't see no chain around your ankle."

The story was, Moses had done time on a chain gang for attempting to murder his ex-mother-in-law some forty years ago when she tried to swipe his whiskey. Reverend Adams was the only one brave enough to steal Moses's bottle these days.

Gracie dropped the Twinkie into a bag. "Now why would there be a chain on my ankle, Moses?"

" 'Cause you're here instead of a hundred other places better than this. What's the matter? You sick?"

"Nope. Not sick, Moses."

Moses offered her a snaggletoothed smile. "You look sick. Tell you what. How 'bout you and me go to Vegas together? I can teach you how to really live. What'd ya say?"

"No thanks, Moses. I'm fine where I am. That'll be two dollars and fifty-nine cents."

Moses threw a five down on the counter and stomped to the door. "You used to be smart. Someone done pulled the plug on your brain."

Gracie felt like she'd been slapped. Moses had been the one to cheer the loudest at her games, even when he'd spent a long night with a bottle in the dugout. She'd lost count of the hotdogs and the egg salad sandwiches she'd bought him with her allowance between games. She and Moses might not have been best friends, but she'd considered him an ally of sorts. In a brave moment, when she was eight, she'd asked Moses how old he was. She remembered being comforted by his answer. He didn't know. His mama had run off, too. Last count, she and Moses were the only ones in Shady Grove who didn't have official birth dates they could put a finger on. Rejection from the likes of someone as self-centered as Moses Day shouldn't have mattered, but it did.

By the time Jimmy offered to relieve her, Gracie couldn't wait to leave. Now, more than ever, she needed to regain a piece of the Gracie Calloway she knew. A pair of jeans would be a good start. If what Chantel said was true, she was missing ninety percent of her wardrobe. She couldn't go around in a dress every day of the week. Sam Fontana's promising grin surfaced in her memory for the hundredth time that day. *Nice dress.* The warmth of his kiss had worn off. All she could think of was slipping into a pair of jeans and curling up in Ben's old chair.

Gracie stepped into the evening breeze and set a course down Pecan Street. She was crossing the second block when she spotted Alice up ahead. She had a large shopping bag tucked under one arm. The lanky Reverend Adams pulled her to a stop and bent over and planted a kiss on her aunt's upturned lips. Gracie froze. Good Lord, her aunt was making a public display. The reverend wasn't in any hurry, either. He lingered over her aunt's mouth, his hand clutching Alice's elbow. Gracie felt a rush of heat race through her blood. Then it hit her: She'd kissed Sam in a much more dangerous situation this morning. What Alice was doing was tame by comparison.

Alice pressed the shopping bag into his arms and turned toward home. The reverend kept a dazed watch over Alice while she made her way across the street.

"The man has it bad." Sam's voice grazed her ear. She turned in time to see him duck out from behind a parked truck.

Gracie's breath jumped out of her lungs. "For monkey's sake, Fontana. My heart just made a home run. Are you trying to collect on my insurance?"

Sam leaned in close. "What do you suppose was in that bag?"

Gracie pulled away and started moving in the direction of the Outpost. "I have no idea."

Sam kept an easy pace beside her. "I do."

After the day she'd had, she was in no mood for games. Gracie pulled to a halt and glared at him, trying, without much success, to keep her eyes off the smile playing on his lips. "Okay, what's in the reverend's bag, Mr. Smarty Pants?"

Sam's smile beamed brighter. "You guessed it —*pants*—jeans, to be exact. If you ask me, Alice has a dark side the reverend doesn't know about. Maybe I should warn him . . ."

Gracie's mind scrambled to make sense of what she'd just seen. *Alice hated jeans. She said they were unladylike.* Then it hit her, she was standing in front of the Outpost—where Alice and the reverend had been standing moments ago—*the place where Alice handed him an overstuffed shopping bag.* Gracie reached for Sam's arm. "*She didn't—*"

"I'm afraid, she did. Bought every pair in your size—*but one.*" Sam had that self-confident gleam in his eye.

This was going to cost her. "Okay, where can I find the last pair?"

Like a regular Houdini, a bag materialized from behind his back. The handle was tied together with a lacy pink ribbon. He dangled it at her eye level. "Size six petite, right?"

Gracie eyed him suspiciously, then swallowed her pride and held up her hand, but Sam moved the bag just out of her reach.

"Okay, Yankee, what do you want?"

"A meeting with an attorney in Montgomery to sign some paperwork. Piece of cake. I'll even throw in some of my old T-shirts to sweeten the deal. Did I mention that I've got a Yankees shirt people pay big bucks for? It could be yours for two hours of your time. What do you say?"

Gracie tried to steer around him. "If I'm going all the way to Montgomery, I can get my own clothes. Besides, I'm a Mets fan."

"Afraid my Mets shirt is history." He danced in front of her. "But you could have these jeans tonight. I have it on good authority these are your favorites."

A breeze caught the hem of Gracie's dress. She

held the fabric down with two hands to keep from exposing her thighs. She eyed the bag with longing. "I'll bet you tied that ribbon on there."

"With my own two hands. Adds a special touch, don't you think?" Sam pretended to admire his handiwork, then flashed her a broad smile.

Alice wasn't the only one with a dark side. The devilish look on his face promised all sorts of things she was afraid he might deliver. Gracie tried to freeze him out. "This is all your fault, you know. You . . . and your nice teeth."

Sam flashed her another glimpse of his pearly whites. "It's a dog-eat-dog world, *princess*."

"Don't call me that."

Another rogue gust lifted the hem of her dress. Sam twirled the bag.

It was downright mean of him to take advantage of her desperation, but sulking wasn't going to get her legs covered in denim. Gracie lifted her chin to the hard angle she used on uppity umpires when they made a bad call. "So, what are these papers I'm signing?"

"Just some routine stuff." Sam gave the bag another twirl. He was tap dancing, and she wanted to know why.

She pinned him with her sternest glare. "Specifically."

Sam sobered. "You're a match. The blood test results came through this afternoon. No surprise, really."

Gracie felt the warmth drain from her cheeks. On the contrary, it was a whopper of a surprise. Up until now, she'd been able to pretend it was all a big mistake. She'd almost convinced herself that she'd wake up someday and see some pretty blonde paired with the words HAMMOND HEIRESS on the front page of *The Atlanta Constitution*. He'd ride off into the sunset and they'd all live their separate lives happily ever after—well, sort of. There'd still be the memory of his cocky grin . . . *and that damn kiss*.

"I thought it took three weeks. When were you going to tell me this?"

Sam didn't miss a beat. "After a nice steak dinner and a bottle of wine."

She lost her composure. Had he taken her flippant remark seriously? Was he angling for lesson two? "Steak . . . ?"

This time Sam beamed. ". . . As in—*filet mignon*. Chantel's offered to cook it just the way you like it."

"That traitor. I can't. I've got to fix Ben and Artie their dinner. It's Alice's bridge night. She and the reverend have been playing . . . for years. *Ohmigod*."

Gracie's mind was chasing its tail: Alice's girlish kiss with the reverend; Alice's constant humming; the rosy glow in her cheeks over the past few months. Gracie had attributed her change in spirit to her clean sweep in the Shady

Grove Bake-Off last spring. Alice was genuinely happy. For the first time, Gracie realized she'd glimpsed the woman who'd taken charge of her female side of her education. She was a fearsome woman with needs of her own. Why had Gracie never noticed?

When she looked up, Sam met her gaze. "Bridge, huh?"

Gracie stared off in the direction where Alice had disappeared. "Artie usually cooks, but he's not been feeling so good lately. He's losing too much weight. I suppose Ben could—"

"Ben's over at the Widow Perkins. He said something about a softener."

"But it's nearly dinnertime, and he fixed her softener two days ago—"

Sam's gaze swerved away from hers. He was giving her space while her mind caught up with the truth. Gracie followed his attention to the sidewalk.

He jabbed the toe of his shoe at a weed coming up through a crack. "Softeners are tricky things—you never know when they'll go on the fritz. I'll send Chantel over with an extra steak for Artie. She can bully anyone into eating. You can wear your new jeans."

Something told Gracie olive branches weren't Sam's usual style. And this was the second one he'd offered her today.

She glanced at the lacy ribbon perched on top

of the bag handle. "About Montgomery and the attorneys—what choice do I have?"

"Honestly? None." The usual brilliance in Sam's grin was missing.

He was pitching it to her straight. Gracie nodded. "That's what I figured."

Sam opened the door of his truck and motioned Gracie inside. He was fighting a smile and winning, so she decided to let him slide for the moment. Gracie accepted the bag, hugged it to her chest.

Sam sprinted around the other side and hopped in. While the engine turned over, he leaned her way. His smile returned, big as day.

Gracie fought off the effect. "I haven't said yes about Montgomery yet, you know."

"Holding out for the steak, are you?"

His confident tone said he'd won this inning, but she wasn't ready to forfeit the next one just because he had a kiss-me smile and a set of nice choppers.

As Sam pointed the truck toward the Parnell house, she had to admit he'd managed to take the edge off her horrible day. Once again, she was feeling the anticipation she'd felt after he'd kissed her. Even the image of Melinda's round belly couldn't keep her from hoping he would try again.

Chapter 17

By the time the sun popped its smiley face over Edna McCoy's rooftop the next morning, Gracie was convinced God had invented jeans to make up for His mistake of letting Eve into the Garden of Eden naked as a jaybird.

Gracie was living proof that Eve would have been safe armored in jeans. Last night, Gracie had faced her own temptation in the form of—Snake Fontana and his dangerous smile. Instead of an apple, she'd gotten a steak with all the trimmings. She'd even come out with the shirt off his back.

As Gracie poked her legs into the soft blue denim, she was ready to forgive the Lord on Eve's behalf. The stonewashed fabric felt like heaven on her bare skin. She was in such a good mood that she might even forgive Alice.

Gracie padded downstairs in her socks and cut a path toward the back porch where Alice relegated old shoes. Muffled voices drifted down the hall from Artie's room. Gracie switched directions, moving closer to Artie's door.

Ben stood in front of the bed. "What'd the doctor say?" He sounded impatient and angry, which wasn't like him.

Gracie held her breath, listening for Artie's answer.

"Ain't you got work to do? Fix a pipe or somethin'?" Artie's voice was hoarse and thready, but she could tell from his tone he was stalling. Silently, Ben waited him out. When Artie's voice came again, he sounded more like his old self. "You done talked to the doctor already, I'll bet."

"I don't need to talk to no doctor. I can look at you and see you're counting days. How many nurses had to sit on you to get that tube running through your nose?"

Artie paused. Gracie heard him draw a sputtery breath before he went on. "Just one. I know when I'm licked."

"You tell Gracie yet?"

"Ain't had time. She's having a hard time wrappin' her mind around being a queen, and all. I feel like I'm running out on her."

Ben cleared his throat. "You're gonna have to tell her. She's been mighty touchy lately about secrets. Alice dropped a whopper on her yesterday."

"So she knows all about Alice and the foxy reverend, does she? Ain't nobody listened to me when I said to tell the girl, instead of all this tippy-toein' around. You done made yourselves a briar patch. Don't ask me to help you out of it; I got my own."

What did Artie mean by, *he was runnin' out on her?* Gracie took a stand in the doorway and glared at her uncles. "Tell me what?"

Ben's face drained of color. "Glad to see you found your clothes. I was worried when I saw Alice out in the yard with a clothes basket and the incinerator smokin'."

Artie shrank into the pillows. He knew what was coming. She wasn't about to let him or Ben off the hook. Gracie glared at Ben first. "Sam . . . Mr. Fontana gave me these."

Ben's face went red. Out of his back pocket came his handkerchief. He swiped at the back of his neck. "Guess I'd better be getting to work. The Widow Perkins decided she wants new faucets in all her bathrooms."

Gracie held her ground in the doorway. "We certainly don't want to keep *Delilah* waiting. How's her softener doing, by the way? She seems to be having a bit of trouble with it lately."

Color rushed into the collar of Ben's shirt. "Softener is all fixed. Good as new."

Artie let out a raspy chuckle. Ben shot him a warning look, grumbling something about nosy, ungrateful folks before he slammed out the door.

Gracie turned a pointed glare on Artie.

He dodged her look with a weak smile. "You won't see him for dinner tonight. He's gonna sulk at the widow's house, just you wait and see."

Gracie perched herself on the stool beside Artie's bed. "What do you need to tell me, Arthur Dubois? Spit it out. Ben's right. I've had enough of secrets."

Artie played with the oxygen tube running across his face. He was stalling again. They both knew it. Gracie wouldn't let up on her glare.

Finally, he stopped fiddling and looked up at Gracie. "You know I ain't been able to play my horn in nearly a year now. Just breaks my heart. My lungs is gone south for good. The doctor is givin' me couple of months, not even the whole season. I meant to tell you, but I know you gonna take it hard. And with all the other things goin' on . . . I didn't think you needed to know just yet."

"That's not very funny, Artie." Gracie felt a loud rush inside her ears. She took a quick breath to stop the swimming in her head, then double-checked his expression for honesty.

"I ain't pullin' your leg, girl." Artie was dead serious. There wasn't even a hint of a smile. No wink, just a plain cold spot of fear in the depths of his brown gaze.

When Artie stopped playing his horn, she'd known something was seriously wrong. Gracie kept her face straight, her words toneless, like Ben taught her, but her stomach ached like she'd taken a hard punch. When she opened her mouth to speak, she could feel a sore lump in her throat rubbing against her words. "How does the doctor know?"

"I've been up to Montgomery. They done poked me and prodded me until I puked. Ain't nothin' nobody can do."

This couldn't be. Of all the times in her life when she needed Artie—this was it. "I'm gonna be dirty rich. Sam's hauling me off to Montgomery tomorrow to sign the papers. We'll get you better doctors. There must be something they can do."

"I don't want to be nobody's lab rat, girl. I ain't got nothin' to complain about, except not seein' you take that Yankee down another notch. He give you that shirt off his back?"

Gracie felt her face go hot. "I won it, fair and square."

"You watch that Yankee. Don't you give him no sugah unless he earns it with somethin' that says forever. You hear what I'm sayin'?"

Gracie couldn't find her voice. She nodded and continued to look down at the worn braided rug under her stockinged feet. A tear leaked out of her eye and plopped onto her hand. Artie was gonna think she couldn't buck it up. Silently, she called herself ten times a crybaby, but that only made matters worse. Pretty soon her tears were falling like a spring shower and her new jeans were sprinkled with dark spots. Her chest ached so bad, she could barely breathe.

Artie sat up and wrapped his hands over hers. "Lordy, girl, you got me dead and buried already."

"This is no joke, Artie. You tell me you're dying and there's nothing I can do about it." Gracie launched herself off the stool, knowing she would burst into a regular hurricane if she didn't move. She slipped her hands into her back pockets and started to pace, like she did when her team was down by two in the ninth and short one run.

She needed something to distract her mind from going down a dark path of panic. As she passed the foot of the bed, she glanced sideways at Artie. "Tell me the story about the day you met Jackie Robinson."

Artie settled deeper into the pillows and folded his hands over his belly. "You know that story inside and out. Why you want to hear that wild tale?"

" 'Cause you like telling it and I like hearing it."

"I wanna hear how you cheated that foxy Yankee out of his shirt."

Gracie stopped pacing and glared at Artie. "Just the way you taught me. Now, tell me the story, *dammit.*"

"Ben's right, you's gettin' mighty bossy." Artie's eyes drifted halfway shut, like Gracie had seen him do a thousand times when he was considering something deep. Then he nodded, and the smile that lurked in the corners of his mouth reached his eyes. "That's okay. You'll do fine." Artie sank back on the pillows and closed his eyes tight. "This time I want you to tell me a story—the one where the big bad princess makes a home run with a Yankee bat."

Sam poured a cup of coffee and scowled at the portable TV in the corner of the kitchen. A reporter, nicknamed Roger the Weasel, flashed onto the screen.

We have another bizarre twist in the Hammond family saga. Clare Hammond, the youngest daughter of the recently deceased financier, Conrad Hammond, has been reported missing. She was last seen shopping at Saks yesterday morning. The Hammond family is refusing to comment on Clare Hammond's sudden disappearance. She is thought to be driving a black Mercedes sedan with Connecticut license plates . . .

Hot java went down the wrong pipe and Sam choked. He had a sudden urge to put a finger on Gracie's whereabouts. He reached for his keys and raced for the garage. Midway down the graveled drive, he cranked his window and poked his head out.

Chantel was shimmying through an overgrown hedge. "Where's the fire, Mr. Fontana? Or should I say—who's on fire? Don't answer that. I can guess. I heard she beat you at poker. Took the shirt off your back. You're lucky you still got your pants."

"Good morning to you, too, Chantel." Sam eased his foot off the brake and let the truck roll, eager to be moving again.

Chantel called over her shoulder as she headed toward the house. "If it's Gracie you're after, you ain't gonna find her at home."

Sam hit the brake and the tires dug into the gravel with sharp *whoosh*. "Where is she?"

"Down at the ball field workin' little Jackie Brown's arm. She's in a mood. Don't say I didn't warn you. Can't be jawin' all day with your fine ass. I got to get to work before my boss fires me from all that easy Yankee money." Chantel turned and hurried up the driveway, but he could see her shoulders shake with silent laughter and knew he was heading for trouble.

Jackie was loading her glove into her backpack when Sam pulled into the parking lot. Gracie was wandering the outfield aimlessly collecting balls.

Jackie ran up to him. "You the Yankee who gave Gracie that shirt?"

Sam tugged the brim of Jackie's hat lower on her head. "Yep, that's me. Has she been telling you lies about me?"

"I hear you got a glove signed by the Babe, for real. Can I come see?"

Gracie was moving in their direction. Her shoulders slumped and the dimple in her left cheek was nowhere to be seen, a good indication that she wasn't feeling sassy.

Sam glanced briefly at Jackie. "Sure, why not, kid. Gracie can bring you by. Now, beat feet or you'll be late to school."

Jackie turned back when she reached the edge of the field. "You'll tell Gracie?"

"You got it."

Jackie did a high-five into the air and took off at a run. The fact that Jackie was a girl would have surprised him a week ago, but since he'd met Gracie, his expectations had shifted.

Sam glanced across the field. Gracie was picking her way past second base toward home plate. Sam leaned against the backstop and waited. He tried to peer beneath her hat to read her thoughts, but the sun was behind her and her face was in the shadow of her brim.

Gracie set the bucket of balls on home plate and glanced at him out of the corner of her eye. "You didn't come to get your shirt back, did you? I won it fair and square."

"You can cheer up; the shirt is all yours. It looks better on you than it does me. But your shoes could use a little work. Whose closet did you rifle those classics from?"

Gracie dropped her gaze to her feet. "Artie's. It was these or the sandals I wore last night." The angle of her chin dared him to make another crack about her choice.

She had nothing to worry about. One peek at the red rims of her eyes dissolved any smart remarks hovering on his tongue.

Sam tapped the bucket with the toe of his shoe. "So you heard the news this morning and you came out here to take a few swings at something besides me. I appreciate that."

Despite the shadows on her face, Sam detected a sudden alertness.

Gracie peeked at him from under her brim. "What news is that?"

He'd really stuck his foot in it this time. Sam kicked the side of the bucket too hard, tipping it over. Balls rolled in all directions away from home plate while Sam tried to find the right words. Better coming from him than someone like Roger the Weasel on the ten o'clock news.

"I've already got your word on Montgomery . . . And don't forget last night's steak—"

"The news, Fontana, let's have it."

He could only guess at the latest secret that had driven Gracie out to the ball field with red eyes. *Artie.* Sam dried the emotion out of his voice. Gracie would want just the facts. "The short of it is, your sister is missing. It seems she took an extended shopping trip. The press is having a field day, jumping to all sorts of conclusions that will never pan out."

Gracie stared at him while she digested his news. "What do you mean—*missing?*"

What could he say about Clare Hammond that Gracie would want to hear? "She's a mousy twenty-year-old. Her mother alternately guards her like she's Fort Knox, then bullies her. Marcia's been like a horse with a bit between her teeth since Conrad's will was made public. My guess is Clare finally got tired of her mother's race for the family fortune and is out to kick some dust in Marcia's face. I wouldn't worry just yet."

"My sister doesn't want the money, either?"

"Knowing Clare—probably not. But, then, I doubt she's had much time to think about it. Marcia is no fence post when money is at stake."

Whatever Gracie's thoughts were on her sister, she kept them to herself—but Sam could hear her mind clicking away: She had two problems to tackle—Artie couldn't wait; he was running out of time. And so far, there had been nothing to suggest Clare was in danger.

The sooner Gracie accepted Artie's situation, the sooner she'd find a way to deal with her fear. He could help her with that much at least. "Clare is not why you're out here."

Gracie gave him the hard side of her stare. "I

need something else before I go to Montgomery." The tone of her voice was all business.

Sam was reminded of Conrad at his most serious. "Okay, shoot."

"I want passes to a World Series playoff game. Box seats, first class all the way."

. . . And like Conrad, she'd asked for the moon. There was no easy way to give her the bad news. "Did Jackie bean you with a couple of those pitches? Last year's strike has made everyone crazy for tickets. The playoffs have already started. The tickets are long gone. Ask for something else, anything."

"Artie is dying. I want to do this for him. A locker room pass; a chance to shake the hands of some of his heroes. Come on, Fontana. If money can't get me that much, I don't want it."

Gracie pushed out her stubborn chin and locked her watery gaze with his. He no longer wondered if she'd just gotten lucky last night at the poker table. She had outsmarted him.

Sam nodded. "Okay, Gracie. I'll give it a shot, but it's going to cost you."

Her gaze narrowed on his. "How much?"

"One well-worn ball glove should do the trick."

It took only a second for his meaning to register on her face. Her chin stiffened. She stuck out her hand and grabbed his. "Deal, Fontana. Set it up. The sooner the better." In that moment, she was every inch a Hammond, tough as nails. Conrad would have been proud, but Sam wasn't fooled. She was still more Calloway than Hammond. He could see the pain lingering in her gaze.

All he could offer her was a watered-down grin. "Fine. But do me a favor?"

Gracie withdrew her hand from his. Her guard went up again. "What's that?"

"Bring Jackie by after school. I told her she could see Babe's glove. It'll be gone by tomorrow."

Chapter 18

Plenty of days in Gracie's young life had the potential for The Worst Day Ever Award, but this one had home run written all over it. When she'd arrived at the doctor's office bright and early, the sassy receptionist had a thick stone wall in place. But it wasn't her refusal to give Gracie any information about Artie's condition that made Gracie leave without a fight. It was the receptionist's sorry look of pity that had convinced Gracie to call in sick and spend the day at Miller's Pond skimming stones across the murky green pool until Jackie got out of school and they went to Sam's for a last look at the Babe's glove. Sam let Jackie slip it on her hand. When Gracie watched Jackie's face light up, she'd forgotten, for a moment, why she and Jackie had been in such a rush. But then Gracie remembered—Artie and the tickets.

Sam had moved heaven, earth, and the sheriff and his best deputy to keep the press from nosing around Peachtree Lane looking for information on her sister. Burgess probably figured it was a safer bet than her sharpening her knuckles on another reporter's nose. The truth was, she was angrier with God than she was with her daddy, his damn money, and all the reporters put together.

What the hell was she gonna do without Artie?

On the ride home, the tears she'd been holding back leaked out over her cheeks and down the sides of her face, trickling into the neck of her shirt. She reached up to wipe her eyes with the back of her hand as she turned into the driveway, barely stopping short at the bumper of a shiny black Mercedes. A skinny girl, all legs and arms, unfolded gracefully from the driver's seat and approached her Jeep.

Gracie glanced at the license plate. Connecticut. Her heart picked up speed as the girl drew closer. An uncertain smile underlined a pair of sunglasses that hid her eyes. She had to be all of one hundred and ten pounds—what Alice's Hollywood magazines called fashionably thin, a polite word for anorexic. She had damn good balance, considering the height of her heels and the unevenness of Ben's driveway.

Gracie fumbled for the door handle. The girl reached out and held the door open while Gracie hopped out. "Thanks."

Before Gracie could step back, the girl caught Gracie's hand with hers. "I'm looking for Gracie Calloway."

Her hand was smooth and bony as hell. Gracie gripped it gently, fearing she'd break it. "That would be me."

The girl sagged with relief, then reached out and roped Gracie into a hug with her long arms. "This is great. I can't believe it. I am so happy to meet you. You have no idea."

"Who are you?"

The girl released her abruptly and stepped back, extending her hand again. "I'm Clare. Clare Hammond—your sister."

"Sam said you were missing. Folks are looking for you—your mama for one."

"I had to meet you. She was planning on sending me abroad for a semester, so I told her I needed to . . . go shopping."

"In *Alabama?*"

"Not exactly. But I stopped in New York and picked up a few things, so it wasn't a total lie." Clare pressed a button on her key chain and the trunk of the Mercedes popped open.

Gracie's words got lost in the largess piled in her sister's trunk. She'd never seen so many fancy shopping bags. There was one for every color of the rainbow. And boxes of shoes—she hadn't owned that many shoes in her entire life. Gracie's first inclination was to send her back, but her sister was looking at her with such hope, Gracie didn't have the heart to say no. She managed an encouraging smile. "So, you're fixing to stay awhile—"

Her newfound sister swooped her back into a fierce hug. "Could I?"

Gracie tensed against her sister's bony chest. Hugs for Gracie usually came in the form of pats on the back after a good game. Ben and even Artie weren't much for displays of affection. Alice barely held still long enough to hug anyone —except the reverend.

Gracie stepped back. "Well then, I guess we'd better hide this dead man's chariot before the sheriff comes nosing around. Alice's house would be best. She lives next door, mostly. And she owes me a favor."

Clare's face brightened. "Really? I can stay? Oh, I almost forgot." She snatched a tiny bag out of the trunk. "I brought you something." She shoved a small velvet box at Gracie. "Open it." She was like a new puppy, overeager for a kind word.

Carefully Gracie slipped a tiny pink ribbon off the box and popped the lid. Nestled against deep blue velvet was half of a gold heart engraved with Clare's name.

Clare pulled a gold chain from inside her shirt. "I have the other half. Mine says, *Gracie*. Katherine sounds so stuffy. I hope that's okay?" Her pasty cheeks bloomed pink.

Gracie knew if she lived to be one hundred, this day would stand out from all the rest as the worst *and* the best day of her life.

When Clare was fast asleep in Alice's guest room, Gracie slipped down the dog path that wiggled between the sleeping houses toward Sam's back door.

She let herself in through the kitchen, then hollered out, "Samuel Fontana, you still dodging the sandman?" At least this time, he couldn't say she hadn't given him fair warning.

She waited, listening for his footsteps to come pounding down the stairs. Instead, she heard the rustle of paper coming through the open office door. Gracie followed the sound to the collection room. Sam slumped in the hard oak chair beside the table in the center of the room. A roll of bubble wrap and a crisp cardboard box filled with Styrofoam peanuts sat to one side. Behind him, the glass door to the case stood ajar.

"You'll have your tickets by tomorrow night. Artie will have his pick of two games. Just name the day and I'll make the arrangements."

Gracie slipped her small hand inside the glove just as Jackie had done earlier in the afternoon. *The Babe's glove.* It felt pretty much like Artie's old glove—a little stiff and heavy with its thickly padded fingers. She closed her eyes and sniffed. Old leather, neat's-foot oil— and the magic of an amazing man. Chills pimpled the backs of her arms. The Babe was a kindred spirit of sorts—a rebel and a family outcast who'd proven an unwanted kid could do miraculous things. She'd bet he'd known what his dreams were early on. Why were hers giving her so much trouble?

"Having second thoughts, Gracie?" Sam's voice sounded subdued and weary, much like the way she felt.

Gracie passed the glove to Sam, then wandered to the cases along the wall, keeping her back to him while she pretended to study the signatures on the balls. "Technically, it's your glove; I should give you an IOU. How much is it worth?"

"It's not about the money, Gracie. I get that."

"Thanks." Gracie glanced away.

Artie's tired face came to mind. What would he say if he knew she'd traded the Babe's glove? She turned briefly in Sam's direction. "Let's just keep this between you and me. Thanks for showing Jackie the glove. It's probably a good thing you're getting rid of it. Every kid in Shady Grove is going to want to have a look. But for Jackie, it will always be extra special."

"If you're not having second thoughts, then what are you doing here?"

Gracie spun her gaze from a row of balls to Sam. Was that hope or an invitation in his voice? Something in his gaze said he hadn't forgotten her challenge, or their kiss. Tonight there was no dinner or small talk about the upcoming playoffs to fill the silences. Artie's news had cleared the air. When she'd mentioned Artie's cancer, a haunted look had drifted across Sam's gaze.

250

His self-satisfied grin hadn't shown up since. And for the first time, she realized she was missing his smile. He was pretty damn magnificent, as men went. At first, his good looks were a deterrent, but lately she'd gotten to know him and things were getting—well, *complicated*. Gracie spun around. "I'm not having second thoughts; I'm not here about the glove."

A teasing smile tugged at his lips. "Don't tell me you're back for lesson two."

Gracie's cheeks flushed hot and kicked her temper up a notch. She turned her back on him and moved in the opposite direction. "I have a visitor."

"Anybody I know?" Sam tagged behind her, his voice suddenly serious.

"My sister."

"*Clare?* Since when?" He sounded surprised.

Gracie turned to face him. "This afternoon. She's sound asleep in Alice's guest room."

She could see his brain clicking away, making a list of the possible snags ahead. "Who knows she's here?"

"Just Alice, but I told her if she said a thing, Clare's mama would be down here in two licks and snatch her back. Alice is guarding her like a mama dog with a new pup."

He seemed to relax. "So Alice has teeth of her own." Sam chuckled. "How'd Clare get here?"

"She showed up in her mama's car with enough new clothes and shoes to outfit half the debutantes in Atlanta." Gracie turned away abruptly and wandered along the row of glass cases lining the wall.

Sam followed her. "I have a few questions for Clare. Can you sneak me into Alice's guest room?"

Gracie crossed her arms over her chest. "I'm going to ignore how easily that question rolled off your tongue."

Sam closed in on her. "I'll make it worth your while." The flicker in his eye said he was teasing. At least she hoped that's what the flicker was saying.

A lock of his dark hair fell over one side of his brow. Artie's hand-me-down shoes ran out of gas as Sam drew closer. Gracie wet her lips with her tongue.

His gaze caught on her mouth. Slowly he slid his hand along the line of her jaw and cupped her head with his fingers. "Lesson two starts like this . . ."

Gracie closed her eyes. His lips were every bit as tempting as she remembered. He didn't jump right into the kiss but eased in, first with just his lips, deepening it and pulling her closer as he went. Day-old stubble brushed her cheek, then grazed her upper lip, bringing with it memories of other parts of his body that were softer but just as male.

A chuckle rumbled in his chest.

"Don't laugh at me, Yankee, or I'll make you pay."

"You already have." His gaze shifted sideways to the glove on the table, but he kept her close.

Gracie had to lean back to see his face. "How's that?"

"I remember when Conrad bought that glove. He let me ride along to the auction. There were other things going for less that would have looked better hanging on a wall, but he wanted that glove, despite the condition."

Gracie pulled back so she could see his face. "We'll think of another way. I've still got my checkbook."

"The seller doesn't want or need money, just the glove. It's a done deal. Courier picks it up in the morning. Artie can go first class all the way. I put Conrad's pilot on standby. Name the day."

Sam knew, like she knew, that Artie's days were limited by his strength. One game would have to be enough. "Why'd you do it? You didn't have to."

"Because if I had the chance to do this for my dad, I would. Besides, all this is yours, princess."

"Stop calling me that. I'm nobody's princess."

Sam leaned in closer. His warm breath brushed her ear. "You were Conrad's."

"So you say. Since he never bothered to tell me, I'm not sure I believe you." Gracie broke loose and again wandered along the row of cases. The mention of her elusive father always ate away at her mood.

Sam hung close to her back. "That's it, isn't it? You're sore at Conrad for not coming to your rescue." He paused, like he was struggling with his words. "As far as I can see, Gracie, you don't want to be rescued. Eddie Fry may have kidnapped you, but you're the one holding yourself for ransom. I just can't figure out for what."

Gracie spun around, ready to deny his words, but she couldn't. He was right. And she didn't have an answer to his question. Asking him for the tickets had cost her pride a lot more than the value of Babe's glove.

Quietly he closed the door to the case. "Your grandmother will be here in the morning. I'll give it two days on the outside before Clare's mother follows her down here." He stopped abruptly and gave her a long look. "Shall we go wake Goldilocks up and see what she can tell us?"

Chapter 19

Even Sam's nice teeth hadn't gotten him past Alice. One dark look and Sam had gone home, agreeing his questions could wait until the morning. He wouldn't have gotten much out of Clare anyway. She was down for the count. According to Sam, her Yankee grandmother had called the dogs off Clare's trail—all but the biggest dog of all, Clare's mama.

So when Gracie tiptoed down the stairs the next morning and heard the knock on the front door, she was only half prepared for the sparkly woman on her porch. Gracie was struck speechless by the sleek vision in white and gold. She didn't look anything like the woman Clare had warned her to be on watch for. It occurred to Gracie that she should have asked Clare for a picture of her fearsome mama.

"Is this the Calloway residence?"

"Yes, but if you're here to see Clare, she's not here. But I'll tell her you stopped by." Gracie started to close the door.

"Clare?" A puzzled frown crossed the woman's smooth features. then instantly flipped into a wide smile. "But Katie, darling, I'm here to see you."

"Me?"

The woman's smile faltered, then brightened. "I'm sorry. I thought your grandmother would have warned you I was coming."

Gracie caught a glimpse of two sleepy reporters stumbling out of a van. She opened the door wider and reached for the woman's hand. "Looks like the vultures are back. You'd better come inside and explain."

The woman glanced over her shoulder and smiled at a reporter, then shoved a frothy pink gift bag at Gracie as she followed her into the living room.

Gracie slammed the door, then leaned against it as the woman wandered the room, searching for a place to sit. Finally, she settled on a wooden chair near the fireplace and looked back at Gracie expectantly.

"You don't remember me, do you? Well, that's to be expected. You were only a couple months old when you were . . . taken. I'm Lillian Hammond. Your *mother*. But you can call me Lillian, if you prefer."

This was her mama. Not Clare's. Gracie gaped at the woman, trying to find a likeness of herself, but she came up empty. Where the woman was fair skinned and blond, she was olive skinned and brunette.

"Look at you—I have a grown daughter." Her smile stumbled on Artie's old shoes, but she rebounded and beamed back at Gracie. "I just know we will be the best of friends."

Gracie's feet refused to move. Speech deserted her as she tried to fit the sophisticated woman dressed in white silk into her childhood fantasy. Words like *elegant* and *social chameleon* came to mind. The gift bag weighed against her chest. The same thick sweetness that clouded around her mama wafted out of the silver and pink tissue.

Impatiently she motioned Gracie toward the sofa. "Open it."

Gracie seated herself in Ben's chair. She still couldn't believe an ounce of her blood ran in the woman's veins. "Someone said you had the bug."

"Yes," she said, frowning. Then, just as suddenly, she brightened. Whatever had troubled her was forgotten. "I did . . . or I would have been here sooner." Lillian's gaze picked its way over the furnishings, then returned to Gracie with a poorly suppressed shudder. "Imagine, you living here all these years . . ."

For the first time, Gracie felt embarrassed by the mismatched secondhand furniture. She'd never given it much thought, even when Alice pointed out the shabby condition of Ben's chair and mud-brown couch. Ben's furnishings worked their way into the conversation at least once a week. Nine weeks out of ten, Alice turned on Gracie, saying she was the woman of the house now and should see to fixing things herself. But Gracie never seemed to find the time, mostly because Alice equated good homemaking skills with finding a husband. And Gracie refused to succumb to Alice's wish.

"You look like your grandmother, but we can fix that. A few highlights in your hair . . . a good foundation . . ." She misread Gracie's discomfort and offered her an encouraging smile.

"I've never met my grandmother."

A brief frown crossed her face. "She seems to know quite a bit about you." Then her expression brightened. "Well, that's for later. Go ahead and open my surprise."

Gracie turned her attention to the gift in her lap. It struck Gracie that Alice would like the bag but not the woman who'd given it to her. But Gracie figured her mama deserved a chance. She untied the ribbon on the handle and was reminded of Sam's surprise present—but this woman wouldn't bring her jeans.

Gracie dug into the bag and pulled out a frilly peach blouse with a drawstring neckline and a silky ruffled skirt to match. The fabric felt soft as butter and must have cost a fortune. The outfit would suit the woman sitting across from her, but Gracie was sure the peach silk would look silly on her. The woman's wide blue gaze waited for her approval. What could she say that wouldn't be a bold-faced lie?

When the long silence felt brittle enough to snap, Gracie heard the kitchen door open and Alice's sandals pump their familiar hiss through the kitchen. "Gracie Lynne?" Alice came to a sharp stop in the doorway. "Where did you get those boy's pants, child? That nice young clerk assured me there were none left in your size—" Alice abruptly stopped speaking as Lillian popped out of her seat. "Oh, excuse me. I see you have company."

Her mama offered Alice a shiny smile. "I'm Lillian Hammond, Katie's mother."

Alice's mouth worked open and closed. Gracie wondered if her mama was in the habit of surprising folks. She didn't seem at all bothered by the sight of Alice's flapping gums. In fact, she seemed to be enjoying herself.

Gracie remembered her manners and bounced out of the chair, dumping her gift onto the seat. "This is my aunt Alice. She lives next door. Nowadays, I'm called Gracie."

"Lucky you, to have your aunt so close. Of course, you didn't have any *real* aunts. Conrad and I were only children. It was your father's idea to name you Katherine, after his mother. To spite them both, I've always called you Katie. It suits her better, don't you agree, *Allison*."

Alice stepped back abruptly, as if the woman had swatted her. "We're partial to Gracie. She was a blessing brought into our lives when we needed her. She'll always be Gracie to us."

The battlefield was clearly set. Alice had the home team advantage, and her mama recognized the fact. Quietly she resumed her seat. But her cold gaze said she'd like to have Alice's liver on a plate. Her smile said she wasn't ready to rock the boat just yet. Gracie would like to think it was maternal instinct shadowing Lillian's features, but she couldn't be sure.

Alice's face said a nasty storm was brewing and it was only going to get worse. Gracie needed a way to head it off. She raced to the chair and grabbed Lillian's gift and ran back to Alice. "Look here, at this fancy outfit. It must be pure silk. Feel the fabric."

Alice didn't even glance at the peach silk. She kept her gaze trained on the woman. "That's very nice, Gracie. I guess you won't be needin' this old dress, then—"

Another new dress was clutched to Alice's chest, a yellow one this time, in a simple calico fabric. Alice backed toward the kitchen. "I'll be going now. I've got to be gettin' to the church."

Gracie latched on to Alice's arm. "Come and sit with us. The Reverend Adams won't mind if you're late." Gracie practically dragged her back into the room.

Alice met Gracie's pleading with a look of reluctance. "All right. I suppose the reverend can spare me for a few minutes. Did you offer your guest some tea, *Gracie,* like I taught you?"

Lillian launched herself out of her chair, shouldering her purse in a rush. "I can't stay. Actually, I just dropped by to invite Katie to have tea with me at my hotel. Tomorrow at the Riverview—say, four o'clock?"

Alice scowled at the woman. "Too bad. She can't make it. Our Gracie's got choir practice."

The whopping fib flew out of Alice's mouth like a well-aimed bullet. Gracie had been asked to leave the choir when she was seven. Even then, her singing voice crackled like a crow's.

Her mother was practically vibrating at Alice's shabby excuse.

Alice glowed. She'd hit her mark, and she didn't look a bit sorry. In fact, she swaggered a little closer.

Gracie jumped into the middle. "Mr. Fontana will bring me . . . after practice." She heard Artie cough and glanced nervously in the direction of his room. Gracie edged toward the door, hoping her mother would follow.

Lillian was quick to take her cue and scurried across the room in Gracie's direction. "Let's make it just the two of us. I have some things I'd like to discuss with you . . . Ciao, *Allison.*" She blew Gracie a kiss and ducked out the door.

Alice slammed the door and raced to the window. "Well, I never—"

Gracie followed at a slower pace. "Who would

261

have thought my mama would be anything like that? She's shiny like a new penny, isn't she?"

"There isn't a thing on her that hasn't got a one-year warranty and isn't made in a foreign country. You aren't going to have tea with *that . . . that woman*, are you? She doesn't even know your name."

Lillian swayed gracefully to the end of the walk, where a chauffeur waited beside a gleaming black car, much like the one Clare had shown up in. Gracie raised her hand to wave from the window, but her mama's attention was directed at the reporters. She offered each of them a blinding smile, then climbed into the car without looking back.

Gracie hid the slap behind a smile. "She must be a mighty busy woman. To think she came all this way—to see *me . . .*"

Alice dithered beside the window. The news vans pulled away from the curb and followed behind her mama's car. Across the street, Edna McCoy's curtains dropped into place. Alice glanced at Gracie. "You'll have to move. The neighbors are gonna keep you up nights with their gossip. I can already hear what they're saying. Hussy, that's what. Hide your man and your money. She's a scarlet woman with a loaded pistol, that's what she is."

Gracie stared down the empty walk. "But Alice . . . she's my mama."

"I'm real sorry, honey. Truly I am." Alice patted Gracie's shoulder and cut a path toward the kitchen door but not fast enough to hide the tears forming in the corners of her eyes.

A big lump of congealed guilt settled in Gracie's gut. Whatever Artie and Ben hadn't given her, Alice had filled in eagerly over the years. She'd taken charge of the female side of Gracie's upbringing, the dancing lessons and Girl Scouts, even though they didn't much stick.

Gracie shouted after Alice's retreating back. "I'd really like it if you left that dress. Yellow is my favorite color. I'll need something to wear when I go to Montgomery with Mr. Fontana."

Alice didn't answer. Gracie abandoned the window and made a beeline for the kitchen. Alice was gone, but Artie was there.

Gracie started for the door. "The dress is on the chair, there. Let her go. A big bad wolf just tried to steal her cub. She's got a right to feel sorry for herself for a while."

What a tangle life was getting to be. Gracie plopped herself down in a chair. "Nobody is stealing me. I'd just like to make up my own mind about my mama, that's all."

Artie eased himself into a seat across from Gracie. The effort made him breathe a little harder. Gracie held her own breath while she waited for him to catch his. Her heart twisted ten ways as she watched him struggle.

When he'd settled his oxygen tank beside his knee, he leaned across the table toward her. "You listen to me, girl. The day you arrived on that doorstep, we all thought you were a miracle sent from the Big Man upstairs. Truth was, life wasn't treatin' us all so good. Ben and Alice snapped at each other like hungry turtles after fat flies. And I was feelin' sorry for myself and drinkin' too much. You gave us good reason to get up off our sorry asses. So you see, when that fancy woman walks in here and tries to steal you away, we naturally want to peck at her."

"She was sort of fancy, wasn't she?"

"Could just be window dressin'. You go right on and have tea with her, then you'll know. Don't worry about Alice; she be jus' fine."

"Thanks, Artie." Gracie felt her eyes fill with tears. When the kettle started to whistle, she jumped at the distraction and poured Artie's tea, then carried it back to the table. "Seems only fair, her coming all the way from New York, or wherever it was she came from."

Artie nodded, stirring his tea. "Best not to judge folks right off."

When Artie used that speech, he usually applied it to folks he thought deserving. Lately his words left questions where the answers had always been. Gracie found herself having to make up her own mind. "You'll be happy to know, I've been cutting that Yankee some slack."

"Cutting him slack? Is that what you call it?" Artie chuckled.

Gracie felt her cheeks flame with embarrassment. "Chantel's been tattlin' on me and Mr. Fontana, hasn't she?"

"I hear he's got a nice backside, and Chantel ain't the only one who noticed." Artie waited for her response, eyebrows up, lips sealed.

She passed him a dark look, but his face was such a mask of comic expectation, she couldn't keep her stubborn chin jutted out for long. "Oh, all right. He does have nice parts and he's a good kisser. There, you satisfied? I swear, you're worse than an old hen."

Artie feigned shock. "Kisser? I wasn't askin' for details, girl."

"The hell you weren't. He thought I didn't know a thing about kissing boys. I had to prove him wrong."

"I bet you showed him." Artie's gaze swerved to the floor but not before she saw the grin jump across his lips.

"Why shouldn't I? I'm twenty-five years old. I've kissed plenty of boys, for your information."

"Mr. Fontana ain't no boy. He's a man. There's a difference."

"I know what Sam Fontana is. And I can handle him just fine. Don't you think I can't." Gracie grabbed the yellow dress off the chair and marched toward the stairs.

● ● ●

Artie might not think Alice needed soothing, but Gracie's female instincts knew better. If she didn't fix things with Alice soon, her aunt would be telling stories in her head, which pretty much amounted to her putting words into Gracie's mouth that never saw the up side of her tongue. If Ben told big fish stories, then Alice told whale tales. The last thing Gracie wanted was to be swimming in Alice's ocean, where Marjorie Finks could take a bite out of her.

She tucked the frilly bag her mother had given her in the back of her closet. If Alice went poking around, it would do no good for her to see her mama's expensive gift hanging in the closet alongside the dresses Alice had given her. Then, just to be safe, Gracie tucked her new jeans and Sam's old T-shirt under her mattress before she donned the yellow dress Alice had left behind.

The dress had a high-waisted narrow bodice that hugged her ribs and emphasized her breasts with tiny gathers. The skirt fanned out over her hips and flounced around her knees. The neckline gave her the most concern. It cut a wide V across her chest with a dainty outline of lace. Gracie climbed on her bed and stood barefoot in the center to study her reflection in her dresser mirror.

The image of the gangly girl she'd been carrying around in her head had turned into a woman.

How had it happened? She hadn't been paying attention. Gracie spun sideways, then slowly turned, keeping her eye on the strange woman. Hints of Lillian were more visible now: her petite stature, narrow hips, and most notably, her womanly chest. The gap between herself and the primped and manicured image of Darla Watson narrowed considerably.

Had Sam Fontana noticed, too? Gracie blushed, then smiled at the woman in the mirror—and wondered what Sam would say if she turned the full strength of her charms on him.

Gracie didn't know whether she should mourn her old self or feel relieved that she wasn't exactly the ugly duckling she'd presumed. As soon as the thought surfaced, she gave herself a quick scolding. What she looked like didn't change a thing. She was still in deep with Alice. No matter what Artie said, she needed to fix things before she went to Montgomery.

Gracie bounced off the bed and raced next door. She let herself into Alice's kitchen. The room was dim and silent. Normally Alice had the lights burning in the morning hours as she bustled through her morning chores. The sinking feeling in Gracie's stomach hit bottom. She had some serious groveling to do. In the past, Gracie would have waited for Alice to come around to her, but this time was different.

Tentatively Gracie tiptoed up the stairs, praying she wasn't going to find a teary-eyed Alice prostrate on her bed. "Alice?"

As soon as Gracie cleared the landing, Clare, not Alice, stumbled into the hall wearing Alice's summer nightgown and waving a note. "Alice went to church. Does she know it's not Sunday?"

Gracie accepted the slip of paper, then wandered into Clare's room and sat down on the end of the bed. "Alice goes to church everyday. She works there—at least she used to. She probably went in early to pray for my mama's soul."

Clare's sunny expression dissolved into confusion. "Lillian's? She's *here?*"

"She's gone now. But I opened the door this morning and there she was. I thought she was your mama. She sure surprised the heck out of me. I had no idea she was so—" Gracie searched for the word. Alice would say *flashy*, but that seemed mean. Gracie glanced at Clare for help.

Clare hesitated, then shrugged. *"Beautiful?"*

"I guess she was. But as soon as she was out the door, Alice branded her a hussy and a gold digger, then she left in a huff. Artie says Alice is just afraid my mama will steal me away. I need to set things straight with Alice."

"This isn't really Lillian's sort of place. She probably won't hurry back."

"I think I was a disappointment to her . . . Lillian, I mean."

Clare absently picked up a shopping bag and pawed through it, then tossed it aside and grabbed another. "I've always felt sorry for Lillian. Mom hates her. But that's because she's jealous." She stopped rummaging and looked up at Gracie. "I mean, who wouldn't be? Lillian's gorgeous and exciting. Dad married Mom because she was all the things Lillian wasn't. But Mom didn't make him happy, either . . . and I wasn't you." Clare shrugged, like it was no big deal. "They broke up when I was four. Mom's been crazy ever since."

Clare held up a long skinny black knit top and pair of gray leggings, considered her reflection in the vanity mirror, then abandoned them on the floor and picked up another bag.

Gracie stared blankly at the growing pile and mulled over Clare's last words. "He didn't even know me. How could he expect you to be like me?"

Clare glanced at Gracie. "All I know is he was obsessed with finding you. My mom said he even demanded custody of you when he divorced Lillian. Everyone thought he was crazy —except Joe Fontana."

Gracie couldn't believe her ears. *He'd demanded custody of a child who'd been presumed dead.*

Gracie thought about her daddy and what Sam had said about her being angry with him for not rescuing her. If he was so obsessed with her, why had he stayed away? Before she could forgive him, she needed to understand why.

And what had he done for his other daughter, besides abandon her to a bossy mama?

"What about you?"

In a flash, the self-conscious girl who showed up in Gracie's driveway reappeared. Clare dodged Gracie's gaze and looked down at her hands. "He didn't want me badly enough to brave my mother. I tried to be what he wanted . . . really I did."

Conrad had hurt Clare with her mama's help. He'd sliced to the core of her self-confidence. Gracie understood what that felt like. She lived all her life with the sort of pain Clare was still wrestling with. But Gracie had had Artie. Clare had had no one. She wasn't sure she could forgive a man who had so blatantly hurt his own child. The fact that she'd unknowingly been part of the cause only increased her anger.

Clare must have read her expression. She quickly offered Gracie a brave smile. "He took me out to lunch the week before he died. It was a first—let me tell you. He just showed up one day. My mom was speechless, which is a rare occurrence." Clare paused and looked at Gracie. "He told me about you. He even gave me your address and said he wanted us to meet—to become friends. He promised to arrange things —So you see why I had to come."

270

"You knew—about me?"

Clare discarded the bag she was holding and plopped down on the end of the bed beside Gracie. "I would have come earlier, but I didn't want my mother to know. It was a secret, just between me and Dad—something I've never had before." Clare glanced away briefly and took a deep breath, then flashed Gracie a watery smile. "My mother was furious with me because I wouldn't give her any of the gory details of our lunch. For once, I realized I didn't care what she thought. I wasn't going to let her spoil this for me." The tears were gone. Clare's chin had a stubborn tilt that Gracie recognized as her own.

Silently she glanced at their joined reflection in the vanity mirror opposite the bed. In the past, mirrors were just a reminder of the physical differences between herself and the people she loved. At an early age, she'd realized she didn't have Artie's dark skin, or Ben's towering stature, or even Rita's ruddy coloring. Whereas her eyes were gray, theirs were brown. She assumed her features came from her father. But now that she'd met Clare, she knew she'd reached another dead end. Clare looked like Conrad Hammond all over again—tall, angular, with green eyes. Though her mother's eyes were blue, they were nowhere near the dusty shade of her own.

Despite that fact that Sam claimed her blood

271

matched Conrad's, she still craved visual proof that she was a Hammond.

Gracie met Clare's gaze in the mirror. "You look like our daddy. Who do I look like?"

Clare's pale face blushed pink. "The old battle-ax—our grandmother, Kate. Sorry."

"She's a battle-ax, huh? Why do I feel like I got the short end of the stick?"

"Mom just calls her that because she's one of the few people Mom can't bully. Actually, Grandmother Kate is awesome, but don't let her know I said so." Clare draped her arm over Gracie's shoulder and pulled her tight against her side in a fierce hug.

Gracie laced her arm around Clare's waist and hugged her back. Clare was an amazing kid, despite her dragon of a mama. Conrad Hammond had missed out. Had he realized the fact during their last lunch together? She sure hoped so, but then she realized it didn't matter because he hadn't left Clare any indication of his love.

Suddenly she felt the fierce need to protect her sister. Whatever decision Gracie made about the money, it would affect Clare, too. Was that why their daddy had left her in charge? Gracie glanced at the mountains of new clothes scattered helter-skelter around the room and knew Clare wasn't ready to deal with piles of money just yet.

Gracie turned toward Clare. "Did anyone ever

ask you what *you* wanted to do with your life?"

Clare flopped backward on the bed and laughed. "You're kidding, right?"

Gracie plopped down beside her. The feel of Clare's shoulder rubbing against hers was a strange and wonderful feeling. Gracie soaked up the moment, then glanced over at Clare. "I'm serious. What would you say?"

"This." Clare thrust her arms into the air above her head and stretched toward the ceiling. "This is what I've wanted all my life—" Clare's voice cracked, then she rushed on. "You know, someone to laugh with and talk to—with someone like me."

Gracie glanced up at Clare's long fingers and polished nails, fluttering overhead. Her sleek graceful sister considered herself to be like her. How about that? Two days ago she would have rushed Clare off to the nearest optometrist, but today she'd give her big gold stars for being brave enough to speak her heart. Clare might have lived in her mama's silk cocoon, but she had a brain and more courage than most men Gracie knew.

Minutes earlier, her knees had been knocking together at the thought of facing Alice. Conrad wasn't the only one who'd underestimated Clare's abilities—she had, too.

Gracie closed her eyes and lay still, focusing on the point where her sister's shoulder touched hers. Silently she soaked up Clare's courage. She was going to need all she could get in the next couple of days—to deal with Alice and face her new mama over the tea table in Montgomery.

When Gracie felt her fear subside, she sat up and glanced back at Clare. "If Alice comes home, tell her I came by. I'll be back later. Make sure to tell her I was wearing my new dress, if she gets sulky." Gracie picked her way through the piles of clothes to the door.

"Gracie?"

Gracie paused in the doorway. "Yep?"

"Thanks for saving me. Dad was so right about you."

Chapter 20

Sam felt a warm hand rattle his shoulder against the mattress. He opened his eyes to see Chantel scowling down at him.

"I hate to disturb your beauty sleep, handsome, but there are two women downstairs who are fixin' to move in. I figured you'd rather see my pretty face roustin' your sweet ass outta bed than them two hoity-toity Yankee women."

Sam sat up and rubbed the sleep out of his eyes. It couldn't be more than eight A.M. "Yankee women?"

"A Mrs. Katherine Hammond and her lackey. And that ain't all. There's an old man with them, too. Looks like somethin' they dug out of the ground."

"Marcus? He's the gardener."

"Well, there you go. Now, where am I supposed to put all these folks? There ain't but three bedrooms in this big house since Mr. Conrad did his remodelin' for his collection."

"Put me in the downstairs office. I'll sleep on the sofa."

"Say what? The sofa?"

Sam paused with his legs over the side of the bed, the covers still drawn across his waist for modesty. "How do you know about his collection?"

"Who do you think cleans that room, Cinderella's mice? I'm leavin' now while you get your fine self outta that bed and take a shower. Since Gracie's got dibs on you, I won't even peek."

Kate had ensconced herself on the sofa by the time Sam padded downstairs.

He helped himself to a cup of coffee, then eased back into a chair. "I assumed you'd be staying in Montgomery where the alligators don't roam the streets."

"I'm not in the mood for your humor this morning, Mr. Fontana. Traveling with Cook and Marcus has been a trial I will not repeat."

Sam suppressed a chuckle. He could imagine the elderly Cook's face and Marcus's grumbles when Kate ordered them to pack for Alabama. Three suitcases sat in the foyer: a small expensive-looking carryon and two enormous overstuffed tattered bags, which completed the story of their crusade south.

"You should have brought Jonesy."

"Mr. Jones is no longer in my employ. I refuse to tolerate his insubordination. He was taking liberties with Conrad's possessions, though he denied it. I saw him give Lillian a packet of some sort. I called immediately and demanded she return whatever it was. She claims it was nothing—just some old snapshots of her and the baby. Nevertheless, Martin Jones lied." Kate stabbed him with a sharp look that said the subject of Mr. Jones was closed. "I've come to see my granddaughters, Mr. Fontana. Wake them up."

Jonesy had always been the epitome of efficiency and loyalty in Conrad's household. He'd held his tongue when Lillian's name was dropped into conversation. But Sam knew that his allegiance belonged, without a doubt, to Conrad. Jonesy had gone so far as to offer himself as a witness on Conrad's behalf during the divorce proceedings. Why would Jonesy change camps? It didn't add up. Lillian was even more of a loose cannon than he'd expected. He'd have to find a way to keep a closer eye on Gracie.

No sooner had the thought crossed his mind than Gracie's head bobbed into view outside the window. "Here comes granddaughter number one. Play nice, Kate. She's had a hard time of it lately."

Gracie breezed through the front door without knocking. "Sam *Fontana,* why didn't someone warn me my mama was going to visit this morning . . . Alice walked in and—" Gracie paused in the foyer. "Excuse me, I didn't realize y'all had company . . ."

Kate's gaze widened with shock. There were so many characteristics in Gracie: eye color, voice, and manner—even the way she moved— that resembled Kate's. He'd been thrown at first, too.

Sam launched himself out of his chair. "Gracie, I'd like you to meet your grandmother, Katherine Hammond. Kate, this is Gracie Calloway."

Sam motioned Gracie to a chair. "Have a seat, Gracie, before Kate gets a stiff neck." Sam took up a post on the chair's arm as silence stretched across the room.

Kate came to life first. "You are hardly a Katherine. I suppose Gracie will have to do. You may call me Grandmother Kate. Be advised, I will not answer to *Grandma* or any such colloquialisms."

Gracie sat up straighter in her seat. "Clare said as much. Truthfully, you don't look much like a *grandma*. Grandmother is a mouthful. How about just Kate?"

Kate's face remained expressionless, but her eyes darkened to smoke. "Well, I can see you're not meek like your sister. That's a small blessing, at least. I suppose Kate will be acceptable. Now, what's this about Lillian?"

"She showed up on my doorstep this morning. Alice ran off in a huff."

Kate's gaze snapped to Sam. "*Lillian's arrived? When?* Mr. Fontana, what do you know about this?"

Sam kept his gaze trained on Gracie. "Evidently, she arrived . . . this morning."

"But it's barely nine now—Lillian rarely rises before noon."

Gracie turned toward Sam. "She's staying in Montgomery, at the Riverview. I've been invited to tea tomorrow afternoon."

Kate sent him a panicked look. "Mr. Fontana, you will not let her out of your sight, do you hear me?"

After Lillian's encounter with Jonesy and his subsequent defection, Kate didn't have to ask. Sam nodded to Kate. "You can count on it."

Kate returned his nod with a silent look that said they would talk later, then Kate pointed her stern gaze at Gracie. "Where is Clare?"

"Unpacking. She's decided to stay awhile."

"She has, has she?" Kate challenged Gracie's gaze.

"Yes, ma'am." Gracie sat quietly, unruffled. She was taking Kate's measure, if Sam didn't miss his guess.

Kate brushed off Gracie's scrutiny and turned to Sam. "Bring me that briefcase near the piano, Mr. Fontana. I want my granddaughter to look at a few things."

Reluctantly, he retrieved the black leather case and handed it to Kate with a warning look.

Kate pulled out a stack of papers and held them out to Gracie. "Your birth certificate. And some family photos. One should always know where one comes from."

Gracie stared blankly at Kate's outstretched hand. Sam kept a close watch on her face. The color had drained from her cheeks. "You okay, princess? You're looking like a regular mashed potato." Sam leaned forward to accept the papers for her.

But Gracie intercepted the stack. "I'm fine."

She was playing it tough again. But Sam knew she was far from fine. Kate had just presented her with the first official proof that she wasn't Gracie Calloway. Quietly he reclaimed his protective post on the arm of her chair and peered over Gracie's shoulder as she took her first tentative look at the evidence.

The first two pictures were copies of the photos above the stairs. Gracie dismissed them quickly but paused over the third one. It was a close-up of her lying on a baby blanket. She was a runty little thing with a tiny little bow of a mouth. Conrad once bragged that he could hold her in the palm of his hand when she was born. Sam had never believed him, but Gracie couldn't have been more than five pounds when the picture was taken.

Kate had aimed straight at Gracie's heart. Why did he feel like he'd loaded the gun? He glanced at Conrad's crafty mother. She sat silently sipping her coffee, her eagle eye trained on Gracie, hungry for a reaction.

When Gracie flipped to the next one, she was rewarded with a sharp intake of breath. The photo was a real heartbreaker. Conrad had baby Gracie tucked into the crook of his arm. He held a book in one hand, but his attention was fixed on her sleeping face. Gracie's head lolled to one side, her mouth gaped open and a dribble of spit oozed down her cheek. Conrad's face was filled with unguarded affection—a rarity for him.

Gracie sat stone still. All of her attention was glued to the photo. He had the sudden urge to snatch the picture away and save Gracie from suffering pain for something she could never have. Words of warning were on the tip of his tongue when Kate shifted her watchful stare to her lap. Both women were on the edge of tears.

His pesky Y chromosome had him at a loss in such situations. He had nothing left to save him but his cocky sense of humor. Sam leaned into Gracie's space. "I'd sue. Definitely not your best side."

Gracie ignored Sam and glanced up at Kate. "Can I have a copy of this one?"

Chapter 21

The morning interview with her grandma and Sam's watchful gaze had taken more out of Gracie than she cared to admit. She still hadn't glanced at the date on her birth certificate. It seemed like a simple thing, just a few numbers—something she'd always wondered about—but just knowing the actual date would make the last week just a little too real. Already she was beginning to lose track of where Gracie Calloway ended and Katherine Hammond began.

Sam had sensed her need to be alone and reluctantly let her leave with a promise to go straight home. Her grandma had backed off when she said she had to pack for the trip to Montgomery to sign papers, which was the truth. But first she had to fix things with Alice.

Old Man Guilt had been following her around all day and wouldn't leave her be. The image of Alice's wobbly lips and dog-sad eyes kept popping into her mind. Alice had come out fighting for her, and she'd just stood there, tongue-tied like a fool with her mind looping around the sparkly image of her flesh-and-blood mama.

Gracie kicked off her sandals on Alice's back

porch and smoothed the wrinkles out of the yellow dress, hoping Clare had delivered her regrets and softened Alice up. Her girlish side had always admired Alice's frilly kitchen in a moth-to-flame sort of way. It was practically a religious experience, complete with a hand-painted statue of a smiling Lord Jesus who stood guard over Alice's row of fancy china cups and saucers.

The smells—a mixture of fresh-baked pies, coffee, and Alice's lavender body powder—hit her as soon she stepped through the doorway. Gracie's apology went still on her tongue.

Alice clutched a rolling pin in her right hand and offered it to Clare. "Now, if the piecrust isn't kept chilled, it will get sticky, then hard as wood when it bakes. Might even break your sweetheart's tooth. And he won't thank you for it. Then you'll have a toothless man smiling at you from across the table the rest of your days. Makes me shudder just to think of it."

Clare looked up from what she was doing. "Your neighbor, Skip Evers, has a nice smile."

Alice quickly swallowed her surprise, then beamed back at Clare. "Why, yes, he certainly does. Mind you, that's because I told Millie Evers to make sure he brushes twice a day." As sly a smile as Gracie had ever seen spread across Alice's lips. "I hear he came by twice to check on you while I was at work this morning."

Clare blushed. "He did, and the second time he brought me flowers. No one has ever brought me flowers before."

"Oh my, but how sweet our Skippy is. Flowers, like teeth, are the mark of a true gentleman. Gracie is immune to his charms. But that's just as well now that she has her fancy mama to make a fuss over her."

Alice let out a sorrowful sigh, then reached over to guide Clare's hands. "Roll it gently now, dear. Not too thin. There you go. Now, that wasn't too hard, was it?"

"This is fun. I could do this all day." Clare's voice had a skip it hadn't had when she arrived in Shady Grove. "What's next?"

"Hand me that pie dish from the table, would you?"

Gracie stepped out of the shadows and hurried toward the dish. "Here you go, Alice."

Alice's hands flew to her chest as she spun around. "Lord Almighty, you scared the livin' daylights out of me, child. Haven't I told you not to sneak up on me when I'm in the kitchen? Clare, bring me my stool, would you? My heart's nearly out my throat. I need to catch it before it runs off."

Clare plunked the stool down beside Alice. "I can finish. Just tell me what to do."

Alice reached for Clare's arm as she lowered herself onto the stool. "Why, thank you. You are such a dear."

"I'm just so happy to be here. I can hardly find the words."

Alice tightened her grip on Clare's hand. Gracie couldn't believe her eyes . . . or her ears. Was that a drawl she'd heard slipping over her sister's New England accent? Alice had turned Clare into her clone, right down to the calico apron hugging her sister's waist. Where was the brave girl she'd been sharing secrets with just this morning?

Gracie felt her temper bump up a notch. "Are you feeling sickly? Do I need to call the doctor?"

Alice pulled a tissue out of her sleeve and dabbed at her eyes. "I thought you'd be packing for your tea party at the Riverview." Alice's sharp gaze was taking in her new dress.

Gracie swallowed the inclination to snap back that she had nothing to pack. "Not yet. I'm only going for one day. I'll be back before you know I'm gone."

Alice leaned toward Clare. "Tell me, dear. What do you think of Gracie in yellow? Did I choose the wrong color?"

Clare's gaze did the jitterbug, flitting back and forth between Jesus and the teacups behind Gracie's head. "Yellow turns my skin green, but on Gracie it looks great."

Bless the teacups and the happy Jesus. The spell was lifted. The Clare she knew was back.

But Alice didn't seem to notice. She was still

considering Gracie's dress with her finger propped against one cheek. "I suppose it will do for tea with your new mama."

Clare dropped the rolling pin on the counter and shot Gracie a panicked look. "But I thought you said she'd gone home—"

Alice's gaze was intent on Gracie's. "She arrived at the crack of dawn with an entourage of paparazzi."

"*The press* was here? Why didn't somebody tell me?" Clare's voice jumped an octave.

Alice didn't seem to notice. She had her laser stare fixed on Gracie. "The street was cluttered with news vans of all sorts, just when that nice Mr. Fontana had told them to stay away. She brought them on purpose, I'll bet."

Gracie glared back at Alice. "You don't know that for sure. She came to invite me to tea."

"Most folks send a proper invitation." Alice's bottom lip jutted out, and her eyes narrowed behind the glare of her glasses. She was still on a snipe hunt.

Clare untied her apron and thrust it at Gracie. "If my mother finds out Lillian is still here, she'll be right behind her . . . I'll have to leave. Where will I go?"

Alice commandeered Clare's hand and patted it gently. "Don't worry, my dear. She wouldn't dare come here, where she's not welcome."

Clare stopped dithering and sent Gracie a look

of apology. They both knew Alice wasn't talking about Clare's mother, but Gracie's own mama. Artie had been right: This wasn't a battle Gracie couldn't win without losing an arm or a leg. She'd only made things worse with Alice.

Gracie slammed through Ben's kitchen and snatched up the envelope Kate Hammond had given her, then peeked into Artie's room. He was lying in a sea of new pillows. The oxygen tube still ran from his nose. Playing cards were spread over the coverlet in front of him.

"Quit your spyin' and get yourself in here. I ain't had nobody but ornery women bothering me today."

She'd spent endless hours playing solitaire with Artie: when it was too hot to move, then again when the rains came and they couldn't go outside and play ball. Artie was the only one she knew who could beat Old Sol with any regularity. Never once had she suspected him of cheating, but Alice claimed he did.

Gracie perched on a stool and studied the cards. "You've reached a dead end. Time to fold."

Artie worked through the cards in his hand one more time. Magically an ace of spades surfaced. Then there was no stopping him. One-by-one, the cards fell into place. A smile tugged at his lips. "You been draggin' your sorry ass around too long, girl. Don't you think it's time for you to pull yourself out of it?" Artie set the last card into place with a snap.

"I'll drag as long as I want. Besides, I've got reason." Gracie fumbled with the envelope of photos she'd taken from her grandmother.

"Some folks would say you don't . . . but they're not standin' in your shoes, so you just go on and wallow, now, you hear?" One of his gray brows lifted her way expectantly.

"I haven't had time to wallow. I've got visitors coming out of the walls."

Artie laid the two of spades on the ace, then shuffled the pile one more time. "That so? You gonna tell me who, or are you gonna make an old man wear hisself out guessin'?"

"My sister showed up in her mama's car with a trunk full of fancy new clothes. Now Alice is in her kitchen teaching her to make pies. And I've got a grandma who puts a whole new twist on the word *Yankee*."

Artie was quiet for a minute, but Gracie wasn't fooled; his thoughts were working at lightning speed, making connections. "I see you's wearing Alice's new dress—even though I knows you never liked yellow."

"I can change my mind, can't I?"

"I told you not to worry 'bout Alice. She might fuss a bit coming out of the gate, but she'll come 'round."

"There was no gate. She cut straight through

the fence. All it took was one look at my mama, and she was like a fast horse heading down the track. I tried to slow her down by putting on this silly dress, but she just ran me down and stole my sister. I give up."

"You know damn well you and Alice ain't never seen anythin' with the same pair of eyes. That's been goin' on long before this new trouble come along. Why you so worried about what she thinks now?"

Artie's look told her he knew why, but he wanted her to say it out loud so she could hear the words for herself. What could she say? "My world is burstin' at the seams. Alice is running off to marry the reverend. Who knows what's going on between Ben and the Widow Perkins? Did I mention Jimmy is squeezing me out of my job? And you tell me you've already bought a space in the Big Man's parking lot—" She didn't even bother to add Sam Fontana to the list. "I got more rights than most to feel out of sorts."

"Yes, you do. But some of those things that's sucking up your smile is things you can't change. Let those go. Worry about the things you can change. Facts is facts." Artie reached for her hand and laced his fingers through hers. "Now, what about your new family? I suppose their faces are witchy and ugly like yours, long-nosed with warts. You bring them along?" Artie pretended to peer past her shoulder. Something told her he already knew the details. From the look on his tired face, she'd guess he'd missed his nap waiting for her to show up and spill the news.

Gracie tucked Alice to the back of her mind and offered Artie a smile. "Chantel's been tattling, hasn't she?"

Artie nodded, then released her hand and settled into the pillows. "She came over to brag about how that Yankee gave her time off, paid. That girl is so busy looking for easy street, she gonna miss the turn—unlike you. You's gonna miss it 'cause you gots your eyes shut so tight you can't see where you're goin'." Artie's gaze dipped to the envelope. "What you got there?"

"A headache."

"I mean, in that envelope you's huggin' so tight."

"Oh, this?" Gracie lowered the package to her lap. "Just some old baby pictures. Nothing much."

"Hand me my glasses, girl. I want to see if you were as ugly as I remember." Artie cracked a smile, but it was a good twenty calibers weaker than his usual sassy grin.

Gracie's heart seized up. He was fading right before her eyes. Reluctantly, she dumped the pictures into his lap, then reached for his glasses while she tried unsuccessfully to press the tears back into her eyes. "Here you go. Knock yourself out."

Artie let her watery voice slide by without a second glance. "Well, look at you. Why, you weren't nothin' but a tadpole. I seen kittens born bigger than you. And this must be your daddy." Artie moved the photo up and down until he found the right focus through his bifocals. "You got his chin. Must have a pair of mules in his britches, jus' like you."

Gracie resisted the urge to grab the picture away before Artie saw something she wasn't ready to admit to. For some reason, the picture was painful for her to look at, but she'd wanted it more than anything. If her grandmother had refused to give it to her, she would have found a way to get a copy, even if it meant stealing.

Artie moved on to the next photo. Gracie held her tongue through his grunts, snorts, and nods. When he'd finished, he tucked the snapshots carefully into the envelope—all but the one.

Gracie reached for it, but he snatched it away.

Slowly he raised his one-eyed laser stare in her direction. "I figured this would be the one you'd like the best. I knowed, if it was me, it would be the one I'd pick. Makes me feel sorta like I gypped your daddy."

Gracie swallowed the lump in her throat. "Why's that?"

"Well, 'cause he's lookin' at you like you could move heaven and earth. I'm thinkin' he was a lonely man and you was his North Star."

"Save your pity for someone else. He lived in this town, shopped in my store, sent me flowers, but he never told me who he was. I had a right to know, and he never said boo. Now I don't know who the hell I am."

"You're Gracie Lynne Calloway—the girl who pitched three no-hitters in a row; the girl who spends her Thanksgivin' deliverin' food to folks who ain't got none, and it wasn't 'cause Alice and her churchy friends made you. You's still the same girl—except for them shoes. They's some kinda ugly."

"They're yours." Gracie blinked away her tears.

"I thought I taught you not to lie. They ain't ever been on my stylish feet. No, siree. Arthur Dubois may be poor, but he gots his pride. You been fishin' in Moses Day's trash heap, that's what."

Gracie felt tears crowd her eyes again. She dashed them away with the back of her hand. "Alice burned my clothes."

Artie laid the picture down on the coverlet. After a long silence, he nodded his head. "Me and Alice don't agree on much, you know that. But I'm thinkin' maybe this time she's right."

She couldn't believe what she was hearing. Artie had always been on her side when Alice got pushy. "Right? About what?"

"That you need to leave the nest. Burnin' your clothes is her way of shovin' you out. Ben and me, we got too used to you doin' for us. Don't you see, this is your big chance, girl, to do something in a big way besides take care of two old men who smell more every year. Ain't you got no dreams?"

Gracie stared back at Artie. No one had ever asked her that. The answer had to be yes, 'cause everybody had a dream, right? She could feel Artie's gaze hanging on hers, waiting for an answer.

But if she was still Gracie Calloway, not Katherine Hammond, like Artie said, then she was the same child who'd been left on the front porch. Even that girl had had dreams at one time—dreams of a fairy-tale mother who thought she was the cat's meow. But she'd learned over the years just because she wanted something to be true, dreaming didn't make it so. Gracie met his prying look with a stubborn frown. "I don't have time for dreams, Artie."

"Uh-huh, that's what I thought. You's been so busy worryin' about other folks, you forgot all about little ol' Gracie Calloway. I'm talkin' about big dreams like the ones Martin Luther King and John Kennedy had."

Gracie felt the day creeping up on her. Her arms and legs ached along with her head. She stared at the forgotten photographs in Artie's lap, then shifted her gaze to Artie's face. "You don't ask for much, do you?"

"I'm askin' 'cause you ain't, don't you see?"

Gracie felt her voice go small in her throat. She propped one foot on her knee and toyed with the frayed shoelace. "I wanted to sing once. But we both know that isn't gonna happen."

"Ain't that the truth. You got the singin' voice of a crow. What else? There's got to be somethin'."

Sam and his grin skated uninvited into Gracie's mind. Gracie tried to shoo the image away without success. As soon as one version of Sam was gone, another replaced it, until she felt a serious frown tugging at the corners of her mouth.

When she glanced up, Artie's eagle gaze fixed on her face. Finally his eyes lit and he cracked that smug grin of his that made his ears crinkle along his cheeks. "You's in love. Hot damn. About time."

Gracie hopped off her perch on the bed. "You're crazy. I've got to go pack. I'm going to Montgomery—just for a day, mind you. Don't go getting any funny ideas about me and Mr. Fontana, because they're just not so." Gracie collected the envelope from Artie's lap.

A broad smile curved his face. "I been prayin' for this day a mighty long time. Yes, siree. My little chick is about to spread her wings."

"Well, don't stop, because it's not here yet. I'm just going to sign some papers."

"You go on, now. And get yourself some pretty

new clothes while you's there." Artie started to cough. The raspy sound was deeper this time.

A rush of fear and lack of sleep the night before made Gracie's head swim. She reached for Artie's hand. "I can stay here. Sam can arrange for them to come to Shady Grove, if they need me so bad. I don't give a damn about the money."

"You met someone else you want to give it to? Someone who will do good with it? From what you tell me, that money could end up in the hands of some mighty shortsighted folks. I know you, girl. You'd never forgive yourself. It would eat at your socks. Seems to me, you gots some serious thinkin' to do."

"I'm beginning to think that's the problem— too much thinking."

"Maybe you're startin' in the wrong place. First off, you gots to know what your dreams is, 'cause if you don't, I don't see how you can know what to do."

They were back to that again. Gracie still didn't have an answer—at least any she was ready to admit to. She prayed that as long as she was still looking for an answer, he'd be waiting. If Artie could trick Old Sol as many times as he had, he could trick the Grim Reaper just once.

Chapter 22

Ben plopped Gracie's newfangled cordless phone into its holder and leaned back in his chair. Artie's door was open at the end of the hall; he could hear the raggedy hiss of his labored breathing. Since Gracie had left for Montgomery, Artie had given up fighting the pain medication the doctor prescribed.

Ben said a prayer for the fact that Artie had not been awake for Rita's call. She would have upset him with a lot of nonsense about how she thought she was being spied on. Her call was quick. She was feeling him out for details. She wanted to know if the authorities were looking to arrest her for her role in Gracie's kidnapping. Ben assured her no one was out to blame her, but when he hung up, her words started to gnaw at him. Conrad had warned him to keep an eye out for folks who might be looking to harm Gracie.

Ben's gaze swung past the coal bucket on the hearth, then to Gracie's baby booties resting on the mantel. His mind wandered through the birthdays and the Christmases they shared since Gracie came their way. Good years. She'd been such a tiny thing, but she'd brought them all back to life. Ben glanced at his watch. Gracie should be sitting down to tea with her mama by now. He'd been holding his breath since she'd left for Montgomery. Her leaving put him in mind of the day Rita left with Tom Robbins's boy. He wasn't ready to let Gracie go any more than he had been Rita, but he knew it was time.

The screen door in the kitchen banged closed. Alice's sandals pumped softly across the linoleum. She paused in the archway to the living room. "What are you doing here? Did Delilah run out of pipes?"

Ben refused to rise to her bait. "Gracie said she wouldn't go with Mr. Fontana unless I promised to stay with Artie until Chantel gets here. I had some thinking to do, besides."

She pedaled to a chair opposite his and settled herself on the edge of the seat. "Thinking about what?"

"Rita. She called."

"What does she want this time?"

Ben steered his gaze away from hers. "She's seen the news reports. She asked to speak to Gracie."

"Surprise, surprise. I don't suppose she mentioned anything about the money."

Alice had had twenty-five years to build up a case against Rita. At first, she went on about a mother being blessed with a child and how she could just abandon her, the way she did. Then, when they'd figured out just who Gracie belonged to, she started in on Rita's lying. She claimed he was too quick to excuse his niece's faults.

Fact was, Rita had not had a fair shake from day one. Her mama loved her but died just when the girl needed female guidance. She'd never known her daddy. Ben had tried his best to fill in the space, but he'd be the first to admit he hadn't done such a good job. Rita had been headstrong and he'd had two left feet around female emotions. It broke his heart when she'd left in a huff for Connecticut with Woody Robbins.

Ben glanced at Alice. "She wants a chance to explain things, is all. Figures she owes Gracie that much. Why is it so hard to believe that she's worried about Our Gracie?"

Alice rolled her eyes. "Now that Gracie's rich, everybody's worried about Our Gracie Lynne. *Humph!*"

Ben shot Alice a stern glare. "It ain't like you to be so mean-spirited. What's eating at you, woman? Did the fancy reverend smudge his napkin at lunch?"

"That so-called mother of hers showed up at the door, not seconds after the sun came up, toting fancy silk clothes and gushing false promises. Our Gracie was sucked right in, like dust to a Hoover. And now Rita's going to add her lies to the poor girl's troubles. I tell you my heart is fractured so . . . Well, I just can't say how bad."

"Her mama came *here?*"

"She raced back to Montgomery as fast as she came." Alice raised her nose in the air like a hound dog that had caught a particularly fine scent. "She's staying at . . . *The Riverview*. My best guest room is for family. But with Gracie's dear sister staying, . . . there just isn't any room."

Ben knew the drill. Alice had been outdistanced by another female and needed reassuring. He stifled his groan and eyed the back door with longing while Alice rattled on.

"She's not so much. Didn't even have the decency to call Gracie by her name. Called her Katie. Can you imagine our Gracie being a *Katie?*"

"Gracie set her straight, I'll bet."

"She said as much, but I noticed she took the woman's fancy present. She's going to look like a fool parading around in those fancy clothes." Alice pulled a hankie out of her sleeve and pressed it to her mouth, stifling a sob.

Ben felt his feet start to itch. But something in Alice's tone kept him from running. She was truly terrified. He let out the breath he was holding. "You think she's gonna steal your baby away, don't you?"

Alice's chin wobbled. She was building up a regular thunderstorm inside herself. But how could he be angry with her when he was worrying about the same thing?

"Look, Allie, Gracie ain't going nowhere. This will always be her home, and we will always be her folks. Can't you see how hard she's fighting to shove that other world away?" As soon as the words were out of his mouth, Ben realized his speech was meant to console himself as much as Alice.

Alice's jaw made several false starts. She was preparing to heap her own lecture on his head. But Ben hurried on before she could sermonize on money and a woman's needs, something they had never seen eye to eye on. "Haven't we taught her to stand tall and do what's right? This is hers—not ours. She'll do a fine job. We've given her most of what she needs. The rest, she'll figure out, or get help from Mr. Fontana. Don't make it hard on her. And don't think I don't know what you were doing out there at the incinerator."

Alice's face turned mutinous. He recognized the stubborn slant of her shoulders, could hear the words forming in her head, and practically taste the bittersweet denial on her tongue. After all these years, she was still trying to bamboozle him. He stifled a chuckle, knowing his laughter would only make her swell up more.

Finally, she turned toward him, still wearing a mulish frown. "It's past time for Gracie to stop dressing like a boy. I was just helping things along. We're gonna be ashes and dust and she'll be here living alone with no babies to take care of her in her old age."

"You been beating that dead horse for twenty years, Allie. You're the one who's worried about not having children to look after you. I'm truly sorry about that, but I did my best."

Alice's face reddened. She visibly deflated and fiddled with a letter in her lap. "Yes, you did. And it wasn't you that was the problem. It was me. I got bad pipes." Her rumpled hankie came out of the sleeve of her blouse. The letter fell to the floor as she held the handkerchief up to her mouth to muffle the sob.

Ben pushed himself out of his chair and shuffled to her side. Normally Alice was more inclined to give a lecture than burst into tears. What was he supposed to do? He could really like women if they didn't spout off every time their noses got out of joint. Gracie and Rita had learned early on to keep their whining to themselves or take it to Artie. But Alice saved hers for him.

He inched a little closer. "Look here, Allie. Our Gracie would take on the whole world for you. You know that. So why are you wasting all that water thinking she won't?"

"I disgraced myself this morning, acting like a jealous she-cat. Gracie tried to apologize, but I was too put off by that woman." Alice held up her hand. "Don't say it, I know what you're thinking—and you're right. I know when I've disappointed the Lord. But the fact is, now she's gone off to Montgomery without even saying goodbye. I just know she's gonna sweep me under the rug and forget me, and I'll deserve it. I said bad things about her mama. Even if they are true, I shouldn't of said them. I feel so ashamed. I'm thinking the reverend should up and run."

Ben glanced down at her salty brown head and set his hand on her small shoulder. "You were a good wife, and I was just too stubborn to make a good husband. Gracie made us both grow up. It'll be better for you this next time, you'll see."

"You're just saying that, Ben Calloway, 'cause I'm making a fool of myself. You never did know what to do with a watery woman."

"Take it, woman. It's the best I got."

Alice peered up at him with a smile and slipped her hand over the one he rested on her shoulder. "You're a fine man, Ben Calloway. We've our share of good times, haven't we?"

Ben nodded. "Remember that Christmas Gracie hitched a pair of paper wings on the back of Harriet Ackers's prize piglet and dragged it in the front door all 'cause you refused to bake a fruitcake with the nuts Delilah sent over. *Not until pigs fly,* you said."

Alice's eyes glazed over with the memory. "She was all of seven years old and already keeping us on our toes. Good thing you caught her before she pitched that poor pig over the stair rail. We'd still be in Harriet's black book." Tears of laughter dripped down Alice's cheeks. She dabbed at her face, then glanced up at Ben. "I'll sure miss not living next door."

Ben swallowed his laughter. "What do you mean?"

"Well, the reverend has a nice house near the church. No sense in me keeping this one. I plan to sell."

"*What?* To who?" He hadn't thought that far ahead. Alice had always lived next door in her daddy's old house, except for the few years she'd been married to him.

Alice's smile turned sly. "Well, I don't know. Delilah Perkins has been saying she wants a smaller house. Claims she's got a ghost in her attic."

Ben pulled his hand back. "You wouldn't. I'll buy it, if you're so set on selling it. I'm not having Delilah next door."

"You're right. Folks would talk faster and louder than they already are."

Memory lane had disappeared. Ben felt relieved. He could deal with hard-nosed Alice better than the softer version of Allie. "Dammit, woman. I take back what I said. The reverend ain't so lucky. You are just as female as ever." Ben reached down and scooped up the letter she'd dropped earlier and handed it to her. "Here you go. I'm sure the reverend is waiting for his dinner."

But Alice didn't budge. She just sat there with an expectant look on her face. "That letter is to both of us." Alice waved it in his face. "See, it says here, 'To: Mr. and Mrs. Ben Calloway.' Gracie's grandma is inviting us to tea."

"I ain't got time for finger sandwiches. Take your fancy reverend to tea. I've got to go to Montgomery and prepare Gracie for Rita's visit, or I ain't ever gonna get out of the doghouse with her."

"But Mrs. Hammond must want our help."

"To do what?"

"Make Gracie do her duty, of course."

"Gracie can make up her own mind. I'll help Gracie if she asks me, but I ain't gonna conspire against her. I'm in enough trouble with her already."

Alice clutched her best handbag closer to her side and fingered the invitation, without sparing a kind thought for Ben for leaving her to do the proper with Gracie's fancy grandma. As soon as she pushed the front gate open, she knew why he'd refused. The place had shirt-and-tie written all over it. Alice had chosen her newest lavender Sunday suit and a pair of black patent leather pumps. Clare had assured her she looked like a young Jackie Kennedy and that her prickly grandmother would be suitably impressed.

The walk leading up to the Parnells' front door was neat and trim. The concrete steps had been overlaid with cream-colored marble. Conrad Hammond had given the Parnell residence a new shine. Alice would give just about anything to see the look on the snooty Violet Parnell's face now. To think she'd snubbed Gracie for being poor and fatherless—

A stout woman in a neatly starched apron answered her knock and motioned her inside. "Mrs. Hammond is expecting you."

Alice followed her into a large room decorated in mahogany and cream. Katherine Hammond sat ramrod stiff in a tall wing-back chair. Alice's gaze paused on her slacks and polished loafers. She was the picture of elegance in silver and gold—slightly mannish, very Yankee . . . and yet, almost the spitting image of Gracie. Alice's breath clogged her throat and froze her steps.

"Cook, you may bring the tea in five minutes." She offered Alice a brief smile. "Come in, Mrs. Calloway. I know it's a shock. We should be grateful the child didn't take after my husband. He was uncomfortably tall and clumsy."

Alice seated herself on the sofa. "Our Gracie is about the most coordinated girl I know. I'd hoped she would have taken up dancing, you know, something womanly, but

Ben and Artie had their say. As soon as they found out the girl could throw a ball, it was a losing battle. My, my, but you do look like her. I must say I'm much relieved that she doesn't take after her mama."

Gracie's grandma offered her a dime-store smile with none of the trimmings. "So, you aren't overly fond of Lillian. I'm glad we agree on something."

Alice glanced at her, feeling ashamed. "It's really not my place to say. Please beg my pardon, Mrs. Hammond."

"You can be frank with me, Mrs. Calloway. Lillian is quite beautiful. However, since I'm a woman, her looks mean very little to me."

Alice didn't much care for Gracie's mama, but her grandma had possibilities. She wasn't quite sure how to deal with the woman she'd come prepared to dislike. "Very nicely put, Mrs. Hammond."

Her compliment caught Gracie's grandma by surprise. "For Gracie's sake, I'm prepared to deal with Lillian, if I have to. My objective is to convince Gracie to accept her role in the Hammond family. I could use your help. There are a number of things she needs to learn before it's my time to go."

"But you only just arrived—"

"*Go,* as in *die.* I'm not young, Mrs. Calloway."

"You don't look sickly."

"I'm not, but the future is uncertain. The loss of my son has made that very clear."

"I was sorry to hear the sad news, real sorry. I take it Gracie's daddy didn't have any brothers or sisters?"

"Childbirth is not a pleasant task. I did my duty and produced a son. I did not feel the need to repeat the experience. And then . . . my husband died and saved me from having to consider it further."

The woman's bitter declaration was a pill Alice didn't feel inclined to swallow. Alice wiped the sympathy off her face. "Children are a blessing I was never able to have. That's why Gracie is so precious to me."

The door to the kitchen swung open. Cups rattled precariously in their saucers as the cook trundled into the room.

Mrs. Hammond shot the woman a sharp look, then glanced back at Alice. "Children are a frustrating but necessary part of life. Thank goodness they grow up."

Alice felt her suppressed dislike bubbling to the surface. She'd been right after all: Katherine Hammond was a mercenary woman and would have a great deal of trouble stealing Gracie's heart.

Silently Alice accepted a cup of tea, then looked Gracie's starchy grandma in the eye. "Just why did you invite me here today, Mrs. Hammond?"

"To discuss Gracie's future, of course. Her marriage in particular."

Alice was taken aback. "*Marriage?* Our Gracie?"

"You seem to think it's an impossibility."

"I've been worrying myself sick for years trying to push her in that direction. She'll have none of it—until she finds someone she fancies."

"I think she's found someone." A smile worthy of the craftiest fox slipped across Katherine Hammond's face.

"And who would that be?" Alice sat quietly waiting for the answer she knew would follow. For the moment, she was willing to forgive Gracie's grandma for stepping ahead of her.

"Sam Fontana, naturally."

Alice took a calm sip of her tea. "He does have nice teeth." She paused, glancing over her cup. "But I don't see what you're saying. Mr. Fontana seems to rub her the wrong way."

"Yes. And she *rubs* him the wrong way, too. But he cares for her. Of that, I'm certain."

"Ben and me were the best of friends, but our marriage was a mistake. Takes a bit more than liking someone to make a good marriage."

Gracie's grandma shrugged and picked up her teacup, gracefully extending her pinkie finger. "I'm not saying I wish for the match, but my son did, so I'm considering his wisdom in this matter. He may be right. It's clear Gracie would never accept any of the young men I have in mind."

Alice set her teacup back on its delicate saucer. "What sort of young men are those?"

"Men with knowledge of business who have strong family ties in the corporate world."

Gracie's grandma had just described the sort of man she would choose but Gracie would have nothing to do with. Alice let out a sigh. "Gracie would run circles around them or strike them dead. She'd never agree."

Katherine Hammond's carefully arched brows dipped together in a fearsome frown. "Yes, well, now that I've met her, I realize my plan will need adjustment. That's why I've called on you. I believe she might accept Sam Fontana, who is the next best thing to Conrad's son."

"Pardon me for saying so, but if that's your new plan, then you should have picked someone else to deliver the Trojan horse. She's got it in her head that he's the enemy. If she has her way, she'll give him the *whole mess,* as she calls it."

"We'll just have to make sure that doesn't happen."

For the first time, she had an ally in her cause. Alice could barely suppress her excitement. "Gracie is wasting herself here, looking after folks who won't be around when she's old. She needs a family of her own. She's got a lot to give and no one to give it to."

An infectious gleam danced in the starchy woman's eyes. "It's settled, then. Let's do it."

Alice eyed the elegant woman across from her. She'd be a tough adversary but a much better ally. Marjorie Finks would never have let her win so easily. And Alice did want grandnieces and nephews in the worst way. Finally, she smiled at Gracie's Yankee grandma. "If Gracie is inclined, you won't have to ask me twice. You are quite a wicked woman, Mrs. Hammond."

"Yes, I am. Then we are in agreement?"

"On one condition—that we have the biggest wedding Shady Grove has ever seen."

Katherine Hammond's expression turned fierce. But Alice refused to back down. Gracie would never agree to a hoity-toity Greenwich society wedding. If it took place at all, it would be in Shady Grove. "It's what Gracie would want."

"You're quite a sly crocodile yourself, Alice Calloway."

"Well, bless your heart for saying so, Katie dear." Alice stood, ignoring the horrified look on Katherine Hammond's face. With Gracie's grandma on her side, Gracie's flashy mama wouldn't stand a chance.

Chapter 23

The lobby of the Riverview Hotel was just the sort of place Alice would love but Ben would hate. Gracie was caught somewhere in the middle. The grandeur gave her the urge to gawk and bolt all at the same time.

While Sam handed the man their bags, Gracie stored up the images so she could share them with Artie when she got home. It was like a scene from one of Alice's old Hollywood movies, with the tiered fountain bubbling merrily in the center of a rotunda and the potted palms racing slender mahogany columns to the glass ceiling two stories overhead. Men wore business suits and women wore soft flowery dresses as they hustled back and forth across the polished marble floor.

The new calico dress that was too fancy for the likes of Shady Grove had her feeling like a secondhand Sally, but Sam didn't seem bothered.

He finished with the bellman and laced her arm with his, pulling her close to his side. "Don't worry, you look fine—actually better than fine. If it makes you feel any better, most of these people have credit card bills that could choke a horse."

Gracie scanned the lobby for Lillian. "Alice says credit cards are God's revenge on the foolish."

Sam chuckled, then propelled her through the entrance to the hotel restaurant. "You give the sign, and we're out of here, *capisce*?"

Across the room, Lillian raised her hand and waved at Gracie. "There she is." Gracie waved back and led Sam in Lillian's direction.

"Just give me a sign when you want to leave. Flick your hair or something."

Gracie stopped abruptly and spun to face Sam. "I don't flick my hair."

"I know. You get this little crinkle in your forehead"—Sam reached out and smoothed his thumb over the spot above the bridge of her nose—"right there."

Gracie's stomach went fluttery for a moment. "I do?"

"Yes, you do."

He replaced his thumb with a warm kiss, a simple gesture that made her tingle in the all the wrong places and her knees feel like jelly.

Gracie caught herself as she leaned into Sam. Suddenly she was aware of all the eyes turned their way. "Maybe you should wait for me in your room."

"Sorry, sweetheart, no can do. I promised Kate."

His husky whisper set Gracie's cheeks on fire. She pulled away to hide her reaction and set off in Lillian's direction, leaving Sam to tag behind.

Lillian's sunny smile faded when they reached the table. "So nice of Mr. Fontana to escort you. But I'm afraid we only have room for two—"

Sam grabbed an extra chair from a nearby table and planted himself next to Gracie. "We've been having a problem with the press lately. I'm sure you'll understand if I stay, Lillian."

Her mama's face cemented into a tight smile. "Well then, Mr. Fontana, perhaps you could find the waiter and tell him to bring the wine list. I've changed my mind. I'd like to order a bottle, after all."

Gracie shot Sam a pleading look. "Wine would be nice."

Sam held her gaze, then rose abruptly from the table. "Be right back."

When he'd disappeared, Lillian reached across the table and slipped her hand over Gracie's, squeezing it lightly. "I ran into one of Conrad's attorneys. I understand you have an appointment tomorrow." She didn't give Gracie time to answer but rattled on. "An unsettling experience, certainly. But I want you to know, I'm here to lend you support."

Gracie was taken by surprise. Without asking, she knew Sam distrusted her mama almost as much as Alice did. What excuse could she offer but the truth? "Sam is going to take me."

Her mama's face looked pinched as she leaned in close and whispered across the table. "Perhaps you are unaware of the fact that Mr. Fontana is the son of the police officer who investigated your kidnapping." She broke off and shuddered. "His father fabricated horrible lies to hide his own lack of diligence during the investigation. He wasted precious hours questioning me, when he could have been searching for you."

Gracie recalled the smiling man standing next to her daddy in the photo. "What do you mean?"

Lillian tightened her grip on Gracie's hand and shot her a fierce look. "Joe Fontana *accused me* of the unthinkable. And your father believed him. I would have come out with little more than the clothes on my back if I hadn't given him custody of you—By that time, they'd presumed you were dead. The media had a field day—*at my expense*. Thanks to Joe Fontana, my husband and friends turned against me. I cannot begin to tell you how much I hated that man."

Gracie spotted Sam looking in her direction. "But Sam needs to be there—" She turned back to Lillian and lowered her voice. "He's what I call my escape button. Meaning no disrespect to my daddy, but this money has caused me no end of trouble. First the reporters won't leave me alone, then Jimmy is giving away my job, not to mention Alice running off with the reverend. And that's only a partial list of what's gone wrong. If I didn't have to wait six months, Sam would be signing tomorrow instead of me."

Her mama yanked her hand away. *"What? Don't be a fool.* Joe Fontana's son is a nobody —*from New London.* He has done nothing to deserve a penny of Conrad's fortune. Tell me you're *not* serious."

Sam reappeared at Gracie's side and offered her mama the wine list. "The 1970 Beaulieu cab comes highly recommended." His voice cut the air with a sharp edge Gracie had never heard him use before. A long silence followed his words.

Her mama shot out of her chair so fast it tipped backward and landed with an echoing thud on the marble floor, effectively extinguishing the buzz of conversation in the dining room. All eyes were on Lillian as she stormed around the table in Sam's direction. "You're just like your father." She turned a fierce look on Gracie. "If you give this . . . *this* . . . *leech* your inheritance, you will be throwing away everything your father worked for—and *died* for, I might add."

Gracie felt her stomach do a somersault. "What do you mean—*died* for?"

"He worked himself to death. His doctor warned him to slow down. Don't look so surprised, *Katherine.* He didn't make all that money sitting on a beach in the Caymans. He was determined to build an empire for you, so you'd have everything your heart desired. I know because I sat alone more nights than I can count so he could build a future for *you*. He was obsessed. He needed more, even though we had plenty. Do you know where he was the day you disappeared? In Japan, making the biggest deal of his career, the one that put Hammond Industries on the top of Fortune Five Hundred list. It was all for you. And you want to *give it away*—"

Gracie felt like she'd been washed out of a deep sleep with a bucket of icy water. Her father had been eccentric—she got that. The temperature-controlled collection room at the Parnell house was odd—the mark of a man obsessed with perfection, she had to admit—but her mama made her daddy sound like a crazy man.

"If you choose to side with Mr. Fontana, I promise you, you'll regret your decision. Call me, when you come to your senses, *Katherine*." Lillian grabbed her purse off the table, withdrew a card, then tossed it at Gracie.

Gracie caught the card before it fluttered to the floor. *Katherine?* The strange name coming from her mama sounded like a dirty word. Gracie felt her insides shrink up. The feeling was not much different from the one she'd experienced when she'd been called *Love Baby* all those years ago.

The last of her old dream vanished in a *poof.*

Of all the voices in her head, it was Alice's that spoke first. *Folks is best measured by what they do, not by what you'd wish they'd do.* Wasn't that the truth? She'd been wishing hard all her years for a mama who didn't exist. But she couldn't figure out how to let go.

Lillian was still fuming when she reached her hotel room. She'd heard Kate had hired the younger Fontana as her errand boy, but she'd underestimated the extent of his role. Never would she have considered him a threat. What was Kate thinking? She heaved her handbag at the bed and headed for the minibar. The truth was, she needed money. It wasn't a secret; Kate was certainly aware of the fact.

A lavish bouquet of pink roses had appeared in her absence. Lord Devon—again. He was persistent. She'd give him that. She'd almost taken him up on his proposal until Kate's name had slipped off his lips. She was convinced his eagerness to wed had nothing to do with deep affection but everything to do with Kate's need to see her out of the picture.

If Devon was still paying court after she'd turned him down, there must be a reason. Chances were Kate's attorneys had a carrot—a prime piece of real estate or, more likely, a donation to Devon's favorite project, the restoration of his crumbling Yorkshire estate—

an archaic monstrosity. Kate's questions regarding Devon's proposal and her unexpected offer to finance Lillian's jaunt to Monte Carlo where he was vacationing suddenly made sense.

But Lillian refused to be consigned to a life in an aging pile of stone in the wilds of the English countryside with a man who loved his house more than his wife.

The announcement of her daughter's existence had come as a shock. She'd actually gotten physically ill and had to excuse herself from dinner. She told those who'd come knocking on her door that she had the flu. But the truth was, she'd been consumed by fear of the old lies and suspicions plastered across the front of every cheap news rag along with her picture. Until this morning, she'd only half believed her daughter was alive. The doubt was gone. The girl who called herself Gracie had grown into the spitting image of Conrad's mother—another horrible injustice.

Lillian poured orange juice and vodka into a glass. The phone rang. Lillian's pulse jumped. Thank God! Her daughter had come to her senses. Carefully she steadied her hand and took a long sip of her screwdriver, then picked up. "Hello?"

"Lillian?" It was a man's voice, one she didn't recognize.

"Who is this?"

"I'm offended, you have to ask. It's Martin . . . Jones. Did you find the envelope I gave you *interesting?*"

Envelope? She'd been so eager to get to Alabama, she'd forgotten about the envelope Martin had handed her at Conrad's estate. He'd said they were photos. She assumed they were shots of herself, Conrad, and the baby.

Lillian crossed the room to her carryon and withdrew the envelope, then spilled the contents on the bed. The poor quality black-and-white photos were of Conrad and an older man standing in the lobby of Hammond Industries.

"Why did you think I'd be interested in these?"

"The man standing next to Conrad is none other than Ben Calloway—"

Lillian moved toward the lamp and examined them more closely. It was the man who claimed to be her daughter's yokel uncle, *Ben Calloway.* She'd seen clips of him on the news. He'd made her blood boil with his pretend indifference. "When were these photos taken?"

"Who knows? The dates are . . . strangely missing. Could have been anytime in the last twenty-five years . . . I thought you would know best."

The last twenty-five years . . . She examined the photo more closely. The lobby they were standing in had been remodeled years ago—*eight, to be exact.* She remembered the double-page spread of the pricey renovation in the Sunday section of the *Times*. It was about the time Conrad began liquidating his foreign investments . . .

The insistence during the divorce that he be given full custody of their missing daughter, should she be found alive, now made sense. Lillian's mind raced through the list of summer homes she'd borrowed from friends who had taken pity on her in her straightened circumstances.

Conrad had played her for a fool. He'd been keeping their daughter a secret, for who knew how long, so he wouldn't have to compensate her for her parental rights.

Resentment returned in a flash, but Lillian caught it before it blossomed into rage. She needed a cool head. Martin was nobody's fool. "Why would you give these to me now?"

A muffled chuckle filtered though the line. "Because I'd like to retire, and your dear departed ex-husband did not make provisions for such an event in my life. I dare say, you of all people know what that feels like." He paused for emphasis, before he went on. "I'd say the originals are worth . . . two hundred grand. Maybe even more—to you. I'm convinced you know where they belong."

His confident tone irritated her. Like Kate, she'd never much cared for the pompous Martin

Jones, but revenge didn't require friendship, and Conrad was only getting what he deserved. Lillian let the silence linger as she studied the photos and considered her options. Kate's animosity and Sam Fontana's smug grin, which reminded her so much of his father's, made the decision for her.

She wouldn't have to do much. Put pressure in the right places. A friendly inquiry from the Fairfield County D.A.'s office to the local law enforcement would be enough to convince the Calloways that she meant business. She wouldn't even have to release the photos to the press. Katherine would pay to avoid more scandal connected to Conrad's name.

"Mr. Jones, I accept your offer."

Chapter 24

Gracie had declined Sam's offer of an evening on the town, then shooed him out her door. Sam left her studying the room service menu and retreated to his own room, giving her time to sort out her feelings regarding Lillian.

Ben's jumbled SOS message had been waiting for him on the phone. Sam hurried downstairs to the lobby. Ben Calloway stuck out like a hooker at Bergdorf's. He'd come straight from work. His khaki work shirt was stained with rust and grease.

Sam stretched out his hand and steered him toward the bar. "You look like a man who could use a beer."

When they had each ordered a bottle, Ben swung his gaze to Sam. "Where's Gracie?"

"Upstairs experiencing the joys of room service. What's up?"

"I got a call from Rita. She wants to talk to Gracie. Knowing Rita, she's likely to show up on the doorstep in the middle of the night. I figure I owe it to Gracie to be straight with her. She's had enough surprises for one year."

"Where's Rita now?"

"She wouldn't say. But she's on her way to

Alabama. The news reports have spooked her. She always was a skittish thing. Not tough like Our Gracie."

Sam knew enough about Gracie to know Ben had pegged her wrong. She wasn't tough at all. She just put up a hell of a good front, like Conrad. Though he didn't doubt the Calloways' love for Gracie, it didn't take a fortune-teller to point out the fact that Alice and Ben were blind dogs, and that Artie Dubois was Gracie's only ace in the hole.

Sam sat silently as Ben dithered with his napkin. "Rita's got it into her head that the FBI is waiting to arrest her for kidnapping Gracie. I told her that was nonsense. It was a long time ago, and like I told Mr. Hammond nearly eight years ago—it weren't her doing in the first place. It was that scalawag, Mr. Fry, who done most of the dirty work. Gracie's safe and sound. That's all that matters." Ben paused, looking at him expectantly.

He wanted reassurance that Rita was in the clear. Sam wasn't ready to let Rita off the hook so easily. She'd hurt Gracie and owed her more than a casual, *Sorry, kid.* "There's no statute of limitations on kidnapping. I can't promise anything."

Confusion registered on Ben's face. "Gracie's daddy said he took care of things. He made sure the case was shut tight."

Sam spotted panic in Ben's gaze. It didn't take a mind reader to know that Rita held a special place in Ben's heart that even Gracie couldn't touch.

Sam couched his resentment for Gracie's sake. "*Closed?* Since when?"

"Since Gracie turned eighteen. Mr. Hammond wanted things kept quiet so as not to upset Gracie. That was fine by me."

If Ben was looking for approval, he wasn't going to get it from him. Sam was on Gracie's side. "When does Rita expect to be here?"

"She didn't say."

Sam nodded, then rose from the table. "I'll give Gracie a shout. You can tell her yourself."

Ben latched on to Sam's arm. "Mr. Hammond figured there was a possibility that someone besides that Eddie Fry fellow might have been involved in Gracie's kidnapping—*not Rita.*"

Ben's news didn't break any sound barriers. "Did Conrad say who?"

"He was mighty closed-mouthed. He told me and Skippy to watch over her. If any strangers were to ever show up in Shady Grove, we was to call him right away."

"Evers was in on it too?" *Why hadn't Conrad asked for his help?*

Ben read his confusion. His gaze took on a fatherly tilt. "He didn't tell you 'cause he didn't want anyone poking around up there who might set off an alarm. He figured we were far enough out of the picture. No one but Mr. Hammond and me knew who Gracie was, after Rita gave up the news. Even Skipper, Alice, and Artie didn't know the whole story."

"Did he say anything about Lillian?" Sam watched Ben's face carefully for a reaction, but Ben's attention had wandered off.

Sam's followed the path of Ben's gaze. Lillian Hammond's unmistakable blond head turned his way as she crossed the room. Her gaze widened with surprise when it latched on to Ben.

Sam stood up as she stopped in front of the table. "Lillian, I assumed you would be upstairs packing."

Lillian ignored him and glared at Ben. Her nose wrinkled slightly. "Where's my daughter, Mr. Fontana? I assume you haven't lost her?"

"She's safe, if that's what you mean."

Ben rose from the table and nodded in Lillian's direction but didn't extend his hand. Sam couldn't blame him. Lillian was giving off death rays.

Her sharp gaze tripped over the name embossed on Ben's work shirt. "So you're the one I have to thank for raising my daughter."

Ben looked confused. Lillian's tone was a long way from thankful. Sam stepped into her line of vision and shot her a warning glance.

But Ben would have none of his interference.

He shifted closer to Lillian. "Yes, ma'am. Our Gracie is a real pleasure. We love her more than words can say."

Lillian retreated slightly. "Well, I hope that will keep you warm at night when I press you with kidnapping conspiracy charges, Mr. Calloway." She turned away abruptly.

Ben reached for her arm. "Now hold on just a minute—"

"*No.* You listen *to me.* You conspired with my husband to steal my daughter. I have proof, and *you* are going to pay—one way . . . or the other."

Lillian spun around and stormed toward the lobby, brushing past a startled Gracie without even seeing her.

Gracie rushed toward Ben. Her eyes flashed with panic. "What are you doing here? Where's Artie?"

"Slow down, girl. Artie's fine. He's got Alice jumping through hoops like a circus dog, fetching this and that. I came 'cause I got news I wanted you to hear from me straight."

Gracie shifted closer to Sam. "Okay. Let's have it."

This time Sam didn't feel sorry for Ben. He'd lost Gracie's trust on his own, and it was his job to earn it back.

Ben pulled his cap out of his back pocket and fumbled with the brim. "The short of it is, Rita called. She's planning on paying us a visit. She's set on talking to you. In case she arrives before you get home, I wanted you to know." Ben inched nervously toward the exit. "I got to get back and relieve Alice. You sign those papers without any fuss like Mr. Fontana says, you hear?"

Gracie cut a path toward the hotel room window and glanced back at Sam. He'd perched himself on the end of her big wide bed while she worked off steam from Ben's news. Sam Fontana really was a saint. He had the patience she lacked, and then some. The fact that he was there gave her comfort.

She took a calming breath. When her heartbeat had finally settled into an even rhythm, she took up a seat beside him. "Thanks for being there this afternoon. I hoped things would turn out different."

"It's not your fault, you know." Sam had turned his head sideways and was looking at her out of one eye. A tentative half smile curved his mouth.

She was conscious of his thigh against hers, but she didn't move away. She needed his solid reassurance. "I'll keep telling myself that. Maybe someday, I'll believe it."

"I'll remind you when you forget." Sam's voice was warm and teasing, but the unsettling evening hung with her.

She couldn't get over the fact that Rita was

finally coming home. Her birthday wish had been answered—too late. It seemed like years instead of weeks since she'd blown out her candles and spied Sam smiling at her through the smoke as she whispered her old wish one last time. So much had happened . . .

She glanced at Sam. "Why would Rita show up now? Maybe Alice is right. Maybe it is the money."

His left brow went up, much the way Artie's did when he wanted her to consider another line of thinking. "Or maybe Rita is worried about you . . ."

Gracie's stomach did a soft flip at the idea. There had been only three people in her small life she could count on to worry about her: Ben, Alice, and Artie. It occurred to her that now she had a few more, starting with Sam. But somehow him worrying about her was different. Sam's worrying was growing more personal with each passing day.

Gracie offered him a shy smile. "Rita worried about *me?* That *will* take some getting used to. So, when is she going to be here?"

"Ben didn't say. I think he's afraid the authorities might be waiting to arrest her for the part she played in your kidnapping."

Gracie had to admit the thought had crossed her mind, too. Rita had been the placeholder for her mama all these years, which accounted for something—and she'd sent cards and birthday presents. . .

"Is Rita in trouble? Even though Ben doesn't like to admit it, he worries about her." Gracie shot Sam a stoic smile. She figured she owed half of Ben's love to Rita. She heard it in his voice every time Rita's name worked its way into the conversation. Now that Lillian was officially her mama, she wasn't so sure where she stood with Ben.

Sam slipped his big hand over hers. "According to Ben, Rita claims Eddie Fry used her as a place to stash his stolen goods—and not for the first time. Eddie and Rita had been an item. Seems he had a history of preying on needy women. Earlier that year, Rita was arrested for stealing booze from the country club where she and Eddie worked. Kate's team of legal beagles checked the records. Her testimony points the finger at Eddie, saying he stashed the bottles in her car. Unfortunately for her, he had an alibi— with the right connections. Because it was her first offense, Rita got off with a heavy dose of community service. But the judge promised to lock her up and throw away the key if he ever saw her in his courtroom again. I know the guy —Honorable John the Executioner. He's tough and has the size to back it up. The man is six foot six and weighs in at three fifty. Got a bellow that could stop a train."

What little Gracie knew about Rita, she'd gathered from hushed conversations over the years. But one thing was clear in all reports—Rita was skittish and tended to bolt at the first sign of trouble, just like Ben. "So, how *did* she get her hands on me?"

"When Rita called Ben to confess your identity, she told him that Eddie dumped you on her, claiming you were his sister's kid. He said he had an emergency to attend to and promised he would be back in an hour to collect you. Ben says Rita is a soft touch and felt sorry for you—evidently you had a strong set of lungs and were crying up a storm." Sam laced his fingers through hers and gave her hand a tight squeeze while throwing her one of his teasing smiles.

Gracie placed her free hand over his, sandwiching his warmth between her fingers. "Keep going. You haven't gotten to the happily-ever-after part."

"Right. Well, according to Ben, when Eddie was discovered drowned in the river with one of your toys and a baby seat in the back of his car, the media went haywire with the story. That's when Rita realized who you were and panicked."

"And ran for the safest place she knew . . ."

Gracie thanked her stars she had no recollection of the event. She thought of all the years she'd branded Rita a lousy mama and chicken, when all Rita really had was a healthy fear of going to jail for something she didn't do. "If Ben had known who I was then, he would have given me back."

"And chances are Rita would have done time in jail, since she knew who you were when she took off for Alabama."

"Ben would never have been able to live with himself. He blames himself for Rita's wild ways. And Alice never fails to remind him of Rita's mistakes. She's the reason Ben and Alice split up. They never could agree about Rita."

"Or maybe they didn't love each other the way a man and woman need to."

"What way is that?"

Sam raised her hand to his lips, then turned it over and kissed her palm with a feather-soft kiss. "Someday, Gracie, you'll find out. And it'll be good. I promise."

His warm lips against her skin set off a vibration unlike any she'd ever felt before. She wanted him to show her, not someday—now. She unlocked her fingers from his and redirected his hands to her waist and leaned close to his mouth. "Show me, Sam. Right now, please."

"All right, Gracie." There was no sign of his cocky smile. He was as shy and uncertain as she was.

She leaned in and pressed her lips lightly to his, giving him the encouragement he needed.

She heard his breath catch in his throat. Then gently he tugged her backward onto the bed and deepened the kiss. His touch was tentative at first, moving over the curve of her hip to the small of her back. He was waiting for another signal from her.

Gracie kicked off her sandals and wrapped her arms around his neck, fingering the long hair at the nape of his neck. "I'm ready for lesson two."

Sam rolled her on top of him and focused on her mouth. "I'm not sure I'm clear on lesson one. How did it go again?"

She reached out to touch his bottom lip with the tip of her finger. "Maybe you need a refresher lesson." She pressed herself against him and was rewarded with a soft chuckle that sent goose bumps up her arms.

Sam pushed his tongue into her mouth, deepening the kiss as his hand drifted from her hip to her front. Gently he rubbed the inside of her thighs through the fabric of her dress, until her breath came in ragged gasps. Gracie arched her body against his hand, guiding the pressure. "Sam?"

"I'm here." He slipped his hand under the hem of her dress and let it ride hot over the tops of her thighs before it dipped deep between her legs. His touch was light—maddeningly so.

Gracie pushed her hips upward. The sensation erupted into a blast of heat that subsided slowly into a deeper yearning. Gracie gulped for air. "Okay, I think you've got the hang of it."

His husky chuckle tickled her ear. "You think so?"

"Yeah. I'd say you're ready for lesson two." Her heart was still beating a hundred miles an hour.

His laughter shook the bed. Gracie pulled back to get a better view of his face in dim light. "Are you laughing at me, Yankee?"

Sam sobered instantly. "Nope, Gracie. I'm not laughing at you. You've shown me things I never knew were out there—good things." She could feel the need rolling off his body. He was ready for the next lesson, and so was she.

"Sam?" Gracie's voice sounded small, breathless, even to her own ears.

"Yeah?"

"Is there a lesson three?"

"Yes, Gracie, there is. Even better than one and two."

Chapter 25

Sam let the conference door slam behind him as he raced down the hall after Gracie. Her good mood had continued through a hasty breakfast, but the meeting with the attorney Jason Myer had ended abruptly. Gracie had signed the documents without bloodshed—just barely.

He deftly dodged a bellman pushing a load of suitcases, then stepped into pace beside Gracie. "What was that? Why did you tell him it may not matter in six months?"

"I never made any promises or kept my feelings a secret. Clare should have been here. This concerns her, too." Gracie's legs might not have been as long as his, but she could cover ground fast.

"Conrad knew Clare wouldn't be interested. She told you so herself." Sam had to use some serious muscle to keep up. He was weighted down by her purse, which she'd left on the conference table in her rush to escape.

Gracie came to a halt and waved a file folder of the recently signed documents in his face. "I don't understand how my daddy could choose one child and ignore the other." Gracie didn't wait for his reply. She set off again down the hall.

Sam stepped into pace beside her. "You know the answer. Conrad knew you would know what to do. Clare would let her mother muscle in. Marcia rarely thinks past the next social function. Clare would be no more than a high-priced carrot. Be honest, is that what you want for her?"

Gracie came to a stop. Frustration, disappointment, and fear all had a turn on her face. "Clare is nobody's fool. She just needs a little more starch in her drawers, that's all."

"You've already got starch. Jason Myer looked almost human when you told him to button his lip."

Myer's veiled innuendoes at her country manners hadn't slipped past Gracie. She'd caught every one of them, until she'd been forced to say what Sam was thinking—*pass the pen and shut the hell up*. Not exactly in those words, better ones that only Gracie could put together. *Mr. Myer, in Shady Grove we have annoying birds that do nothing but chatter in the most gawd-awful pitch. Your ears just want to fall off the sides of your head, rather than listen to them. You know why they chatter? 'Cause they don't know how to sing, can't hold a tune to save their lives. They don't last long in Shady Grove if they squawk. Everyone keeps a slingshot or a pelt gun handy. And you know, those birds are learning to hold their tongues if they want to live to lay an egg.*

Myer had turned an angry red—but sure enough, buttoned his lip until the signing was complete. Even now, Sam smiled at the memory.

Gracie propped one hand on her hip and leaned in close. He could feel her warm breath on his lips. "That man reminds me of all the reasons I don't want to have anything to do with his kind. What do you suppose his mama was thinking of when she raised him?"

"Guys like Jason Myer hardly ever saw their mamas. They were raised by a string of nannies and maids, a different set in each of his parents' households."

Gracie looked thoughtful, not shocked, like Sam had expected. "What if I have children? What if they turn out like him? Money changes the way you think even when you don't want it to. That man's folks didn't set out to make their son into a callous worm."

"I suspect he was born that way. But Gracie, you're different. Look, already you see the difference between people like Jason Myer and who you want to be."

Gracie shot him a look of disbelief, then marched toward the elevator. "I have shopping to do before we go home. You sure you want to come?"

He couldn't unleash her on the city alone. Her mood was still stomping through the swamp, ravaging evil gatorlike attorneys. "Why not? You go into a store and buy stuff, right? No big deal."

Gracie dodged his gaze, but he caught the pink glow of her cheeks beneath the curtain of her hair. Her voice practically dropped to a whisper. "Yeah, but I need *girl stuff*. Alice burned those, too."

Sam glanced down at his shoes. "Oh . . . well, fine. I'm okay with that." The elevator doors opened. Sam ushered Gracie inside, then hit the button for the floor to their rooms. While they waited for the numbers to pass overhead, Sam ran his finger under his collar to loosen his tie. The thought of Gracie in anything with lace sent his body into a spin.

"You look a little flushed. Maybe I should go by myself."

"Sorry, princess. I'm afraid you're stuck with me. Remind me to pick up the tickets at the front desk. They were delivered this morning."

"Really? Wait until I tell Artie—"

The smile on Gracie's face did things to his heart he didn't want to think about. After their lovemaking last night, he'd realized Conrad's imp of a daughter owned a piece of him. What really surprised him was the thought that he'd been saving it for her all along. Conrad had had a way of slipping ideas into people's heads.

Sam tried to keep what they'd shared last

night in perspective as they stopped in front of Gracie's door. He hadn't kissed her since they'd gotten out of bed four hours ago. He leaned on the door with an ease he didn't feel. "Here we are. Got your key handy?"

Gracie slipped her card into the slot. The look she gave him as the green light flashed said she'd forgotten all about Jason Myer.

Sam reached past her hip and yanked on the door handle. Slowly he backed her into the room, his lips brushing hers with promises before realizing that they weren't alone.

Skip Evers lounged in a chair near the window. Sam whirled around, shoving Gracie behind his back. "What are you doing here? And how'd you get in?"

"Ben asked me to come. I need to talk to Gracie." Evers stood up. His gaze jumped past Sam's, then followed Gracie as she stepped out from behind him. Waves of silent communication zipped past Sam's ear.

Sam shot Skip a questioning look. "Evers, who's keeping an eye on Clare?"

"She's with Alice. Reverend Adams is supervising." Evers was answering Sam's question, but his gaze was intent on Gracie's.

Sam reached over to steady Gracie, but a sob broke from her chest as she bolted past him. The next thing Sam knew, she was locked in Evers's big bear hug and wetting his shirt with tears.

Evers's watery gaze caught his. This time the silent message was for him. Artie Dubois was gone.

The packet of freshly signed legal papers he'd cajoled Gracie into signing felt insignificant in his hand. Artie might never have been rich, but he'd had one thing money couldn't buy—Gracie's love. For all his millions, even Conrad hadn't had that. And God knows Conrad would have traded his money for that one thing. Maybe that's what he'd tried to do in the end. Maybe that's why he gave Gracie a way out. He'd wanted her to have a choice—because he loved her and always had. For the same reason, Sam knew that he'd step in, if she chose not to do it herself.

Ben collected the letter with Gracie's name scrawled across it from the lamp table beside Artie's bed and slipped it into his shirt pocket. A car pulled up outside in the drive. A shadow moved passed the bedroom window toward the back door. That should be Chantel coming to pick out a suit for the burial. She said she had instructions from Artie; knew just which one he wanted. Ben had to admit he was relieved he didn't have to be the one to choose. He was still carrying around the image of Artie's still body lying there with the quiet laughter gone from his eyes.

Ben shook off the ache in the back of his throat. Plenty of folks would be crying. He was a grown man, too old to blubber about losing his best friend. Noisy grieving belonged to the women.

Above the light switch was a photo of him and Artie in their uniforms. He hadn't seen the picture in thirty years, maybe more. Ben slipped it off the hook. Artie was wearing a big smile. Ben felt one of his own tug at the corners of his mouth. "Arthur Dubois, you are one sly, sorry man, leaving me your picture—like I'd forget. I'm sure as hell gonna miss your ugly face."

Ben tucked the photo under his arm. He knew just about everybody in Shady Grove, knew where they'd been born, who their mamas and daddies were, and even knew how they took their coffee. But he didn't know any of them like he'd known Artie.

They'd been young and immortal, full of dreams of glory when they'd set off for Korea. They'd stuck together through the horrors of war and bad-luck marriages, the death of Artie's boy, then Artie's fight with Jim Beam. When they'd run out of ways to save each other, Gracie came along and saved them both.

Ben was halfway across the living room when the back door burst open and Chantel stumbled in huffing and puffing. "Burgess is on his way over here right this minute. He's got a warrant for your arrest. You better run. I'll tell him you're out tangling with that big catfish you spotted in Miller's Pond."

"What are you talking about, girl?"

"Gracie's mama gonna string you up on kidnappin' charges. You need to vamoose."

"Well, she did say she would. Nice to know she's a woman of her word, in some respects."

"Has that Witch Perkins put a hex on you? You're gonna be spendin' Wednesdays with Burgess's pet alligator in a room with bars. His time on the loose has given him a taste for live meat. You need to scoot."

Ben plopped down in his chair. "I didn't kidnap Gracie. Her mama knows that. I ain't gonna run away 'cause of somethin' I didn't do. You go on and get Artie's suit like he told you. Then you give Mr. Fontana a call and tell him I expect him to look after Gracie while I'm—"

"While Burgess's lizard makes *a snack* out of you. Uh-huh, I'll tell her. Maybe I better be pickin' up a suit for you. too. Brown don't show the blood so much. I'd go with brown."

"Calm down, girl. Burgess don't believe I snatched Gracie. There's lots of folks who know I wasn't anywhere near Connecticut when she disappeared."

A hard knock echoed on the front door. Chantel marched toward Artie's room. "I ain't gonna tell my best friend that I handed her fool uncle

341

over to the law. No, sir. You'll have to answer it by your own self."

Ben set the photo down on the table and pushed out of the chair. Chantel was just upset over Artie. They all were. Burgess would come in and they'd sit at the kitchen table, kill a couple of beers and he'd be gone, leaving Ben with a warning not to leave town before sunrise.

Ben wrenched the door open with a howdy on his lips, but Burgess wasn't alone. An Amazon-like woman in a neatly pressed uniform towered beside him. It was the shiny U.S. marshal's badge that held his gaze.

Burgess fumbled with his hat. "I'd heard you was fishing. Why ain't you?"

Burgess knew why. They'd both been by Artie's bedside near midnight when Doc had pronounced him dead. Neither one of them had had any sleep after that.

"You heard wrong." Ben nodded to the woman next to Burg's shoulder.

Burg tipped his head toward the stranger. "Ben, this here's Marshal Bailey from Montgomery. She'd like to have a talk with you about Gracie. Mind if we step inside?" Burgess didn't wait for Ben's reply. He ushered the marshal into the living room while Ben remained standing.

"I'm real sorry about Artie. My condolences to the family."

"Thank you. I'll tell Gracie you stopped by." Ben parked himself inside the open door. The long-legged woman stood at attention close by. Nothing about her made Ben think this was going to be a friendly call. Gracie's mama had been busy.

The sheriff paced the floor, stopping to glance at the picture Ben had set on the table. "I was always jealous of you and Artie getting to see action, while I was stuck behind a desk in North Carolina. You got to be heroes, and I got food poisoning."

When Ben shifted in front of the doorway, the marshal took a long step to block his movement, then motioned toward his chair. "Why don't you make yourself comfortable, Mr. Calloway."

Burgess stopped his pacing. "Might as well, Ben. This might take a while."

He didn't like this any more than Ben did. For Burg's sake, he eased himself into his chair. "There, y'all more comfortable now?"

Burgess sent him a relieved smile but didn't stop his dithering.

Marshal Bailey, on the other hand, was calm as a rock. He'd bet she could stare down ten men his size with her cool blue eyes. She took a stand in front of him. "Mr. Calloway, how did you come into possession of the Hammond baby?"

Ben glanced at Burgess, but it was clear the

situation was out of his control. One way or the other this woman was going to get the answers to her questions. "My niece left her on my doorstep. When I went out to get the morning paper, there she was."

"And you just assumed the baby belonged to your niece?"

"She left a note saying as much. I figured she was doing what she thought best for the child. Burgess, here, seen the note."

"That's right. Ben showed it to me when I came over to pay my respects to the little girl."

The woman looked unimpressed by Burg's testimony. "Did you ever try to find your niece and verify the child's identity?"

She was starting to get on his nerves. "I figured she'd tell me when she was ready."

The woman's face swelled up like a red balloon. "Tell me, Mr. Calloway, what deal did you make with Conrad Hammond?"

There was only so much nonsense a man could take sitting on his behind. Ben stood up. "Now, you're trying to put words in my mouth. I don't have to say a thing until I talk to a lawyer."

"That's your choice, Mr. Calloway."

"No, ma'am, it's my right. Seems to me, y'all are *making* it my choice."

Chantel lingered in the doorway of Artie's room, her eyes as big as dinner plates. The woman had been so intent on getting her answers, she hadn't noticed her standing in the shadows.

Ben turned her way. "You get that suit to your mama now, you hear? And tell her not to worry about a thing. I took care of the funeral arrangements. She just needs to pick out the color of the flowers she likes best."

Before Ben got to the door, he remembered the letter in his pocket. He held out the envelope to Chantel. "See that Gracie gets this."

Chapter 26

Sam glanced over at Gracie as they left Montgomery behind. She'd been silent since he'd trundled her into the car. She was beating herself up over Artie and the fact that she wasn't there when he needed her. In another thirty miles, he'd have to work up the courage to tell her about Ben's arrest. Chantel had called him in a panic with news about Ben while Gracie was crying her heart out on Evers's shoulder.

As the miles disappeared, he could feel Artie's presence, almost see his gray brow raised over one eye in that knowing way that made you dig deeper and tell the truth.

When the silence got the better of him, he glanced over at Gracie. "It isn't your fault. You know that, right?"

Gracie kept her gaze trained out the window. Her bottom lip wobbled. A tear broke loose and trickled down the tip of her nose and dropped onto her lap, making a dark spot on her new jeans. "We didn't keep secrets from each other. He shut me out."

"Maybe he wasn't shutting you out so much as he was shutting himself in—making peace with himself."

He'd been where she was now. His dad had been his other half. He knew from experience there was little that could be said that would ease the kind of pain she was going through. He wanted to stop the truck and offer his shoulder, absorb her grief, but it wasn't time yet.

He drove on, glancing occasionally in her direction as the buildings thinned out and the trees took their place. A myriad of images of his father's face were interspersed between the passing landscape and roadside signs. With them came his father's rich baritone and unchecked laughter.

Gradually, Joe Fontana's voice faded as Gracie's words rose above the hum of the tires. "I couldn't have had a better mama or daddy. Our skin might not have been the same color, but our hearts beat faster over the same things."

Sam listened while Gracie's gaze clung to the swirl of green outside the window. He was beginning to need her words as much as she did. Her voice was a soft but steady rhythm inside the car.

". . . Sometimes we would walk into town and chat up a pretty widow woman who worked at the newsstand on Pecan Street. Artie's wife, Leonie, ran off and left him when their son died. Artie said he didn't want to get married again . . . he just liked to hear a woman's voice now and then. The widow woman had a fine set of lungs.

Artie would make me close my eyes and listen, but I could never carry a tune like her."

Gracie turned his way. "I am what Artie made me, not Conrad Hammond's little rich girl. I swear and I go barefoot. I'm proud of the people I love, and my home. I can't abandon those things."

"I don't think Conrad would want you to. That's why he left you in Alabama. That's why he gave you an out . . . if that's what you want."

"Some out. You don't want the money any more than I do." Gracie was silent for a minute. Then her attention zeroed back on him. "Just what sort of man was my father?"

"Well, he couldn't carry a tune, either. But he did have good teeth, like me. Alice would have approved."

Gracie shot him a warning glance that said she wasn't in the mood to laugh.

"Okay. He was a private sort of guy. Not many people could get close to him. I guess my dad was one of the few people he confided in."

"What about you? Did he confide in you?"

"Not so much. I was younger . . . and I turned down his job offer. He said he respected my decision, but I think he was disappointed that I didn't want to be like him. He was a lonely guy. Sometimes when we would go fishing, and he and Dad had had a couple of beers, he'd loosen up. He'd talk about your mother."

Gracie turned away. He could only see the side of her face. "Oh yeah? What did he say?"

"He had it bad."

"Had what bad?" Suddenly she was all ears.

He felt a white lie form, then die, on his tongue. His thoughts on Lillian, admittedly, were jaded by his father's opinion. Sam let the silence run on until she looked back his way expectantly.

"Love? Lust? Probably both." Sam focused on the road but monitored her reaction from the corner of his eye.

"Oh." Gracie glanced at her lap. She was remembering last night, and so was he.

To cool the moment, he hurried on. "She cured him of beautiful women, at least as far as wives went."

Gracie jerked in her seat. "What do you mean? How many did he have?"

"Just two, Lillian and Marcia. You couldn't find more different women if you tried."

"So why did he marry Marcia?"

Sam smiled. At least her mind was off Artie. The raw emotion moments ago had made them both vulnerable. Sam took advantage of the reprieve and offered her a teasing smile. "You never struck me as being a gossipy type, Gracie."

"I need to know."

What could he say about Clare's mama that wouldn't paint Conrad in an ugly light? "It wasn't her batting average. I'd say it was her hips. Good breeding stock is my guess. Shortly after Clare was born, he realized another kid wasn't enough to make a happy marriage."

"Poor Clare. Why do you suppose he even bothered?"

Sam turned away to check his sideview mirror, then zoomed past a poultry truck. "Everyone wants a piece of happiness, Gracie. Conrad thought kids would relieve his loneliness. He figured Marcia wouldn't wander since she wasn't shaped like Lillian. She was content as long as the money kept flowing. And Conrad liked the fact that she had little in the way of family to interfere with his plans—just one estranged brother overseas."

Gracie flashed him a worried look. "What about Lillian? Who has she got for family? Guess I should know the worst, since they're mine, too."

"Lillian was like Conrad. She was born with a silver spoon in her mouth. Unfortunately, her mother died before she was a teenager and her father made and lost several fortunes. He was a brilliant but unstable man. She married Conrad when her father's finances hit a low point. Her father died shortly afterward."

"So, she has nobody but me . . ."

It wasn't really a question. Sam knew what was going through her head. To her, family was the Holy Grail. That's why she was having such a hard time saying no to Conrad's request. Sam was counting on her sense of loyalty to accomplish his goal. In another few miles, he was going to have to drop the other shoe—Ben's arrest. He prayed the attorneys had pulled some magic strings and gotten Ben released.

Gracie could feel Sam's tension rise as they neared Shady Grove. Conversation had faded into silence. Gracie stared out the window the last few miles, hardly daring to breathe. He was probably worrying about how he was going to handle her tears once they reached home. Minutes ago, she would have said she was doing fine, but since they hit town the memories were thick with images of Artie—the clear fall light glancing off the flat top of his cap as he shuffled unhurried down the sidewalk, Artie carrying on with Eldon Bird, the newspaper delivery man from Montgomery, the two of them like twins with cups of coffee in one hand, cigarettes in the other. Artie always walked her to work on Fridays so he could catch up with Eldon . . . Eldon didn't know there would be no more Fridays . . . Eldon was a lucky dog.

Gracie looked up as Sam pulled into the driveway behind Ben's work truck. "The widow's pipes must be all fixed." She turned to grab the door handle and offer him a brave smile.

Sam latched on to her arm. "Gracie, wait—"

She released the handle and felt herself curl up inside as she braced herself. "I'm tired and hungry and feeling like a marked target. Whatever it is, can you tell me tomorrow?"

Sam's gaze slid away from hers. "Unless something's changed since we left Montgomery . . . Ben isn't home."

It wasn't like Sam to shuffle his feet. She was running out of patience. "You can do better than that, Yankee."

"Lillian had Ben picked up on kidnapping conspiracy charges this morning. The attorneys are working on getting him released."

"But what about Rita's note? Burgess has seen it. And what about the dead man in the river? I read the news reports. Where's Rita?"

"I wish I knew."

Gracie bolted out of the car and marched toward the porch. Sam's footsteps echoed behind her.

Gracie came to an abrupt halt in front of the door. She reached into her purse to fish for her key. "It's been twenty-five years. Do *I* have a say in any of this?"

Sam reached for her key and unlocked the door. "I'm afraid not. Lillian produced photos of Conrad and Ben shaking hands in the lobby of Conrad's office. We suspect they were taken during Ben's trip north, shortly after Rita told him the truth. But we're having trouble verifying the dates."

Gracie started through the door. "Where are they holding him?"

"Burgess has him."

"But Burgess wouldn't—*lock* him up. He and Ben have been friends forever."

"Lillian's got a U.S. marshal breathing down Burgess's neck. Evidently Lillian has connections in the D.A.'s office in Fairfield County. Someone called Burgess, asking questions, and made a few not-so veiled threats, then set the local marshal on his tail when he balked. So far, they're keeping it local, which makes me think Lillian is using the photos as a scare tactic to force us into a quick settlement. If she weren't your mother, I think Kate would hire vigilantes to deal with Lillian, once and for all. She's that hot under the collar."

"I've got to fix things—Ben doesn't deserve this." Gracie turned back toward the driveway.

Sam cut her off. "Wait, Gracie. I spoke to Burgess. Ben is beating himself up over Artie, but otherwise he's fine."

The look on Sam's face did nothing to relieve her growing panic, but she felt the fight go out of her. It was obvious Sam blamed himself for the turn of events. "Okay . . . as long as Ben is safe. He'll be home by tomorrow, right?"

"Kate has a team working on it. We don't want to set off the wrong alarms. The FBI has a lot of red tape. We don't want this to go that far."

Gracie stepped into the living room and was immediately hit with a sense of emptiness. The twenty-four hours she'd been gone felt like years.

The hallway leading to Artie's room was silent. It would be easy to pretend he was taking his afternoon nap. Gracie felt the pull of Sam's gaze and turned around. He was working hard to muster up something that didn't fall on the side of pity.

"Give it some time, Gracie. If you want, we can stay with Kate."

He'd said *we*. He wasn't going to be leaving her alone without a push. "Don't think I'm up for that yet, but you go on, if you want. I'll be fine."

"Still trying to get rid of me?"

His grin didn't quite ring true. He was holding his breath, hoping she would say *no*. Fact was, at one time she would have told him that that was exactly what she was doing, and leave him to deal with the bad news. But now, even though she felt the need for time to herself, she didn't want him to go. And even more unsettling was the fear that someday he would go and she'd be alone for good.

Gracie set her purse down on the lamp table near the sofa and glanced down the hall. Sam was right—she wasn't ready to face Artie's room. "I'm going to take myself upstairs for a bath."

From the angle she was standing, she could see

his throat work to swallow. "I'll get the suitcases from the car."

Gracie wasn't the only one who'd been affected by their time in Montgomery. As Gracie climbed the stairs, she had to wonder about a man who could be cool as a cucumber when big things were on the line but who turned to jelly when a woman announced she was taking a bath.

Sam Fontana was shy. How 'bout that? She'd missed the signs before. When she reached the top of the stairs, she glanced back. He was watching her with something akin to fear. Then she remembered something Artie had prophesied when she was pining over the loss of her high school sweetheart, Johnnie Bean, to the voluptuous Marianne Talbot: "Someday a man is gonna walk through that door, take one look at you, and know you's the bee's knees."

She'd asked, "How am I supposed to know? He could just be after my lucky ball."

"When he looks like the Devil hisself has snatched him by the throat—then you know that's him."

Something had hold of Sam Fontana's throat because no sound was coming out.

Gracie was halfway to a prune when a tap sounded at the bathroom door. "I'm fine, go away, Fontana."

The door flew open and Gracie lurched against

the back of the tub, pulling a towel into the water to cover herself. It was one thing to lose yourself to a man as naked as you in the dark but a whole 'nother kettle of fish to face a fully dressed one in the light of day without a stitch on.

Chantel's dark head poked around the door. "If you talk to your man that way, he ain't gonna be your man for long." She padded into the bathroom and plopped down on the toilet seat.

Gracie tossed the dripping towel over the faucet and pulled the drain plug. *"Dammit, Chantel,* you scared the bejesus out of me. You looking for another funeral to plan? 'Cause I'm sure my heart isn't anywhere near my chest anymore."

Chantel shook her head. "You are some kind of puzzle, girl. And I know you better than just about anybody. There's a handsome man down there all by himself, and don't tell me you ain't noticed . . ." Chantel leaned closer and narrowed her eyes at Gracie. "In fact, . . . I'd say you did a whole lot more than notice while you was in Montgomery . . ."

"While you're trying to figure out my love life, make yourself useful and get me a dry towel."

"I should make you parade down the hall and get it yourself."

"Chantel—"

"Oh, all right. Hang on to your socks." Chantel ducked out into the hall. Her heavy footsteps clumped toward the linen closet, then stopped short. "She's still got on her ugly face, Mr. Fontana. I'll see what I can do to pretty her up. You just keep yourself all handsome like you're doin', you hear?"

Gracie hissed through the door. "*Chantel,* for God's sake—"

"Say what, Mr. Sam? You want to dry her off yourself? Sure enough. Bring your sweet self up here and I'll step aside."

Gracie pressed herself against the cold tile and covered her shivering body with the dripping towel. "*Chantel Dubois,* your liver is on a plate. Five seconds, *I swear*—"

Chantel stepped back into the room wearing a broad smile. "Relax, girl, he's in the kitchen fixing your supper. You don't deserve him."

Gracie snatched the dry towel. "I don't deserve you, either."

"*Humph.* Haven't I always told you that?"

Gracie wrapped the towel around herself and marched out of the bathroom toward her room. Sam had set her suitcase on her bed. Beside it sat a frilly gift bag, not unlike the one she'd received from her mama. She tossed it at Chantel. "I bought this for you at the hotel shop."

"Artie always did say you had a sweet side." Chantel danced with excitement as she reached into the bag and pulled out a glittery copper-colored dress Gracie had seen in the display window. The look of admiration in Chantel's eyes was all the thank-you Gracie needed. She'd finally done something with the money that made her feel good.

Chantel held the dress in front of her and swished around the room. "I'm going to wear this tomorrow for Artie's services and do the Dubois side proud."

Gracie tried hard to smile. "Artie would have liked it."

Chantel stopped her twirling and sat down on the bed next to Gracie. "I got the arrangements all set. Alice is seein' to the food." Her voice lost its push.

Gracie's heart squeezed hard in her chest. It was all she could do not to bawl like a baby. She'd been waiting all day for him to walk into the room and tell her it was all a mistake and he'd just had a bad case of indigestion. She'd heard his voice so clearly. . . . She felt the weight of Chantel's arm slip across her shoulders.

Tears welled in Chantel's eyes. "I'm gonna miss him, too, honey. We all are, even Alice." Chantel reached inside the pocket of her skirt and pulled out an envelope. "Ben told me to give you this."

Gracie stared at Artie's loopy letters scrawled on the front, then swallowed the lump in her throat and tried to put on a brave face for Chantel. If she started crying, she'd never stop. "You ought to consider taking a job as mail lady."

"There ain't nothin' wrong with bawlin' when you feel like it, you hear. I know you think cryin' is for sissies, but if you keep that all bottled up inside, Gracie Lynne, you're gonna explode."

"I'll be fine. Thanks, Chantel."

"Yeah, well, there's a mighty nice shoulder downstairs going to waste. Sam don't look like the kind of man who's afraid of a little water."

Gracie smiled back at her. "When Ben gets home—"

"Your daddy's money will see to that."

"If it weren't for that *damn* money, Ben wouldn't be in this fix. Nobody would give a fig who I was or how I got to Shady Grove—not even my own mama."

Chantel rounded on her with a raised finger. "You listen to me, Gracie Lynne. This ain't your fault. What were the chances of you, a Yankee, landin' here in Shady Grove? God done put you here for a reason. You think he didn't know your daddy had them piles of money? You bet your sweet ass he did. It's up to you to figure out what he wants you to do with it. You always did know how to add and subtract better than anyone in school. You'll figure it out. As for your mama, well, she ain't your fault neither. Sweep her under the rug with the rest of the dirt. That's what I'd do."

"I wish I could, but—"

"But nothin'. You are all the good that woman is ever gonna do in her life."

What Chantel said made sense, but Gracie still felt like she had her foot caught in the door. She was letting go of a dream she'd had since she was a child—her very own mama—and she didn't have anything to replace it with. And now Artie was gone and she had no one to help her figure it out—except Sam. But he was on the other side of the fence, praying she'd not dump it on him. Her head hurt and her stomach burned, and she didn't feel like being at all reasonable.

"Money changes people. They do stuff for it that they should do for better reasons."

Chantel raised a doubtful brow at Gracie. "Folks got to buy bread. It's a fact of life. Artie was talking 'bout folks who use money to get what they want and hurt other folks along the way 'cause they're greedy and just plain don't care. I don't see you doing that. And I don't see Sam asking you to, neither. So, don't go dumping this at his door, you hear? You're gonna have to be a chicken-baby all by your own self."

Gracie wanted to stomp her feet and throw something, but she'd run out of energy. "I've been Rita's castoff baby girl all my life. Up until Sam found me, only the folks of Shady Grove knew it. Now the whole world knows. Don't think my daddy naming me in his will has changed that, 'cause it hasn't. I've seen what they're calling me in the papers."

Chantel hadn't heard a thing Gracie said. She was fingering the coppery fabric of her new dress. "Look, you already put that money to good use. I am gonna look like the Queen of Sheba. Thanks for the dress." Chantel waltzed out of the room, closing the door behind her.

Making a friend happy with a silly dress was a long way from knowing what to do with the kind of money her daddy had left her.

Sam poked at the lump of bread and cheese on the griddle with a spatula.

Chantel stopped on her way through the kitchen and peered over his shoulder. "A little more butter. You want to make sure it gets nice and brown all over."

"Butter? Are you trying to kill me or Gracie?"

"That's the way Gracie likes it. And hold the salt. Gracie don't like salt. Just smear the butter over it and serve it to her hot."

"You *are* trying to kill me."

Sam dumped the sandwich off the skillet onto a plate. It was mostly white with black spots and edges. "Does it look edible to you?"

"You're one brave man. I bet you're brave enough to take that upstairs to Gracie. She's hungry and she don't even know it. She'd eat just about anythin' right now. I can tell."

Sam shot her a suspicious glance. "How can you tell?"

"Scrape off the burnt edges, slap a pad of butter on it, then brown it. She'll swallow her tongue and won't have nothin' to lash your Yankee hide with. Now, I've got to go. Mrs. Hammond needs my help with your house. I'm growin' on her. She's even offered me a job . . ."

Sam poked his head out of the refrigerator. "I hope you told her you've already got one."

She was hugging the dress Gracie had bought for her and smiling. He knew enough about women to recognize the artful look.

Chantel's smile widened with each slow step she took toward the back door. "Mrs. Hammond offered me a whole lotta money . . ."

Sam grabbed the butter and marched toward the stove. "I'll double it."

"I'll take it, 'cause you're gonna need me here. Besides, I already done you a big favor, so it's not like I was robbin' you blind."

Sam poked absently at the sandwich. "What favor was that?"

"I told your woman to treat you nice. Remember, lots of butter and make it hot."

"My woman?" Sam turned around, but Chantel was gone.

Sam carried the sandwich to the sink and

scraped off the black edges. Then he carried it back to the stove and smeared butter on both sides, like Chantel had instructed, and plopped it back on the griddle.

When Gracie's sandwich was browned, he set it on a plate and sliced it diagonally, the way they did in restaurants. It looked lonely. He ducked back in the refrigerator and pulled out a jar of pickles, speared one with a fork and dropped it in the middle, then grabbed an extra one and placed it on the side. It actually looked edible. Sam's stomach let out a groan. If he was hungry, then Gracie must be starving. She'd barely eaten before the morning meeting with Jason Myer.

He grabbed a napkin and headed for the stairs. He tapped twice, and the knocking eased open the door a crack. Gracie was stretched out on her stomach fast asleep. Sam sat down in the rocking chair to watch and eat her sandwich. The salty warm cheese melted in his mouth. Not bad. In fact, it was damn good. He loved hot buttered grilled cheese . . . and Gracie's smooth thighs where they curved under the towel. Both ways, he figured he was a doomed man.

Chapter 27

Gracie rolled over in her damp towel and opened her eyes long enough to identify her surroundings. *She was home,* thank God. Then she remembered —Artie was gone, and not just to the Blue Jay for a night out with friends but for good.

The last vestiges of a dream niggled at her sleepy brain. Artie was there, and Ben, too. Alice stood beside the reverend, holding his hand, looking happier than Gracie had ever seen her. They were in a church. She could practically smell the thick sweet smell of lilies clustered along the main aisle. Someone was getting married. Artie's smile was big as day. He wore a creamy white rose in the lapel of his best brown suit. His arm was joined with hers. She could feel the warmth of his touch on her hand as he reached over to steady her. They were walking slowly up the aisle . . . *It was her wedding.* The groom's back was to her. She squeezed her eyes tighter, trying to recall the details. Nothing came, not even the name of her intended.

She finally gave up and forced her eyes open. It was just a dream, a wishful one at that. Artie was gone. Ben was warming Burgess's jail. And Sam was downstairs . . .

Gracie pulled the towel tighter around her and glanced around the room. The late afternoon sun bathed the walls in warm gold light. This had been Artie's favorite time of year. Baseball and pumpkin pie were only part of the reason. Artie claimed all the good things that had ever happened to him came in the fall. He'd shaken Jackie Robinson's hand, bought his first horn, and found Gracie on the front porch. And if he could comment on dying just now, Gracie was pretty sure he'd find a way to make it sound like he'd planned to leave during his favorite season all along. But why this fall?

The rumble of male voices echoed up the stairs. She held her breath, listening for Ben's easy drawl. Sam's voice, and then Skippy's filtered through the door. No Ben.

Gracie dug under the mattress for Sam's shirt and the pair of jeans she'd hidden from Alice. When she was feeling safe and legal, she raced downstairs.

Sam lounged against the counter, looking as handsome as ever in his bare feet and rolled-up shirtsleeves. She was pretty sure he was the dark nameless figure standing at the end of the aisle in her dream. Gracie felt heat rise to her cheeks and transferred her attention to Skip and Clare.

Gracie's gaze stopped dead on their joined hands, then flew to their smitten faces. "Is there something you need to be telling me?"

Skip beamed back at Gracie. "Clare has decided to rent Alice's house when she and reverend get married. Isn't that great?"

Gracie checked her sister's expression.

Clare's pasty cheeks bloomed pink. "I'm sorry about Artie, Gracie. We all are."

Skippy offered Gracie a sheepish look. "Anything you need, you just name it."

"Thanks." She managed a brief smile for Clare and Skippy's sake, then glanced at Sam. "When's Ben coming home?"

Sam's face sobered. "We're working on it. The marshal is a by-the-book kind of girl. We're trying to prove that the photos Lillian produced were taken eight years ago when Ben made his trip north."

Gracie flinched at the reminder of Ben's betrayal but kept silent and waited for him to finish.

"They're searching the security company's archives for the originals, but they seem to have gone missing. Lillian claims Conrad was behind the kidnapping and made a deal with Ben so he could keep her from gaining custody of you when he divorced her. Ben has a hefty sum of money in his bank account, which isn't helping things. The evidence is flimsy, but they can keep Ben another forty-eight hours while they search for more."

Gracie felt the panic rising in her stomach.

"But he'll miss Artie's funeral—I need to fix this."

"I'm not going to let that happen. Trust me." Sam read her frustration and moved in her direction, but she shot up from the table.

"I should be helping Chantel get things ready."

Skip stood up but kept hold of Clare's hand. "Take it easy, Gracie. Chantel said she doesn't need any more help. She's got Alice."

"Alice? She and Artie never saw eye to eye on anything. And Chantel is Artie's clone."

"Kate's offered my house for the wake. She'll keep them under control."

"I need to do something besides sit here."

Gracie was halfway across the kitchen when Chantel burst through the door. The whites of her eyes were wide with panic. She fixed her wild stare on Clare. "Your mama . . . she's here and is doing her best to chew your grandma's head off. But that Ms. Kate, she's doin' some chewin' of her own. Just thought y'all should know."

Clare shrank against Skippy's shoulder, then swung an alarmed gaze to Gracie. "She must be getting desperate if she came here."

Skip glanced back and forth between Gracie and Clare. "What's she want?"

Gracie checked the fear on Clare's face. "Money . . . and someone to bully. Skippy, you keep Clare out of sight, you hear? And if you break my sister's heart, I will do some chewin' of my own."

Gracie moved toward the door, but Sam stepped into her path. "Wait, *Gracie*—"

"Not this time, Sam. I can't let one more nasty thing happen while I sit by doing nothing." In one quick sideways movement she was around him, down the back steps, and on her way through the rear gate. When she was out of his reach, she glanced back in time to see him snag his tender Yankee foot on a twig.

Gracie slowed down, but the feel of the damp red clay beneath her bare feet was what she needed. At least for a little while, she could pretend nothing had changed and she was still Gracie Calloway, the girl who had the meanest pitch in town and the coolest uncle to cheer her on.

Gracie bounded to a stop on the dog path at the end of Parnell Street. The shadow of a shiny black limo stretched in front of Sam's gate in the late afternoon sun. There were no reporters in sight, but little Jackie Brown leaned on the side of the car with her nose pressed to the window. A ball cap was pulled down over her shorn hair. From a distance, she looked like a boy even in her pink shorts.

Gracie felt guilt shimmying around inside as she padded across the asphalt to the car. "Hey, Jackie. Sorry about your hair."

Jackie pressed her finger to her lips, then pointed at the driver's door. *"Shhh."*

A chauffeur was out for the count in the front seat with his head cocked against the window glass and his cap shading his eyes.

Jackie grabbed a handful of Gracie's shirt and towed her toward the rear of the car. "Who's visitin' Sam?" Jackie whispered. Her wide eyes rounded on the front door.

Gracie followed her gaze. "I suspect it's Clare's mama."

"Is she rich?"

Gracie shrugged. "Maybe so."

Jackie's face twisted up. She looked like an elf, with her ears poking out either side of her cap. "Whatcha mean? Either she is or she ain't. If she's got somebody to clean her dishes and sweep her floor, and she eats steaks on Fridays, then she's rich. If she don't, then where'd she get the money for this fine car and that lazy man in the front seat?"

"That's what you think rich is, huh? Well, then I guess she is. But Clare likes it here with us and doesn't want to go home with her mama, so I figure there's better things than steaks on Friday nights and not having to do the dishes."

"My mama says you're gonna be rich and that you're goin' away now that Artie's gone. She told me I'm gonna have to play ball with my brothers instead. They get sulky when I strike them out. Baseball with no brothers is the only thing that can top steaks and no dishes."

369

Jackie's snub nose and mouth scrunched so Gracie could see her white teeth pressing against her gums in a fierce frown. Gracie tried not to laugh. She reminded Gracie of herself years ago, when the world had seemed like it was tipped sideways. Everything she did seemed to go wrong—except baseball. The more she played, the more level the world got. She counted herself lucky she hadn't had five brothers who felt threatened by their younger sister. Poor Jackie was getting it from two sides.

Gracie unhooked Jackie's hand from her shirt and placed it securely in her own and gave it a firm shake. "You tell your mama that I'm not going anywhere. That's a promise." Just saying the words made Gracie feel better. It was a small decision, but it was all hers. In her mind's eye, she could see Artie nodding his approval, if not for her decision, then for that fact that she'd finally made one. Her heart felt a little less heavy.

Jackie threw her arms around Gracie's waist and gave her a quick squeeze. "I told her so, but she don't listen."

Gracie unhooked herself from Jackie's arms and glanced at Sam's front window. Katherine Hammond moved into view. "There seems to be a lot of deafness going around. Now I've got to go have a talk with Clare's mama. She's a little slow to catch on, too."

Jackie snatched her bicycle away from the fence

and straddled the seat, then beamed up at Gracie. "My mama was just pullin' my leg when she said you was rich, huh? Anybody can see you ain't. You got no shoes and I seen you do the dishes lots of times."

Jackie was right. She had no shoes, just one pair of sandals and Artie's old cast-offs. She hadn't gotten around to buying a new pair. Gracie watched as Jackie zoomed down the street.

The chauffeur stumbled out of the car and shot Gracie a menacing glare. "Now look what you gone and done. You got smudges all over my glass. I got important folks to attend to." He reached into his back pocket and pulled out a handkerchief, started polishing Jackie's sticky fingerprints off the glass. Then he nodded toward the house. "That there is the home of Ms. Katherine Hammond. I heard all about her in the papers. She even been on the national news." He glanced sideways at Gracie, this time narrowing his eyes on her face. After a long pause, he shook his head and went back to his polishing. "But I don't guess you know nothin' about her or you wouldn't be smudgin' my windows."

"Oh, I might smudge your windows—But I can say for a fact that Ms. Hammond wouldn't care two cents about a few fingerprints."

"What you say, girl? I heard she laid a reporter low. You go on now and keep away from the car before she comes out here and gives you what for. You best be scared."

Gracie steered around the car toward the walk. "That's just it. She doesn't scare me so much anymore."

Kate Hammond shifted her gaze from Marcia's face to the view out the window. When Gracie's brown head bobbed into view, Kate felt a large bubble of relief. Seconds later, the front door burst open and Gracie bounded into the room looking suitably hoydenish in her jeans and bare feet.

Kate suppressed a smile. "I see Chantel found you." She ignored Gracie's startled expression. "Marcia, I'd like you to meet my granddaughter, Gracie Calloway."

Marcia exploded out of her chair. "Where's my daughter?" She spun toward Kate. "Make her tell me where Clare is—*this instant.*"

Gracie skirted Marcia and came to stand beside Kate. "Clare's free to go anytime she wants. She just doesn't want to, that's all."

"I knew it; she's locked my daughter in a swamp. Just look at her. *Sh-sh-* . . . *she's—unwashed.* Kate, I *demand* you do something."

Silently Kate applauded her new granddaughter. "You can see Clare, if she's willing. If she's not, and you persist, I will advise her to obtain a restraining order against you."

"You wouldn't dare—"

"Gracie, get Mr. Fontana on the phone. I've had quite enough."

Kate trained a watchful eye on Marcia. Gracie retrieved the cordless from the dining room, dialed a number, then passed the handset to Kate. "Mr. Fontana? Put Clare on."

"Will do. And Kate . . . keep Gracie busy, will you? She's turning my hair gray. Hey, Clare, it's for you, kid."

Her granddaughter's timid voice came on the line.

Kate was in no mood to placate Marcia. The woman hardly deserved the courtesy. But then she remembered what was at stake and stiffened her chin. She would do this for her son.

"Clare. Your mother is under the impression that we've hidden you in the swamp. Would you reassure her that you are not being held hostage by large carnivorous lizards?"

"I can't—"

"Of course you can. Show some backbone, child. You're a Hammond, after all."

Marcia snatched the phone from Kate. "*Clare*, is that you? *Answer me*—I've had quite enough of this silliness. I expect you here in five minutes. We *are* going home—*together.*"

Kate watched as Marcia's face drained of color. Good God, was the woman going to faint? Kate reached forward and intercepted the phone as

Marcia's knees buckled and she landed in a chair.

For a brief moment, Kate felt sorry for her. She'd been in Marcia's shoes—a single mother with no family but one child. She knew what it was to be alone.

Kate eased back a safe distance. "Clare, I take it your answer was *no*. Good girl." She handed the phone to Gracie, then turned back to Marcia. "Pull yourself together, Marcia. Your child is finally growing up. Be happy. If you don't smother her, she may actually speak to you again."

Marcia recovered from her swoon, stood up, and advanced on Gracie. "You've brainwashed her, *you greedy little bitch*."

Gracie stood tall in the face of Marcia's attack. "The fact is, ma'am, Clare says she doesn't want the money, so I'm wondering why you're here . . ."

"Kate, you're not going to let this miscreant waste a fortune. Even you aren't such a fool."

"Children grow up, Marcia. They make their own decisions. It's your job to support them . . . even when you happen to disagree." She glanced at Gracie, then rounded on Marcia. "I think I know my granddaughter well enough to know that she wouldn't be protecting her sister if you were doing the job yourself."

Marcia blanched, then glared at Kate. "You have no idea what it's like to be a mother."

Gracie stepped toward Marcia; Kate cut her off. She was quite capable of defending herself, but the idea that Gracie was ready to go to battle on her behalf went a long way toward taking the sting out of Marcia's remark.

"You're forgetting, Marcia, that I lost my child. You, at least, have a chance to get yours back."

Gracie watched Clare's mama storm down the walk as her grandmother sank into a chair. Kate's bony shoulders poked at the shoulders of her soft blouse. Her gray head bowed over her lap. She raised one hand to her face and dabbed at her eyes. Gracie didn't know what to say that wouldn't bring on more tears and embarrassment on both their parts. Maybe Ben's habit of silent retreat would be best. Gracie inched toward the kitchen.

"Don't run away, Gracie. I need to talk to you." Without turning around, Kate motioned her toward an empty chair, but Gracie chose to remain standing.

Her grandmother had never addressed her as Gracie before. That alone gave her pause. She studied the woman who sat hunched in the chair. Kate Hammond was tired and that made her human, far from the hard-edged general who ordered folks around like they were her personal army. For the first time, Gracie felt a connection to the tough woman she looked so much like.

She weaved her way through the maze of

polished furnishings toward a chair opposite her grandmother, not sure whether before she sat down she should offer to fetch her a glass of water, a fresh hankie, or a shot of whiskey. Anyone who had to deal with Clare's mama needed a stiffener.

"I'm afraid you've seen the worst of the Hammonds. I can imagine what you must think of us." Her grandmother's voice rose from her lap.

Gracie inched closer and laid a tentative hand on Kate's shoulder. "Begging your pardon, ma'am, but she's not really a Hammond, blood-wise, and all. You can be sure whatever she's got is not our doing."

When her grandmother's head snapped up, Gracie was surprised to see a smile. Kate motioned her to the chair. "Very diplomatic answer, child. Good grief, sit down. A stiff neck at my age could kill me."

Gracie eyed the cream-colored damask skeptically, then perched on the edge of the seat. "What is it you wanted to say?"

"You're direct. I like that. Few people are these days. I won't waste your time. I want you to accept your inheritance. I shouldn't have to explain why, after Marcia's display. As grateful as I am to Sam Fontana for his assistance, he's not a Hammond. You and Clare are the last."

Gracie opened her mouth to protest, but her grandmother held up her hand.

"Clare has possibilities, but she isn't prepared to deal with people like Marcia. Your father liquidated his assets so you could make your own choices. It was against my better judgment, but there you have it. I understand you have a passion for baseball." Her grandmother paused and gave her the full benefit of her shrewd gray eyes. "Surely there must be something, an enterprise, you'd like to invest in . . ."

Once again, Artie and his question about her dreams came to mind. It was almost as if Artie was coaching the old woman from heaven. She had a familiar wily gleam in her eye.

Gracie chose her words carefully. "I'll think on it some more. My checkbook has taught me a few things."

Her grandmother straightened. Suddenly she was all business. "Sam Fontana can help you. Conrad tutored him for several years. It's time he grew out of his father's detective shoes. I expect you to prod him for his own good."

Prod Sam? Was she kidding? "He's sweating just thinking I might dump this all on him."

"I'm confident he's about to change his mind." Not so much as an eyelash flickered on her grandma's face.

Gracie couldn't help but think her namesake was more than just sly. She was downright snake-like, to be sure. She gave her grandma Artie's one-eyed stare. "Chantel hasn't been taking you down to see Voodoo Sal, has she? Because I've got to warn you, that woman is only after your money. She can't see into the future. Fact is, she can't see a darned thing. She's as blind as a bat. Has been, going on ten years."

Her grandma puffed up a bit. "I have no need for Voodoo Sal's services. I'm quite capable of arranging the future without her help. Thank you."

As soon as her craw was emptied, her stiff Yankee features lapsed into a genuine smile. For a moment, Gracie felt herself slipping under her grandmother's spell. Kate was tiny but regal. Her sharp gray eyes flashed with passion. Could she match this woman? Shuffle her personal life into a closet and take on the world with so much courage? Kate Hammond seemed to think Gracie was up to the task. Gracie wasn't so sure. Most of all, she wasn't sure she wanted to, though she had to admit Kate painted an exciting picture that made her blood run a little faster.

"And if I say no—what happens?"

Sadness, instead of disappointment, rolled through her grandmother's gaze. "Then the buzzards will circle until there is nothing left."

"What about Sam?"

"It's not his by right. He won't take it. He's stubborn, like you. He'll arrange for Clare to deal with it, eventually. Every money-hungry hyena will be sniffing around her. Marcia will only be the first."

Gracie knew Kate was right. Though Clare had promise, she wasn't ready. Skip, if he figured in Clare's life, would put up a fight against the buzzards but would end up miserable, too. She was back to herself—and Sam. What made her grandma so sure little Gracie Calloway, who'd spent her life trying to be invisible, could handle standing in the spotlight?

Kate sat erect and emotionless, waiting for her response.

Gracie shifted uncomfortably in her chair. "If you're looking for a straight answer, I can't give it to you now. But there's one thing I need to know—"

"What would that be?"

"Why did my daddy never claim me?" Gracie's voice wavered, but she kept her gaze steady on Kate's.

Her grandmother exhaled. Her shoulders sank. She looked smaller, more fragile. "I imagine he was afraid of losing you again, in the event you rejected him. Sometimes it's easier to pretend the relationship we want than it is to experience the one we actually have. Hammonds excel at pretending. It's worked well for us in the past."

Gracie's first instinct was to deny the Hammond habit, but then she thought about Lillian and the lonely moments of her own child-hood when she'd pretended her mother to life.

"What about you and me? What if I don't take my daddy's money?"

"If you mean, will I disown you—my answer is *no*. I'd like very much for us to be friends—more than friends . . . and not just because your father would wish it."

Gracie felt her chest heave with relief. She'd been holding her breath, waiting for Kate's answer. "That's mighty generous of you."

"Not at all. I've learned my lesson." The sad tilt of her mouth said she was talking about Gracie's daddy.

Gracie pushed out of her chair and offered her grandmother's hand a squeeze. "The ones who love you, forgive you; the folks who won't are like yesterday's lunch, done and gone. Leastwise, that's what Artie always said. And he's as close to God as you can get."

Chapter 28

Gracie set the last dinner plate in the cupboard. She'd sent Alice and Chantel home to rest up for Artie's services tomorrow. But Gracie couldn't stop. As long as she kept busy, she wouldn't have to think.

Sam pulled the stopper from the sink, then reached for the hem of her apron, pulling her toward him as he dried his hands. "Leave something for the ants."

"You say that now, but you haven't seen the size of the ants around here. They could swallow a grown man."

"Still trying to scare me away, Gracie?"

"Is it working?"

"You forget. I come from a family of risk takers. My Aunt Sophie smokes like a chimney and plays poker every Friday night. She makes enough money off her winnings to feed her five kids. Uncle Tony owns an Italian restaurant. He was a small-time bookie when I was a kid, until he took a six-month fall for the town doctor who had a bigger racket going. Then there's Uncle Carlo who made his hobby legal; he's a licensed gambler. I could name a few more, but you get the general idea. If life is too predictable for my blood, it gets boring. I look forward to an alligator or two."

"That Marcia woman is the biggest one yet." *Next to her very own mama—that is.* She was still trying to figure out what to do about Lillian. Gracie tore her gaze away and pretended to straighten the plates of cookies. "She'd run her own child off for money. What makes folks like her so damn blind?"

Sam smiled, then followed her lead. "I think it starts early. People like Marcia and Lillian don't have anything more substantial to hold on to. They think money will give them the admiration and respect they lack. It does, in a way. People open doors for them; they get preferred seating at the opera. All of it makes them feel special. It's just a substitute for what they really need."

"What about my daddy?"

Sam laughed. "To Conrad, making money was a game, one he played particularly well. Sure, he enjoyed the nice cars, the trips to Monte Carlo, but I don't think he had many illusions about the value of money. Basically, he was lonely. That's why he bummed around with Dad and me when we went on fishing trips and to ball games. Money can isolate people. It may cut out some of the bad stuff life throws at them, but it cuts out the good stuff, too. Losing you made Conrad reexamine what was important. But not everyone gets such a painful wake-up call."

Gracie remembered the looks on folks' faces when she took their money for their groceries. She'd swear they thought she was stealing their last penny. She wasn't Gracie Calloway anymore. She was Katherine Hammond, daughter of multi-millionaire Conrad Hammond. It didn't matter that she wore the same clothes and did the same job she'd always done. She had more than they did, and she was taking what little they had for things like food.

And worst of all, the ones who'd thought she was beneath them because she was Rita's abandoned love child now showed her the respect she should have gotten from them all along—all because of the money.

Gracie looked up at Sam. "If I give it back, things are still going to be different, aren't they?"

"I'm afraid so. People will either think you're crazy or you're lying and you stashed it away so you don't have to share. You'll be guilty, even with the best of intentions. Sorry, princess."

Sam was being straight with her; at least he was learning. This time Gracie let his pet name for her pass. Fact was, she was getting used to being his princess but was still a long way from wanting to be queen. "If I take the money—?"

"—I'll be relieved." Sam threw her a hopeful grin. "I might even owe you another steak."

"Don't swallow your tongue yet. I haven't said yes."

Sam moved closer, forcing her to look up his way. "Gracie, none of us are going to run out on you. Kate and the attorneys . . . minus Jason Myer will be here for you. For what it's worth, I'll be here, too."

"You just said you didn't want it." Gracie swallowed the lump forming in her throat.

Sam backed off, giving her space, but his look of promise stayed with her. "It's not mine to want."

All this talk about wanting things put her in mind of Artie and his big question. She was only a teensy bit closer to knowing what to do. It seemed like the whole world was holding its breath waiting for her to choke out the easy answer. So far, all she'd decided was she was staying in Shady Grove—she'd promised Jackie —not just for Jackie's sake but for her own.

Gracie let her gaze wander along Sam's jawline, then drift to his eyes. He'd tucked his cocky attitude away and was waiting patiently for her response—the way Artie used to do. He wasn't going to give her the answers. He wanted her to come up with them herself.

It occurred to her that she'd asked Clare about her dreams, but she hadn't asked Sam. "What *do* you want, Sam?"

"The same thing you want, Gracie."

It was pretty clear from the way he was looking at her that they were no longer talking about money. He wanted her the way she wanted him.

Gracie's gaze locked with his. "Then, I'd say, we're in trouble."

Gracie stared into the dark outside Ben's back porch, listening to the silence. Sleep had eluded her. She'd wandered to the kitchen out of habit, hoping to conjure up Artie's ghost. She'd spent countless late nights with Artie drinking milky tea and talking to him about everything from the new bumps growing on her chest to the odds on Braves winning the Series. There were only a couple of subjects that made him button up tight: his son and the wife who'd run out on him. As long as Gracie steered clear of those, Artie would talk all night and forget she was supposed to be sleeping.

The clock on the stove clicked onto the twelve. Artie's letter was still tucked under her pillow upstairs. Though she was hungry for Artie's voice, she was saving the letter because she knew it would be the last she heard from him. Tears poked at the back of her eyes. Gracie forced herself out of the chair and wandered to the hall, peered into the living room.

Sam was asleep on the couch. His dark hair spilled over his forehead.

Just when she began to wonder whether what had happened in Montgomery was real or just a dream, she would catch him looking at her in that way that said he hadn't forgotten a thing and wanted more when she was ready to ante up.

Sometimes she felt like she'd been waiting for him her whole life. Maybe it was how he read her thoughts and answered with that quirky brow of his. But that couldn't be. He was everything she wasn't: self-assured, able to laugh at the absurdities in the world the way she never could, and a Yankee. The novelty he found in the South would lose its charm and he'd be off to someplace more exciting. And she would have one more empty spot in her chest, like the one Artie had left her with. As soon as the thought was out, she realized she was wallowing. That's when she heard it—Artie's voice as clear as day.

What's the matter with you, Gracie Lynne? You gots the world by the tail and you's sitting there feeling sorry for yourself. Get up off your monkey ass and sing a little, girl. You's in love. You got to trust some folks. You can begin with that Yankee. Don't you bring that mopey face to my funeral tomorrow, you hear?

The hairs on Gracie's arm prickled. She whipped around, searching for a body to go with the words. Was the voice in her head, or was it coming from the room? She hurried toward the hall. "Artie?"

No answer. Gracie felt her way back to the

kitchen. Her toe caught the leg of a chair, but she grabbed it before it crashed to the floor. Slowly she regained her bearings and stood quietly, listening. Nothing but silence.

Great. She was hearing voices, which could mean only one of two things in Shady Grove: She was either crazy or dead. Since her toe was still throbbing, she was pretty sure she wasn't dead. There was a third option that Alice didn't like to speak of, but at the moment it was looking like the better choice—Artie was a ghost and had decided to hang around a while longer and pester her for an answer.

Gracie plopped herself down in the chair. "I've got a few things to say to you, Arthur Dubois. *Come back here and listen, dammit.*"

"I'm listening." Sam's husky voice came at her from the living room.

Gracie started in her seat. "If I'm not dead yet, I will be shortly. My heart just skipped ten beats."

"Sorry." His voice moved closer to her back. "It's not uncommon, you know. My dad visited me the day he died. Sat on my bed and gave me a lecture. Now I'm a way-too-cocky P.I. instead of a Wall Street suit. Best lecture I ever had."

Gracie turned toward his voice. "Around here, they bring out the white coats if you admit you hear voices . . . unless you're as old as Methuselah. In that case, they figure you could be gone by the next sunrise, so they prop you on the front porch in the morning and bring you in at night, like laundry."

Sam reached over and tore off a sheet of paper towel and handed it to her. "Alice?"

Gracie blew her nose. "She caught me talking to Rita's mama's picture when I was a kid. I spent Wednesday nights and Sundays in church getting the devil preached out of me."

"Alice is a tough cookie."

"But Artie could outmaneuver her better than anyone else. She'd rarely suspected a thing until it was too late. Used to drive her nuts."

"He left me a message, you know. Alice relayed it to me this evening."

Gracie spun around, searching for his face in the dark. "What'd he say?"

Sam pulled up a chair and sat opposite her. "He told me to ignore those two mule ears of yours. Said you needed to be pushed out of your rut and I was just the man for the job, seeing how you've nearly slain every man in the county at one time or another with that rocket pitch of yours. They're too embarrassed to come near you, let alone ask you for a date."

"That sounds like Alice's sermon. You sure she didn't make it up herself?"

"He said you've never been in love before and that I was to go easy on you."

Gracie was grateful for the darkness and the

fact that Sam couldn't see her blush. "He had no business saying that. What does he know about who I've been sweet on?" Gracie abandoned her chair, but Sam reached for her hands before she could get away.

"Maybe it was about me. I do twenty-four-hour relationships pretty well, not much more than that. I guess he figured me out."

Gracie wasn't ready to give in. She wanted to hear the full skinny from his lips. "A regular Casanova. I knew that, too."

"Guilty before proven innocent. You need to watch that." He pulled her closer. "So, what did he say just now?"

If she told him, would she be giving him too much power? Gracie hesitated, waiting for that cocky grin of his to erupt on his face, but it never came. "He said I was to stop feeling sorry for myself." Gracie paused and checked his expression, then went on. "He said I should trust some folks more."

"That's it? Seems a little general for all that effort."

Gracie reclaimed her hands and crossed her arms over her chest. "Okay, he said, *you*. I should *trust you*. Don't go getting all smug on me. I'm not saying he's right. Maybe I am crazy. Maybe I'm hearing things."

"Like the phone ringing?" Sam picked up the cordless from the counter.

Gracie stared blankly at the phone as Sam passed it to her. "Hello?"

"Gracie?" A woman's hesitant voice came across the line.

"Who is this?"

"It's Rita."

Relief worked its way through Gracie's body. She sagged gratefully into a chair. "Thank goodness. *Where* the heck are you?"

"Is Ben okay? Tell him I'm real sorry." Rita's voice wavered, then dropped softly.

"He's in jail. They think he kidnapped me. You need to get here, real quick."

"I'm in Texas with a blown head gasket. Tell Ben to hang on. I'll be there as quick as I can."

"But Artie's services are tomorrow—*Rita?*"

Chapter 29

After Rita's call, the sandman was more elusive than ever, despite Sam's warm presence beside her. Gracie inched toward the edge of the bed, then glanced at Sam. He'd dozed off an hour ago, but her mind kept circling back to Ben. She needed him to be at Artie's memorial service. She couldn't say goodbye alone. Aside from Rita, only one other person seemed to have the ability to make it happen—*Lillian.*

Gracie punched her mother's number and told herself she wasn't selling out. She was taking care of business, using the resources Conrad had given her.

"Hello?" Lillian's sultry voice sounded rattled.

"This is Gracie. We need to talk."

"I'd given up on you. I have a flight scheduled for noon." Despite her words, Gracie detected a hopeful rise in her mother's tone. She'd been waiting for her call.

Gracie's patience snapped. "I want Ben released —*now.*"

"*It's five A.M.* Why don't we meet for breakfast? There's a little place around the corner from the hotel—"

"Meet me at the ball field in Shady Grove in

one hour. It's in Parnell Park, just as you come into town." If she was going to pull this off, she needed all the confidence she could muster. She wasn't going to find it at a fancy restaurant in the city.

"But I'll need more time than that—" Lillian's voice sounded panicked.

Artie was gone. Ben was in jail. Gracie figured she had nothing left to lose that mattered. "Drive fast."

"Wait—"

Gracie didn't give her another chance to argue. She hung up, feeling satisfied with herself for finally taking action.

Sam materialized out of the dark. "Where are we going?"

Gracie jolted in her seat. "You're supposed to be sleeping."

He circled her chair. "I was—until I realized you weren't. By the way, your bed has a lump."

She could feel the intensity of his gaze through the dim veil of light as he passed behind her. He knew who she'd called and wasn't a happy camper. "That's my 1991 Series ball."

"You keep it in your bed?"

Gracie shrugged. She was beyond worrying about what Sam, or anyone, thought. "It's signed by Tom Glavine, and it's lucky."

"Lucky, huh? You don't need it anymore, now

do you? That is—you don't *if* you're not thinking of doing something stupid."

They'd never gotten off the subject of her mystery call. Silently she turned and paraded up the stairs.

When she got to the top, his voice stopped her. "Where are *we* going?"

"*I'm* going to settle things with Lillian."

"Before you do, there's something about Lillian you should know."

She wanted to tell him not to bother, to keep whatever secrets he had left to himself. She'd had all the bad news she could handle. But she was on her way to make a deal, not just for Ben's freedom but for her own future. Artie had said she needed to trust Sam. Gracie steadied the quiver in her throat. "Okay, Fontana. Let's have it—all of it."

"My pop believed Lillian's negligence made it possible for Eddie Fry to get his hands on you. Whether it was deliberate or not, Pop was never able to prove her involvement. But knowing Conrad, I'd say that's why he left you in Alabama when he discovered your whereabouts. Ben knows more about Conrad's motives."

"So, you're saying Lillian has a legitimate gripe against Ben?"

"Call it posthumous revenge. She's got a lot of rage to unload. Ben is an available target."

"Your daddy must have had a theory . . ."

Sam started up the stairs, but Gracie signaled him to stop. She didn't want comfort right now. She needed her wits about her. Cold facts were all she could handle at the moment.

"The theory is straightforward. Conrad was discussing divorce with his attorneys. Lillian got wind of his intentions. You were her bargaining chip—but something went wrong."

Straightforward or not, being reduced to a bargaining chip hurt. There was nothing more to say. Gracie left him standing at the bottom of the stairs and hurried to her room and threw on her clothes. With Sam's theory still roaring through her brain, she raced back downstairs.

Sam hovered at the front door. When she'd tried to brush past him, he blocked her path. "I promised Artie I wouldn't let anything happen to you. I'm coming along for the ride."

Sam had a stubborn streak. She'd recognized it right off, mostly because she had the same one. She knew she'd be wasting precious time arguing with him. "Fine, but I call the plays—*all* of them."

Sam eyed her purse. "You don't happen to have a gun in there, do you?"

Gracie hugged her purse against her side. "Nope, I have something even better."

"You're not going to tell me, are you?"

"Nope."

Silently they drove through the dark to the ball

field. Twenty minutes later, a Lincoln Town Car pulled up beside Gracie's Jeep.

Gracie climbed out but stuck her head back in the door before Sam could follow her. "I'm benching you, Fontana. I mean it. Stay put."

He gave her a look, like he was itching to sass her back, but then thought better of it and settled back into his seat. "Okay, as long as I can see you. If you suddenly decide to take a stroll in the woods, I'll be there with the squirrels."

"Just keep your bushy tail out of sight, you hear?"

Sam grabbed her arm. "Hey, Gracie, be yourself, not Lillian's daughter, not Rita's kid, or Alice and Ben's glue, not even Artie's girl. Just be Gracie. *Capisce*?"

She'd been worried about Sam growing Alabama roots, but now he was speaking Italian and throwing her slightly threatening looks. Pretty soon he'd be back in Connecticut eating pasta instead of cluck-in-a-bucket. She nodded to Sam, then walked toward the bleachers where her mother sat inspecting her nail polish.

The morning sky was lightening, throwing blue shadows across the playing field. A chipping sparrow and its mate pecked their way over the outfield. Gracie took a deep breath, exhaling slowly as she approached the bench where Lillian sat. She faced her mother from the ground. "I want Ben released. I have a funeral to attend today. I need him to be there."

Lillian remained seated, with one leg crossed over the other. If she was intimidated by Gracie's manner, she didn't show it. The planes of her face remained calm. She smiled briefly in Gracie's direction. "*That man* and your father didn't just cheat me, they cheated you, too. They kept you here—in *this place*. You should be as furious as I am. It's time someone paid."

A wall went up in Lillian's gaze, but Gracie warmed to the challenge. She'd played this game with Alice more times than she could count.

Gracie crossed her arms over her chest and shifted her weight to one foot, resisting the urge to tap out her impatience. "Eddie Fry paid with his life, from what I hear. I'd say we're done collecting. I'm prepared to sweep the past under the rug, *if* you tell them to let Ben go."

Red patches blossomed on Lillian's cheeks and she glanced away.

Across the field Sam hovered on the bumper of her Jeep. She borrowed courage and patience from his presence and quietly waited for Lillian's answer.

When her mother finally turned her way, her features had settled into a puzzled expression. "I don't understand how you can be loyal to some-one who would keep you living in this place when he knew you didn't belong here. I could show you another world—the one you were born to live in."

"You mean the one Clare came from? No thanks."

Lillian's eyes narrowed at the mention of Clare's name. "Marcia has no vision or connections. Her child has grown up in a virtual closet. I'm talking about dining on yachts in the Mediterranean, movie premieres, preferred seating at the Met . . ." Lillian's voice brightened with excitement the way Alice's did when she'd found a new recipe. Lillian hadn't just grown up in the world she described; it was part of who she was—her identity.

If Sam's father's theory held the slightest bit of truth, could she forgive her mother? She never would have known Ben, or Alice, or Artie, if not for the series of events that had landed her on Ben's porch. Who was to say that she would have been happier in her mama's world? She knew one thing for sure: Money all by itself didn't make folks happy. Happiness was something that came from having the freedom to be who you really were—not someone's else's version of your ideal self but the deep down you, with all the good and bad mixed up thick.

Gracie let her gaze wander over her mama's neatly tailored pants, polished nails, and designer handbag, then took a seat beside her. "We're really not so different, you know." Her mother's delicate features dipped into a frown, but Gracie wasn't intimidated. Instinct told her she was on the right track. "You're scared, just like me. So scared, you'd do almost anything to hang on to all those things that make you feel like *you*— the fancy boats, the movie premieres . . . If I were to hold that against you, I'd be the same as the folks who go to church on Sunday, then salt their neighbors' roses on Monday. Lord knows, I don't want to be one of them."

Lillian squared her shoulders and fumbled absently with the clasp of her purse, refusing to look Gracie in the eye. "I never meant to hurt you."

"I'm going to try to believe you." Gracie reached into her purse and pulled out her checkbook. Her mother's features smoothed out. But just before a serene mask slid fully into place, regret touched the corners of her mother's mouth.

Gracie focused her attention on the checkbook in her lap. This time around, her hand was steady as she neatly scrawled a check for the remaining balance of her christening money— one million one hundred fifteen thousand dollars —then logged it in on the line below the entry for Moses Day's shoes. Quietly, she handed it to her mother. "I want the charges against Ben dropped and him home by lunchtime."

Lillian examined the check silently for a

moment, then glanced up at Gracie with wonder. "Conrad knew there was something special about you the day you were born. He said we didn't deserve you. I thought he was just being spiteful. But I have to admit, he was right. Whatever it was he saw in you is still there." She bowed her head. Her carefully arranged blond hair fell forward, covering the sides of her face and blocking her expression from Gracie's view. Gracie had to strain to hear her next words.

"I suppose Ben Calloway did a better job of preserving that quality than I would have."

Lillian uncrossed her legs and rose gracefully from the bench. But Gracie stayed seated. Despite her mother's confession, she still had a lot to answer for. She'd put Ben in jail, knowing he was innocent. Gracie knew she was stretching Artie's idea of trust by giving her the check in advance.

Her mother covered her embarrassment with a shaky smile. "They haven't had time to distribute the proceeds from the estate. Whose money is this?"

"Your daughter's—but she wants you to have it."

Lillian blanched, then dropped her gaze to the check, quietly smoothing the edge with her fingers. "Thank her for me, would you?"

Lillian started to walk away, then paused and turned back. Her face was wet. Dark streaks of mascara trailed down her cheeks. "Tell my daughter . . . I'm sorry. And tell her goodbye."

Gracie nodded. Her words jammed up like logs. She prayed her mother would leave before she embarrassed herself, but Lillian just stood there looking at her. The pretense was missing this time. Gracie held her breath as she realized her mother had something else to say.

"Gracie?"

"Yeah?" The sound of her name on her mother's lips nearly undid the dam in her throat. All she could manage was the one syllable.

"There's nothing your father left you that you need—but you've already realized that, haven't you?"

Out of the corner of her eye, Gracie glanced at Sam perched on her bumper watchful as ever. *There was one thing . . .*

Lillian followed Gracie's gaze. "Goodbye, Gracie, and good luck."

Chapter 30

Gracie glanced at the clock beside the bed, then rolled back against the pillow and closed her eyes. She had two hours before Artie's services began. The last thing she remembered before falling asleep was Sam guiding her toward the stairs with the phone pressed against his ear as he worked out the details of Ben's release with the attorneys.

Lillian had kept her word. She'd tricked Kate's wily butler into coughing up the original photographs with the correct dates and gotten Ben cleared. In the end, Gracie had to admit her mama had surprised her. It wasn't so much her unspoken apology as it was her acceptance of who Gracie was that had wiped the anger clean. Her mama was done salting folks' roses, just as Gracie was. Despite the melancholy of the day ahead, she felt lighter than before. How could that be? Artie was gone. Her dream mama didn't exist. *But she had a sister, who was growing into her own set of lungs . . . and a grandma who had distinct possibilities . . . not to mention a handsome Yankee who was showing no signs of leaving.*

Gracie opened her eyes. It wasn't Artie's voice

she'd heard this time but her own. She lay motionless, listening. Then realized she wasn't alone. Someone was rustling around her room.

"You're awake. Good. I thought for a minute there, you'd lapsed into a coma or something. Never seen anyone sleep without moving a twitch."

Gracie searched the room for the woman's voice. She found her in the rocking chair. Rita was much taller than Gracie had envisioned. She had short auburn hair that curled softly around her face. Her eyes were a deep brown like Ben's. Her nose followed the same line as his, straight with a slight hook on the end. Apart from her height, she was just as Gracie had imagined her.

Rita seemed to read her thoughts. "I don't blame you. I'm a bit shocked to see you all grown up. I mean, I imagined what you looked like a hundred times . . . but I'm happy to say you don't look anything like what I expected."

Gracie still had an ax to grind with Rita. She didn't try to soften the suspicion in her voice. "And what would that be?"

Nervously Rita popped out of the rocker and paced in front of the window. "Well, I always thought you'd look like your mother. Blond and, you know—"

"Flat-chested?"

Rita paused and looked over at her, then burst

into laughter. "Glad to see you've got a sense of humor. You didn't get it from Ben, so I assume Artie's responsible."

But Gracie wasn't laughing. She sat quietly and let the silence do the talking for her.

Rita was quick to pick up on her mood and sobered quickly. "I know what you're thinking."

"What's that?"

"That I should have put you back where you belonged." Rita crossed the room and stopped in front of Gracie. "But it wasn't that simple. I was young and scared, not brave like you, Gracie."

Gracie stared at her in disbelief. "You let me go on thinking you were my mama all these years—A card would have done the trick."

"Believe me, Alice didn't waste five minutes before she grabbed the nearest stick and beat that horse to death. She told me you used to have a picture of me in your room." Rita glanced around. "I don't see it, so I guess that pretty much says it all."

"I gave it to Ben."

A brief smile touched Rita's face before her gaze dropped away. "I wanted to tell Ben the truth. By the time I figured I'd done something really wrong, it was too late to undo it. I must have picked up that phone a hundred times, but I figured he would be the one who got hurt the most. He didn't deserve that after all he put up with from me over the years. Your daddy had

403

enough money to hire an army of attorneys to make sure Ben paid for my bad judgment. So I kept silent—until I got homesick and drunk one night."

"Is that why you took the long route through Texas while Ben had to sleep behind bars?"

Rita had the good grace to bow her head and look ashamed. "I panicked when they arrested him. Someone was watching my apartment. I didn't know who it was. Turns out, it wasn't me they were watching but my neighbor, who's been sneaking around on her husband."

Gracie stared down at Rita's chipped toenail polish and worn sandals. She wanted to park all the dirty names she'd endured over the years at Rita's door, but she couldn't. She wasn't her love baby any more than she was Conrad Hammond's lost baby girl. She was Gracie Calloway and all the things Shady Grove had made her.

Rita sagged down on the bed. "One thing I've learned is that sometimes we try to do what we think is best, but later it turns out we were wrong. Maybe your daddy was working up to telling you. Alice says he bought a house here."

"The Parnell house."

Rita's face screwed into a frown much like Ben's did when he was contemplating something tricky. "Never had any use for the Parnells."

Gracie had heard as much. The accounts of Rita's childhood weren't all that different from her own. Gracie nodded her understanding. "The Parnells did seem to have it out for us Calloway girls."

Rita glanced away and gathered her breath in a noisy gulp. "That's because my daddy was a Parnell."

Gracie kept silent while Rita struggled with another breath.

"He was what Alice called—*the Parnell black sheep.* They drove him into the army when they found out about him and my mama planning to marry. He died in Korea never knowing about me. Of course, they laid the blame at my mama's door every chance they got. I don't think it was the cancer that got my mama so much as it was the Parnells' meanness and her broken heart. When I got to be older, I looked more and more like my daddy. And the Parnells got nastier and nastier, till I could think of nothing but going someplace far away. So you see, it wasn't you they hated but me."

"They thought I was yours . . ."

"That's right—another Parnell *mistake* that would haunt them forever. But we surprised them, didn't we? Boy, I would have loved to have been a fly on the Parnells' wall when they picked up that paper and read the truth." A mischievous gleam twinkled in Rita's brown eyes.

Though Gracie was surprised by Rita's

confession, it didn't discount the fact that Ben had hidden the truth about her daddy from her for eight long years. Gracie launched herself off the bed. She still had a bone to pick with Ben. "Ben had plenty of time to work up the courage to tell me the facts."

"I asked him not to. I was afraid." Rita picked up the photo of baby Gracie in her daddy's arms. Gracie kicked herself for leaving it out for public inspection. The last thing she wanted to do was to answer questions about her feelings for her daddy. How could you feel something for someone you never knew?

Because there's evidence that he loved you.

Rita was examining the evidence. Was she seeing what Gracie saw? What Artie saw? Her dark brows knitted together in a worried frown.

Gracie wanted to grab the picture back. But then she noticed the tremble that shook Rita's shoulders.

When Rita looked up at her, her eyes were glassy. "I'm sorry. He must have loved you very much. I didn't know." Gracie knew she'd seen what Artie had seen, what Gracie herself had seen . . .

Gracie accepted the photo back. "Neither did I. That's what makes my decision so hard. If it weren't for that, this would be a piece of cake."

Rita's gaze skipped past Gracie's to Grandma Lynne's picture. Gracie could tell by Rita's expression that she understood. Was she thinking about her own daddy and wishing she had some scrap of proof that he would have loved her the same way?

Finally her gaze zeroed back on Gracie's. "Yeah, love really complicates things." She rose and ambled toward the door, her voice fading with her footsteps.

Gracie thought of Sam. What would he say when she told him about her decision?

Her gaze stumbled on Artie's letter. It was still waiting, offering one more bit of his tough wisdom. She'd finally made her own choice, but she desperately craved his approval. She reached for the letter and slipped it into her pocket, then set Conrad's picture back in its place beside her bed and prepared to say goodbye.

Artie's funeral was an event Shady Grove would long remember. Ben made it in time. There had been more flowers and fancy clothes than Easter Sunday. Gracie suspected her new grandmother had something to do with the huge fuss. After Kate Hammond had overseen the setting out of the food and wine, she had discreetly disappeared.

Artie's letter still crinkled in the pocket of her blue dress. Gracie waited for a lull in the condolences, then slipped into the gazebo and tucked herself into a seat obscured from the open doorway. She took a deep breath and opened the envelope, shoving the tears back into her eyes with quick blinks. The handwriting on the inside was Alice's, not Artie's. Gracie's gaze raced to the bottom of the page, then skidded to a halt on his signature. It was every bit as perfect as the one on the front of the envelope. She exhaled her relief and let the slow rolling rhythm of Artie's voice come back to her one more time:

Dear Gracie Lynne,

I got to say I'm mighty proud of you. I ain't never been prouder of anything 'cept maybe my daddy's mule. That's a joke, girl. You's supposed to laugh. I know you don't feel much like it, but you go on and give it a try.

The best Gracie could do was a teary smile before she started again. Artie's voice moved on in her head, even before her eyes caught up with his words.

I know you just done a sad job. You'll get better at it. Sooner, if you let folks help you instead of being the old rusty iron princess. You know what I'm talking about.

Gracie knew. She'd earned the dreaded title when she got so bottled up she shut down. No laughing, no crying, nothing—usually around her birthday. Gracie cleared her vision and focused on Alice's measured script.

For the rusty princess days, I'm leaving you my horn. So when you feel yourself clogging up, you play and I'll be listening.

I'm getting tired. But there's something I got to say that you need to hear. Take off those mule ears for a minute and listen up.

I know you got your heart set on not taking that money your daddy left you. You's thinking about all the folks who is more deserving than you, even Moses Day. And you know that just ain't so. Fact is, honey, they wouldn't know what to do with it if they had it. That's the truth. Chantel, she'd buy herself a closet full of fancy dresses and get herself a big ol' fancy house and a maid. Then she'd get fat and lazy. Folks wouldn't like her much.

This is your turn to dream, Gracie girl. When you was just a little thing, you wanted to sing. But the Big Man got the order wrong and He give you a good pitching arm and a head for numbers instead of a voice. The bases are loaded. You gonna bring your runners in with a home run or are you gonna let that pitcher walk you?

"Yeah, well, that's the six hundred and fifty million dollar question, Artie, isn't it? It's always been your job to supply the answers."

A pair of footsteps echoed on the gazebo floor. Gracie spun in her seat.

Sam stood in the archway with one arm braced above his head, a bower of Violet Parnell's prize Cecile Brunner contrasted his lean dark silhouette against the pale pink blossoms. "Maybe he already has and you were just . . . *distracted.*"

She felt the pull of his gaze but shifted her focus back to Artie's letter. "He wanted to know what my dreams were. I'm not sure I have any."

He abandoned his spot and took a seat on the bench beside her. "Dreams are tricky. Sometimes they're there without you even being aware of them. It's not until someone tries to take them away that you realize you have any at all."

When she was a kid, she'd wanted plenty of things—a mama and a daddy, a chance to go to baseball camp like the boys she played with. They didn't happen, so she'd told her dreams to keep quiet so Ben and Artie didn't feel bad because they couldn't make them come true.

When Gracie glanced up, Sam was waiting for her with a tiny, perfectly formed rosebud between his fingers. He leaned in closer and tucked the bud behind her ear. "You tell me yours, and I'll tell you mine."

She could hear Artie chuckling inside her head. She smiled, fingering the notorious Parnell rose against her temple as she glanced up at Sam. Could she say it? Would he laugh? Gracie took a whiff of the faint sweet fragrance, then smoothed Artie's letter against her dress. Stirring up her courage, she glanced up at Sam. "Baseball camp."

The surprise she'd expected was missing from his expression. "I had the same dream. How about that?" His excitement for their shared dream came through loud and clear.

She felt her somber mood lighten as she pictured Sam in his Little League uniform, looking tough and sassy. "So, did you go?"

Sam shook his head but didn't look too disappointed. "Nope. Broke my arm that summer giving Roddy Henderson his just deserts after a brutal session of crack-the-whip. Roddy was bigger than the average bully, and I'd appointed myself to take him down a notch."

Sam had had to deal with bullies? Gracie almost felt sorry for Roddy Henderson. Though she hadn't experienced his tough side, she had no doubt it was there, standing tall beside his strong sense of justice. "So did Roddy go to camp?"

Sam's smile was just short of a laugh. "He did, but he got sent home with a bad case of poison ivy. Roddy now sells lemons in Detroit—just in

411

case you have a yen for a new set of wheels . . . Be warned."

Gracie couldn't help but laugh. "Artie always said Old Man Justice might be slow, but if you give him time, he gets around to fixing things." She folded Artie's letter and slipped it into her pocket for safekeeping.

Sam reached for her hand and laced his fingers through hers. "So, what about you? You going to camp?"

His touch as well as his suggestion caught her by surprise. He was joking, of course. "That's not my dream anymore. That's Jackie's."

Everyone was making plans for her to leave. Jimmy had practically given her job away to Melinda. Alice couldn't wait to set up house with the reverend. Even Ben was talking about retiring and spending his days fishing, since Clare had cut the Widow Perkins out of the equation by deciding to rent Alice's house.

Sam just sat there looking at her expectantly. She tried to reclaim her hand, but he held fast. Like Artie, Sam wasn't going to let her off the hook until she came up with an answer. Gracie sagged against the bench. Ever since Kate had suggested she come up with an idea related to her passion, an idea had been niggling at her unconscious. Or maybe it had been there before that and Kate had finally forced her to recognize the power Conrad's gift had given her and her

412

freedom to put her own stamp on her choice.

"There *is* one thing—a patch of ground west of town—about forty acres of flat land that would be perfect for a baseball camp for girls like Jackie." Her dream spoken out loud made her blood rush in her ears. She glanced at Sam in wonder.

His brow was creased in concentration. He was already working out the details. "Build it and they will come . . . is that it? Since you're not looking to do ten to twenty in a white coat, I'm going to assume you'll be looking for live bodies. I've got some ideas. We'll want to run it as a nonprofit, which will minimize the tax burden on the estate . . . We can set up a generous scholarship program, name it after Artie."

Sam wasn't much of a P.I.—he had a better head for business. She suspected her daddy had his number and had set up things not just to test her but to challenge Sam as well. Gracie offered him a sly smile worthy of Artie in his most devilish moment. "Or . . . I could give it *all* to you."

"*No,* no. A camp is a great idea. If it's bodies you need, I can find them."

Gracie felt the idea catch fire, but her confidence wavered. "I don't know . . . Actually, I'm thinking *you* might do a better job. But if it's any consolation, I feel bad about dumping it all on you."

Sam's face went still. "*How* bad?"

The tone in his voice made her sit up straighter, suddenly wary. "What do you mean? How bad do I have to feel?"

Sam shot her with a suspicious look. "Are you still after my baseball collection? 'Cause you've got three premium passes that say we're square."

Gracie ignored him and plunged ahead. "We're taking Jackie to the game, by the way."

"Artie would have insisted on as much. So, what about the six hundred fifty million reasons for you to soothe your guilt? I'm ready for the soothing to begin—" The gleam in his eye said he was expecting a good dose of lesson one and had hopes they would progress to lesson three.

Gracie felt her palms ache with the need to touch him. "You look fine to me. I think you'll live."

"I don't know. I've got six hundred and fifty million reasons to feel bad. That's a lot of reasons. It would practically take a whole lifetime to undo all the sadness—fifty years at least."

A hot rush warmed her face. Now she was the one who needed her ears checked. "Sam Fontana, are you asking me to marry you?"

Sam deserted the bench and stood in front of her, his eyes dark with promise. "You want a straight answer?"

He was shuffling his feet, nervous as heck.

Pretty amazing, since the only boys she'd ever made tremble with fear were the ones staring at her down the end of her pitch. Gracie reached for his hand and wove her fingers through his, then offered him an encouraging smile. "Straight would be best."

He seated himself beside her, claimed her free hand and towed her closer. "The fact is, Gracie Calloway, I love you."

Gracie thanked her lucky stars that Sam wasn't the sort to profess undying love on a bended knee. As it was, she was having trouble keeping the joy inside of her from bursting out in silly girlish laughter. Sam wanted her—for the long haul. When she'd managed a sober face, she whispered back, "You love me, huh?"

"Shall I get a tattoo?"

"Don't you dare. Then I would have to get one, too, and I would never hear the end of Alice's disgrace."

"Just for the record, tell me what yours would say?" Suddenly he was looking pretty cocky.

But she could be cocky, too. Gracie raised her chin the way she'd seen her Grandma Kate do. "I love a Yankee." There, she'd said it aloud and he was still looking at her with a big ol' happy grin. Gracie smiled back.

Sam reached for her hand and towed her off the bench into his arms. "Okay then, it's a deal, you and me?"

She heard them before he saw them. Hoots and whistles came from all sides of the gazebo. Kate and Alice parted from the group and marched up the steps, side by side.

Gracie turned, giving Sam easy access to her lips. "Quick, kiss me."

"Yes, ma'am." Sam covered her mouth with his. Out of the corner of her eye, Gracie could see Alice and Kate pause on the steps, then scurry back down, shooing the crowd with them.

When they were alone again, Sam pulled her onto his lap. "Alice sent over a set of knives this morning. Said they were a present from Artie. Should I be worried?"

Gracie offered him a watery smile. "Your worries are over. You're officially *a somebody*."

Author Insights, Extras & More...

from Lorelle Marinello

Reading Group Guide

1. Gracie's biggest fear is that the money will destroy her quiet life in Shady Grove and that the relationships with the people she cares for will be changed forever. What would you do if you suddenly inherited a large fortune or won the lottery? How would money change your life path? How would it affect your relationships with members of your family and your friends?

2. Gracie discovers, once the news of her inheritance is out, that folks in Shady Grove treat her differently. Does money, or the lack of money, influence your perception of people's character? Celebrities, neighbors, co-workers, and family members.

3. One of Gracie's greatest fears is that her inheritance will eventually lead her down the path of greed and selfishness. Do you think it is possible to have great personal wealth without your economic status influencing your attitude about your place in society?

4. Do you think Conrad had good reason for not revealing his true identity to Gracie? Would you consider his actions self-serving? Or admirable? How do you think Gracie would have responded to the news of her inheritance if Conrad had introduced himself into her life sooner?

5. Should Ben have told Gracie the truth from the outset? How do you think Gracie's life would have been changed if she had known her true identity at age seventeen?

6. We have the saying "money talks and people listen." How would our society be changed if more decisions were based on character and need instead of the bottom line?

7. Lillian's actions were not solely motivated by greed, but also by fear. In the end, Gracie realizes her attachment to Shady Grove is no different from Lillian's attachment to her lifestyle. Should Gracie have forgiven Lillian for her indiscretions? Can you find parallels in Lillian and Gracie's characters?

8. The novel shows us how culture and social standing influence our decisions. What values

and beliefs have shaped your decisions regarding wealth?

9. Which of Gracie's characteristics is a result of the Southern culture she has been raised in? Had she been raised in another cultural setting, would her decisions have been different? How so?

10. Forgiveness is a strong theme in the novel. Name three incidents in which Gracie had to overcome her strong ideals and demonstrate forgiveness. How did these actions change her?

11. Alice felt the only way to force Gracie to shed her old life was to burn her clothes. Was this too drastic a measure? Was Alice fulfilling her own desire or thinking of Gracie?

12. Artie, Alice, and Ben considered Gracie their saving grace. Why?

13. Which aspects of Gracie's character do you admire? Why?

14. Artie realizes Gracie has set aside her needs to take care of other people for so long that she has lost touch with her own dreams.

In order for her to know what to do with the money, she needs to know her own heart and her own desires. What are your dreams? What steps can you take today to make them a reality?

Lorelle Marinello

Although Lorelle Marinello is a native of Southern California, she spent much of her childhood in the home of Alabama-born grandparents. When she began to write, the familiar voices of her childhood came back to her through her characters.

She makes her home with her husband and three children in the mountains near San Diego. She received a B.A. in Fine Arts from San Diego State University. When she is not writing, she enjoys researching her Southern genealogy and gardening.

Center Point Publishing
600 Brooks Road ● PO Box 1
Thorndike ME 04986-0001 USA

(207) 568-3717

US & Canada:
1 800 929-9108
www.centerpointlargeprint.com